Women, Murder, and Equity in Early Modern England

Routledge Studies in Renaissance Literature and Culture

Women, Murder, and Equity in Early Modern England

Randall Martin

Routledge
Taylor & Francis Group

NEW YORK AND LONDON

First published 2008
by Routledge
605 Third Avenue, New York, NY 10017

Simultaneously published in the UK
by Routledge
2 Park Square, Milton Park, Abingdon, Oxon OX14 4RN

First issued in paperback 2021

Routledge is an imprint of the Taylor & Francis Group, an informa business

© 2008 Taylor & Francis

Typeset in 10 point Sabon by IBT Global.

Library of Congress Cataloging in Publication Data
A catalog record has been requested for this book.

ISBN 13: 978-0-415-54256-2 (pbk)
ISBN 13: 978-0-415-96115-8 (hbk)

For Madeline and Hermione

Contents

List of Figures

Acknowledgments

Researching original news texts for this book has extended the hunt that began with my facsimile edition, *Women and Murder in Early Modern News Pamphlets and Broadside Ballads, 1573–1697* (2005). I have many librarians and their institutions to thank for making these searches fruitful and pleasant: Aude Fitzsimons, The Pepys Library, Magdalene College, Cambridge; Geoffrey Groom, The Bodleian Library, Oxford; Susan Halpert, The Houghton Library, Harvard University; Rachel Howarth, The Houghton Library, Harvard University; Christine Jack, Harriet Irving Library, University of New Brunswick; Adrian James, Society of Antiquaries of London; Susi Krasnoo, The Huntington Library; Ann Mar, The Huntington Library; Mona Noureldin, The Huntington Library; Sandra Powlette, The British Library; Monica Petraglia, The Newberry Library; Stephen Tabor, The Huntington Library; Georgianna Ziegler, The Folger Shakespeare Library.

Besides the people named above, I wish to thank Josie Lister of The Bodleian, Richard Palmer of Lambeth Palace, Bettina C. Smith of The Folger, and William Stoneman of The Houghton for granting me permission to reproduce material from their collections.

This project was substantially supported by a grant from the Social Sciences and Humanities Research Council of Canada. I am also grateful to David S. Zeidberg and Robert C. Ritchie for awarding me a Huntington Research fellowship in Spring 2003 that allowed key sections of this book to be researched and drafted. The Dean of Arts of the University of New Brunswick also generously underwrote part of the cost of reproduction and permission fees.

Colleagues and friends have also generously offered information and encouragement. Many thanks to Jennifer Andrews, Sabrina Baron, Graeme Clark, Phillip D. Collington, David Gants, Elizabeth Hanson, Barbara Hodgdon, Peter Kuling, Helen Ostovich, Anne Lake Prescott, Edith Snook, Betty S. Travitsky, Paul Werstine, and Julia Wright. Research assistants Elizabeth Harding, Jane McLean, and Alison Toron provided invaluable contributions to this project at various stages. Dana Hope's technical knowledge greatly speeded preparation of the illustrations. My department staff, Susan Miller and Vera Zarowsky, have helped me produce the volume with their usual patience, efficiency, and good humour. Carey Nershi of IBT Global provided singular expertise at the copy editing and proofreading stages, and Max Novick and Liz Levine were supportive editors. And I am particularly indebted to Susan Amussen for reading a draft of the entire manuscript and suggesting key improvements. Any shortcomings which now remain are my own.

Hospitable friends have enabled me to spend the necessary time away researching this book. My personal thanks to: Elizabeth Archibald, Jonathan and Henrietta Freeman-Attwood, Linda McJannet and Michael O'Shea, Peter and Betsy Newell, and Amelia French and Andrea Sella.

RM

1 Introduction

NEWS FOR THE PROSECUTION;
READERS FOR THE DEFENSE

On 25 or 28 February 1608, Margaret Ferneseede was burnt to death in
St. George's Field, Southwark for allegedly killing her husband. She had
refused to admit her guilt despite intense pressure during the trial and before
her execution. Dressed in a "kirtle [i.e., gown] of Canuasse pitched cleane
through, ouer which she did weare a white sheet," she was escorted to the
pyre by two women holding her hands. As she was being tied to the stake,
a clergyman

> admonished her that now in that minute she would confesse that fact for
> which she was now ready to suffer[;] which she denying, the reeds were
> planted aboute, vnto which fier being giuen[,] she was presently dead.
> Finis. (*The Araignement & burning of Margaret Ferne-seede*, B4v)

Only 6 weeks later on 11 April, Elizabeth Abbot was hanged for allegedly
murdering her drunkard landlady, ironically named Elizabeth Killingworth.
She too had refused to confess. A gibbet was purposefully erected close to
the victim's house near Aldgate, towards which Abbot was faced and "bad
[to] let the sight of that where she had committed so foule a fact, be a
remembrance to haue her cleare her soule." When this arrangement failed to
stir her conscience, Abbot was forced to her knees in the cart and made to
pray "that [god] would be pleasd to open her harte, and make her fit for him
in this her houre of death" (*The Apprehension, Arraignement, and execution
of Elizabeth Abbot*, C3v). This too failed and led to an extraordinary scene.
While one sheriff rode away to inform the Mayor of London "how she still
persuered in pleading her innocency" (C4r), another hauled Abbot from the
cart into nearby St. Katherine Cree Church where all the prosecution witnesses were summoned to reiterate their testimony against her. The writer's
account of this postverdict tribunal revealed that crucial allegations against
Abbot had never been proved:

[They urged] that she wold yet tell whither shee knew Mistris Killingworth, or if she shamed to open that sinne, that she would but discover
who was partaker with her in the roberie yt he might, be found, or what
manner of man he was. (C4r)

Still unmoved, Abbot was quickly brought back to gallows and hanged. Her
story ended as starkly as Ferneseede's: "Finis."

Though their crimes were unrelated, the women's stories became intertwined by virtue of their legally questionable convictions and steadfast denials of guilt. These issues were opened to public debate when Henry Gosson
published black-letter pamphlets about each crime, possibly written by the
same anonymous author.[1] Unlike many seventeenth-century news writers,
he was not primarily concerned with constructing homiletic biographies (in
this case of extreme wickedness rather than pious repentance). Rather his
(or their) main aim was to defend the integrity of officials who handled each
case and to justify the legal verdicts. The narrative voice—more distinctly
in the Abbot pamphlet—was that of an authoritative insider with privileged
access to examination records, arraignment and trial testimony, and notes of
the presiding assize judge, Sir Edward Coke.

Given these sources of information, it is not surprising that neither pamphlet judged the women's protestations of innocence to be credible. Like most
English news about women murderers published before the Restoration and
much of it afterwards, the reports made no conscious effort to represent the
defendant's perspective or offer possible justifications for her actions. The
narrative point of view was squarely that of the prosecution, epitomized
during the trial by the allegations of the Crown indictment. Legitimate legal
fictions at best, fictions *toutes courtes* at worst,[2] indictments were composed
at the request of prosecutors based on pretrial examinations taken by local
magistrates. The suspect was invariably charged with the maximum offence:
wilful and malicious homicide.[3] If grand jurors accepted the prosecutor's
arguments and sent the indictment forward (which they often refused to
do), and if the prisoner pleaded not guilty (which she almost always did),
the assize judge and petty jury questioned the prosecutor's evidence and
defendant's testimony—including her public reputation—to determine if she
or he had indeed acted with malice aforethought.

Ferneseede's and Abbot's denials of guilt meant that the outcome of their
trials hinged on their personal characters and competing interpretations
of the victims' deaths. As W. Lance Bennett and Martha S. Feldman have
shown in their seminal study of trial narratives, the rhetorical structures
of prosecutors and defendants differ in their persuasive aims. The prosecution strives for a logically consistent interpretation of the accused's actions
as well as congruency with the materially discovered facts of the case. In
other words, the assertions of the prosecution's story must match precon-
ceived assumptions about the defendant's social identity, temperament, and
motives.[4] In early modern assize trials, such preconceptions were constituted

by a traditionally gendered repertoire of criminal types and behavioral habits. The colloquially fictionalized details of *The Araignement & burning of Margaret Ferne-seede* presented early modern readers with familiar images of the shrewish, sexually disordered, and therefore incipiently murderous wife, interwoven with narrative manipulations to compensate for an absence of directly incriminating evidence.[5] Early modern readers with knowledge of classical rhetoric could have regarded these as valid forensic techniques.[6] Other readers might have understood their paramount significance to be an allegorized justification of the story's moral lessons and the symbolic restoration of social order. But in a period when traditional forms of knowledge based on similitude and correspondence were being challenged by emerging empirical and skeptical methodologies,[7] their mythologizing constructions probably spurred some Jacobean readers to question their truth claims and to reconstruct more legally consistent or rational versions of the crime that queried the prosecution-oriented narrative.

In contrast to modern English-speaking trials, the accused was not allowed the benefit of defense counsel, nor was she or he presumed to be innocent of the charges.[8] Indeed the opposite was true. During the arraignment, the grand jury heard evidence only for the prosecution before deciding whether to find a true bill (i.e., accept the prosecutor's evidence supporting the indictment). During the main trial, the judge was, in theory, the only possible counsellor for the defendant, in so far as he decided whether to accept the prosecutor's evidence or challenge it.[9] Sir Edward Coke's extensively reported charge to the jury at Elizabeth Abbot's trial accurately conveyed the more familiar pattern of Crown arguments being positively reinforced by the authority of the bench (*The Apprehension, Arraignement, and execution of Elizabeth Abbot*, C2r–C3r).

It was this version of the crime, obtained either first- or second hand from magistrates' examinations, indictments, and assize proceedings that constituted one of two main sources of information about condemned murderers in early modern printed news, beyond local rumor and hearsay. (I shall discuss the second source in the next section of this introduction.) News titles later in the century made this perspective explicit; for example: *A True Account of the Proceedings on the Crown-Side at this Lent Assize Held for the County of Surrey . . . Thursday the 13th of March, 1683, and ending on Saturday the 15th* (1684). The Ferneseede and Abbot crime narratives were remarkable for their density of circumstantial detail and lengthy report of the Crown's arguments, but not for their prosecution bias. As we shall see, these salient features betrayed official anxiety about how the public would judge the trial and outcome of each case.

It was up to the accused persons to find the right words, if any, to defend themselves. In theory, as Bennett and Feldman also explain, defense strategies might take several routes. The defendant could question the internal consistency of the prosecution's narrative by highlighting missing facts or evidence, logical weaknesses, or semantic ambiguities. With the help of friends and neighbors as witnesses, they might try to reinterpret the prosecutor's account of their actions in the light of their individual circumstances and good character. Or they could try to reconstruct the indictment's allegations of wilful malice in exculpatory ways.[10] In the pressured and estranging atmosphere of early modern assize trials, however, few commoner defendants—who were often famished and sick after languishing for months in foetid county jails—managed any kind of cross-examination or rebuttal of the prosecutor's arguments. Most could utter only the briefest denial of the formal charges. As J. M. Beattie has shown, even on the infrequent occasions when the prisoner managed to organize witnesses, his or her defense "might well remain seriously limited."[11] The whole legal mechanism of early modern assizes put defendants charged with murder at serious disadvantages.

Women faced additional technical and cultural obstacles that affected verdicts, sentencing, and the news stories that followed. In the absence of legal counsel or customary courtroom strategies, early modern defenses had to be invented which would mitigate the gravity of the offense and neutralize the prisoner's culpability. In homicide trials, the aim was to persuade the jury to bring in a reduced conviction of manslaughter, or excusable killing in self-defense or by accident. These lesser degrees of homicide allowed men to avoid execution by claiming benefit of clergy. If they demonstrated their claim, they were branded on the thumb or palm of the left hand.[12] Women, however, were ineligible for clergy for any serious felonies.[13] Garthine Walker has also shown that they derived no benefit from a lesser charge of manslaughter or excusable homicide since these were capital offenses and they would still face execution if convicted.[14] Walker and Susan Dwyer Amussen have further argued that female defendants faced profound cultural difficulties in justifying any kind of physical retaliation or self-defense because these categories of behavior were regarded as proper only to male temperaments and masculine roles.[15] Homicides by men often took place either in public spaces such as alehouses where certain levels of violence were tolerated and killings could be rationalized as temporary drunken lapses or hot-bloodedness, or in private quarrels where principles of masculine honor were at stake. By contrast, the author of *The Apprehension, Arraignment, and execution of Elizabeth Abbot* treated Mistress Killingworth's addiction to drink as self-incriminating, while also avoiding any possible justification for Abbot's allegedly murderous reactions to her abuse. Both women were morally culpable, though Abbot's alleged violence transgressed obvious legal as well as social boundaries.

The absence of procedural and rhetorical strategies for constructing legal defenses for women did not lead to any weakened ability to avoid prosecution, conviction, or execution, however. In fact county records show that the courts treated early modern female defendants more leniently than their male counterparts, and that they were discharged or acquitted in greater proportions than men.[16] The origins of these benevolent discrepancies appear to be cultural as well as jurisprudential, and are a main focus of this book. Joining recent scholarly interest in the material production of early modern texts and reader-generated interpretation, I argue that the growth of printed murder news and diversity of public reception nurtured discourses of social and legal equity towards female homicide, while at the same time reproducing traditional negative images of murderous women.[17] Contentious responses to topical news in periods such as the 1650s and 1680s demonstrated that readers could challenge reports on any subject according to their political interests. Readers of news stories about female killers in these and other periods were no less capable of questioning prosecution evidence or imaginatively constructing counter-arguments that mitigated the defendant's moral or legal culpability, whatever the trial's decision. Such readers included people at all levels of the community who participated in the discovery and arraignment of local suspects: neighbors, officers, magistrates, sheriffs, clergymen, jurors, and judges. Their recollection of ambiguous or mitigating perspectives shaped their responses to later cases in which they became involved directly or read about. For their part, news writers often invoked readers' memories of notorious but controversial murderesses such as Anne Saunders, Alice Arden, and Anne Turner to analogize present-day cases. Popular murder news thus became a significant form of *preknowledge*, to borrow Roger Chartier's term, that determined readers' understanding of future crimes as recurring events, "but not necessarily in conformity with [the meanings] desired" either by prosecuting officials or by similarly positioned writers.[18] Legal records of the period confirm that in cases of women accused of homicide or infanticide, individual or collective reactions were often divided and/or effectually mitigating.

Alternative possibilities of interpretation were enabled by long-established and widely diffused concepts of equity. Equity was (and is) the legal principle by which formal application of written statutes and absolute legal principles is mitigated or remedied by extenuating individual circumstances and humane considerations.[19] Aristotle originally defined equity's modifying impulses as imaginatively expansive and temporally progressive since they spring from suppositions about what past framers of the law would decide at the present moment if the unforeseen complicating details of a particular case came before them.[20] In Thomas Aquinas's adaptations of Aristotle, which provided the basis for early modern theories of equity, the harshness of strict applications of the law and judicial power was ameliorated by the moral virtues of fairness, mercy, and compassion as authorized by natural law and Christian precept. The gallows contrivances used to pressure Elizabeth Abbot into confessing at her place of execution could have been regarded by contemporaries, paradoxically, as both desperate and merciful gestures in so far as they were based on natural-law assumptions that a guilty conscience would always reveal and/or redeem itself in the end.[21] Natural law was the broad set of traditional moral beliefs that humans are attuned by their divinely created hearts and minds to follow virtue and shun vice, and are intrinsically capable of distinguishing good from evil. Operating as manifest rational conscience, natural law in theory justified all criminal laws and state punishment, making it a fundamental component of equity.[22]

As a dynamic field of legal and social theory, early modern equity validated popular as well as elite practices and discourses. The influential Church of England divine, Cambridge don, and sometime prison chaplain William Perkins attempted to bridge these constituencies by synthesizing Aristotelian and Thomist views in *E'ΠΙΕΓΕΙΑ* (*Hepieíkeia*): *or, A Treatise of Christian Equitie and moderation*, published two years after his death in 1604. Writing in the plain and trenchant style that made his systematic exposition of Protestant doctrine known across Europe, Perkins defined public equity as an integrated moral, social, and legal concept. Equity underpinned the social contract between rational agents in all human relationships, and connected the private and public spheres. Perkins cited the normative early modern correspondence between the family and the nation: if equity is the foundation of "sound [and] lasting loue, betwixt man & wife . . . which is the nearest coniunction, and the most excellent and perfect societie, which is in this world[,] then it is much more true, in all other societies of men" (A1–A2r). Because strictness in the application of laws, or what Perkins called "extremity," serves the powerful in society more advantageously than mitigation, justice should always shake "hands with her sister mercie[;] . . . all laws allowe a mitigation" (A8v). Severe poverty and personal vulnerability, for instance, were social conditions Perkins repeatedly cited as mitigating circumstances for crime (A6r-A7r, B3v, D5v).[23] His treatise nonetheless revealed tensions between early modern righteousness about hierarchical order, and Christian imperatives of mercy and forgiveness (B8r). He excluded repeated serious offenses, "manifest & public enormities, as of treasons against the Prince of state," and "gross and palpable crimes" from equitable consideration. Yet the latter remained contingent categories dependant on their positive identification as both "plainly evil" and wilfully intended, thus reserving a role for rational identification of ambiguous and potentially excusable behaviors (C8r).

Writing partly with legal officials in mind, Perkins argued towards the end of his treatise that equity was a broad-based social practice, not limited to legal knowledge or restricted areas of conduct. Rather, it was "known before all men" from day-to-day interactions as well as oral and written exchanges. In these guises, concepts of equity and natural law fed popular ideas about the desirable limitations on, or the necessary flexibility of, the instrumental application of early modern criminal and common law.[24] Negotiating these legal boundaries, as Cynthia B. Herrup, J. A. Sharpe, and Steve Hindle have argued, constituted a significant part of the public interplay of political power and cultural authority between elites and the governed.[25] The popularity of the numerous early modern courts of equity, especially among female litigants, illustrated a widely dispersed desire for fair and practical remedies to common-law restrictions and silences.[26] The spiky personal complications of individual homicides and child murders, although ostensibly flattened by the weight of formal statutes and trial procedures, and subsequently by the moralizing rhetoric of news writers, could nonetheless be re-appraised by readers' observation of extenuating or conflicting details, especially in multiple news stories by rival publishers.

Early modern legal commentators also vigorously debated the theoretical relationship between common-law and equity. Christopher Saint German's continually reprinted *The Dialogues in Englysshe/bytwene a Doctour of dyuinyte & a Studēt in the lawes of Englēde* (1523), for example, drew on Aquinas's reformulations of natural law to define equitable justice as legal interpretation based on moral conscience and the unique material and human particularities of each case.[27] This contrasted with common-law determination of cases in strict conformity with parliamentary statutes, recorded precedents, and proverbial analogies.[28] The widely read sixteenth-century law commentator Edmund Plowden argued that equity (*epicaia*) was a critical practice concerned with enlarging the interpretive possibilities of written laws to avoid injustices. Equitable readings could open up the literal or conventional signification of legal texts in response to unforeseen differences presented by individual cases:

> For the further exposicion of an estatute there is well to be considered the wordes, the sentence, & the meanynge thereof, for sommetymes it shalbe construed straictelie—that is, according to the wordes & no further. Sometymes the wordes by equytye are stretched to lyke cases. Sommetymes they are expounded againste the wordes. And sommetymes there happen cases upon statutes for which there is no wordes in the statute, and then is the exposicion made at the commen lawe.[29]

Similarly, Sir Christopher Hatton's *Treatise Concerning Statutes*, widely circulated from the last quarter of the sixteenth century though not printed until 1677, drew on Plowden and Saint Germain and argued that:

> All statues may be expounded by Equity so far as *Epicaia* goeth forth, that is, an exception of the Law of God, and the Law of Reason, from the general words of the Law of Man. . . . And, to be short, there are few Statutes Penal, which may not be expounded by Equities.[30]

These moral and rational imperatives to analyze beyond the settled understanding of legal texts carried progressive implications. Plowden's and Hatton's equitable values anticipate, and are clarified by, Stanley Fish's and Jacques Derrida's poststructuralist arguments about the enabling relationship between radical openness of textual interpretation and the discovery of alternative paths of legal justice. Fish observes that the law's foundations are linguistic, and that its power derives from "authoritative marks" of language, or the interpretive force of self-sufficient and impersonal principles.

This situation appears to render the law's "plain" core of meaning immune to challenges from contextual or differential criteria. Yet the legal standard of interpretive immutability is always the product of a previous history of debate resulting in the triumph of a particular set of meanings. Its inherent temporality can be suppressed but not erased. At later moments in history, the circumstances of a present-day case will generate contending perspectives arising from different perceptions of the legal rule and its paradigm cases, and thus open new interpretive horizons. These may in turn become "authoritative" until the process begins afresh.[31]

Derrida connects Fish's arguments about the historically contingent basis of legal decision making to the moral and humane values which inspired Plowden and Hatton:

> To be just, the decision of a judge . . . must not only follow a rule of law or a general law but must also assume it, approve it, confirm its value by a reinstituting act of interpretation . . . as if the judge himself invented the law in every case. No exercise of justice as law can be just unless there is a 'fresh judgment' [Fish's term in *Doing What Comes Naturally*[32]]. This 'fresh judgment' can very well—*must* very well—conform to a preexisting law, but the re-instituting, reinventive and freely decisive interpretation, the responsible interpretation of the judge requires that his 'justice' not just consist in conformity, in the conservative and reproductive activity of judgment . . . [but] must, in its proper moment if there is one . . . reinvent it in each case, rejustify it, at least reivent it in the reaffirmation and the new and free confirmation of its principle.[33]

Like Plowden and Hatton, Derrida argues that textual interpretation and equity (*la droiture*) share the same goals of identifying significant legal aporia through critical comparison of statutes and individual cases.[34] Both kinds of intervention create the imaginative space necessary to achieve fuller or truer justice from what is lacking in, or exceeds, the mechanical application of written laws (*droit*). Equitable approaches to law reflect broader cultural desires for expansive legal and social justice. They propose an intellectual journey from narrow interpretation of an alleged crime based on statutory deference and prescriptive categories to a differential reading made in the light of variable human contexts. The result in both instances is a fresh interpretation of what seemed to be foreclosed situation: a "poetic" practice of legal inventiveness.[35]

Although Plowden's and Hatton's theories of statute interpretation became subordinated to stricter approaches to laws and precedent during the course of the late sixteenth and seventeenth-century jurisdictional dispute between equity and the common law, personified by Lord Chancellor Francis Bacon and Chief Justice Sir Edward Coke, respectively,[36] their principles of humanely individualized judgment did not disappear. They were instrumentally rechannelled through the legal system's discretionary and flexible approaches to trials and sentencing.[37] Prosecutions for murder and infanticide were regularly (though not always steadily) tempered through the local applications of historical memory, community interests, juror discretion, and judicial mercy in the form of discharges, acquittals, reprieves, and pardons. Writers and readers of early modern murder news were fully able to recognize those exceptional aspects of an individual case that exceeded its interpretation according to the letter of the law and/or normative moral and cultural categories. As this book hopes to show through close readings of the full range of sixteenth- and seventeenth-century news about women homicides and infanticides, historical contexts of literary representation, commercial production, and public reception generated contested legal interpretations as well as empathy towards the social origins and personal circumstances of extreme female violence.

In terms of possible outcomes at assize trials, the most influential readers in these respects were jurors and judges. Typically the former were drawn from the ranks of lesser gentry, yeoman freeholders, and substantial merchants. Their attitudes generally reflected governing-class interests and religious affiliations. *The Araignement & burning of Margaret Ferne-seede* attested to the dominance of these perspectives in its fulsome praise of the presiding judge and juries. Yet it was palpably uneasy about how the public would accept the court's handling of the case. The writer carefully laid out the prosecution's circumstantial evidence and character testimony against Ferneseede in what must have been an unusually long—and hence controversial—trial. He also highlighted the solicitous attention paid to Abbot, including the privilege of being called to the inner-court bar before the jury foreman and being prompted to speak in her own defense.[38] He even mimicked courtroom procedures by reproducing lengthy quotations from Sir Edward Coke's charge to the jury and summing-up of evidence, attempting to place readers in the same subject-position as jurors.

In theory the function of grand and petty juries was simply to evaluate the evidence presented to them at arraignments and trials. But in practice both groups acted on prosecutors' or judges' recommendations with increasing independence, especially from the 1650s onwards.[39] Early modern jurors were not vetted for their susceptibility to personal bias, nor were they sealed off from outside media influences as they are today. Indeed pretrial news such as *Murther Murther* (1641), *Bloody Newes from Dover* (1646), *The Unnatural Grand Mother* (1659), *Bloody News from Clarken-well* (1661), and many post-Restoration newspaper reports clearly represented pre-emptive strikes to mold public opinion before assizes began. Implicitly such accounts assumed juries and judges were news readers whom they could influence.[40]

The emergence of juror discretion (or defiance) coincided with two related social factors: the increasing education and literacy of jurors, and the impact of serialized trial and execution news on common forensic knowledge and public opinion.[41] In 1618 Michael Dalton complained that grand juries regularly interpreted (or subverted) the law by challenging and altering indictments according to their own understanding of a case.[42] Zachary Babington objected more strenuously in *Advice to Grand Jurors in Cases of Blood* (1677) to juries evaluating indictments on points of law in which they were supposedly not trained (B3v–4r, C8v). Dalton's and Babington's criticisms indicate that grand jurors did not feel their interpretations had to defer either to the letter of the law or the authority of Crown prosecutors, but could be guided by social values and local interests.[43] Laypersons involved in early modern law enforcement likewise regarded themselves as knowledgeably empowered agents. Cynthia B. Herrup, Malcolm Gaskill), and Steve Hindle have demonstrated that early modern decision-making and opinion-forming processes related to criminal enquiries, legal charges, and court verdicts were widely dispersed and integrated. Participation in the mechanisms of the criminal law were communal and its administration was locally responsive.[44] The criminal law's legitimacy also depended on broad acceptance of a just correlation between criminal and punitive violence. Susan Dwyer Amussen has argued that ordinary English men and women had sufficient social and legal knowledge to assess individual cases of domestic violence, a category that included husband murder and its gendered execution in the form of burning at the stake.[45] Public spectators and lay officials were increasingly news readers (or listeners), aware of rhetorical conventions and legal biases in contemporary narratives as well as the ideological and commercial rivalries of publishers such as David and Elizabeth Mallet and George Croom in the 1670s and 80s. These contexts demystified the authority of assize courts while stimulating public debate about verdicts and the social assumptions underlying them, including those related to men and women's asymmetrical legal rights and punishments.[46] In such instances, as Richard A. Posner has observed, gender-differentiated interpretations of controversial crimes are proto-equitable readings of the law and its judgments.[47]

In this study I explore the interplay of criminal justice and legal and social equity that characterized the reception of early modern news about women murderers. I argue that discourses of equity supplied readers with the conceptual means of plausibly explaining, and in certain cases partially justifying or mitigating, the motives of women in the absence of normative defense narratives and cultural approval of female violence. Equitable perspectives were always available to some degree because they were reader centered and affiliated with nonofficial public desires and opinions. Readers were capable of imagining alternative interpretive choices despite the news writer's dominant—typically prosecution and Protestant—viewpoint. Different political or religious loyalties could lead them to dispute official verdicts.[48] Textually, differential perspectives were latent in narrative evasions, ambiguous material details, or (as the Ferneseede and Abbot pamphlets demonstrate, and I explore in greater detail in chapter 2) fleeting allusions to public controversy surrounding the trial that the news writer had marginalized but not expunged. By isolating these semiotic gaps and discrepancies, one can re-animate counternarratives that circulated during the trial and afterwards, and thus restore a more accurate history of contemporary responses to local cases, individually and collectively.

This book proposes that printed crime news generated a paralegal culture of equitable perspectives that enabled early modern jurors, judges, and other officials to conceptualize the rational options of leniency extended towards female suspects in the many arraignments and trials ending in dismissal or acquittal. (Not surprisingly, these anti-climactic outcomes went largely *un*reported in popular news before the Restoration; they are now only austerely documented by the surviving evidence of county assize records.) Three major historical developments fostered conditions of equitable news reception: (1) the emergence of writers presenting circumstantially contexualizing, skeptical, and/or sympathetic accounts; (2) competitive social and political discourses generated by the growth and consumption of commercial journalism; and (3) conflicting interpretations by diversely positioned readers. Seventeenth-century news made economic, physical, and emotional circumstances related to female homicide and child murder increasingly visible. This empirical evidence underwrote reading practices of comparison and differentiation that vied with reductive images of female wickedness and traditional jurisprudence.[49] An emergent dialectic of identities gradually challenged—without ever abandoning and in some respects strengthening—caricatures of murderous wives and unnatural mothers. In chronological terms, therefore, the popular profile of the female murderer exhibited both representational continuity and change. Such conditions militate against a teleological analysis of the period's news texts. Chapters 3 to 5 of this book will therefore be arranged primarily according to historical categories of crime, narrative structures, and topical contexts rather than by strict date of publication. Most of the homicides and infanticides discussed in these chapters are reported only in single news accounts. A relatively small number of the period's cases, however, survive in multiple or substantially contested reports. These tended to mingle prosecution-oriented narratives and *de facto* defense arguments in the absence of legal remedies and customary approval of female violence. Chapter 2 will examine a selection of these diversely versioned texts, which invited the public to assess the motives and circumstances of individual women critically and, potentially, equitably.

CONFESSION, EXECUTION, AND CRIMINAL BIOGRAPHY

Official examinations, arraignments, and trials were one of two main sources of information for news of convicted murderers. The other was a prisoner's confession of her life and crime. This information could be extracted either before the trial, usually by local officers, or after her conviction up to the moment of her execution. As the passage about Margaret Ferneseede quoted at the beginning of this introduction illustrated, posttrial and gallows confessions were largely the responsibility of clergymen who counselled the condemned woman or man facing public execution and tried to bring her or him to repentance. The often conflicting legal, spiritual, and human objectives made the relationship between condemned murderers and prisoner visitors (as such clerics were called) far more complex and intimate than that of a trial reporter narrating a murder according to the Crown's version of events.

As servants of government and ecclesiastical policy, prison visitors had access to privileged sources of information. They were in a unique position to offer news readers brief biographies of the defendant based on her own words and experiences, however reconstituted through trial and gallows rituals to produce official justifications of court decisions. On the other hand, prison visitors were also motivated by personal interests and career ambitions. These sometimes created visible conflicts with their charitable and spiritual duties that could compromise their narrative authority and, by implication, the legitimacy of the criminal law.

As we shall see throughout this book, many murder pamphlets were written as one-off ventures by anonymous clergyman-reporters. A revealing exception to this situation was the early to mid-seventeenth-century author Henry Goodcole. His unprecedented half-dozen news pamphlets were among the most innovative and visually arresting of their kind and established him as England's first professional real-crime writer.[50] Goodcole's discussions of homicide, petty treason, and child murder opened new social perspectives on the causes of female violence that broke with the stridently moralizing, self-censored, or patently fictionalized approaches that had characterized earlier murder news. In collaboration with several publishers, his pamphlets targeted a broad audience ranging from semi-literate to educated readers. They drew concentrated attention to the huge commercial potential of domestic crime news, which post-Restoration publishers eagerly exploited in a rapidly expanding market for crime journalism.

Looking at an example of Goodcole's work is a convenient way of introducing the biographical model of early modern news. *The Adultresses Funerall Day* (1635) was one of three pamphlets published towards the end of Goodcole's career that began consciously, if provisionally, to represent a female defendant's point of view. His report based on personal interviews offered readers comparative stories of an unnamed woman and Alice Clarke.[51] Both were burnt to death in Smithfield in 1635 after being convicted of killing their husbands by poisoning. Smithfield was known in English historical memory as the site where heretics or martyrs were executed during the sixteenth century, and it might have been this association that prompted the publishers, Nicholas and John Oakes, to include an otherwise incongruous image of a man being burnt at the stake on the title page. The publishers also probably supplied the pamphlet's sensationalizing title, although the narrative was written by Goodcole, then Visitor of Newgate

Prison. His job was to obtain a full confession of the murder event from condemned persons that supported the court's verdict, and to prepare them for a publicly penitent death.

After offering a potted history of homicide, poison, and notorious early modern domestic murderers, Goodcole invited readers to contrast the women's lives and crimes. The unnamed wife, "much commiserated, much lamented," suffered "injuries, and harsh and unmanly usage" at the hands

The Adultreſſes Funerall Day:
In flaming, ſcorching, and conſuming fire:
OR
The burning downe to aſhes of *Alice Clarke* late of *Vx-bridge* in the County of *Miadleſex*, in *Weſt-ſmith-field*, on *Wenſday* the 20. of *May*, 1635. for the unnaturall poiſoning of *Fortune Clarke* her Husband.

A breviary of whoſe Confeſſion taken from her owne mouth, is here unto annexed: As alſo what ſhe ſayd at the place of her Execution.

By her daily Viſiter H. G. *in life and death. And now publiſhed by Authority and Commaund.*

LONDON
Printed by *N.* and *I. Okes*, dwelling in *Well-yard* in lit-tle St. *Bartholmews*, neare unto the *Lame Hoſpitall* gate, 1635.

Figure 1.1 The Adultresses Funerall Day (1635). Reproduced by permission of the Houghton Library, Harvard University.

of her husband. Mismatched in age, class, and temperament, their wretched marriage degenerated to the point where he "used not onely to beat her with the next cudgell that came accidentally unto his hand, but often tying her to his bed-post to strip her and whippe her, &c." Goodcole's voyeuristic portrait of wife battery and rape culminating in the imaginatively provocative "&c." was unusually graphic for early modern murder news and unequivocal in condemning the husband's viciousness.

Suffering acutely but prevented by social codes of feminine modesty from revealing her predicament, the wife sank into suicidal despair, "pondering with her selfe how she might end both their lives by poyson." Continuing to narrate from the wife's viewpoint, Goodcole related how she administered poison first to her husband and then resolved "with her selfe to drinke the rest" but was overcome with guilt. Revealing what she had done, she begged her husband "to take some present *Antidote* to preserve his life, which was yet recoverable" (B1v). Switching to dramatized first-person speech, Goodcole presented her husband rejecting this advice:

> nay thou Strumpet and murderesse, I will receive no help at all, but I am resolved to dye and leave the world, be it for no other cause, but to have thee burnt at a stake for my death: which having said, and obstinate in that *Heathenish* resolution, he soone after expired. (A4v–B1r)

With an eye to the legal implications of these actions, Goodcole suggested the battered wife's motives were defensive and nonmalicious, though premeditated. The invented or embellished final speech repositioned the husband as a vengeful reprobate. This first narrative seemed to show Goodcole moving between the boundaries of his official position as Visitor of Newgate, which prevented him from directly challenging the court verdict, and the new conceptual territory of rational empathy for the condemned woman who came into his care, and whose story he not only heard from her own mouth but also sought out from "those of credite, who were well acquainted with the conditions of them both" (B2r).[52] In suggesting that the abuse suffered by the wife "almost compled her to what she did," Goodcole daringly invited readers to reconsider the homicide as a possible case of self-defense or manslaughter rather than wilful murder.

Alice Clarke's more complicated story followed in two parts: a "free and voluntary Confession" on 8 May,[53] and a "second Confession" two days later on the 10th. Goodcole opened by blackening Clarke's reputation and anticipating her temptation to murder by reporting her illicit relationship with Henry White, a lover she refused to stop seeing after being married.[54] Her ties to White were financial as well as emotional, since she had been made pregnant by her master, who, promising her money for silence, "matched her unto *Fortune Clarke* her Husband . . . whom she could not love, or have any matter of maintenance." The master failed to follow through with the money, leaving Alice impoverished in a loveless marriage. Goodcole did not name the master but directly implicated him in the chain of events: "A great clog unto such a mans conscience, if it be true; to seduce a woman unto his will, and so leave her" (B3r).

Alice's relationship with White enraged her husband, who "outragiously fell from words unto blowes" (B2v). The situation reached a crisis when Fortune discovered Alice and White "shut up together privately in a Chamber in the house," whereupon he "freshly fell foule upon her, and so cruelly added blowe upon blow upon her body, that the markes thereof were very visible on her body at this present" (B2v). Afterwards White provided Alice with money to buy mercury from an apothecary. As she explained later to Goodcole, when she returned home, her husband bolted down the poison after rifling her pockets to search for drinking money. Goodcole doubted this explanation, but admitted he could not discover other details to refute it. This left the reader anticipating further revelations and set up Goodcole to demonstrate conclusively his powers of interrogation and narrative closure. On the basis of her reported testimony so far, he knew there was reasonable doubt as to whether Alice was legally responsible for her husband's death. While unsympathetic since she was resisting an admission of guilt, Goodcole's report represented ambiguous motives and intentions as well as multiple sides to the story that almost certainly reflected conflicting public opinion.

Alice's second confession did not follow directly. Instead Goodcole inserted "A Short Tract Vpon The *hainousnesse of Poysoning*" (B3v–B4v). This brief collection of moral, legal, and historical observations was more scholarly than the preceding confessions and seemed aimed less at a "popular" readership than at members of Goodcole's professional class. As a rhetorical diversion, it shut down the relative openness of the first interview and retreated from legal possibility of judging Fortune Clark's death to be accidental or Alice's actions to be chance medley. It was as if in the two days between the interviews that Goodcole recognized he had possibly undermined the official verdict that had found Alice guilty and needed to show which side he was on. And yet this backtracking, if it was such, did not lead him to erase Alice's first confession or the free play of competing interpretations of the crime, which included arguable claims for legal mitigation based on uncertain evidence of wilful murder.

Goodcole reoriented Alice's second confession towards repentance. Adjusting his rhetoric, the tone became judgmental: "this obdurate Malefactor . . . in Adultery was so Rooted, and insensible of the heavy burthen, and most intolerable plagues insuing" (B4v–C1r). As accounts by Goodcole and other early modern writers demonstrated (and I examine in greater detail in chapter 3), pressure on the condemned to confess and perform penitently on the gallows was enormous, both from state officials and spectators.[55] Stubborn prisoners could be blackmailed by prison visitors,[56] and Alice Clarke was one of these, "of a stout angry disposition, suddainly inraged, if you began to touch her to the quicke of her husband poysoning" (C1r). To break her resistance, they decided to deny Clarke her last rites. Making as though she "was no fitting guest for the Table of the *Lord Iesus*," they

> would have excluded her thence, in denying the benefit of the holy Communion, of the Body and Blood of Jesus Christ. . . . Whereupon, it pleased God, so to mollifie her heart, that teares from her eyes, and truth from her tongue proceeded, as may appeare by this her ensuing Confession at the very Stake. (C1r–v)

According to Goodcole, Clarke confessed she bought mercury with the initial intent of giving it to her husband. She reiterated the disastrous circumstances of her master's getting her pregnant and forcing her to move to London to wed her husband, "whom shee could not love, nor no way affect, or haue any matter of maintenance" (C1v). She continued to deny actually causing her husband's death, now explaining in greater detail that

> hauing no conuenient opportunity to dispose of [the poison], she put it into her sleeve, which her husband as she said tooke it out of her hand, then being overcharged with drink he immediatly swallowed it down, was thereat so perplexed, that she uttred these words unto her Husband, that he had undone both him selfe and her. (C2r)

Having supposedly "disburdned her loaded conscience" by this declaration, Clarke allegedly grew more self-possessed, "and by her countenance, which was very ruddy[,] confirmed her inward new begotten chearfulnesse . . . and surrendered her soule into the hands of the Lord *Iesu*" (C2r). Goodcole encoded Clarke's performance with conventional physical signs of religious conversion and—going back to memories of Smithfield preserved by John Foxe—Protestant martyrdom that ambiguously justified his own professional conduct. Seen from Clarke's perspective, Alice voiced her independent conscience, drew boundaries around her moral guilt, problematized the legal verdict of petty treason, and possibly left some readers skeptical about the truth of her repentance. She seized this last public opportunity to reconstitute her future identity as a domestically martyred and unjustly tried woman, which Goodcole had in fact abetted through his socially contextualized biography and his revealing comparison with Alice's unnamed counterpart.

The Adultresses Funerall Day thus presented both condemning and critically compassionate views of female homicides. On the one hand it denounced the mythical evils of discontented wives, and on the other it vividly condemned the physical violence inflicted on the bodies of two women by their brutal husbands. The unnamed wife, free of any ambiguous sexual history, became a more sympathetic foil to Alice Clarke. While stopping short of presenting robust defense arguments, Goodcole's account of the former's values and behavior undermined any simple legal position of wilful malice, as the trial indictment claimed. In both cases, moreover, the dialogic structure of his prison and gallows interviews called into question the culturally privileged prosecution narrative by drawing attention to questionable facts and culpability, redefining the crime in the light of each woman's individual circumstances and experience.

Goodcole located the origins of Alice Clarke's criminal identity in personal sin and marital infidelity as well as the material and legal constraints of her enforced impecunious marriage. Drawing on his subjects' prison confessions and the testimony of neighbors and witnesses, he evaluated the social and economic factors that contributed to both dysfunctional marriages. His pamphlet also made wife battering shockingly visible, and so contributed to changes in seventeenth-century attitudes towards "acceptable" levels of "corrective" physical violence by husbands.[57] For some female readers of Goodcole's pamphlet, his vivid reports might have forged memory links with their own experiences of domineering, unfaithful, or abusive husbands. And in such cases, as Cynthia Marshall has argued in the context of early modern executions and the formation of public identities, they might have "over-read" Alice's Clarke's ambiguous "surrender" at the stake as a subversive form of martyrdom, a scenario made possible by the generic title page illustration.[58]

Along with *The Adultresses Funerall Day,* Goodcole's other two pamphlets from this period, *Heavens Speedie Hue and Cry sent after Lust and Murther* (1635) and *Natures Cruell Step-Dames, or Matchlesse Monsters of the Female Sex* (1637), presented readers with a gallery of female murderers in a decade when prosecutions for serious felonies peaked.[59] His writings were pivotal interventions in the history of English crime news. Before Goodcole, murder reports going back to Arthur Golding's pamphlet about Anne Saunders (*A briefe discourse* [1573]) had been framed mainly by Calvinist moral dichotomies and regressive views of female deviance and human nature. (The Ferneseede and Abbot pamphlets are secular exceptions to these conventions.) The chief rationale for reporting news had been to exemplify inevitable detection and punishment of crime and thereby affirm public values of order, justice, and piety. This agenda was justified by Reformation ideologies emphasizing divine omniscience and vengeance operating through the state machinery of criminal law. Goodcole's pamphlets rehearsed these cultural legacies, which continued to be written and read into murder news until the end of the seventeenth century and beyond. Yet they also began to represent new forensic perspectives being opened up by print journalism that documented the material and personal circumstances of individual murders, thereby explaining the motives of female killers according to epistemological categories of social and economic power. By implicitly questioning traditional jurisprudence, court verdicts, and dominant public attitudes towards female murderers, Goodcole's criminal biographies introduced ideas of social and legal equity into popular representations of deadly female violence.

HOMICIDE AND GENDER DIFFERENCE

Public curiosity about murder was heightened if the killer was female, since women committed crimes of blood far less often than men, even though disproportionate numbers of early modern news stories about them suggested the opposite.[60] A stronger threat of contagious social disorder was conveyed by the settings in which women normally acted out their violence. For many turned to murder in their homes: spaces more publicly open in the early modern period than they became later, yet thoroughly infused with traditional (though continually contested) ideas about proper gender and marital relations. As domestic microcosms of civic and national governing hierarchies,[61] households were saturated with cultural obligations for women to fulfil prescribed roles as obedient wives and dutiful mothers. Within these ideologically charged spaces, when women murdered husbands, servants, and children, their violence seemed to represent more disturbing outbreaks of disorder than homicides by men, which typically occurred during drunken brawls or highway robberies and might be socially or legally mitigated as momentary excesses of otherwise admirable virile aggression.[62] When women killed in their homes, or indeed elsewhere, their actions inverted cultural norms. The sense of moral transgression was often aggravated by the means of death, since many female murderers turned to poison. Long regarded as the most heinous form of murder and behavior culturally foreign to England, poison combined the devious and the extravagant in its betrayal of domestic trust.[63] Because it was deliberate, relatively slow to reveal itself, and ultimately agonizing, poison defined the accused woman's actions as calculated cruelty and usually put her beyond the scope of mitigated charges such as manslaughter or killing in self-defense.[64] The strong cultural and legal associations of female homicide with poison thus made it a highly gendered category of murder news. Furthermore, poison was associated with some of the period's most politicized murder conspiracies, including the notoriously byzantine case of Thomas Overbury in 1615–16, which established a new threshold for public debate about class privileges and culpability involving male and female defendants. The chemical properties and physiological effects of poison also made it a touchstone for new developments in forensic science and the competing opinions that followed in printed news. These contexts kept alive possibilities of contrary or equitable interpretations. I shall examine their relationship to news of female poisoners in chapter 4.

Another fundamental difference between news reports of homicide in this period and our own was the virtually synonymous association of murder with sin, which had the effect of suppressing economic and circumstantial explanations. According to Calvinist theorists such as William Perkins and the many clerical news writers he inspired, original sin created a universal human disposition towards spiritual and literal murder. From this perspective, ordinary readers and citizens were distinguished from homicides only by their degree of self-control and not by human ontology or what we would now call environmental causes. Only the hard-to-identify elect possessed the justified will to resist slipping from sinful offenses into murders and child killings, as Gilbert Dugdale argued with some strain in the course of implicitly defending Elizabeth Caldwell (*A True Discourse*, [1604], discussed in chapter 2).[65] Biblically and classically derived ideas about the flawed nature of woman aggravated assumptions about their intrinsic tendencies to kill. The origins of murder in fallen nature could be related by analogy to any form of suspect behavior in the defendant—in women typically sexual activity—since they all shared the same origins. Hence the reflexive association of female homicides in popular printed news before the Restoration with whoredom and/or adultery, and the emphasis in women's murder trials on a public reputation for chastity (in both early modern and modern senses). Detecting and publicizing cases of sinful murder to deter crime and urge more rigorous personal and state discipline explained much, but not all, of the clamorous moralizing found in many murder pamphlets, especially earlier in the period.

For less-than-zealous or skeptical readers, however, responses to *Matchlesse Monsters of the Female Sex* (publisher Francis Cole's sensationalizing subtitle for Goodcole's *Natures Cruell Step-Dames*) might have been similar to political or religious satire: the caricatured representations allowed ordinary readers to distance themselves from any mental identification with them. Thus, news pamphlets not explicitly premised on Calvinist ideology began to shift thinking about crime away from murder representing the final destructive stage of irremediably reprobate lives, although not in any theorized or systematic way. Crime instead came to be framed as a secular legal problem arising from real individuals or social classes who had experienced personal or social misfortune, or who threatened ordinary citizens in identifiably risky zones. A materially oriented analysis of crime invited new kinds of personally defensive conduct based on self-informing recognition of danger signs, rather than blanket exhortations to self-examination and punitive rigor. Such representations also identified relational motives for murder that were linked to certain categories of anti-social behavior. These epistemological shifts altered assumptions of blame. Although writers of virtually all seventeenth-century accounts of female homicides continued to assign primary guilt to the woman who killed, some authors such as Henry Goodcole or Roger L'Estrange (*A Hellish Murder* [1688])—to cite examples of two named writers from the vast majority of anonymous ones—were willing to focus on physical and psychological abuse that led to the deadly response, rather than collapsing explanations of motive into seduction by the devil or atavistic female nature. In the case of domestic crimes especially, violence towards women by husbands, masters, or mistresses reciprocated by murder became a focus of horror and revulsion in later seventeenth-century trial- and execution-reports (e.g., *Great and Bloody News, From Farthing-Alley* [1680], or *Dreadful News from*

Southwark [1680]). This viewpoint divided human responsibility more equitably among conflicted personal agents, and it dispersed blame situationally and ethically if not always legally.

In law a charge of murder and the key issue of determining malicious intent to kill were prosecuted in the same way for men and women. If juries decided that a person's life had been taken violently and wilfully, there was virtually no question in this period that the aggressor's life should be forfeit. This kind of murder story was the safest—in the sense of being secure from judicial or government censorship—for early modern reporters and publishers, because it illustrated an uncomplicated relationship between crime and justice. Stories of wilful murder followed by swift apprehension, trial, and execution usefully publicized the violation of moral and legal boundaries that were widely assumed to be clear and immutable. Reaffirming those boundaries by showing murderers brought to justice in turn justified exploiting a sensationally violent crime for commercial profit.

Yet in disputable cases and rival claims by competing news accounts, gender differences often altered normative correlations between crime, judgment, and punishment. Most sixteenth- and seventeenth-century murder stories were framed by traditional assumptions about social order and female behavior, beginning with the law itself.[66] When wives killed their husbands, the felony was petty treason rather than murder, and the punishment was burning at the stake rather than hanging.[67] Reducing women to ashes—as many news reports put it chillingly—provoked visceral reactions from spectators, and a greater likelihood of disagreements with court sentences and damage to the law's reputation. Writing to Sir Dudley Carleton on 8 July 1616, Sir John Chamberlain questioned Anne Wallen's condemnation for petty treason in light of the manner of her execution and her defensive response to her husband's violence:

> That morning [22 June 1616] early there was a joyners wife burnt in Smithfeild [*sic*] for killing her husband. Yf the case were no otherwise then I can learn yet, she had *summum jus* [extreme right, or excessive rigor of the law], for her husband having brawld, and beaten her, she took up a chesill or such other instrument and flung it at him, which cut him into the bellie, wherof he died.

Chamberlain emphasized the husband's threat to Anne's life and her lack of premeditation, since she, in apparent desperation, had seized a tool related to the household business that would have been casually at hand. His interpretation implicitly mitigated her actions to manslaughter or accidental killing, and his Latin formula pointedly criticized the court's lack of equitable justice in privileging the husband's legal rights over the wife's. Chamberlain's justification of Anne stood in contrast to T. Platte's ballad version of the crime, *Anne Wallens Lamentation* (1616), in which Anne appeared as a traditional railing wife who deliberately revenged herself on her husband after he cuffed her on the ear.[68]

In general, juries seem to have been more reluctant to convict female murderers knowing that burning would be their fate. Judges seem to have had similar hesitations, occasionally accepting face value pleas of pregnancy after conviction or sentencing. By doing so they would grant the condemned woman a reprieve that might eventually turn into indefinite clemency if she managed to give birth. Or judges could choose an alternative mechanism of contingent equity by impanelling a jury of "matrons" or local women to examine the woman "pleading her belly."[69] These women would possibly know the condemned woman, and they were given flexible scope to return a favorable or negative verdict based on their evaluation of the crime's local context as well as the woman's physical condition. If they returned a positive verdict, they could effectively reroute the whole judicial process, since contemporary documents indicate that women were not invariably put to death after they had given birth to a child. Because early modern prisons were essentially holding tanks for semi-annual assize-trials rather than institutions for correction, these women presumably returned to their own or other communities.[70]

Similarly, although infanticide—strictly, the killing of newborn children— could in theory be committed by either women or men, in practice it was regarded almost entirely as a female crime.[71] Because it normally took place within households and violated deeply held assumptions about the natural bond between mothers and children, it was defined legally and socially as a uniquely transgressive form of behavior. A 1624 statute distinguished infanticide from murder by making it illegal for an unmarried woman to conceal a birth, regardless of how the child subsequently died. Those charged were usually single female servants, most vulnerable to patriarchal intimidation. The 1624 statute proved to be controversial, however, because it altered the customary burden of proof and required the woman to prove her innocence with witnesses and material evidence. Its application also had to contend with pliable local attitudes about the woman's actual intent, the interests or absence of the father, and practical calculations about parish support of bastard children. For these and other reasons, juries increasingly resisted convicting women under the 1624 law after an initial wave of indictments in the 1630s and 1640s, when prosecutions for all felonies reached or had just passed their highest levels in this period. Another temporary upturn occurred around 1680.[72] Early modern readers would not necessarily have recognized the actual peaks and valleys of these prosecution trends from news pamphlets and newspapers, however,[73] which circulated the greatest number of infanticide reports after the Restoration, especially in the late 1670s and early 80s, during lapses in the Licensing Act. Like poisoning, infanticide constituted another distinct historical category of female homicide, but one that was more amenable to legal redefinition and equitable counterinterpretation. It will be examined in chapter 5.

NEWS SOURCES, READERS, AND CIRCULATION

The historical evidence supporting this study can be divided into three broad categories defined by commercial or noncommercial publication and readership: official records and artifacts; personal, critical, and fictionalized commentaries in manuscript or print; and popular printed news.

Archival work by early modern historians over the past forty years has made the variably surviving legal records from county and metropolitan assizes more readily available. Assizes were public sessions where the most serious crimes—apart from state treason—were tried by judges appointed by the Privy Council who travelled on established circuits (e.g., the Western circuit, Home counties circuit, etc.). They took place twice a year except in London, where the higher volume of indictments necessitated holding Old Bailey sessions eight times a year.[74] Official accounts from county assizes included indictments, coroners' inquests, depositions, and gaol books. These documents provide invaluable quantitative evidence of variable frequencies in crime, changes in juror and judicial attitudes, and gendered differences in rates of prosecutions, convictions, and executions. News reports, especially after the Restoration, often relied on official documents publicized at assize trials such as indictments and coroners' inquests read aloud in court, though they were written in an archaic mixture of Latin, French, and English (except during the Commonwealth, when they were written exclusively in English).[75]

Where they survive, indictments and other court records should in theory be of great value. In practice their usefulness is limited by their brevity and questionable accuracy. Historians who have worked closely with assize records have shown they were routinely distorted by formulaic conventions and the subjective interpretations of court clerks, who briefly summarized rather than transcribed trial proceedings to produce documents conformable with prosecution objectives.[76] My research has confirmed these tendencies. Although court records can establish that a particular crime and trial took place, they lack information about motives, intentions, or circumstances, and their factual details often contradict those in pamphlets and other popular publications.[77] The discrepancies may clarify differences between official and popular criteria for interpreting criminal events and personal responsibility. They may also draw attention to contexts that contemporaries viewed as equally if not more important than the material facts of the case (which were by no means the highest priority in determining guilt or innocence). But given the large number of infanticide cases reported very briefly in Restoration news formats as well as the limited usefulness of formulaic indictments, it was neither practical nor meaningful to attempt to track down every extant court record. I have instead tried to locate surviving documents related to the most substantially reported murder cases.

Personal sources are noncommercial writings and correspondence, while original critical and fictionalized sources consist of commercially published texts that either mention or comment on the crime under discussion. Personal accounts include manuscript correspondence and notes such as John Castle's letter to James Miller describing Anne Turner's murder trial in 1615 (reproduced in *The Court and Times of James the First* [1849], edited by Thomas Birch), or Dr. William Petty's medical notes on reviving Anne Greene after she was hanged for infanticide in 1651 (BL Add. MS 72892). Critical works encompass legal manuals and advice books such as T. E.'s *The Lawes Resolutions of Womens Rights* (1632) or Zachary Babington's *Advice to Grand Jurors in Cases of Blood*. An anonymous play about Anne Saunders, *A Warning for Faire Women* (*ca*. 1590, printed 1599), which draws on contemporary accounts of the crime in addition to Arthur Golding's *A briefe discourse* (1573), is an example of fictionalized evidence. These sources vary in historical usefulness, especially when defined according to "documentary" standards. Yet they all possess value as witnesses to the political and religious contexts of women's murder trials, and the different cultural uses to which their lives and crimes could be put.

The same evidential flexibility must be extended to printed news texts, which in most cases provide the only source of information about female subjects in this book. These women were rarely public or high-ranking figures. In terms of literary conventions as well as commercial marketability, their crimes rarely generated recorded personal responses from contemporary readers. Even though women murderers were less common than men, assumptions about the impact of commercial news on readers, especially powerful ones such as jurors and judges, must be based on: (1) general material evidence of the production and consumption of news; (2) the innovative development of genres and formats to serve expanding consumer interests and markets; (3) the growing distribution of crime news through extensive and well-established commercial networks; and (4) the purchase and reception of murder news by a wide spectrum of buyers, who included local officials interested in crime as part of their working lives and civic knowledge. In addition, the growth of competing versions of the latest crime among rival publishers makes it reasonable to assume that public debate of female homicides and child murder grew proportionately, informed as it was by an array of often intense political perspectives and topical associations (e.g., the Exclusion Crisis of 1680–81, which temporarily altered the popular profile of infanticide; see chapter 5).

Commercialized news culture emerged vigorously, if spasmodically, after the Restoration until 1695, when deregulation of press began to direct practices of news reporting towards modern journalism (e.g., lengthy verbatim reports of individual testimony rather than trial summaries).[78] Changes in seventeenth-century print technology and news formats also shifted the dominant popular medium of murder news from broadside ballads and black-letter pamphlets presenting didactic exempla, to documentary accounts in half- or folded-broadsheet newspapers and news reports using roman lettering. For both ideological and commercial reasons these formats were better able to represent the perspectives of the defendant—implicitly ignored or marginalized in earlier genres—and the prosecution simultaneously, allowing readers to judge their merits more equitably.

The claims of this book rest on accounting for the full range and volume of popular printed news about women homicides and infanticides to the end of seventeenth century. Previous studies of female crime news have confined themselves to selected cases represented by ballads, pamphlets, and plays, mainly before the Restoration.[79] Before exploring the period's diverse and changing popular attitudes towards women homicides and infanticides, it is essential to identify the ways in which these perspectives were mediated by various news genres and bibliographic formats. The remainder of this introduction will outline distinguishing features of the period's traditional and emerging printed news: ballads, pamphlets, gallows speeches, trial- and execution-reports, and newspapers. It will conclude with a discussion of news distribution and popular readership.

BALLADS

News ballads were published at the cheapest end of the market for printed texts and aimed at the humblest readers, although they were not restricted to that readership. They were the country's most widely and frequently distributed news form until the later seventeenth century. The highly accessible—and much disparaged—ballad genre made its transition into print in the mid-sixteenth century from a flourishing oral tradition of itinerant minstrels who transmitted topical events and folktales through simple narratives written in rhyming verse ("ballad metre" or "poulters' measure") sung to popular tunes. Before the development of printing, the written counterpart to this oral form consisted of ballads recorded in manuscripts, many of which were later printed.[80] Although print technology rapidly commercialized news ballads, it did not suddenly displace oral and manuscript media, which continued to co-exist with the newer public forms. As Tessa Watt has demonstrated, manuscript versions of news ballads such as *The vnnaturall Wife* (*ca.* 1628) and *A warning for all desperate Women* (*ca.* 1628), recounting Alice Davies's husband-murder, remained current well into the seventeenth century, creating a fluid zone between oral and print cultures that served the needs of illiterate, semi-literate, and educated buyers.[81]

First issued in broadsides (i.e., large single folio sheets printed on one side), the cost of ballads rose from a halfpenny in the sixteenth century to a penny from the mid-1630s: "For a peny you may have all the Newes in England, of Murders, Flouds, Witches, Fires, Tempests, and what not, in one of *Martin Parkers* Ballads."[82] Prices could go higher if the ballad was illustrated. Woodcut illustrations extended the accessibility of ballads, and thus of crime news, to semi-literate buyers or even nonreaders who might hear the ballad sung or read. Commissioned woodcuts directly illustrating the contents could double the cost of a ballad. Yet most ballad images derived from old woodblocks that printers recycled to advertise the basic genre, subject, or emotional mood. For murders, the most common images were of a person being hanged or burnt at the stake, or of a woman stabbing a man at the prompting of a nearby devil. Printers and publishers included images more and more frequently during the seventeenth century to broaden the market of broadside ballads.[83] Illustrated ballads also seem to have had decorative and public-notice functions. They were commonly posted—and thus presumably listened to as well as read—in alehouses, coffee-houses, markets, and other public spaces. Izaak Walton described an "honest Alehouse" in 1653, "where we shall find a cleanly room, Lavender in the Windowes, and twenty Ballads stuck about the walls."[84] Thus was news of the latest female homicide most economically circulated.

PAMPHLETS

Occasional pamphlets were the news form English readers before the Restoration probably associated most closely with homicide and child murder. They provided the most detailed stories and striking images. Pamphlets were also the most flexible medium in terms of presenting different kinds of testimony from the accused and witnesses. By making all or some of the entire legal process of arrest, examination, imprisonment, trial, judgment, and punishment publicly visible, they not only informed readers but also opened procedures and verdicts to challenges. Reports of confessions and execution speeches also provided the government with opportunities to propagate official ideologies, to demarcate boundaries between obedient and disorderly public conduct, and in theory to deter future crime, which arguably affected most the interests of propertied classes.[85] Despite their commonplace stereotyping and moralizing, they are more complex semiotic artifacts than many scholars have hitherto recognized.[86]

Materially, a pamphlet or chapbook referred loosely to any short piece of printed writing, sold unbound. Before the Restoration they appeared in octavo (small format) or quarto (somewhat larger format). Earlier in the sixteenth and seventeenth centuries they were usually printed in black-letter type, an older font style that came to be associated with popular news ballads and crime reports (and became a vestigial generic marker on later seventeenth-century title pages, similar to certain uses of gothic script today). Otherwise pamphlets were printed in roman and italic type. From the 1670s onwards, publishers of news pamphlets competed (or in some cases co-operated) with those of broadside newspapers that employed similar rhetorical structures (discussed further below). Typically pamphlets consisted of four leaves or eight pages, but some could be as little as two leaves and many were much longer. More expensive than ballads or broadsides, most pamphlets sold for a penny or two, more if the pamphlet was substantial or illustrated. Although now classified as subliterary ephemera, their readership at the time was narrower than ballads because it did not extend down to the humblest semiliterate readers, yet it was still very broad. The expansive format allowed room for moral and social commentary as well as more sophisticated forensic detailing. Certain longer accounts by named authors, such as Arthur Golding's *A briefe discourse* (1573), Gilbert Dugdale's *A True Discourse of the practises Of Elizabeth Caldwell* (1604), Henry Goodcole's *Heavens Speedie Hue and Cry sent after Lust and Murther* (1635), John Quick's *Hell Open'd* (1676), and John Newton's *The Penitent Recognition of Joseph's Brethren* (1684), as well as anonymous reports such as *Two most vnnaturall and bloodie Murthers* (1605) and *A Perfect Narrative of the Robbery and Murder Committed near Dame Annis so Cleer* (1669), made a clear bid to interest educated and/or godly readers in serious legal, theological, and political issues. In short, pamphlets were the most activist medium for relating individual crimes to wider social contexts and interpretive perspectives, including equitable ones.

In most cases, however, the murder pamphlet's immediate appeal lay in presenting fascinating or bizarre stories of bloody violence, illicit sex, and monstrous cruelty set in everyday houses, towns or cities. Juxtaposing the sensational with the commonplace heightened the shock value of the murder and extended its social implications beyond the local community in which it took place. In this way murder pamphlets shared an attempt to exploit responses of wonder, strangeness, and outrage with more traditional news ballads.[87] Publishers in fact often entered a ballad and pamphlet about the same crime in the Stationers' Register. Other pamphlet writers justified themselves on the basis of correcting misleading reports circulated by more fictionalizing news ballads. Henry Goodcole vowed "to defend the truth of the cause" of Elizabeth Sawyer's trial for murder by witchcraft, "which in some measure, hath receiued a wound already, by most base false Ballets" (*The wonderfull discouerie of Elizabeth Sawyer* [1621], A3v). Although such claims were conventional and self-interested, pamphlets were able by virtue of their flexible format to lay substantial legal and circumstantial evidence open to public scrutiny.

GALLOWS SPEECHES

The news pamphlet was dependent on emerging print technology and thus an experimental genre. Authors dealt with the problem of inventing suitable styles and structures of representation by appropriating treatments of existing themes and subjects, such as monsters and prodigies (e.g. *The Most Cruell and Bloody Mvrther committed by . . . Annis Dell* [1606]). Initially, many of their productions were fancifully heterogenous (*viz.*, T. I., *A World of wonders. A Masse of Murthers. A Covie of Cosonages* [1595]). Eventually they began to concentrate on particular stages in the prisoner's journey from crime to execution. The interim between sentencing and execution created a uniquely stressful period with great potential for dramatic revelations. The condemned woman could be pressured—or sometimes volunteer—to divulge new information about a murder that rapid assize trials were unable or uninterested in drawing out. Confession and conversion speeches delivered from the execution ladder, cart, or scaffold were also a much anticipated part of the early modern theater of capital punishment. In theory and often in practice, the condemned person stood before assembled spectators with a noose placed loosely around her neck while she confessed the killing and repudiated her past sinful life. She warned the crowd to avoid her fate by repenting their own sins, and she occasionally ended with prayers for the monarch and civic authorities as well as her own soul. Michael Harris has summed up the genre's appeal: "Public curiosity about the circumstances of a convict's life and the events surrounding his final exit was apparently insatiable. In the period between conviction and execution the condemned prisoners became a very hot literary property indeed."[88]

These were not spontaneous outbursts of remorse and piety, however, but pieces rehearsed in advance with the help of the prison clergyman who supplied the condemned with sententious phrasing and selected scriptural quotations to interweave with her personal sentiments.[89] Spectators looked forward to seeing how the condemned person would perform her words and gestures in the charged liminal space between this world and the next (or how she *refused* to perform them, as Margaret Ferneseede, Elizabeth Abbot, and many other women did). The visitor who had coached the condemned prisoner accompanied her to the gallows on the day of execution and shared her performance with his own homily, prayers, and hymns, which crowds might join in singing. Government and judicial authorities were eager to have the condemned person play this role because it legitimized their personal power and exemplified divine justice operating through the courts. I shall discuss these conventional performances and prisoners' frequent resistance to them in chapter 3.

Public confessions and gallows speeches evolved as a specialized subgenre published either separately or within longer "relations" of criminal lives and trials. Arthur Golding appended Anne Saunders's confession to *A briefe discourse*, and Gilbert Dugdale presented Elizabeth Caldwell's *Letter from Prison to her Husband* as well as her execution speeches in separate sections of *A True Discourse* (1604). Prior to the 1630s, however, confessions and gallows speeches were the exception rather than the rule, with most pamphlets simply recording the verdict or the fact of execution. From then onward, when clergymen such as Henry Goodcole began to be officially appointed as prison visitors, gallows speeches became a regular feature of the murder-pamphlet genre. All but one of Goodcole's crime pamphlets contained confessions or reports of gallows' speeches (the exception was *London's Cry* [1620], a celebration of the jury-trial system). As he declared in his first pamphlet: "Dying mens wordes are euer remarkable, & their last deeds memorable for succeeding posterities, by them to be instructed, what vertues or vices they followed and imbraced, and by them to learne to imitate that which was good, and to eschew euil" (*A True Declaration of the happy Conuersion, contrition, and Christian preparation of Francis Robinson* [1618], A2v).

Since the public could circulate quite freely in prisons such as Newgate, condemned prisoners could also be besieged by news writers for information, and sometimes they seem to have co-operated to counteract fictionalized or bogus reports. Or they may have wished to raise money to pay for funerals and family support, or to shield friends and relations from guilt by association. Although the fear of being ridiculed by ballad-mongers and coffee-house customers seems to have inhibited some prisoners from telling their stories, selling accounts to rival publishers could be a way of resisting the pressure prison visitors put on the condemned to confess. As one early eighteenth-century male murderer declared in the preface to his story:

> I hope it may not here be taken amiss, to acquaint the Reader, that he told the author of this, He had given no Account of Himself to the Ordinary of Newgate; and the Reason he said, why he was not willing to give him any proper Satisfaction, as to his Life and Conversation, tho' often importun'd by him, was this, That he had not a Mind to be the Sport and Ridicule of vain, idle Fellows in Coffee-Houses; who only laugh at unfortunate dying Men, who are frighted into a Confession of their private sins; which he was satisfy'd in his conscience, he was oblig'd to confess to none but his Heavenly Father, who knew the Secrets of his Heart.[90]

The cultural fear and power of gallows speeches was also demonstrated by attempts to control or strategically exploit their publication. As *A Perfect Narrative of the Robbery and Murder Committed near Dame Annis so Cleer* (1669) revealed in its final pages, government authorities could commission pamphlet-publishers to gather reports by legal and church officials to discredit dissenting public opinion.[91] Visitor writers also sometimes supplied serial news reports with information. David and Elizabeth Mallet issued three pamphlets entitled *News from Tybvrn* in 1674, 1675, and 1676. The first of these related the *Confession and Execution of . . . Francis Bennet, [sic, and] Ellen Bayly . . . on Wednesday the 16. of the Instant September 1674*. Bennet and Bayly had each allegedly killed their newborn children. Because it opened with a detailed précis of the execution sermon, the account indicated that the visitor's papers were the source of information rather than a trial and/or execution reporter's summary.[92] In 1684 the Court of Aldermen decided that sheriffs, who managed public executions, should act as licensers for "The speeches of any Malefactors."[93] Since the Court appointed the visitors of Newgate, Ludgate, and other London prisons, this was probably an attempt to regulate their activities as well as the publishers'. The fact that sheriffs' involvement—as indicated by printed notices in visitors' accounts into the eighteenth century—was sparse suggested their main concern was controlling legally sensitive and public-opinion shaping news, since the contractual buying and selling of crime news was otherwise privately arranged between publishers and visitors.[94] By the end of seventeenth century visitors such as Samuel Smith had standardized these post-conviction reports in regularly issued publications. His accounts and those of his successors became some of the most popular sources of criminal lives in eighteenth century crime fiction.[95]

TRIAL AND EXECUTION REPORTS

Occasional brief summaries of the most serious or sensational criminal trials began to appear sporadically in English newsbooks during the 1640s. Serial accounts of Old Bailey trials date from the 1670s. The Old Bailey's jurisdiction covered the areas of Middlesex, Westminster, and London north of the Thames. Murders committed south of the Thames were tried at Southwark assizes, and soon these began to be reported too, although less regularly. London prisoners were held in Newgate, adjacent to the Old Bailey sessions house. Southwark prisoners were held in the equally insalubrious Marshalsea. Assizes tried relatively large numbers (45 to 54) of felons over three or four days (hence the term "sessions") who had been arrested and jailed over the preceding months (hence "gaol-deliveries" preceding every assize). Sentencing of those convicted came at the end of each sessions, and executions followed swiftly, usually within a day or two, unless the judge granted a reprieve on a plea of pregnancy or to give the condemned more time to prepare herself for death.[96] These final stages in the criminal narrative were often reported in follow-up gallows-and-conversion pamphlets, such as *Gods Mercy and Justice Displayed, In the Wicked Life and Penitential Death of Dorothy Livingstone* (1679), a ventriloquized confession published after Livingstone's execution at Kennington Common in Surrey, or the briefer report about Sarah Dent in *The Behaviour, Confession, & Execution Of The several Prisoners that suffered at Tyburn On Friday the ninth of May, 1679*.

The extended wording of trial-report titles was formulaic but could vary to include specific notice of the most sensational crime of that sessions to pique buyer interest; for example, *A Narrative Of the Proceedings at the Sessions-House in the Old-Bayly, From Wednesday the 7th of July instant, to Saturday the 10th . . . And also an Account of the Tryal and Condemnation of Eliz. Lillyman, who killed her Husband, for which she was condemned to be Burned, with the manner of her Deportment at her Tryal* (1675). The highlighted crime was usually discussed first in the paper, regardless of when the trial took place during the sessions. It was often printed using a slightly bigger font and normally given the greatest room in the limited space of the two- or four-page folded broadside.

During the next decade titles became longer and sounded a more legal or official note, although the contents, consisting of brief summaries preceded by the name of the accused, remained the same; for example: *The True Relation Of The Tryals At the Sessions of Oyer and Terminer. Held for the City of London, County of Middlesex, and Goale [sic] Delivery of Newgate; which began in the Old-Bailey the 17th of this instant January, and ended the 18th of the same. As particularly of Elizabeth Wigenton For Whipping a Girl to Death at Ratcliffe* (1681). These changes in wording reflected a significant shift in the relationship between publishers and legal officers. Prior to the 1670s, printed reports of trial proceedings were officially discouraged and in some cases explicitly banned by judges.[97] Summaries of individual crimes and trials from assizes were inevitably brief not only due to pressures of space on the page, but also because publishers had to rely on verbal reports written down outside the court or from local hearsay, with correspondingly variable levels of factual accuracy. The aggregate impression of serialized trial-reports was away from deviant individuals and towards criminal classes. From the beginning they sold briskly and generated intense competition amongst publishers. City of London officials sought to regulate (and profit from) this unauthorized circulation of court proceedings. In 1678 the Court of Alderman required publishers to receive the consent of the Lord Mayor or his deputies and officiating assize judges before printing trial-reports, probably for a fee.[98] This arrangement gave the sessions paper an official status and greater continuity. Both aspects were reinforced by allowing sessions-paper publishers to use agents to take down reports of court proceedings in shorthand. Sessions papers therefore became partly controlled publicity for the legal machinery of local and central-government justice. This arrangement gave publishers of sessions papers a competitive advantage over newspapers, whose reports of assize trials were not officially sanctioned—although they were not banned—and remained more reliant on personal hearsay or information that emerged after the trial and at the execution. For example, *The True Protestant Mercury*'s account of the sensational trial of Margaret Osgood, which was extensively covered by several trial- and execution-reports (see chapter 2), managed only a couple of lines about an unnamed woman tried and burned for killing her husband, "who seem'd very little concern'd at her Tragical end" (Number 24, Wednesday 16 March–Saturday 19 March, 1680/1).

NEWSPAPERS

Before the 1650s printed newsletters or newsbooks were concerned mainly with overseas political events or bizarre local incidents, with titles such as *Newes come latle[y] frō Pera* (1561) or *Strange news out of Kent*

(1609). Corantos, the first newsletters, appeared in the early 1620s mod-
elled on Dutch newsbooks and established the first serialized news format
in English. Although popular from the beginning, their runs throughout
the 1630s were short lived and contained no news of domestic crimes.[99]
Thus, before the 1640s, news of English murders appeared only in bal-
lad- or pamphlet-accounts or digests of crimes derived from the other two
sources. At first this exclusion seems surprising, given the popularity and
profitability of murder stories. The explanation seems to have been the
content-profiles of original Dutch and French models, greater public interest in continental and English political news, and publishers' wariness of
government censors.[100]

Murders and other serious crimes emerged as sporadic items in weekly
or bi-weekly newsbooks such as *Severall Proceedings in Parliament*, issued
from 1651 onwards, or *The Weekly Intelligencer of the Commonwealth*,
published in the mid-1650s, sometimes to fill space when other news was
lacking but increasingly as a routinely reported event. Number 78 of 16–23
January 1654, for example, recounted "*The barbarous and horrid act of a
jealous Woman at* Cobham *in* Kent; *and the most abominable Diet which she
presented to her Husband.*" An unnamed woman invited her husband's suspected lover to drink with her, and, after plying her freely, "demanded of her,
if she would have her nose cut off, or her bearing parts." Aided by a servant,
the vengeful wife proceeded to "excise that part of [the lover's] body which
she thought had most offended." When the husband came home and asked
what was for dinner, his wife replied that "she had got the best bit which hee
loved in the world, and did present him with that most ungratefull object"
(Monday, January 22). The amazed husband rushed to the local constable
who arrested the wife and her maid and committed them to Maidstone jail.
Just as remarkable in its way as the violence itself, and of apparently equal
interest to the anonymous reporter, is *The Weekly Intelligencer*'s concluding information that the "dismembered woman" did not die immediately of
her wounds. The wife and her maid were charged only with assault rather
than attempted murder, which allowed them to "put in great baile to bee
answerable to Justice" and presumably to be released on recognizances. By
drawing readers' attention to the incongruity between the repugnant crime
and the fortuitously mitigated charge, the *Intelligencer* might have wished
to arouse public indignation before the trial to pressure the prosecutor
and grand jurors into elevating the offence. Moreover, presumably the bail
money would not have been supplied by the husband, nor is it likely to have
come from his wife's private resources, since she is not identified as a gentlewoman. The *Intelligencer*'s interest in reporting these details must have been
opposition to the friends or relations who came to her aid. Besides personal
or family loyalty, they may have known of the husband's adultery and sympathized with the wife's grievance, as the maid apparently did (although she
would have been under the authority of her mistress and might have been
pressured into participating as an accomplice).

Joad Raymond has argued that newspaper publication in this period initiated a shift in the "widespread assumption of the right to read, hear, and discuss news," and it established the first print-media network for public discussion of political and social policy.[101] His studies have revised Jürgen Habermas's still influential arguments about the wider emergence of a secularizing culture of rational debate, which he termed the public sphere. Habermas argues that this culture relied in large measure on the growth of sectarian journalism and contending reader opinion in the late seventeenth century, especially after the lapse of the Licensing Act in 1695.[102] His theory accurately reflects intensified post-Restoration competition among commercial crime-news publishers, as well as the liberating impact of judicial licensing on assize-trial reporting. These changes opened the criminal law, trials, and court judgments to unprecedented scrutiny by diverse classes of readers. Yet Raymond's studies of the impact of Civil War and Restoration newspapers significantly backdate the emergence of a commercial news culture fomenting political dissent and debate. David Zaret also points out that Habermas's public sphere is too idealized and restrictive in terms of what constituted early modern critical thought about religion, science, economics, and other subjects of emerging knowledge.[103] In terms of crime, pioneering authors such as Henry Goodcole, for example, or publishers such as David and Elizabeth Mallet, also experimented with what we would now term sociological modes of analysis and reporting. These departures widened possibilities for readers' independent interpretations of legal categories and individual assize judgments from earlier in the century.[104]

Oliver Cromwell's government re-introduced censorship of the press in the mid-1650s, and it was continued after the Restoration in the Printing Act of 1662 under the supervision of royally appointed licensers such as Roger L'Estrange.[105] Despite L'Estrange's vigilance, newspaper publication and readership continued to flourish. Parliament was more favorable towards the press than the court and allowed the Licensing Act to lapse temporarily in 1679 and then permanently in 1695 (with a brief re-introduction in 1685 to 88, and notwithstanding vested opposition from the Stationers' Company).[106] After the first lapse in press control, 1679 to 81, over 40 newspapers sprang up, many surviving for only weeks or months. The genre became more accessible owing to changes in bibliographic format. The traditional quarto was abandoned in favor of single-leaf broadsides, folded in half to create four pages, sold at 1d, and issued once or twice weekly (or sometimes a more compact half-broadside of one leaf with two columns on each side for a halfpenny, with more limited room to report events).[107]

To take one prominent example, Langley Curtiss's *True Protestant Mercury* (December 28, 1680 to October 25, 1682, half broadside) included accounts of serious felonies every two or three numbers. Otherwise it fed readers a mixed diet of overseas news, court appointments, lawsuits, scandals, riots, assaults, and so on. Male homicides were reported if they had a political angle linked to other recent stories or if they involved Catholic figures the *Mercury* wished to defame. Murders by women appeared relatively rarely and were generally unspectacular.[108] When they did appear, they were represented mainly in terms of associations with political and religious conflicts, rather than as epiphenomena of universal moral or metaphysical conditions, as they had been framed earlier in the period. Because newspapers in part used crime reports analogously to stigmatize public figures or government policies, even the humblest female felons could become political symbols.

Besides difficulties of space, the relatively low frequency of crime news was also partly due to the fact that newspaper publishers such as Curtiss issued separate assize-trial reports or individual accounts of the most notorious criminals.[109] This situation drew attention to the intertextuality that characterized Restoration printed news.[110] Ballads, pamphlets, trial- and execution-reports, and newspapers all responded to, anticipated, and plagiarized each other in bids for market advantage (as indeed earlier news had done, but less thickly).

Reports of Letitia Wigington's trial on 17 January 1681 and its surrounding events illustrated the intensive interrelationships of Restoration printed news and their capacity for generating multiple public interpretations of a domestic murder. The crime, which took place in Ratcliff on 24 to 25 December 1680, attracted attention for its cruelty, its grotesque imitation of a naval flogging, its intimations of sexual perversion, and perhaps its seasonal ironies. It centered on the fatal whipping with a cat-o'-nine-tails of a thirteen-year-old maidservant, Elizabeth Houlton, at the hands of a man named John Sadler, and on the alleged instigation of his landlady and Houlton's mistress, Elizabeth Wigington. She was a seamstress who took in female apprentices and had three children of her own. Her family was extremely needy because her estranged sailor-husband had deserted his ship and stopped supporting them.[111] Elizabeth Houlton's father was also a seaman. In September 1680 he paid Wigington £5 to apprentice his daughter and promised a further £5 when he returned from his voyage. Wigington had a local reputation for treating her girls harshly, and on Christmas eve she accused Houlton either of botching some work and/or of cheating her of a few shillings after being sent on a shopping errand.[112] Although Elizabeth denied the charge(s), Wigington had her lodger John Sadler (who according to one account also accused Houlton of stealing some of his linen[113]) punish the girl.[114] Several news reports described Sadler as a bailiff's follower, but according to Wigington's more detailed version of events, he was a former sailor who had become a "runner of Goods," which included supplying Wigington's household with "hot Victuals" in exchange for lodging.[115] She ordered him

> to make a terrible Whip, which they called a *Cat-with-nine-tails*, which it was proved he owned to be about an hour in making, and then stript the poor Child barbarously and immodestly stark naked, and the Prisoner

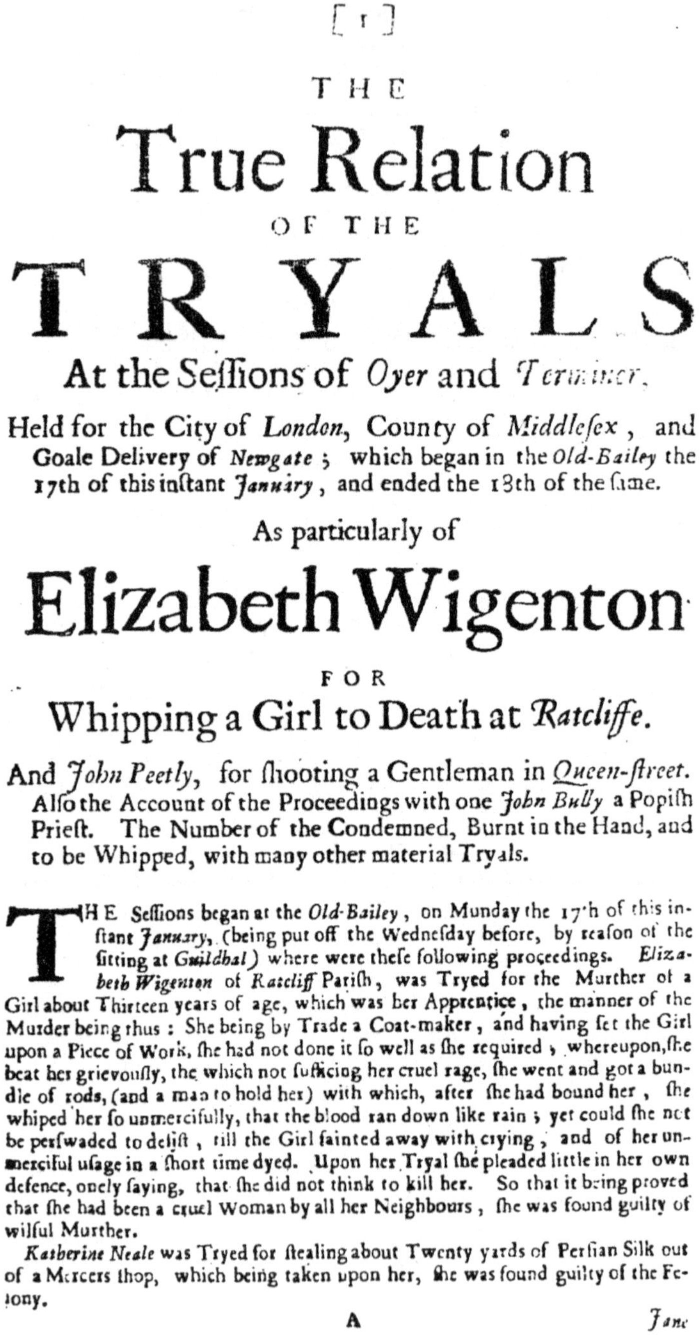

[1]

T H E

True Relation

OF THE

T R Y A L S

At the Seſſions of *Oyer* and *Terminer,*

Held for the City of *London,* County of *Middleſex* , and
Goale Delivery of *Newgate* ; which began in the *Old-Bailey* the
17th of this inſtant *January* , and ended the 13th of the ſame.

As particularly of

Elizabeth Wigenton

F O R

Whipping a Girl to Death at *Ratcliffe.*

And *John Peetly,* for ſhooting a Gentleman in *Queen-ſtreet.*
Alſo the Account of the Proceedings with one *John Bully* a Popiſh
Prieſt. The Number of the Condemned, Burnt in the Hand, and
to be Whipped, with many other material Tryals.

THE Seſſions began at the *Old-Bailey* , on Munday the 17th of this inſtant *January,* (being put off the Wedneſday before, by reaſon of the
ſitting at *Guildhal*) where were theſe following proceedings. *Elizabeth Wigenton* of *Ratcliff* Pariſh, was Tryed for the Murther of a
Girl about Thirteen years of age, which was her Apprentice , the manner of the
Murder being thus : She being by Trade a Coat-maker, and having ſet the Girl
upon a Piece of Work, ſhe had not done it ſo well as ſhe required ; whereupon, ſhe
beat her grievouſly, the which not ſufficing her cruel rage, ſhe went and got a bundle of rods, (and a man to hold her) with which, after ſhe had bound her , ſhe
whiped her ſo unmercifully, that the blood ran down like rain ; yet could ſhe not
be perſwaded to deliſt , till the Girl fainted away with crying , and of her un-
merciful uſage in a ſhort time dyed. Upon her Tryal ſhe pleaded little in her own
defence, onely ſaying, that ſhe did not think to kill her. So that it being proved
that ſhe had been a cruel Woman by all her Neighbours , ſhe was found guilty of
wilful Murther.

Katherine Neale was Tryed for ſtealing about Twenty yards of Perſian Silk out
of a Mercers ſhop, which being taken upon her, ſhe was found guilty of the Felony.

A   *Jane*

Figure 1.2 *The True Relation Of The Tryals At the Sessions of Oyer and Terminer
... As particularly of Elizabeth Wigenton* (1681). Reproduced by permission of the
Houghton Library, Harvard University.

[Wigington] held her and ram'd an Apron down her Throat, to prevent her crying out, and the foresaid Bailys Follower [Sadler] most inhumanely whipt her for 4 hours or more, with some short intervals of their Cruelty, and, having made her body raw, and all over bloody, sent for *Salt*, and salted her wounds, to render their Tortures more grievous, *&c*.[116]

This description of the weapon echoed an extant court indictment against Wigington: "a Whipp vocat a Catt with Nyne tayles."[117] Sadler evidently drew on his naval background in administering the beating, which bore a vengeful relationship to the career of his victim's father, and possibly to Wigington's estranged husband as well.[118]

After receiving a sadistically prolonged version of this correction, Elizabeth Houlton died on Christmas morning 1680.[119] When searchers came to the house, Sadler fled but Wigington was apprehended. According to one of Curtiss's newspaper rivals, at her trial "she pleaded little in her own defense, onely saying, that she did not think to kill [Houlton]."[120] But neighbors alleged she was a cruel woman, thus discouraging prosecutors or jurors from possibly mitigating the charge of wilful homicide to accidental or felonious killing. The fact that Sadler was still at large and not captured until 20 January, according to another newspaper account, also made Wigington the prime suspect, and precluded her from testifying against him.[121] The court found her guilty on 17 January. Sadler was tried and found guilty of murder on 25 February and executed on 4 March, and was not allowed to plead for a royal pardon with 43 other prisoners condemned to death at that sessions.[122] Wigington meanwhile had pleaded pregnancy and was reprieved until late August. She may not have been pregnant at the time of her trial, since "pleading the belly" was a strategy commonly used by convicted women to buy time to gain a pardon or an informal reprieve after childbirth. There is no evidence about whether Wigington did or did not bear a child, and in any event the strategy failed when her estranged husband, to whom she had turned for help, heard about her reprieve on the grounds of pregnancy and publicly denounced her presumed infidelity, retracting the money he had initially sent to her.[123] She was executed on 9 September.[124] In Curtiss's last published account of the case, *The Confession and Execution of Leticia Wigington* (1681), written in collaboration with her Newgate prison visitors, Wigington laid the blame for Houlton's death on Sadler and protested her innocence of any intent to murder Houlton or participate in the whipping. She also claimed to be wrongfully convicted on the testimony of one of her eleven-year-old apprentices (Rebecca Clifford, who later retracted her testimony), and slandered by hostile news pamphlets and ballads alleging her adulterous relationship with Sadler.[125] This version of events sharply contradicted attitudes expressed in previous news versions, including Curtiss's own. Whatever readers made of divergent accounts of the case, this last version demonstrated Curtiss's enterprising ability to keep varying Wigington's story to outpace his competitors.

CONFESSION and EXECUTION

O F

Leticia Wigington

Of *Ratclif*, who suffered at

TYBURN,

On *Fryday,* the 9 h of this inſtant *September* , 1681. written by her own hand in the Goal of *Newgate,* two days before her death, being Condemned for whiping her Apprentice Girl to Death.

We are fully ſatisfied, that the following Paper was written by this unhappy womans own hand, a while before her Death, and though at her Tryal for this horrid Fact, the Evidence againſt her, was full, clear and undeniable, yea which is more, though ſhe was then ſo ingenious to confeſs her ſelf really guilty thereof, having lain ſo many Months in *Newgate,* we have very great reaſon to judg ſhe has been too well acquainted with that curſed crew of Popiſh Prieſts and Jeſuites, who it is to be feared have debauched her with their own damnable Principles, whereby they have perſwaded her to deny what ſhe before had ſo fully confeſſed, which ſhe does in the very words of thoſe Jeſuites who lately deſervedly ſuffered for Treaſon againſt his Majeſty, &c, who though they were Tried and condemned (as well weíl as her ſelf) upon the cleareſt. Evidence imaginable, yet *Atheiſtically* even with their laſt Breath affirmed, *That they were as innocent as the Child unborn.*

Micah the 7th Chap. and 8 9. Verſes.

Rejoyce not againſt me, O mine Enemy : when I fall , I ſhall ariſe ; when I ſit in darkneſs, the Lord ſhall be a Light unto me.
    I will bear the Indignation of the Lord, becauſe I have ſinned againſt him, until he plead my cauſe, and execute judgment for me : he will bring me forth to the Light, and I ſhall behold his Righteouſneſs.

THis place of Scripture I made choice of, as being ſomewhat pertinent to the buſineſs, and troubles and afflictions that are inflicted on me, wherefore upon my bended Knees I humbly deſire all you that have been my loving Neighbours and Friends, and all other good Chriſtians, that have heard of this horrid and dreadful misfortune that hath befallen me, and you that ſhall read theſe doleful Lines, let pity move your hearts to read them, and you that have had any hand in taking away my Life wrongfully, I pray God forgive you all ; but let me admoniſh you not to abuſe the dead by giving out your cruel ſpeeches by me, as you have done in my Life-time (that never did you any harm) firſt to Impriſon me wrongfully, and that not ſatisfying, but to prompt on one, that was my Apprentice, *Rebecka Cliffword* by Name, who was not full 12 years of age, to ſwear againſt me, ſhe not being ſenſible of the danger of taking a falſe Oath, ſo that you have uſed me at your pleaſure. I ſpeak to you all, Rich and Poor, great and ſmall, that have had any hand in my Death, whoever you are, for you cannot be ignorant of the great evil you have done me, (a poor friendleſs Creature) for you have made it your buſineſs to take away my life, who am as innocent as concerning the Murder for which I ſuffer as the Child unborn : but why ſhould I reflect upon my Innocence, and the abuſes put up-

▲   on

NEWS DISTRIBUTION AND READER AGENCY

News reports of Wigington's and Sadler's actions showed in greater than average detail that sensational murder trials could be dissected in print in ways similar to other political and social topics. Such cases compensate for the relatively low survival rate of crime news publications overall, which makes it difficult to extrapolate production and sales figures using statistical calculations. Moreover, empirical evidence of readers who bought and read news of women charged with murder is limited, especially before the Restoration, because most readers, from all social classes, did not record their reactions to popular crime news. (Notable exceptions are Robert Burton, author of *The Anatomy of Melancholy* [1621], and the Oxford antiquarian and biographer Anthony à Wood, *Athenae Oxonienses* [1691–20]; their lightly annotated personal collections of crime pamphlets survive in Bodleian Library collections.[126]) In the absence of direct bibliographic evidence of readership sales or extensive comments by readers, including those who served as judicial officials, the reception and reinterpretation of individual murder stories must be inferred circumstantially from well-documented networks of distribution and sites of exchange for early printed news materials.[127]

Markets for early modern news ballads expanded rapidly within long-established circuits for the sale of manuscripts in both London and the provinces, and pamphlets, trial-reports, and newspapers followed the same routes as the century advanced. The early modern book trade, as Margaret Spufford and Tessa Watt have demonstrated in meticulous detail, consisted of a rich spectrum of printed materials accessible to both humble and elite buyers in many public spaces. Goods streamed back and forth between the provinces and London even after the latter location came to dominate print production when the Stationers' Company was granted a royal charter in 1557. This reader demographic included a "silent 'listenership'" of people who heard printed news read aloud in alehouses, army camps, and marketplaces.[128] Alehouses were traditional sites for the local exchange of oral and written news, as were landmark London spaces such as the Exchange and St. Paul's. The latter was the most important market of bibliographic commerce in the country. Ben Jonson was quick to satirize what he regarded as the *mêlée* of uneducated opinions attributable to rampant metropolitan news culture in *Every Man Out of His Humor* (1600), whose central scenes take place in St. Paul's, and *The Staple of News* (1626). As Jürgen Habermas and Joad Raymond have shown, the seventeenth-century coffee house was also closely associated with news reading and promiscuous public debate. "[E]very Coffee-house [is] furnished with News-papers and Pamphlets (both written and Printed) of personal Scandal, Schism, and Treason," complained Roger L'Estrange.[129] L'Estrange's contempt and anxiety were widely shared by government and legal authorities: "The common people talke anything, for every carman and porter is now a statesman; and indeed the coffee-houses are good for nothing else."[130] Although the elite lamented the proliferation of opinions about political and social issues as well as challenges to ruling privileges posed by news-reading culture, they also implicitly recognized that interpretations of public events by individual readers could never be absolutely regulated. At best they remained open to continual appropriation and transformation by interested parties.[131] A radical versioning of opinion followed daily instalments of stories reported in various news genres. In turn, discursively energized spaces such as coffee-houses became public forums for public debate about politically and legally inflected events. Widely distributed, consumed, and exchanged news forms empowered even humble readers with individually limited, but real and potentially mobilized agency.

These contexts of news consumption and reception involve definitions of early modern literacy and "popularity." Growth in literate and semiliterate readers accelerated rapidly throughout this period. David Cressy has compiled the most comprehensive studies of early modern England to date. His research suggests that the ability to read grew from 10 to 30% among husbandmen, 40 to 60% for tradesmen, and 45 to 75% for yeomen in the period up to 1580. A temporary decline in education and literacy rates followed for about 30 to 40 years, prior to a significant rise in the 1630s and steady improvements throughout the rest of the century.[132] Margaret Spufford partially revised this picture, demonstrating that these figures probably underestimate a basic ability to read amongst husbandmen and laborers, because reading was taught before writing. The evidence of signatures on documents, on which Cressy partly based his conclusions, is not a completely reliable indication of primary literacy, which by the mid-seventeenth century had spread widely, especially in London, although the ability rates for girls and women were probably not as high as for boys and men.[133]

It is the broad public fascination with murder, above all perhaps, that best defines early modern news on the subject as popular. As this book will show, murder news varied widely in bibliographic formats, rhetorical styles, and related cultural contexts. Relatively few publications were restricted by price to particular classes of buyers and readers. In seeking to define popular crime news, Bernard Capp rightly traces its origins to pre- and post-Reformation folk entertainments and pre-occupations with subjects such as wonders and romance published in sixteenth-century broadside ballads and chapbooks. These texts bridging traditional oral and emergent print cultures were aimed at "the lowest levels of the literate" and subliterate, but not exclusively at those readers alone.[134] Yet such categories fall short of accounting for news pamphlets such as *The Araignement & burning of Margaret Ferne-seede* or *The Apprehension, Arraignment, and execution of Elizabeth Abbot*, whose formal dedications, complex narrative structures, density of reported detail, and elevated vocabulary indicate that their main implied readership was the legal and clerical elite, even though the accounts were published in modest printed formats with aesthetic markers of popular taste (i.e. black-lettering and recycled woodcuts). These publications, like others by educated writers during the seventeenth century, especially clergymen visitors, represent learned writers speaking to their *confrères* and employers as well as to the general public. To situate these pamphlets in relation to Peter Burke's question about early modern popular culture—"who was saying what to whom?"—they were crime and trial news written *by* people above, *for* people below *and* above.[135] Given the dominant prosecution viewpoint and confessional sources of narrative information outlined in this chapter, it could hardly be otherwise. Yet as discussion of these texts in the following chapters will show (to invoke Burke's functional criteria as well as Roger Chartier's), the message transmitted was not necessarily the message received.[136]

It is also tempting to cleave to a more materialist definition of popular murder news: that is, regardless of whether the stories were written "from below" (news ballads), in between popular and learned cultures (newsbooks, newspapers, trial- and execution-reports), or from perspectives above (prison and gallows speeches, conversion exempla), they were targeted at ordinary buyers in cheaply printed formats that ensured wide accessibility. Because prices for short texts declined in relation to wages over the period, production and affordability increased.[137] Restoration journalism published in broadside news sheets further encouraged a democratization of crime and trial news. Both before and afterwards there were exceptions to this trend, however, such as John Quick's seven-sheet, ninety-six page *Hell Open'd* (1676) and Roger L'Estrange's six-sheet, thirty-nine page *A Hellish Murder* (1688). Published in octavo and quarto formats respectively, their cost of about 4 to 5d would have been out of reach for modest consumers. It was up to hacks to transmit L'Estrange's judicially mandated and technically demanding "enformations" (official examination testimony) into popular genres, such as Elkanah Settle's verse account, *An Epilogue to the French Midwife's Tragedy* (1688), published by Randal Taylor (who also published *A Hellish Murder*), or the balladizing, archaically decorated, and anonymously written and narrated *A Cabinet of Grief* (1688), issued by J. Blare (all discussed in chapter 2). Overall, the vast majority of murder news can be defined as popular in two senses: heterogenous in rhetorical style and ideological content, with the latter more likely to be directly accessible to buyers with legal and clerical backgrounds; of interest as a subject to all classes of readers by virtue of the imaginative appeal and cultural notoriety of women who killed.

2 Equity and Self-Defense in Female Homicide News

Popular early modern opinions about what constituted culpable female violence and appropriate punishment often differed from the formulations of written statutes, court decisions, and proverbial wisdom. Alternative perspectives emerged from humane local responses to individual accused women, whom neighbors and friends defended by singling out extenuating circumstances or ethical ambiguities that challenged standard legal reasoning. When such counterarguments were reported by commercial printed news, whose viewpoint normally coincided with the Crown's, they tended to be veiled by fictionalizing maneuvres and moralizing rhetoric. This screening process was never absolute, however. Overall, early modern murder news was characterized by legible tensions between generic conventions and official ideologies on the one hand, and semantic openness to rational judgement by individual readers on the other. The historical effects of these negotiations were contingent rather than systematic. With the partial exception of infanticide, they did not lead to any short-term revision of national laws or gender stereotypes. But popular knowledge of personal and/or mitigative aspects of female homicide cases had demonstrable effects on literate parish and court officers who administered the criminal law, as evidenced by the significant number of arraignments and trials that ended in dismissal or acquittal at county assizes.

Readers could recognize possibilities for contested or compassionate legal interpretation most readily in murder news that preserved doubtful evidence in substantial detail, or different sides to a story in multiple printed accounts. Textually, these cases constitute exceptions to the majority of homicides that were reported (or have survived) in single news stories, often with a didactic religious agenda. My aim in this chapter is to examine this smaller category of circumstantially rich or multiple-reported cases to show how they catalyzed early modern practices of equitable interpretation. In these instances, reports tended to validate both prosecution-oriented narratives and *de facto* defense arguments in the absence of legal counsel and customary rhetorical or forensic strategies for female suspects. Readers interpreted opposing perspectives according to their lived, and presumably in some cases direct, experiences of female criminality, legal justice, and social fairness—knowledge that was continually being memorialized by previously published news stories.

I begin by looking more closely at the two news pamphlets discussed briefly in the Introduction: *The Araignement & burning of Margaret Ferne-seede* (1608), and *The Apprehension, Arraignement, and execution of Elizabeth Abbot* (1608). The debate between official and extra judicial viewpoints in these accounts illustrated the beginnings of a public culture of paralegal interpretation. Their evidential and social analysis constituted the rational and humane distinctions that magistrates, jurors, and judges used elsewhere to extend equitable mitigation to women accused of homicide, even though such positive outcomes only began to be reported in serialized trial-reports after the Restoration. Having examined these and other paradigm cases to near the end of the century, I show in later chapters how the same modes of news production and reading are discernable in stories with relatively few circumstantial details and/or reported by single textual witnesses.

BURN, MARGARET, BURN

Official perspectives on Margaret Ferneseede's trial for husband murder begin chronologically with an extant assize record:

> Fernesede, Margaret, spinster,[1] wife of Anthony Fernesede of Peckham, indicted for murder. On 20 Apr. 1607 at Peckham she stabbed her husband in the throat with a knife (1*d.*) and killed him. Guilty; to be burned.[2]

Ferneseede pleaded not guilty to this charge, and *The Araignement & burning of Margaret Ferne-seede* may have implicitly explained why by substantially contradicting this information—presumably inadvertently. Given the pamphlet's semi-official character, the discrepancy between its version of the story and the assize record's suggested the indictment lying behind the latter was a legal fiction designed to paper over the absence of material evidence of murder that is plainly obvious in the pamphlet.[3] Reflecting the dominant perspective of the trial overall, the writer instead represented Ferneseede's bad character as *de facto* evidence of guilt, and fictionalized her identity accordingly. She was presented as a brothel keeper married to Anthony Ferneseede, a taylor who was estranged from Margaret and lived away from home. His maggoty corpse was discovered in Peckham Fields, "his throate cut, a knife in his hand, golde ringes vppon his fingars, and fortie shillings in money in his pursse" (A3v). Unknown to local residents, Anthony's identity was traced by an apprentice's indenture found in his pocket. When told of his death Margaret showed little sorrow.[4] She rebuffed several friends' offers of condolence, and she claimed she would hardly recognize her husband because he had been home so seldom (details the pamphlet later corroborated). Questioned about her possible guilt, she "answered with such constancie, that no suspition could be grounded against her." But a servant-boy later testified that she had quarrelled with her husband and committed adultery "in his view" with a manservant who had since fled, and that she had sold her goods in preparation for following him. Neighbors backed the boy's allegations and Margaret was examined again. She did not deny their "generall assertions," but "touching the death of her husband, that she forswore & renounced the fact or practise thereof . . . with such a shameles constancie, that shee strooke amazement into al that heard her" (B1r). Ferneseede complained angrily when imprisoned in the White Lion in Southwark, and was disruptive with other prisoners being held there in anticipation of the forthcoming assize.

Her trial was delayed for ten months after the murder in April 1607. The pamphlet writer does not mention that Ferneseede was pregnant, so one must assume that examiners were still searching for evidence that would implicate her. At the trial in late February 1608, she pleaded not guilty. Robert Throgmorton and others condemned in another higher profile murder case at the same assizes persuaded Ferneseede in prison to repent her life as a bawd, but she continued to deny killing her husband. Several witnesses gave presumptive testimony of her guilt by stating that she had tried to poison her husband with "powdered broth."[5] Despite the contradictory circumstantial evidence (e.g., Margaret's alleged greed for her husband's money; the purse and ring left on his body), she was convicted on the basis of her sexual reputation, alleged verbal threats to be rid of him, and a lack of proper remorse for her husband's death. The latter seemed to be a tipping point in determining public opinion about her guilt. In illuminating analogous evidence from early modern Germany, Ulinka Rublack has shown that accused wives' behavior towards their husbands' dead bodies was crucial. To signify their innocence, women were obliged to perform a repertoire of sorrowful responses: "Arms were raised, women fell on their knees, and, most importantly, tears had to flow."[6] If, like Ferneseede, they refused to show signs of grief or even feign them convincingly, their lack of "natural" female pity and patriarchal deference condemned them. Had Ferneseede expressed these emotions, she might have avoided prosecution, given the absence of material evidence linking her to her husband's death.

The judiciary first moved to defend the doubtful verdict by including a report of Ferneseede's prison repentance—but not for the murder—in a semi-official news pamphlet issued by Henry Gosson: *The Liues, Apprehension, Araignment & Execution, Of Robert Throgmorton. William Porter. Iohn Bishop* (1608).[7] A similar report appeared in *The Araignement & burning* after a brief description of "How Margaret Ferne-seede spent her time in prison" prior to her execution. Ferneseede's obstinace created narrative difficulties for the writer, who was forced to admit the confession of her sinful life was "truly related" while disparaging her denial of the crime.

THE
Araignement & bur
ning of *Margaret Ferne-ſeede* ,
for the Murther of her late Husband
Anthony Ferne-ſeede, found deade in Peckham Field neere Lambeth, hauing once before attempted to poyſon him with broth,
being executed in S.Georges-field the
laſt of Februarie,
1 6 o 8

LONDON
Printed for *Henry Goſſon*, and are to be folde at the Signe
of the Sunne in Pater-noſter-rowa.
1.o.8

Figure 2.1 The Araignement & burning of Margaret Ferne-seede (1608). Reproduced by permission of the British Library.

He accordingly demonized her character in an otherwise lively section in which she boasts about employing disgruntled urban wives as *belles du jour* for weekly salaries of 10s (B2v–3r).[8] At this point some readers may have felt that Margaret's independent spirit positively recuperated her alleged criminality in the same way that other female outlaws were transformed into festive anti-heroes in popular ballads such as *The sorrowful complaint of Susan Higges, who for twenty yeeres, maintained her selfe by robberies on the high-way side* (*ca.* 1630).

Whether he sensed this ambiguity or not, the author backtracked to testimony allegedly given at the trial by two bargemen, fictionalized in first-person dialogue, to fabricate an impression of legal closure. After being entertained in Margaret's house one night, the men were confronted in bed by her husband returning home unexpectedly:

> I am (quoth he) the maister of this house (if I had my right) but I am bard of the possession and commande thereof, by a deuilish woman, who makes a stewes of it to exersice her sinnefull practises. (B3v-B4r)

Anthony reportedly stormed out, and when the men related his words to Margaret, she exclaimed, "hāg him slaue and villaine: I will before God bee reuenged of him (nay ere long) by ones meanes or other" (B4r). This vow, "which making good in the iudgement of the Iudge, to gether with her life & practises," justified his recommendation of a guilty verdict to the obliging jury.

This culminating scene of patriarchal dystopia attempted to fix Margaret's character as an emasculating wife. It also reinforced her married name's legendary associations with illicit sexuality and witchcraft. For in folklore the minute spores or seeds of the female fern, or bracken (*Pteris aquilina*) were thought to be generated supernaturally. They were said to be visible only on St. John's Eve (23 June) and to render the gatherer invisible. As some early modern readers would have recognized, these associations relate to Margaret's role as a brothel-keeper, because fern fronds had also been used since ancient times in herbal medicine as an abortifacient.[9]

The printer of *The Araignement & burning*, Edward Allde, activated related associations of witchcraft by recycling a woodcut that had appeared on the title page of *News from Scotland, Declaring the Damnable life and death of Doctor Fian, a notable Sorcerer* (1592).[10] Fian was a Scottish warlock burned at the stake with several women. Allde removed the devil emerging from a tree in the original image and substituted a woman at the threshold of a door. She looked outward towards a man lying on the ground and two groups of women, one stirring a cauldron with a ladle over a fire. The image domesticated and feminized the vague impression of illicit activities and can be related to the wider shift in Jacobean news illustrations from masculinized devils to women as principal agents of witchcraft and murder.[11]

The symbolism of Margaret's execution performance was similarly ambiguous.[12] Dressed in a white sheet and led abreast to the stake by women, the visual imagery of public martyrdom competed with that of ritual penance in ways that were later repeated at the contested executions of Sarah Elstone and Margaret Osgood (discussed below).[13] The author of *The Araignement & burning* fictionalized, ventriloquized, and marginalized but never quite managed to erase Margaret's personal voice and claims of innocence. Both manifested an irrepressible "ethics of tenacity" in the face of legal bullying and government co-option that certain readers, especially with legal knowledge, might have recognized.[14]

"THIS WORSE THAN WOLUISH WOMAN"

The more factually packed news-story of Elizabeth Abbot, who was tried by Sir Edward Coke, then Chief Justice of Common Pleas, soon followed the Ferneseede trial and execution.[15] The prominence of civic and legal officials in this text, from local constables and bailiffs to the mayor and chief justice, and the remarkably detailed twists and turns of the crime, indicated that the writer possessed privileged legal knowledge and was likely one of the participating magistrates.[16] Other than a few conventional passing remarks about Abbot serving the devil and God's providence working in wonderful ways to reveal her crimes, the pamphlet's viewpoint, like that of the Ferneseede pamphlet, was legal and secular. The writer was above all concerned with Abbot's refusal to confess[17] (although her moral reprobation, he implied, legitimated the verdict regardless of her denials [C4v]).

The pamphlet's murder story was grim, with none of the gender inversions that imparted comic overtones to the Ferneseede account. Elizabeth Abbot, a north-country woman, came to London to seek work. She took up lodgings with a Mrs. Killingworth, an abusive recluse who was shunned—though not ignored—by her neighbors. The writer assumes Abbot suffered while living in her household (A3v), although he is ambiguous about revenge as a motive. On the evening of Wednesday 21 January she laid in a larger than normal quantity of beer, presumably to supply more than Mrs. Killingworth's usual needs. Abbot allegedly strangled her, placed her body upright in a chimney, and incinerated it, leaving only a few bones to be discovered two days later by neighbors who had not seen either woman stirring and called the constable to break into the house. In the chimney, searchers spied a "locke of [Killingworth's] haire tide in a hairelace, and her stay which went vnder her chinne pinde to it," while a surgeon identified the bones as human (B1r). Abbot had by then long fled. She disappeared for several months, "light enough in all things but in a burthened conscience" (B2v).

Killingworth's death grotesquely parodied an execution for petty treason. The writer insinuated this profile by detailing her reputation as a thrice-widowed and bestially drunken neighbor. He spared her no sympathy: "drunkennes was her sinne, drunkennes was hir punishment: the neglect of hir neighbours was hir sinne, and their neglect toward hir for that sinne, was an excuse to hir murtherer and a furtherer to hir death" (A4v). The reader was asked to assume the killing was deliberate ("I pray you suppose that she is murdered") and that Abbot's motive was robbery, although the writer openly admitted these were conjectures. His gestures of imaginative collusion with readers did not foreclose alternative theories about the crime, such as that Killingworth died whilst in drink and Abbot, terrified, tried to dispose of the body, or that others were involved besides herself.

An unnamed woman was arrested at Gravesend on suspicion of the crime after being linked to a stolen gown that neighbors misidentified as Killingworth's. After sifting the evidence, magistrates were just about to release her when a poor man turned up to identify the gown as his wife's. The woman confessed and was convicted for robbery, but was reprieved "by the favour of the bench" (B3r). This by-path of scrupulous equitable justice prepares the reader for the narrative return to Abbot, who was apprehended near Nonesuch in Surrey while allegedly attempting to burgle a house with her husband or lover. He is a shadowy figure throughout the story, described as a taylor in the Strand (like Anthony Ferneseede), but about whom Abbot refused to talk and nothing more could be discovered. As with John Sadler's disappearance during Elizabeth Wigington's trial (Introduction, p. 35), his absence focused the force of legal allegations exclusively on Abbot. She was cornered by an astute dog while her husband or lover escaped. Examined initially by Sir Edward Saunders, son of the infamously murdered George Saunders (see chapter 3), she was committed into custody at the White Lyon in Southwark. While en route there, she was identified and questioned by one of Mrs. Killingworth's neighbors who was visiting the area, a Mrs. Cox. During their conversation, reported in first-person dialogue, Abbot defensively revealed knowing about Killingworth's death:

> O I found your meaning: you goe about to intrap mee about the woman that was burnt by Aldgate, but you are deceiued in that in faith, as they that did it were deceiued of their expectation . . . they lookt for much and had little, she was a good old gentlewoman, and she had beene a proper young gentlewoman. (B4v)

As in the Ferneseede pamphlet, this dramatized passage created a rhetorical proxy for missing factual evidence of Abbot's guilt. In later conversations with the victim's neighbors, Abbot inadvertently contradicted herself on the question of knowing Killingworth personally, but she denied any involvement in the alleged murder, for which she was indicted on Friday 8 April. She pleaded not guilty but was convicted.

Readers of *The Apprehension, Arraignement, and execution of Elizabeth Abbot* could have understood its complicated narrative in various ways: a story of irredeemable wickedness ultimately brought to light by wonderfully timed acts of providence; of inner fortitude pointing to doubts about her actual guilt (for the crime itself); of absent material evidence linking her to the murder, to which the desperately impromptu re-trial in Cree Church drew attention; or of taxed but justified civil and judicial authorities. Yet while the writer's execution report ostensibly vindicated the rationality and good faith of the criminal law—above all that of the presiding judge Sir Edward Coke, whose charge to the jury and exchanges with prosecuting examiner Sir Henry Montague are quoted approvingly—it also betrayed the authorities' palpable anxiety over the absence of proper evidence in the face of Abbot's denials, and the fairness of her conviction. The pamphlet's narrative complications and mass of circumstantial detail provided ample material for readers (e.g., Coke's numerous enemies) to seize on gaps and ambiguities and reconstruct alternative versions of the crime and trial. The pamphlet's handling of the case may have served as a cautionary example to later writers seeking to defend court officials who anticipated strong public reactions to their decisions. Virtually no other seventeenth-century news pamphlet or trial-report described a female murderer's pre- and post-rial obstinacy in such detail. While the writer presumably intended Abbot's stubbornness to be understood as *prima facie* evidence of guilt, his assumption strained against natural-law assumptions about guilty consciences inevitably revealing themselves.

"AS JOB . . . PICKT OUT BY THE HAND OF GOD"

In his *Treatise of Christian Equitie*, William Perkins observed that the ultimate remedy for verdicts rendered too narrowly in law, or in mitigating moral but not legal circumstances, was a royal pardon (B2r). Pardons were granted after sentencing on the recommendation of assize judges through the equity court of Chancery at the petition of friends of the condemned person. Such negotiations formed the significant backdrop to Gilbert Dugdale's account of Elizabeth Caldwell in 1604, the same year, perhaps not coincidentally, in which Perkins's *Treatise* was issued. Caldwell was a Cheshire woman who in May 1602 had attempted to poison her husband Thomas with the help of her lover Jeffrey Bownd and a widow-neighbor Isabel Hall. Thomas survived, but a little girl visiting the house with whom he had shared buttered oatcakes laced with ratsbane did not. Caldwell, Bownd, and Hall were examined and then charged with murder on 16 May and brought to trial on 4 October at the Court of Great Sessions in Chester.[18] Bownd was pressed to death after he refused to plead. Caldwell was convicted and reprieved because she was in her final month of pregnancy.[19] She was hanged eight months later on 18 June 1603, at which time Hall was finally tried and executed also. In the interval between her apprehension and execution,[20] Caldwell transformed herself into a flamboyantly penitent offender. Following the example of William Perkins (about whose activities in this regard, more in the next chapter), she converted numerous prisoners and offered spiritual advice to the hundreds of people who, according to Dugdale, visited her daily in prison. She also corresponded with divines to seek their assurance "that GOD had pardoned her offences" (B2v). During her lengthy gallows performance she led spectators in the singing of psalms and prayers and gave exemplary warnings, vowing "that if shee shoulde liue yet many yeeres, her desire would be in serving the Lord" (D2v).

Caldwell might have been hoping for a pardon right to the end, because she had gained powerful local advocates who had been working strenuously on her behalf. The title page of *A True Discourse* describes the murder conspiracy as a provincial crime with which Dugdale became connected after Caldwell's apprehension. Immediately before the appearance of *A True Discourse*, Dugdale sought the patronage of the new court by writing a flattering account of James's coronation pageants, *The Time Triumphant* (1604), his only other known publication. According to his "kinsman" and *A True Discourse*'s publisher, Robert Armin (a.k.a. Shakespeare's fellow actor[21]), Dugdale had been Caldwell's prison visitor (D4r). He dedicated his account to Mary, Lady Cholmondeley and twenty-seven other members of the Cheshire gentry—the entire social and judicial elite of the county (A4r). These included John Savage and Thomas Brooke, the magistrates who examined Caldwell, Bownd, and Hall and who presumably remained sympathetic dedicatees.[22] Cheshire's palatine status concentrated local power in a handful of families, and many of its state and legal offices were hereditary.[23] This is evident from the repeated family names in Dugdale's dedication. All appeared in William Smith's *The Vale-Royall of England. Or, The County Palatine of Chester Illustrated* (1656, partly written *ca.* 1616), which listed "all the Knights, Esquires, Gentlemen and Freeholders in the County." Elizabeth's father Thomas Duncalff appeared there (60) but Thomas Caldwell did not. Although he was styled "Ma[ster]" on the title page (probably by Armin), Dugdale's account did not do so. In the Chester Gaol Book he was designated "y[eoman]."[24] These discrepancies indicate Caldwell was not a member of the county set but became a "gentleman born" by virtue of his marriage to Elizabeth and her substantial dowry, which he wasted in foreign travel (A4r).

Mary Cholmondeley (1563–1626, née Holford), on the other hand, was connected to one of the county's oldest families. Anticipating more common successful intercessions by high ranking people at the request of convicted felons in the eighteenth century,[25] she provided companionship and material comforts to Elizabeth throughout her imprisonment, and she tried unsuccessfully to obtain an additional reprieve by appealing to the new monarch after Elizabeth Caldwell's execution date was finally fixed in June 1603 (B4r).[26] This may have been a second appeal following earlier unsuccessful petitions to Elizabeth, who granted very few pardons during her reign. We now know, moreover, that Elizabeth Caldwell was fighting impossible odds;

for according to Garthine Walker, sample records of royal pardons awarded from 1595 to 1673 show that no woman convicted of murder, other than infanticide, was pardoned.[27]

Cholmondeley had her own reasons, however, for sympathizing with Elizabeth's plight and investing her family name and personal credit in defending her. Elizabeth had brought to her marriage an annuity of £10 as well as "a good dower." These represented her family's jointure and portion (A4r). Jointure was meant to provide for a woman in the event of being widowed and un- or underprovided for by her husband. It remained the wife's independent possession after marriage and protected that part of her family's legacy otherwise lost as the portion, which under the laws of coverture passed to her husband.[28] The usual ratio of portion to jointure in early seventeenth-century marriage settlements was five to one. If one reckons the rate of return on Elizabeth's £10 annuity at 5%, then the value of her jointure was probably about £200 and her family's (presumably cash) portion about £1,000—respectable sums for nontitled county gentry.[29] Thomas Caldwell consumed this legacy on his trips abroad, "leauing [Elizabeth] often times verie bare, without prouision of such meanes as was fitting for her, y^t by these courses hee did withdrawe her affection from him" (A4r). Under these circumstances the attractions of Jeffrey Bownd, "a man of good wealth," became financially as well as emotionally irresistible.[30]

Cholmondeley could identify with the class and gender imbalances of Elizabeth's legally sanctioned impoverishment, and she perhaps also came to admire her spiritual fortitude. She had fashioned a distinct public identity as an indefatigable litigant, for which James I ambiguously dubbed her "the Bold Lady of Cheshire."[31] Although she was sole heiress to her father's estate, when he died in 1583 her claim was contested under common law by her father's half brother on the grounds he was the nearest male relation. Her predicament mirrored other lengthy disputes over the rights of female inheritors such as Grace Mildmay's and Lady Anne Clifford's.[32] Cholmondeley fought her uncle's common-law claims in the Exchequer, the county equity court in Chester Castle (where Elizabeth Caldwell was also imprisoned)[33] and elsewhere for over 40 years. Ultimately she secured only about half her father's bequest. In supporting a petition (or petitions) on Elizabeth's behalf for a royal pardon, Cholmondeley was following a familiar female appeal to equity over patriarchally biased common-law justice.

Dugdale's pamphlet vindicated the efforts of Cholmondeley and possibly others to obtain a pardon by reconstructing Caldwell's public identity as a morally justified offender rather than a reprobate criminal, besides expressing their "generall griefes for the fall of so good a Gentlewoman, and when no remedy could be, to comfort such a godly soule" (A3v). Dugdale's equitable framing of Caldwell's actions created palpable ambiguities with the normative legal and didactic assumptions of the murder-and-conversion genre. Unlike most petty treason reports, Dugdale said nothing positive about the husband but instead focused on his lower rank, shirking of masculine responsibility, and squandering of Elizabeth's dowry as causes of the marital breakdown. These also became understandable, if not condonable, motives for Elizabeth's adultery. Dugdale consistently portrayed her as a passive or reluctant agent, first victimized by Thomas and then cajoled by Bownd and Hall (A4r–B1v).[34] Adopting a classic defense tactic in cases of poisoning, he also tried to sow an element of doubt about the exact cause of the little girl's death by noting that "she had beene long before visited with sickness." Whether she died "vppon the force of that poyson or no" was indeterminable, he claimed, challenging the Crown's claim (B1v). He reduced Caldwell's active desire for a pardon and her friends' negotiations for reprieves to narrative traces. Caldwell appeared primarily concerned with securing divine remission of her sins. Only during her gallows speeches did Dugdale allow her to make the pragmatic connection between her self-constructed marks of election and the hope of mitigation:

> shee spake thus, that it was not in the power of man to repent when hee list, but the only gift of God, protesting . . . that during the time of her imprisonment . . . she had sought the Lord with many bitter teares, with broken and contrite heart, to see if his Maiestie would be intreated, and yet she found not such assurance as she desired: but auouched what she did, was done in simplicity of hart, whatsoeuer the world did other was censure. (D2r)

Not everyone was convinced. Dugdale noted earlier that "some disdained" that a convicted murderess should presume to lecture people about their faults. He argued, however that "none might better doe it than shee, hauing smarted euen at her soule for her sinnes" (B3v). Rhetorically, Dugdale attempted to erase distinctions between Caldwell and her detractors by invoking the Calvinist notion popularized by William Perkins that all humans are innately capable of murder because of their sinful nature, and that they differ only in their shifting states of self-control.[35] Yet this belief in the corrupting effects of the Fall and intrinsic human wickedness contradicted the natural-law principles underlying equitable remedies such as pardons.[36]

Dugdale also gave Elizabeth the unusual privilege of defending herself in her own words by including a separately documented *Letter* allegedly written to her husband from prison. Her text opened an adversarial space using the language of spiritual conversion and spousal amendment. Based on the same grounds—"for the soul's health"—as ecclesiastical courts proceeded in cases of martial breakdown,[37] the *Letter* set up a dialogue between the asymmetrical rights of husbands and wives that paralleled the gender-marked jurisdictions of common-law and equity. Elizabeth opened the *Letter* with her only explicit acknowledgements of adultery and murder. These were quickly superceded by condemnations of Thomas's domestic abuse and moral failings. In a daring move, she refigured her coming execution not as punishment for her own crimes but as a heroic opportunity to sacrifice herself for the sake of catalyzing Thomas's personal reformation:

> Call to remembrance the desoluteness of your life … [and] remember in what a case you haue liued, how poore you haue many times left me, how long you haue been absent from me, all which aduantage the devil tooke to subvert mee. (C1v)

After castigating Thomas's "worldly pleasures, drunkennes, & filthinesse," she focused on two specific "abominations:" adultery and sabbath-breaking. The first she insinuated by referring to the destruction of Belshazzar (Daniel 5), whose "banqueting with his Concubines" manifested his idolatrous sensuality. His captive Daniel correctly prophesied Belshazzar's overthrow by interpreting God's handwriting on his palace wall (C2r-v). Sabbatarianism represented not merely a call for social piety but also a practical means of inducing domestic equality: it would keep Thomas at home, where he would not be tempted to waste Elizabeth's dowry on masculine amusements, and it would encourage the mutual companionship idealized by Protestant theorists of marriage. Like Daniel portending Belshazzar's ruin, Caldwell warned Thomas: "You see the judgements of God are already begun in your house." Reversing the traditional link between female sexual infidelity and murder, his philandering became the root cause of the homicide, and in turn positioned Elizabeth as a scourge of providential justice urging him to convert before it was too late.

Dugdale's bold pamphlet demonstrated that well-advertised contrition in prison and public conversion on the gallows could serve multiple audiences. For the government, Caldwell's co-operative repentance validated the judicial process, deterred future criminals, and prompted spectators to internalize the moral and social norms implicit in the punishment of crime and disorder.[38] For Caldwell herself, however sincere her beliefs, her contritionally extended reprieves gave moral and procedural encouragement to supporters such as Lady Cholmondeley. They also sought to rewrite the stereotype of the homicidal adulteress by substituting a class-privileged identity based on her gentle upbringing and spiritual transformation. By representing Elizabeth's defense directly in the *Letter* and implicitly in his biographical narrative,[39] Dugdale's pamphlet insisted that marital injuries such as chronic infidelity and the misuse of family dowries were conscionable motives for her actions that complicated their legal interpretation as straightforward felonies.

SELF-DEFENSE

In early modern law homicide could be mitigated to manslaughter, which was still a capital offence but avoidable by benefit of clergy, or to excusable murder by accident or in self-defense, which might be acquitted or pardoned. Because women were ineligible for benefit of clergy for serious felonies, they derived no legal opportunity to avoid execution from a reduced conviction for manslaughter. Fatal accidents and self-defense were also much harder for women than men to prove. As Garthine Walker has shown, unlike the 1624 infanticide statute that created unique opportunities for women to mitigate or avoid charges, early modern homicide laws were conceived in terms of male anger and violence based on assumptions about physiological differences and traditional behavior. These distinctions excluded women from responding "naturally" to life-threatening danger with violence.[40]

Early modern criminal law and negative cultural attitudes towards legitimate female violence thus seemed to invalidate any defense arguments for women who killed their fatally abusive husbands. Both in practice and in terms of public discourse, however, court records and news accounts suggest that legal and imaginative possibilities for self-defense were more flexible. For example, in theory grand juries did not determine guilt. Yet as "the legal conscience of the shire" they had considerable discretion to throw out insufficiently substantiated charges, or to mitigate indictment "accusations they believed to be miscast."[41] Zachary Babington's complaints about grand juries blocking the passage of indictments and taking it on themselves to reduce initial charges from murder to manslaughter indicated that they routinely challenged the prosecutor's authority.[42] In cases of women charged with homicide, grand juries were well aware that they were ineligible for benefit of clergy, and that defendants, once they came to trial, were more likely to be found guilty and executed. This legal bias had the potential to undermine the public legitimacy of the criminal law, which was based on the concept of selective exemplary punishment. In analyzing this practice, P. G. Lawson has argued that different levels of conviction for women and men at late sixteenth- and early seventeenth-century Hertfordshire assizes can be explained partly on the grounds that "[t]he sight of too many [women] suffering the ultimate sanction" through strict application of felony law "would have brought the whole ceremony [of exemplary punishment] into disrepute."[43] If magistrates and grand jurors wished to avoid this danger, they had to embrace the option of equitable mitigation at earlier points in the examination and arraignment process, before the case proceeded to trial.

Garthine Walker's examination of late sixteenth and seventeenth-century evidence from the Court of Great Sessions at Chester bears out such practices of selective pre-emptive mitigation. It indicates that more women suspected of homicide were dismissed before formal charges were laid than men.[44] Moreover, once proceedings began, more female than male defendants were likely to be acquitted by grand and petty juries.[45] J. M. Beattie's analysis of homicide records from Restoration and eighteenth-century Surrey assizes presents a similar picture. It shows that 34.5% of grand jury bills charging female principals with homicide were returned *ignoramus*, as opposed to 12.8% for men. The figures for female accessories was 66.7%

versus 27.6 for males. Trial jury verdicts were 41.4% not guilty and 6.9% guilty of manslaughter for women, and 38.4% and 29.7% for men. Guilty verdicts were 17.2 and 19.6, respectively.[46]

Walker cautions that such figures are not absolute indications of leniency towards women suspects and defendants, because after the trial men were more likely to be pardoned than women. Also, women's guilty verdicts were rarely mitigated because there were no legal criteria to invoke (other than the fortuitous and unassured course of pleading pregnancy, which might or might not result in indefinite reprieves). Nonetheless, figures from the Cheshire and Surrey sessions—at which nearly half the women were acquitted—demonstrate that both before and during trials, magistrates and juries were making equitable interpretations of prosecution evidence and *internally* mitigating homicide suspects in the knowledge that a guilty verdict would result in the woman being executed. Informed tactical avoidance of this outcome was built up by personal experience at assize trials, memories of previous cases reported in popular news, and topical crimes debated in the court of public opinion. Local news of the unique individual circumstances of female homicides constituted part of jurors' social conscience when they came to determine the latest charges against accused women.

The relationship between news culture and assize proceedings was also underpinned by the increasingly literacy of local jurors—in particular, long-experienced ones who manned late seventeenth-century Old Bailey juries and whose major concerns, according to J. M. Beattie, were effectiveness of public punishments, class and property interests, and public morality.[47] J. S. Cockburn also argues that middling- and merchant-class jurors familiar with puritan modes of thought (*viz.* William Perkins's systematic theology) would have regarded it as a serious responsibility to sift moral points when deciding on possible verdicts leading to sentences of life or death, and he observes that education and literacy were crucial factors in the rise of juror independence, discretion, and partial verdicts after 1650.[48] These trends parallel the expansion of popular crime news, which contributed to the public's growing forensic knowledge. Moreover, if controversial reports of accused women were *pretrial* accounts, any support for the defendant had greater potential importance than it would for men, because women enjoyed fewer culturally approved or legal criteria for mitigation. Like Dugdale's *A True Discourse*, a certain percentage of later news accounts engaged readers in varying degrees of imaginative advocacy on behalf of female murderers, often by way of tendentiously arranged narrative details and/or ambiguous generic markers. *Murder and Petty-Treason*, issued by David and Elizabeth Mallet in 1677, provided a notable example. Its title page tempted buyers with a sensational tale of domestic murder:

Or, Bloody News from Southwark. Being A lamentable Relation of a barbarous Murder committed by a Wife upon the person of her

*Husband, on Munday the 25th of this instant September 1677. How
she stabb'd him into the Breast with a pair of Shears, so violently, that
when the body was open'd, his Liver, Lights* [i.e. lungs], *and Heart were
all found wounded and pierced through.*

The eight-page quarto pamphlet opened conventionally with a moralizing
preamble about Satan's discords and an allusion to Ephesians 5 enjoining a
wife's proper subordination to her husband. The main story began, however,
with the narrator's self-conscious acknowledgement of its own factual and
interpretive instability: " 'tis said" the unnamed wife had been married to
a tradesman for about twelve years and she had had several children from
this and a previous marriage. None had survived, however, "indulgent Fate
seeming in kindness to take all the issue of her body out of the world, that
they might not with grief behold the Tragical End wherewith she is threatened, from whom naturally they deriv'd their being" (A2r). Some readers
might have empathized with the presence of loss, disappointment, and possible conflict in these circumstances, all of which partly explained why the
couple lived "untowardly together."

Continuing to remind the reader of alternative interpretations of the
event, the writer described their most immediate falling-out as "differently
related." Some said the husband came home drunk and his wife began to
scold him. Others said he surprised her on stairs while carrying away her
best clothes with the intention of leaving her. A quarrel ensued,

> insomuch that he took up a pair of Tongs and struck his Wife: who does
> relate her self (as 'tis reported, for I cannot learn that any witnesses
> were present) that she wish'd him not to strike her again: which he,
> it seems, not regarding, would not for all that give over his unnatural
> blows; whereupon she snatch'd up a pair of Shears used by persons of
> that trade, and in a rage stabb'd him therewith into the breast at two
> several places, (though 'tis thought at one blow) of which wounds he
> immediately after died. (A3r)

The couple's violence was overheard by neighbors; but given that these
events happened unseen by anyone (a fact later emphasized again by the
writer), their narration must have derived primarily from the woman herself
or through third parties. Either as a first-hand or mediated account, her version of the event was a self-defense argument clearly aware of its legal position. The husband wounded his wife first and she asked him to stop, thus
implying a rational nonvindictive response to potentially lethal violence,
without prior malice. Only after he ignored her and continued to strike
her "unnaturally" (implying transgression of the boundaries constituting his
legitimate moral authority as a husband) did the wife respond. Her speed
implied a lack of premeditation, a crucial factor distinguishing manslaughter from murder in early modern trials. The murder weapon was a common

household instrument lying to hand rather than a preselected item. This too was common mitigating evidence of manslaughter. The writer's interjection "it seems" signalled his acceptance of the wife's explanations. Her "rage," however, was problematic, insofar as it suggested aggression, which early modern trials generally disallowed women in self-defense. On the other hand readers might have understood "rage" to mean sudden anger and lack of forethought. The concluding parenthetical detail "though 'tis thought at one blow" was also ambiguous. Rhetorically it countered the potential damaging information about two stab wounds. Yet as anyone familiar with indictments would have known, "at one blow" was a common formula, as was the claim that the victim died instantly (see instances quoted below). Because this was a pretrial account, it cannot have drawn on the actual document pertaining to this case, even though it mimicked typical indictment language. Some readers might have understood the phrase to confirm there was no second blow and no malice aforethought.

The story continued to emphasize the wife's impulsiveness as she fled, leaving the body to be discovered by callers, who caused a search to be mounted. Her disappearance raised suspicions because, as the writer put it, "she was thus unusually absent" (A3v). His comment implied she normally stayed close to home and took her household duties seriously. Neighbors recalled the couple's recent quarrels, but the writer avoided incriminating the wife by stating neutrally that "they could not say particularly what passed between them." He thereby avoided any negative suggestion that she had vowed previously to get rid of her husband—a detail commonly invented or reported by hostile writers such as that of *The Araignement & burning of Margaret Ferne-seede* to demonstrate prior intent to kill.

In the penultimate section of the narrative a moralizing tone returned. The inevitability of divine vengeance allegedly caused the wife to wander "in intolerable perplexity" of conscience before seeking refuge with a friend to whom she confessed "in what manner she had done it" (suggesting a source for the writer's account). Although sworn to secrecy, the friend, "knowing the danger and unrighteousness of such a Concealment" (A4r), reported the wife to a constable, who arrested and conducted her to an examining magistrate. The story ended with "the Criminal" awaiting trial in prison.

The pamphlet concluded with a generic twist, however. The writer contextualized the murder historically by referring to another local woman (unnamed but presumably familiar to readers) burnt for petty treason two years previously. This was probably Elizabeth Lillyman, whose crime, as shall see in a moment, was publicly disputed in several news pamphlets, including one published by David and Elizabeth Mallet. The writer lamented that Lillyman's fate had failed to deter the wife in the present case. He then offered readers some unexpected advice:

> And if [husbands] prove unkinde, cruel or unreasonable, [wives] ought to mollifie and amend such depravity of their humours by mildness and

compliance as far as they can; to endeavour to win them by the admonitions of Friends; to be earnest in Prayers to Almighty God to turn their hearts, and make them see the evil of their doings: And at last (if all other means prove ineffectual) to use such Remedies for tying up their injurious hands, procuring maintenance, or obtaining Separation, as the Laws allow of. (A4r-v)

Taking the problem of wife abuse seriously, the writer listed real social and legal options in ascending order of urgency. The initial remedies echoed conventional advice recommended by writers of conduct books such as William Gouge's *Of Domesticall Duties*. Unlike Gouge and many news writers, however, the author recognized that physical restraint and legal separation might be the only alternatives to serious violence. Who precisely should "tie up the hands" of a dangerous husband was left unexplained. Presumably Gouge would expect a wife to call upon civil and ecclesiastical authorities for help. Yet as Martin Ingram has shown in his study of church courts where domestic disputes were arbitrated, women in life-threatening situations faced obstacles to obtaining legal protection and formal separations from violent husbands, especially if they did not have the substantial support of neighbors and relations.[49] The author of *Murder and Petty-Treason* did not condone wives resorting to violence to defend themselves in life-threatening situations, and presumably could not in the context of government licensing of crime news. But readers who had direct experience of such situations would have agreed that legal remedies were not always effective, and individual cases would sometimes exceed formally graded boundaries. The implied audience of *Murder and Petty-Treason* included readers who would recognize the practicality of these arguments and weigh the pamphlet-writer's historically and forensically nuanced representation of the crime in anticipation of the suspect's arraignment.

Like Alice Clarke and the unnamed woman in Henry Goodcole's *The Adultresses Funerall Day* (Introduction, p. 12), *Murder and Petty-Treason* invited readers to compare the wife's motives with those of a previous female homicide: " 'Tis but a few years since a Woman near *Goodmans*-fields was made exemplary, by being burnt to Death for killing her Husband" (A4r). The conclusions to be drawn in this instance from memories of the earlier crime were more ambiguous than those in *The Adultresses Funerall Day*, however, because assessments of Elizabeth Lillyman's actions and trial were strongly contested in two extant news pamphlets.[50] Each argued over her intent to kill, the absence of any witnesses to her husband's death, and the defendant's consistent denials of guilt. Both suggested, however, that Lillyman's passionate grief was feigned to conceal her culpability. *A Compleat Narrative of the Tryal of Elizabeth Lillyman. Found Guilty of Petty Treason ... To be Burned to Death, For the Barbarous and Bloody Murther of William Lillyman her late Husband* (1675) alerted readers that this was an unusual case by altering the normal crime narrative sequence. It began with a brief account of Lillyman's execution speech on the title page verso (A1v), which eight-page news pamphlets normally left blank. The speech's position and typographical peculiarities indicated that the publisher, Phillip Brooksby, added it afterwards to the main pre-execution account to bolster the prosecution's arguments, because here she protested any intent to kill her husband but admitted doing it "in [her] passion." Bibliographical manipulation also probably explains the main story's anomalous final paragraph, which is squeezed into the last page of the single-sheet quarto pamphlet using a smaller type font (A4v). It backtracks to the first night after Lillyman was sentenced for killing her husband. She had found him drinking with a serving maid in a neighborhood tavern, and the woman had teased her about their familiarity, apparently in jest. Lillyman had allegedly also been drinking and grew enraged. After waiting until everyone else had left the room, she stabbed her husband "under the left papp" to the heart.[51]

This physical detail echoes an extant indictment dated 27 June 1675, which directly or indirectly supplied the news reporter with key information.[52] The indictment states that the day before, Lillyman stabbed her husband with her right hand in "the Breast . . . [in] the left papp." It later reiterates (in the legal macaronic of Frenchified Latin and English):

> Elizabetha Lillyman cum quondam cultello aug^te: a knife de ferro et chalybeconfect valor unius denar . . . in manu sua dextra adtunt . . . in . . . the Breast ipsius Willi Lillyman prope sinistram mamillam aug^te: the left papp . . . did strike et stabb dans mammillam ipsius Willi Lillyman vnum vulnus mortale aug^te: one mortall wound latitudinis vnius pollicis et profunditat.

This genealogy of evidence is complicated by the fact that the wording of all early modern indictments was formulaic and tendentious. Court clerks routinely inserted the details "right hand" and "left breast" to validate the prosecution's allegations of wilfully malicious and fatal violence.[53] Moreover, according to this pamphlet writer, William Lillyman lived long enough to accuse his wife of murdering him before witnesses, a scenario reproduced (i.e., invented) in melodramatic first-person speeches (*viz.* "Ah wicked woman thou hast kill'd me"). The indictment undercuts this victim's fantasy by stating that Lillyman died instantly of his wound ("instanter obiit")—another formulaic detail.[54] There is no way of knowing which, if any, of these claims is correct. They demonstrate that official and popular representations of the alleged crime were intertextually related but often contradictory, and left readers to sift them. Those with some knowledge of court procedures and documents could have reconstructed the court's version of events in various ways.

A Compleat Narrative reported that Lillyman acted "very strangely" at her examination, insouciant in the face of questions. During the trial she "fell into a kind of raveing, crying out, *she must see her Husband, and she would not plead till she had him there"* (A4r-v). What she meant by this outburst is uncertain, but it may have indicated that she wished to view her husband's body to prove her innocence by trial of cruentation. This was the ancient folk-belief that a murdered person's corpse would start to bleed if the murderer touched it or came into its presence. Lillyman might have hoped she could prove this would not happen. The other news report about this case implied the same hope: "[she] desired of the Court that she might see her dear Husband before she pleaded, which she insisted upon with seeming earnestness for some time" (*A Narrative Of the Proceedings at the Sessions-House in the Old-Bayly, From Wednesday the 7th of July instant, to Saturday the 10th* [1675], A2v). Trial by cruentation, a remnant of medieval justice, was occasionally used in doubtful cases prior to arraignments throughout the seventeenth century, although skepticism about its validity increased steadily as the office of coroners became professionalized and folkloric beliefs were abandoned.[55]

The writer of *A Compleat Narrative* dismissed Lillyman's pleas as "a faigned Artifice or piece of Dissimulation." He tried to confirm her untrustworthiness by stereotyping her as a concupiscent widow and an unruly defendant at the trial. Lillyman had allegedly become well-off by caring for plague victims in 1665 and now "lived a life somewhat extravagant and expensive" without doing "any considerable matter of work." William, a cooper, was her sixth husband. Twenty to thirty years younger than she, his initial infatuation had turned to jealousy. Lillyman's flouting of normal standards of work, thrift, and sexual continence coded her aptitude for violence. Later at her trial "she fell into another passionate fit, calling [the maidservant] many base, scurrilous, names in open Court" (A4v). Although Lillyman continued to deny murdering her husband, the nonclerical reporter dismissed her protests as impudency. He countered a final time with the appended paragraph, which reported that visitors had been successful in inducing a sense of contrition for her past sins, including the fact itself. Although this assertion was flatly contradicted by the execution speech (probably inserted independently by publisher) at the beginning of the pamphlet, the writer's narrative implied a conventional journey from sin and crime to confession and repentance.

A Narrative Of the Proceedings, issued by David and Elizabeth Mallet, covered multiple trials at the July sessions and thus contained a shorter account of Lillyman. There are also signs it may have derived some details from *A Compleat Narrative*. As usual in trial-reports, the author adopted the prosecution viewpoint, placing greatest emphasis on the incriminating evidence of the dying man's accusations and the coroner's report about the deepness of the stab wound (A3r). The court also judged her passionate outcries "to be but a mad kind of Artifice, designed out of her feigned passionate Zeal to her Murthered Husband to take off the suspicion of her being instrumental to his death" (A2v, echoing the wording of *A Compleat Narrative*). When Lillyman came to the bar to be sentenced and was given the opportunity to make her allocutus, or final statement after the verdict, she "did, as formerly, passionately request to see the body of her husband before she died, saying she could not else dye in peace." Either the court or the reporter dismissed this plea as "a fit of raving." *A Narrative Of the Proceedings* represented Lillyman's mental instability and unruly behavior after the crime as signs of her guilty conscience (A4r-v).

Discrepancies between trial verdicts and the morally complex domestic circumstances in which women defended themselves from violent husbands were displayed in several more news reports published during the 1670s, before the Popish Plot hardened journalistic attitudes towards female offenders. Publisher David Mallet's *Proceedings At The Assizes in Sovthwark . . . Begun on Thursday the 21th* [*sic*], *of March, and not ended till Tuesday the 26 of the same month, 1678* highlighted the controversial "*Tryal of the Woman for murdering her Husband; with the exact proof that came in against her, and her Confession and Pleas at the Bar*" (A1r). Like *Murder and Petty-Treason*, its narrative mingled prosecution and self-defense allegations while justifying the defendant's actions overall.

The heart of the story was that on 25 September in the previous year an unnamed wife dwelling in Fishmonger's Alley had accidentally killed her husband with a pair of scissors when he attacked her with a frying pan. Because this was a trial-report officially warranted by the government licensor Roger L'Estrange (title page), the journalist at first stayed close to the formulaic wording of the indictment read in court: the woman "wickedly, traiterously, and of her malice aforethought . . . [gave] unto him one mortal wound on the left side of Breast near the left Pap, of the breadth of half an Inch, and the depth of 3 Inches, of which he immediately died" (A2r).[56] Unusually, as the title page advertised, the wife was allowed to plead her case at some length. As in the Elizabeth Abbot trial, this judicial consideration indicated her guilt was disputed and the bench was concerned to justify the ultimate verdict. The wife testified that she and her husband had been drinking in an alehouse beforehand and that she had felt light-headed, although she claimed to have drunk no more than a pint and a half. They quarreled over some items of silver he had taken from her and vowed to give to another woman. When they came home she demanded her possessions. Her husband struck her on the head with a fire shovel, knocking her down in a trance; next-door neighbors witnessed his attack and testified to it. When the wife revived she got a pair scissors "intending to go to work with them according to her custome at the Ally gate till his fury were over." The reporter's wording stressed the wife's restraint and the absence of retaliation. But the husband seized a frying pan to beat her again, and "she held [the scissors] forth to keep him off, who was so violent, that, having his Bosom all open to the skin, he run upon them, and thereby got this mischief" (A2v). The reporter did not say whether neighbors also witnessed these incidents. His description was tendentious, however, presenting the wife as passive and the husband's death as self-inflicted, thus contradicting the prosecution's allegations. The narration continued from the wife's perspective in claiming that when her husband fell down she tried to comfort him by giving him syrups. "[B]ut finding him ready to die," she ran into Whitechapel to tell people "she had unfortunately killed her Husband: she now protested very passionately her innocence as to any intention of murdering him." The wife's immediate concern for her husband and lack of concealment authenticated her humane conscience, thus marking her socially as a mitigable offender rather than an irremediable criminal.[57] The writer clearly favored the wife's testimony. He could have been more skeptical or hostile towards her claims if he had wished, and as other trial reporters routinely were towards defendants.

His report concluded by turning briefly to prosecution witnesses who testified that the wife had previously sworn "to do his business" and, in one instance, to poison him. One young woman coming into her house and seeing the dying man asked the wife if the husband had fainted, to which she allegedly replied "surlily, bidding her meddle with her own business," and the girl left to tell neighbors. This circumstantial evidence apparently undercut the wife's testimony, and the jury found her guilty. Perhaps more determining in law was that self-defense by women carried little mitigating force against prosecution for homicide.[58] The reporter's narrative, on the other hand, validated the moral argument of accidental death in self-defense and upheld the wife's actions as nonvengeful and inadvertent. Implicitly—it could be only thus given the shadow of official censorship—his story exposed an equitable gap between the law's conceptual boundaries and a layperson's greater openness to alternative interpretations of the event.

It was not until a month later that the wife's identity was revealed in print by two execution pamphlets: *The Last Speech and Confession of Sarah Elestone . . . Who was Burned For Killing her Husband* (1678), and *A Warning for Bad Wives: or, The Manner of the Burning of Sarah Elston* (1678). These contrasting narratives demonstrated how public debate over Elstone's conviction had intensified. As publishers competed for readers' custom and opinions, they added distinct ideological interpretations not only to the crime itself but also to related questions of domestic violence.

The Last Speech and Confession, issued by T. D, re-presented Elstone's crime as a moralized conversion narrative. Here Thomas, a hard-working felt maker, was victimized by his slightly younger but drunken, rapacious, and emasculating wife. Their marriage spiralled into chronic violence after a series of provocations. First Sarah fell into the company of "lewd" women who inveigled her into drinking, swearing, profaning the sabbath, and spending her husband's money. When he tried to curb these habits, she sold off the household furniture to the point that they had "scarce a Chair to sit on, or a bed to lye on" (A3r). The "perplexed" Thomas then tried beating her, "which she was not wanting to repay." Their brawls often compelled neighbors to intervene "to part them at all hours in the night." On the day of the crime Sarah had been out drinking with her gossips. She came home to demand money and threatened to kill Thomas. He thrust her downstairs (no fire shovel or frying pan here), shut his door and went back to work. When he thought her "heat was over" he came down in his shift for a drink, where she met him on the stairs "and with one side of a pair of sheers gave him a mortal wound on the breast, of which he immediately dyed." She fled but was apprehended after a hue and cry was raised, and condemned to be burnt. She asked for time to prepare, and while in Marshalsea prison, visiting ministers (one of whom was probably the author) converted her to plangent repentance a few days before the execution. At the stake she recited some prayers and piously exhorted the crowd to fear God's laws.

The differences in fact between this prosecution-oriented account and the earlier trial-report are striking but not surprising given the well-established— although at this time often skeptically regarded—conventions of the confession-and-conversion genre (discussed fully in the next chapter). *A Warning for Bad Wives* unexpectedly provided another viewpoint because it was also issued by David Mallet, publisher of the earlier *Proceedings At The Assizes*, who again advertised Roger L'Estrange's imprimatur on the title page.[59] Taking Elstone's posttrial penitence as his frame of reference, the writer (probably another prison visitor) reconstructed her life as a *felix culpa*: "The rashness of a wicked Fury drew her into Affliction, that Affliction humbled her, and God took the advantage of her Humiliation for her Conversion" (A3r). This author offered readers a more factually varied account, however, rather like the one in *Proceedings At The Assizes*. Although he ultimately positioned himself against Elstone's defenders, his representations were nuanced by empathetic details. He dealt with competing interpretations right away by acknowledging "some now would partly excuse the woman, and alleadge the principal Cause of their Differences by [Thomas's] ill husbandry, cross carriage, ill company, and other provocations, not here to be mentioned" (A2r). Presumably these unmentionables included the fire shovel and frying pan. Selectively collating trial testimony, he reminded readers that other persons claimed that Sarah had threatened Thomas's life, and that she did not deny killing him. His version of the main incident endorsed the indictment allegations yet was morally and circumstantially far more ambiguous:

> he having beat her severely, she with a pair of Sizzars gave him a wound on the left breast; whereof, without speaking one word, he died. Yet all along to the last she denied that she had any murderous intention or designe to kill him, onely thought to do him some slight Mischief in revenge of his Cruelty in beating her. (A2v)

In terms of the key legal criteria of moral culpability and *mens rea*, Sarah was suddenly provoked into defending her life in an act of excusable homicide, even though the prosecution defined her alleged retaliation as wilful murder.

According to this account, after her sentencing on 26 March to the day of her execution, Elstone was "extraordinary penitent." Executions normally followed soon after sentencing; so in being granted more than her requested fortnight's time to prepare, there may have been some anticipation of a reprieve being gained by friends, and her penitence may have been tactical, as it had been for Elizabeth Caldwell and Alice Clarke. This context was also suggested by her execution performance, despite its being played down typographically in smaller type and squeezed into the last pages of the pamphlet.[60] Conveyed to Kennington Common on a hurdle, Elstone appeared "clothed all in White, with a vast multitude of People attending her" (A3v). Descriptions of spectators' attitudes and reactions at executions were relatively rare in early modern news about women murderers. Here as elsewhere there is no indication of hostility or lack of compassion. People wished to hear what Elstone had to say, and her deliberately planned appearance and speeches suggest she anticipated some sympathy from her audience. After praying, she spoke "some few words tending to clear her Innocency as to any intent of murdering her Husband, and the horror, confusion, and surprize she was in when she saw him fall." Positioning herself uncontroversially, she gave wives St. Paul's advice to defer silently to furious husbands. These details attested to the prison visitor's coaching, as the writer had stated earlier that Elstone was "extreamly ignorant of the nature and very foundations of the Gospell" (A2r). Sandra Clark observes that her "co-operation with the ideology of state punishment enables her crime to be represented in the pamphlet in a way that is near to being morally neutral."[61] It also eased the major shift in voice that followed. After regretting "lifting up her hand against her Husband, and offering to revenge herself of him," she

> protested again most seriously, that she never in her life had the least designe or thoughts of killing of him, onely it was an unfortunate Accident; and whether it came by a blow from her, or his violent running upon the point of the Sizzars as she held them out to defend herself, she could not to this minute certainly tell; but she hoped God had pardoned her all her Miscarriadges in that matter. (A4v)

An interpretive gap again opened among published versions of the event. Transferring the moment's agency to her husband, Elstone asserted that his death was self-inflicted, and then distanced herself further by regretting any prior behavior that might be connected to it symbolically.[62] Such distinctions were made by every early modern woman who denied committing an alleged murder. But they struggled against the prevailing Calvinist ideology of linked and incremental sins, which (as we shall see in the next chapter) was fundamental to confession-and-conversion narratives. After the pyre was lit, Elstone gave "two or three lamentable Shrieks" and was mercifully strangled before her body was consumed. The pamphlet concluded with a report of two highwaymen whose education, poverty, and previous good behavior, according to the author, mitigated their crimes but didn't save them from the noose.

These accounts opened epistemological fissures between ideological assumptions familiar to readers from gallows-speech news genres, and the legal and moral complexities of individual lives such as Elstone's, particularly in relation to her dissenting testimony and sympathetic representation in *Proceedings At The Assizes*. By circulating varied perspectives in the arena of printed news, commercial publishers and writers ensured, however fortuitously, that the alleged crime's meanings would be interpreted according to personal and social criteria that exceeded the limits of institutionalized justice, gender commonplaces, and perennial bio-allegories of sin and redemption. The transformative impact of such controversies on criminal-law jurisprudence was apparently negligible before the statutory reforms of the second half of the eighteenth century. Even in popular news, their revisionary potential in terms of assessing the origins of female violence was restrained by the dominant—and profitable—tendency to focus on notorious murders that ended in uncontestable verdicts and re-affirmed traditional gender roles. But their practical consequences can be inferred from the greater skepticism towards court testimony and judgments seen in later seventeenth-century trial-reports, as well as the diminished credibility among educated writers and readers of crudely allegorizing narratives. The cultural effects of controversial verdicts such as Elstone's were also reflected in the independent decisions of officials and jurors, who rejected the formulaic reasoning of prosecution indictments or gave female defendants involved in cases of extreme domestic abuse the benefit of reasonable doubt. Their willingness to consider mitigation coincided with growing public disapproval of violent husbands that, in emergent polite society at least, well-publicized cases such as Elstone's helped to strengthen.

DOMESTIC CRUELTY, HOMICIDE, AND INSANITY

Changing attitudes towards spousal abuse in seventeenth-century news were signalled by the expanding gender boundaries of morally culpable domestic violence. Earlier in the period, printed news categorized abusive husbands according to degrees of legitimate or excessive physical violence and/or economic deprivation, and in relation to stereotypical female provocations and deviance.[63] As the dominance of religious perspectives waned after the Civil War, popular news began to represent serious marital violence against women, and long-term mental degradation in particular, more openly. Homicide committed in a state of temporary "distraction" or "frenzy" (as contemporaries called insanity) also began to be considered as a reasonable way of explaining and possibly mitigating newborn child murder. Its use as a defense in instances of adult homicide was rarer and usually ineffectual. Insanity was not recognized either in law or culturally as a legitimate defense for female violence, which tended to be defined in trials as wilful aggression and revenge.[64] Nonetheless, as with other aspects of the relationship between the law and printed discourse, later seventeenth-century murder news began to depict lethal insanity in the context of domestic strife not just as satanic hysteria (e.g., Margaret Vincent in 1616, discussed in chapter 5) but as a plausible psychological disorder with physical origins.

The five news accounts of Margaret Osgood's killing of her husband on 30 to 31 July 1680 provide illuminating comparative evidence of changes in reporting techniques and societal assumptions about the motives of marital violence.[65] This gruesome murder prompted two unknown publishers to rush sensational accounts into half-broadsheet formats before the trial. *Great and Bloody News, From Farthing-Ally . . . Of a Horid and Barbarous Murther, Committed on the Body of Walter Osily, by his own Wife*[66] may have been the first of the two, since it managed to get the Osgoods' name wrong and contradicted its own title page summary that Margaret had "first strangled [Walter] with a Bow-string, and afterwards cut him with a Hatched on the bare Head" (A1r). In the main text strangling is Margaret's *coup de méchanceté*. The reporter's main source of information seems to have been the coroner's inquest, because he reproduces a remarkably exact physical description that was unlikely to be invented or obtained by hearsay:

> with a down-right blow [Margaret] struck her sleeping Husband . . . on the Forehead, making there a wound three inches in length and an inch in depth . . . with a second just under his right Ear, the which was about an Inch and a half deep . . . and after that another that slit his Nose, and a fourth on his hand between his Fingers, the which he was supposed to receive in making resistance. (A1v)

The rest of the account built conjecturally on incomplete details gleaned from the inquest and magistrate's examination. It presented Margaret's motive as revenge for her husband's drunken violence. Walter came home at 9.00 p.m. on 30 July "somewhat disordered in drink" (A1r). After quarrelling, Walter beat Margaret, and then, being overcome with drink, fell asleep. She complained to neighbors of his "grievous abuse," returned home, locked the doors and bludgeoned him with a hatchet "she chanced to light upon." (Here the casual tool does not denote her lack of forethought but fortuitously enabled malice. It also worth noting that though "the Devil prevailed with her," Margaret's actions are otherwise presented as entirely human.) She went to bed and next morning privately confessed what she done to an alehouse keeper, who afterwards told a neighbor. They visited the Osgoods' house, found Walter's body "welterred in Blood all mangled on Flore," and set in motion Margaret's arrest and examination. Only at the end did the writer briefly mention that Margaret had married her apprentice and possible lover Walter, who was twenty years younger, after the death of her first husband, and allegedly slept with him the night after the husband was buried. Walter squandered the £200 she inherited, "which extravagance of his and abusing her a[s] it is conjectured were the causes for which she murthered him for which no doubt she gave him cause, being a Woman of a Turbulent spirit" (A2v). With this garbled passage, the pamphlet ended, leaving three quarters of a page blank.

By contrast the writer of *Dreadful News from Southwark: Or, A true Account of the Most Horrid Murder committed By Margaret Osgood On her Husband Walter Osgood* relied on personal interviews with neighbors for his information.[67] His representation of Margaret's motives was contexualized by a history of her violent marriage, and his moral assumptions about husband killing as a response to spousal violence were contingent on the woman's circumstances. Margaret's crime was indeed horrifying, he argued carefully, because it was

> perpetrated *deliberately*, and by one of the softer *Sex*, and by a *Wife* upon her Husband, and without any proportionate provocation. (A2r)

If Margaret *had* been faced with immediate life-threatening violence, this might have justified her response. The violence was not "proportionate," however. One neighbor "aver[red], he heard the deceased threaten to kill his Wife, which she likewise affirms, and as it seems by the bloody sequele, was resolved to prevent and anticipate him therein" (A1v). The writer confirmed this scenario by paraphrasing Margaret's morning-after conversation with the alehouse keeper:

> she thought it was better to *Kill than be Killed*; he observing her Distracted looks and words, said, *I hope you have not Killed your Husband? Yes*, said she, *I have, come to our house and you will see it done ... I will not run away, but go home and look out things for his Burial.* (A2r)

Neighbors testifying about the Osgoods' dysfunctional marriage confirmed this morally extenuating scenario. They alleged "they were both too much to blame" for their increasingly rancorous relationship, "each of them following loose and extravagant courses" and "continual fewds and ill-language," "insomuch, that (as an antient Neighbour attests) they seldom went to bed without a storm of Oaths and mutual Curses." Margaret was "a handsome and well-proportioned Woman," yet "too *free* and liberal of kindnesses both to [her first husband's] *Servants*," of whom Walter Osgood was allegedly one. The writer discounted the stereotypical speculation that the difference in their ages—forty and twenty respectively—was a significant factor, although he was not above misogynist remarks ("but no *wild Beast* is so cruel as an incensed woman") and graphic depictions: Margaret gashed Walter's forehead, slicing the fingers "of both his hands almost to the Wrist," and cutting off his ears, "or so far mangl[ing] them, that she could (as afterwards they were found) turn them over his face" (A2r). This account mentions nothing about strangling, though witnesses—let alone

[1]

Dreadful News

F R O M

SOUTHWARK:

O R,

A true A C C O U N T

O F T H E

Moft Horrid M U R D E R committed

B Y

MARGARET OSGOOD,

On her Husband *WALTER OSGOOD* a Hat-maker,
On Saturday the 31th of *July* 1680.

Whom fhe moft barbaroufly Murdered, by Cleaving his Head
whilft he was afleep, cuting off his Ears, and Wounding him in
feveral other places in an inhumane manner.

Together with her Examination and Confeffion of the whole Fact before
the Juftice of the Peace, and commitment of her to Prifon till Tryal.

IN other Cafes long *Preambles* may be neceffary, but here
is too much *matter*, and too horrid, to need either *flourifh*
or *Aggravation* ; therefore we fhall immediately come to
the naked *Fact*, which being truely related, muft be acknowledged one of the moft difmal *Tragedies* this Age has been
guilty of.

Murder at all times is a black and crying fin, no lefs abhor-
rent to Humane Nature, than punifhable by all Laws of *God*
and *Man* ; but to find it perpetrated *deliberately*, and by one
of the fofter *Sex*, and by a *Wife* upon her Husband, and without any proportionate provocation ; and to be perfifted in,
ftood unto, and in effect juftified, this feems to be the height
of malice, and a feared Impiety.

The perfons concern'd in this wicked Deed, lived in *Southwark*, in a place called *Farthing-Alley*, not far from St. *Thomas's*

A   Hof-

Figure 2.2 Dreadful News From Southwark (1680). Reproduced by permission of
the Bodleian Library.

many readers—might not have noticed given Walter's sanguineous state. The attention to horror in these physical details may have derived from the reactions of neighbors, who also made much of the fact that Walter's blood was dripping through the ceiling from the upstairs chamber when his body was found. The writer repeated this vivid image twice. When arrested and examined, Margaret admitted the deed but showed no remorse, and "did in effect declare, were it undone, she would yet do it." On this point *Dreadful News from Southwark* agreed with *Great and Bloody News*, although the latter typically embellished her remark: when told "she would be burnt . . . she replied, she burn'd already and that would prepare her for the Flames to come" (A2r).

Notwithstanding the sensationalism of both pamphlets, the author of *Dreadful News from Southwark* was more self-aware in presenting material evidence. His account *sounded* more forensically authoritative because it was apparently based on neighbors' variably credible testimony. Perhaps for the same reason, only he recorded the local opinion that Margaret might have been "Distracted" when she killed her husband. This plausible observation was prescient because it became the defense argument at her murder trial eight months later. The delay was owing to her lack of repentance, according to David Mallet's *The True Narrative of the Confession and Execution Of the Prisoners . . . the 16th of this Instant March, 1681*. It gave prison visitors time to work on her to produce a confession that would justify a conviction for petty treason.[68] Mallet highlighted Osgood's case both in this postexecution account and in his earlier *True Narrative of the Proceedings at the Assizes Holden at Kingstone-upon-Thames . . . on Monday the 7th of this Instant March, and ended on Tuesday the 10th following* (1681).[69] The trial-report stated concisely:

> The defence she made was thus, That by his extravagancy he had brought her to Distraction, and so desperate she was under that sence, that she had several times attempted her own end by violence, and was not capable of her actions when she did commit that horrid Murther on him; but her confession and the Evidence against her contradicting that Apology she was brought in Guilty of Treason and Murther. (A1v)

The True Narrative of the Confession and Execution endorsed the defence of insanity deductively. This more substantial account declared that the powers of darkness often turn "jealousies and discontents" to despair and suicide, "or to desperate revenge by which we destroy others[;] the effects of the latter has been amply proved in this Tragical Exploit with which we shall Usher in this Scean of Death one *Margaret Osgood*"(A1r-v). *The True Narrative of the Confession and Execution* connected Margaret's argument that she was suicidally depressed before the killing to their violent brawls ("notwithstanding the Mediation and Perswasion of several Neighbours") and to financial distress, Walter having "in a short time [wasted] almost all that her former Husband had left her (which was considerable)" by spending "lavishly to keep Horses and Spannels [*sic*]" (A1v). When he came home drunk on the 30th, "after some contest[,] she got him to Bed" and bludgeoned him three times on the head with a hatchet, slit one of his arms "whilst he extended his dying Hands for mercy," and strangled him with a whip-cord, "sitting by the Corps [a] good part of the Night." In Marshalsea Prison "she remained very careless and negligent of her futer state" until her trial, at which she pleaded that "she was not (*Compes Mentis*) but *Distracted*" when she killed her husband. However the alehouse keeper, Mr Fowler, and several other witnesses deposed that on the morning after the attack "she was as at other times and they saw no Distraction in her." Unable to add anything at her allocutus, she was found guilty by the jury.

This narrative sharpened the legal interpretation of Margaret's guilt by making Fowler's testimony pivotal to the jury's decision about her mental state. As reported by *The True Narrative*, Fowler's statements left open the question of whether she was criminally insane before and/or during the killing, a condition the rest of the pamphlet appeared to validate. The report of her morning conversation in *Dreadful News from Southwark* also contradicted Fowler's alleged claims here. To modern eyes, her behavior after the killing looks like a state of deep shock. This was certainly her condition after sentencing, when "she seemed as it were stupified with the horror of guilt." Her mental condition and moral consciousness fluctuated between feelings of guilt for her adultery, and passionate defiance about her deed: "she answered she was sorry for the Murther, but were her Husband now alive she would rather be burnt according to sentence than to live with him."

Like Margaret Ferneseede and Sarah Elstone, Osgood dressed in white for her execution, but already "she seemed as one half dead" (A2r). *The True Protestant Mercury* echoed this observation in Number 24 for Wednesday 16 March to Saturday 19 March, describing the unnamed woman burned in the marketplace at Kingston for killing her husband as "very little concern'd at her Tragical end" (A2r). *The True Narrative* reported that Margaret's only speech to the crowd was to ask them "to pray for her, and take warning for her sad end." Its last piece of information was a bit of hearsay: "It is said during her Imprisonment she did what she could to be got with Child, thereby to respit [*sic*] her Execution, but her Expectation failed her, for she proved not pregnant" (A1v–A2r). This rumor was likely occasioned by the lengthy period between her arrest and trial.

TO KILL OR BE KILLED

It was not long before a far more spectacular story about a wife killing her serially abusive husband rivetted and divided Londoners. The remarkably detailed accounts of Mary Hobry's wretched marriage, desperate killing, and uncontested verdict created a controversial news-event that escalated already extensive word-of-mouth debate. As Roger L'Estrange, presumed compiler and editor of *A Hellish Murder* (1688), put it in his preface:

> The late Barbarous Murder of Denis Hobry, (what with Malice, Prejudice, Credulity, and Mistake) has put more Freaks and Crotchets into the Heads and Minds of Common People, then any Story of that size perhaps ever did in this world before. (A2r)[70]

L'Estrange's statement may be more than puffery, because he had acted intermittently as government censor of the press since 1663.[71] He became directly involved in Hobry's case as an Old Bailey examiner and translator, having published translations of literary works from several languages, including French, Hobry's mother tongue.[72] News title pages about this and other recent murderesses advertised his warrant to legitimate their authority.[73] L'Estrange seized his own opportunity to profit from publishing an account of Hobry's crime after she had pleaded guilty—although not before being asked to reverse her plea by the court—and no official airing of examiners' evidence had ensued. As he explained,

> The Womans Confession has Prevented the Publick Notification of the Foulness of the Cause, that would otherwise have been made, by a Printed Account of the Tryal: So that it remains only to supply that Disappointment by True Copies of the Following Enformations, which would have been the Foundation at last (in case she had put her self upon her Defence) for the Court to Proceed upon. (A2v)

L'Estrange and his publisher Randal Taylor offered readers 37 quarto pages of bilingual testimony ("Enformations") taken from relations and neighbors in preparation for the trial.[74] At least four popular interpretations flowed from his official report.[75] *A Hellish Murder* and its discursive offspring tried Hobry in the court of public opinion and refracted the event into an ideological spectrum. All viewpoints were concerned with defining what L'Estrange called "the Foulness of the Cause." Speculations about the crime's motives were initially dispersed among the sometimes byzantine testimony of multiple "Enformants" in *A Hellish Murder*. Readers' opinions depended on interpretations of Hobry's own story (as narrated by L'Estrange and his colleagues) in the light of deep-seated assumptions about the limits of a husband's domestic authority and a wife's right to survival in the face of extreme sexual violence. Although the effects of Hobry's retrial in print do not seem to have been as legally and culturally influential as Anne Greene's in 1651 (see chapter 5), the memory of Hobry's husband killing was long lasting, and its social meanings continued to be debated. The crime was still being recalled at the end of the next century when publisher James Caulfield (1764 to 1826) issued a bizarre image of a satanically inspired Hobry butchering the classically sculpted body of her headless husband. Her gormless

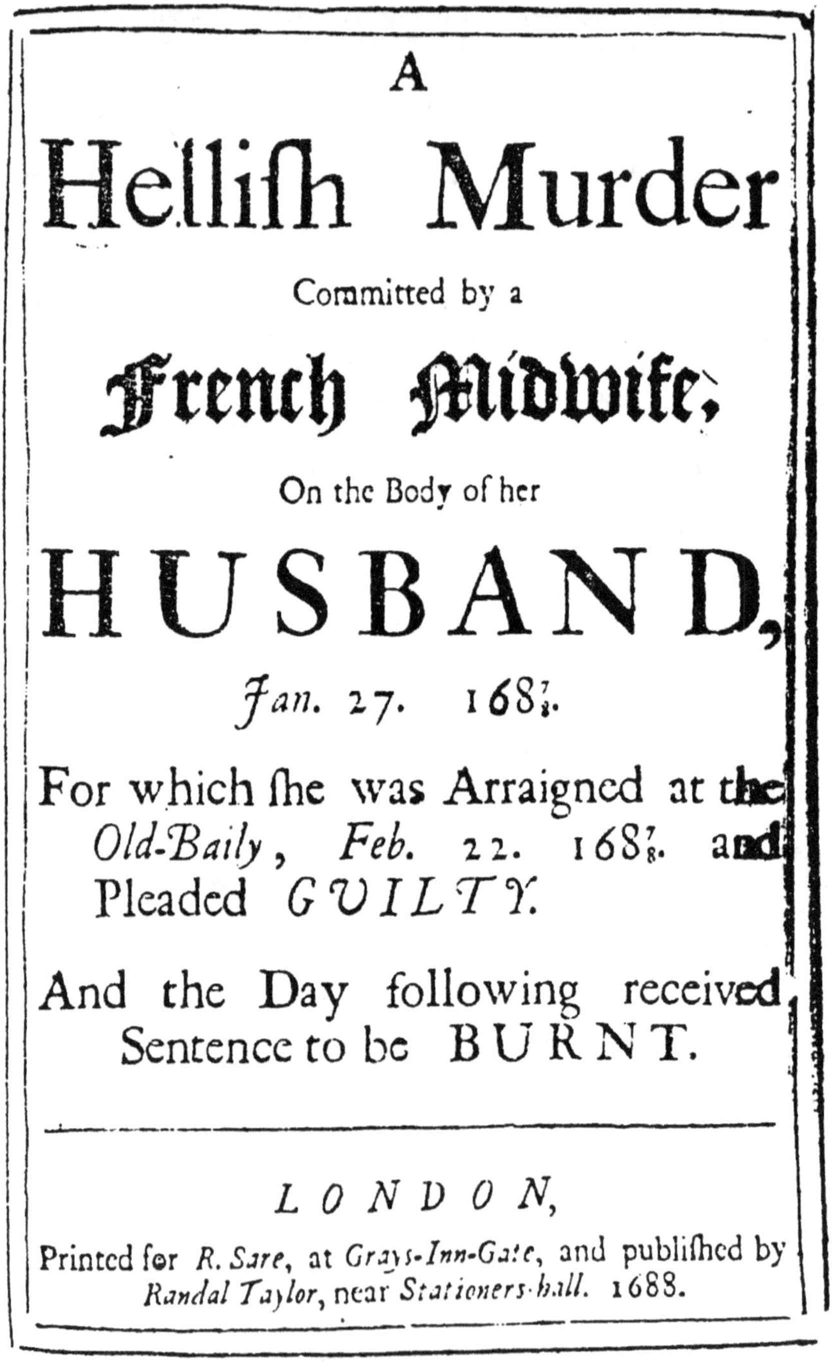

A
Hellifh Murder

Committed by a

French Midwife,

On the Body of her

HUSBAND,

Jan. 27. 168⅞.

For which fhe was Arraigned at the *Old-Baily*, *Feb.* 22. 168⅞. and Pleaded *GUILTY.*

And the Day following received Sentence to be BURNT.

LONDON,

Printed for *R. Sare*, at *Grays-Inn-Gate*, and publifhed by *Randal Taylor*, near *Stationers-hall.* 1688.

Figure 2.3 A Hellish Murder (1688). Reproduced by permission of the Huntington Library.

son held his father's head in one hand and gestured to his mother with the other what to do with it (*Mary Aubrey A French Midwife who murdered her Husband in Long Acre. Anno 1687–8* [1798]). An inset image depicted a strangled woman being burnt at the stake.

Hobry's killing seems to have struck most contemporaries as less "foul" than either its provocation or the aftermath. On 27 January 1688, Mary strangled her sleeping drunken husband to death with one of his garters. He had come in at five in the morning after being out "among Bougres and Rogues" that made him "mad" (F1r).[76] Mary had been asleep and left the doors open, and Denis had announced his arrival by punching her violently in the stomach. After several more blows, he squeezed her so hard "that Blood started out of her Mouth:"

> Immediately upon this, he attempted the Forcing of this Examinate [i.e. Mary] to the most Unnatural of Villanies, and acted such a Violence upon her Body in despite of all the Opposition that she could make, as forc'd from her a great deal of Blood, this Examinate crying out to her Landlady, who was (as she believes) out of distance of hearing her. (F1r)

The narration of such brutality was remarkable even by the often highly sensationalized standards of early modern murder news. It surpassed Henry Goodcole's more coded description of spousal rape and sodomy, for example, in *The Adultresses Funerall Day* (1635). There Goodcole did not record the unnamed wife crying out. Here Hobry and/or L'Estrange did, clearly signalling her rejection of consent and defining the violation legally as rape.[77] But Goodcole's aporetic "etc." has not disappeared; it has returned to establish a new horizon of domestic cruelty. When Mary tried to get up and tell neighbors what had happened, Denis threw her on the bed and "Bit her like a Dog, *&c.—*this Examinate saying to him, *Am I to lead this life forever? Yes, and a worse too, ere it be long, you had best look to yourself.*" Denis fell asleep and Mary

> lay in Torments both of Body and of Mind, thinking with her self, *What will become of me? What am I to do! Here am I Threatned to be Murder'd, and I have no way in the World to Deliver my self, but by Beginning with him.* (F1v)

L'Estrange's reconstruction of her interior monologue expounded the same dilemma resolved by Margaret Osgood and Goodcole's unnnamed wife: "it was better to *Kill than be Killed*" (*Dreadful News from Southwark*, A2r; *The Adultresses Funerall Day*, B1v–B2r). Yet by positioning her words immediately before rather than after the killing, L'Estrange avoided characterizing Mary's actions as vengeful frenzy or fearful guilt. Instead they seemed a rational and morally justified response to her husband's life-threatening abuse. *A Hellish Murder* (1688) validated her identity to this point as a legitimate agent with legal rights to her personal safety, and it mitigated her actions as justifiable homicide.

If that had been the end of the crime, the grand jury might have dismissed charges against Hobry. Initially, like the unnamed woman in *The Adultresses Funerall Day*, she reinforced the cultural distinction between an offender and a criminal by trying to revive her husband with brandy "in the hopes that he was not yet Dead, repenting with all her heart." But Mary had left the body overnight and the next morning visited her thirteen-year-old son, John Desermeau, to ask for help disposing it. The petrified boy refused, and that afternoon Hobry dismembered her husband, wrapped up the body parts—including the head, after her son advised her not to throw it in the river—and carried them to various dung-heaps and privies around the city. The head was found and identified, however, and Hobry readily confessed after she was arrested.

Elkanah Settle attempted to define public interpretation of the crime in *An Epilogue to the French Midwife's Tragedy* (1688), a verse-report written after Hobry's execution on 2 March,[78] by focusing readers' emotional reactions on Mary's desecration of her husband's body. Using a historically resonant comparison, he argued that this action transgressed an absolute moral boundary, whereas the murder itself had crossed a socially ambiguous one:

> Had some girl by covetous Parents Doom,
> In Natures Prime, in Youth and Beauties Bloom,
> Betray'd to some old jealous Misers Bed,
> To Impotence, to Age and Aches Wed;
> Her Chamber-walls, her Dungeon, and her Tomb,
> Lockt up from Foraging, yet starv'd at home:
> Had this mew'd slave, to meet some dearer Charms,
> And run to a more darling Lovers Arms,
> A Cawdle spiced, or cut a Jugular Vein,
> He Jaylor laid asleep to break her Chain;
> The Murdering Blow her pitied hand should give,
> Would scarcely to a Nine Days wonder Live.

Settle's scenario recalls almost exactly the period's most iconic story of enforced marriage leading to husband murder: the 1591 poisoning-homicide of Thomas Page of Plymouth by his wife Eulalia and her lover George Strangwidge, continuously known through often reprinted ballads (discussed in chapter 4). The nine days wonder reference also invoked news readers' memories of earlier printed reports of discontented wives killing their disagreeable or abusive husbands, some of which, such as Elizabeth Caldwell's, had generated considerable public sympathy and moral outrage towards a bad husband's legal privileges. But for Settle, Hobry's infamous scattering of her husband's limbs translated her criminal identity into the realm of mythic murderesses such as "Great *Medea*."

A Cabinet of Grief: Or, The French Midwife's Miserable Mean (1681) shifted this interpretation further by fictionalizing Hobry's first person confession and execution lament in the archaic style of a news ballad.[79] The pamphlet's title page presented readers with an equally antiquated woodcut of a smiling woman being martyred in flames with both hands raised away from the stake, while a soldier looking rather pleased with the spectacle watches from the bottom left. The text of this octavo pamphlet only stretched to the recto of the eighth leaf, so the publisher added another old woodcut of a woman being burnt at the stake on the final verso page. Billows of black smoke rise from her tightly hemmed-in pyre as a multitude of what look like shaven heads and three soldiers with halberds wearing wide-brimmed hats look on impassively. The scene looks Continental rather than English. But this made the image fortuitously apt.

Neither the anonymous author nor his publisher, J. Blare, bothered to identify Mary, although her husband was named. Textually depersonalized, the murderesses' criminal identity was freer to be reconstructed according to contemporary suspicions of Frenchness, Catholicism, and midwives. All three profiles had recently converged in the "popish midwife" Elizabeth Cellier, tried twice in 1680: once for conspiring to murder the king, for which she was acquitted, and again for libel, for which she was convicted. Cellier was also pilloried for allegedly helping fellow Catholics plot the destruction of the fleet at Chatham.[80] *A Cabinet of Grief*'s prose *adieu* activated these popular prejudices by associating Denis's abuses, extravagances, and marital "confusion" between Mary and himself with "ramble[s] into Forreign parts." It also stereotyped the narrator's "business" with the devil as the chief inspiration for her bloody thoughts. After being assaulted on the morning of January 26th [sic], she took revenge and made no attempt to revive her husband after killing him. Eventually her guilty conscience moved her to reveal her crime to her (presumably French) friends, who condemned the murder but kept it secret (A3v–A4r). The concluding ballad, sung to the tune of "The Pious Christian's Exhortation," possibly alluded to Mary's reported attempts to pledge her husband to good behavior, thereby accentuating the ideological failure of these socially approved methods:

> When him I strove to reconcile, saying, thou know'st how 'tis
>   with us,
> Maliciously he'd me Revile, and swear it should be worse and
>   worse.
>
> Though he to Wickedness was bent, and show'd himself so cross and
>   grim,
> I own this was no argument that I, alas! should Murder him.
>   (A6v)

By contrast, *A Hellish Murder*'s self-defense argument was ambiguously affirmed by an anonymous 164-line broadside verse-report, *A Warning-Piece to All Married Men and Women. Being the Full Confession of Mary Hobry, The French Midwife* (1688). This was published by George Croom, the Mallets' long-time commercial rival. Its final thirty lines described the dismemberment and dispersal of Denis's corpse fairly briskly. Before then, as the title promised, it presented readers with a cautionary example of a dysfunctional marriage. "The cause that mov'd him to those Tyrannies, / Was her aversion to his Villanies;" and as the report unfolded it chronicled Mary's virtuous resistance to a deepening pattern of abuse and dereliction, the latter a result of Denis often taking French leave after literally squeezing money out of her.

A Warning-Piece recalled the advice to battered wives presented at the end of *Murder and Petty-Treason* in narrating Mary's incremental attempts to secure her husband's good behavior through institutional channels, and it implicitly answered the question of what might be necessary when these failed. On Denis's first return from France "he Courted her again" and "swore a thousand times to please her Mind." Mary persuaded him to make a formal pledge before a priest and witnesses that "he would no more vex her during his Life." The abuse soon resumed and Denis again fled to France. When he returned, Mary asked him for a separation, which he refused and Mary was unable to enforce in the church courts, notwithstanding the support of relations and neighbors, perhaps because she was a Catholic.[81] Mary began to ponder killing her husband, particularly after one neighbor named Yard (an examinee in *A Hellish Murder*, which supplied virtually all the factual details here) warned her that Denis was preparing "for her Ruine:"

> For . . . it was commonly his way
> When he did want, to threaten night and day,
> If she could not him furnish, no Excuse
> Could get place with him, but still her abuse.

A Warning-Piece explicitly interpreted Mary's decision to leave her door unlocked on the evening of the 27th as legal evidence of "bearing no kind of Spight / Or Malice to her Husband." Thereafter its account closely followed her testimony in *A Hellish Murder* of being brutally attacked and raped, her decisive interior monologue, and her attempted revival with brandy after the killing. It eliminated any suggestion of sodomy, however, and arguably moved the boundary of Denis's villanies back into the extreme although legally condonable zone of "natural" male authority. The broadside's central illustration ultimately left the meaning of Mary's actions in the eye of the beholder. It depicted four persons being burnt at the state, possibly two women and two men, before a large crowd of soldiers and civilians. At the right a man prepares to toss a sprawling naked baby on to the raging pyre.

A WARNING-PIECE
TO
All Married Men and Women.
Being the Full
CONFESSION of MARY HOBRY,
The *FRENCH* Midwife,

Who Murdered her Husband on the 27ᵗʰ of *January*, 168¾. (As alſo the Cauſe thereof.)

for which ſhe receiv'd Sentence to be Burnt alive: And on *Friday* the Second Day of *March*, between the Hours of Ten and Eleven in the Morning, ſhe was drawn upon a Sledge to *Leiceſter-Fields*, where ſhe was burnt to Aſhes.

ALL you that Married Men and Women be
Give Ear unto this woful Tragedy,
That now befell a *French man* and his *Wife*,
Who liv'd together in continual Strife;
One *Denis Hobry* about Four years ſince
Took to his Wife a Woman Born a *French*,
Whom he Abus'd at ſuch Inhumane rate,
That ſhe a thouſand times wiſh'd him ill Fate,
and thought within herſelf to end the Strife,
ſhe were forc'd, to take away his Life :
The cauſe that mov'd him to thoſe Tyrannis,
Was her averſion to his Villanies;
At length into a private Room ſhe fled,
Intending never to Embrace his Bed,
Where ſhe remain'd four Months, and then by chance
Her Husband went beyond the Seas to *France* ;
But when return'd, he Courted her again,
Tho firſt he fear'd it was all in vain.
He ſwore a thouſand times to pleaſe her Mind,
And prove a Husband, faithful, chaſte, and kind.
His Words prevail'd ſo much, that ſhe did yield,
Upon theſe Terms, to give him up the Field,
That he would firſt confeſs before a Prieſt
And two Witneſſes more, as he own'd Chriſt
To be his God, the was his lawful Wife,
And would no more vex her during his Life.
Father *Gaſper* wrote this every Word,
Who plac'd it afterwards upon Record.
But ſcarce two days, or three at moſt, were paſt,
When he on her the old Reproaches caſt.
In two months time he went to *France* again,
And gave the Woman juſt cauſe to complain ;
For, not ſeeing that he could come at or find,
But he brought with him, and left none behind.
When three months paſſed he returned home,
And with diſſembling Words to her did come ;
Not ſoon found him to be the ſame Man ſtill.
She often beg'd of him, with weeping eyes,
A Separation, or that otherwiſe
He would be civil ; who gave this Reply,
He would her ruine ; which cauſt'd her to cry,
And think to take his Life, or loſe her own,
Which ſhe did often tell him in her moan.
Long ſhe endur'd, at laſt ſhe told her Caſe
To Neighbours that dwelt near about the place,
And ſaid, the fear'd Miſchief would be the end
Of his ill Actions, or be from would mend.
Three months being paſ'd, one time ſhe took a Knife,
With an intent to take away his Life :
But God did then beſtow on her his grace,
Which made her give her Husband longer ſpace.
So twice ſhe did intend upon her Bed
To ſtab her Husband, and to leave him dead :
And to Himſelf ſhe did declare her mind,
Who dared her in a moſt fooliſh kind.
Now he was going from her into *France*,
And the told him, If that it were his chance
E're to come back, and follow the old Rule,
He muſt become unto him ſomething cruel :
Who promiſs'd her moſt earneſtly, and ſwore
He never would abuſe her as before.
In three weeks after he return'd again
Unto his Wife, who did him entertain ;
And ſaid, dear *Hobry*, welcome thou to me
So that you henceforth a good Husband be.

I will, ſaid he, taking a thouſand Oaths,
If you'll me furniſh preſently with Cloaths.
She anſwered Him, The Times were very dear,
And hardly ſhe her honeſt Debts could clear.
He hearing her, moſt wickedly did curſe,
And ſwear he would to her be ten times worſe
Than e're he was: who then this Anſwer had
From her, That he already made her mad,
For that it was moſt commonly his way
When he did want, to threaten night and day,
If ſhe could not him furniſh, no Excuſe
Could get place with him, but ſtill her abuſe.
One *Yard* to her did openly declare,
That for her Ruine her Husband did prepare.
Thus they continued in the ſame degree
To th' Twenty Seventh of laſt *January* ;
When ſhe, about Ten of the Clock at night
Took her Repoſe, bearing no kind of Spight
Or Malice to her Husband, as before,
But open, for his Coming, laſt the door;
Who came at Five a Clock next Morning home,
And did in Rage and Choler fret and fome,
And to his Wife, as dead as in a grave
(With Sleep) a blow upon the Stomach gave,
Which made her ſtart ; What, you are drunk (ſaid he,)
If I am not, 'tis like you are, quoth ſhe :
He anſwer'd, I with Rogues all night did lie,
Which made me mad, and you muſt pay for it ;
Whereupon he gave her another Blow
Upon the Breaſt, which did renew her Woe :
To weeping ſhe immediately did fall.
And he then took her in his Arms with all
His force, till he did ſtop her Vital Breath,
So that ſhe wiſhed for a ſudden Death :
He forc'd on her ſuch barbarous Violence
In ſpight of what ſhe did in her Defence ;
Forcing much Blood from her, ſhe cried out
To her Land-lady, who did not hear the Shout ;

Unto the Neighbours I'll (ſaid ſhe) complain ;
Wherewith he threw her on the Bed again,
And bit her like a Dog kept in a yard,
Shall this ſaid ſhe, be always my Reward?
Yea, anſwer'd he, be ſure thyſelf to keep
Well, and with that he fell in a dead Sleep ;
Which ſhe beholding, and feeling the ſmart
Of his ill uſage to her ; in her Heart,
What ſhall I do, (ſaid ſhe) muſt I now Die ?
Or Murther him that makes me thus to Cry ?
With that ſhe ſtarted full of Wrath and Evil,
Being thereto Spurr'd by th' inſtinct of the Devil,
And pull'd his Garter off his Leg in haſt,
Being a Pack-thread, which ſhe thought no waſt,
And doubling it about his Neck, ſhe drew
The ends ſo faſt, that ſhe him quickly Slew;
But ſoon Repenting, hop'd he was Alive,
And thought that Brandy would him then Revive:
But when all was done, her labour was in Vain,
For Life once loſt, can ne'er be had again.
Till *Monday* following the Corps was there,
For ſhe could not convey it any where,
Untill ſhe brought her Son out of the *Strand*,
Who durſt not ſpeak againſt her cruel Command :
When he beheld the Corps lye at this rate,
He did bemoan his Mothers wretched Fate :
What will you do ? you muſt (ſaid he) now Die,
Or out of *England* you muſt quickly Flie :
She told him Money ſhe had none in hand
That would buy Paſſage to another Land,
My way ſaid ſhe is to Cut off his Head,
His Thighs and Arms, now that he is Dead,
And none can tell what Country man he's then,
Though he were found by the moſt wiſe of Men.
At Four or Five paſt Noon, this Curſed Wife
Cut off her Husband's Head with a ſharp Knife :
His Arms and Thighs came off, his Legs again,
And though his Neck did Bleed, he felt no Pain.
At Eight a Clock this Night through *Caſtle-ſtreet*
And *Drury-lane* ſhe went, and none did meet,
Until at *Parkers lane* to pleaſe her will
She laid the Corps near by a naſty Dung-hill,
She did in Linnen next the Thighs convey
Into a Privy that's in the Savoy,
Where ſhe again the Arms and Legs did caſt,
Nothing remaining but the Head at laſt :
She then adviſed with her Son to know
Where they might cloſely put the Head alſo ;
Who ſaid the Water was for it the Place,
But ſhe then fear'd ſome Man might know his Face;
And ſhe at laſt reſolved to this end,
To throw't into the Privy of her Friend,
A Fringe-maker, that lives by the Savoy,
For they do ſtill two Privies there imploy.
The Corps being found, and all the truth well known,
She did her ſelf no word of it diſown ;
But did confeſs that no untruth is here,
For God will not let Murtherers go clear.
She is now Burn'd, and beggs of all Mankind
And 'Women too, Wiſdom by her to find.

With Allowance.

LONDON, Printed and Sold by *George Croom*, at the *Blue-Ball* in *Thames-ſtreet*, near *Baynard's-Caſtle*. 1688.

Figure 2.4 A Warning-Piece (1688). Reproduced by permission of the Bodleian Library.

Probably recycled from an earlier account of (French?) religious conflicts, the image was at odds with the narrative, yet possibly mingled semiotic associations of petty treason, political and domestic rebellion, and foreign martyrdom that readers from the English or French communities in London might have found relevant to Hobry's case.

Though *A Hellish Murder* portrayed Mary's escape from her husband's patriarchal tyranny as necessary rather than gratuitous rebellion and in no way defended Denis,[82] it raised material questions about the dismemberment. In his Postscript, L'Estrange admitted to initially sharing public doubts over a woman's physical ability to dispose of an adult male body: "But still that which stuck with *other* people, stuck with *Me*: That is to say, How all this could be done without *Complices*" (F3v). Flourishing his self-authorizing skepticism, L'Estrange argued that Desermeau's testimony had in the end agreed so closely with his mother's that it was impossible to doubt his claims of refusing to touch his father's body. Besides, L'Estrange observed, if one considered the weight of man's trunk without its limbs or head, "a Woman's carrying such a Burthen in the Truss of her *Petticoat*, will be found no greater a Wonder, than he shall see ten times over in *oue*[*sic*]-*Days Walk* betwixt the *Old Exchange* and *Westminster*" (F4r).

For Settle, on the other hand, Hobry's putative strength was a sign of monstrous femininity and domestic treason: "Her vigorous Arm with youthful sinews fill'd, / And stoutly following the Triumphant Stroak, / Unbrancht, Unlimb'd, She hew'd the falling Oak" (*An Epilogue to the French Midwife's Tragedy*). Hobry's treatment of her husband's body bore a parodic resemblance to execution rituals on bodies of male traitors, which as Susan Dwyer Amussen has demonstrated "sought to obliterate the criminal and remind the onlookers of the perils of such behavior."[83] Hobry's actions challenged the state's limitation of domestic petty treason to women only, and to its exclusive power over the criminal subject. Her implicit political challenge to the law's gender imbalances explained the vehemence of detractors such as Settle, who interpreted the scattering of Hobry's ashes to the wind as an appropriate material retribution for her aggravated husband murder. Less abstractly, Hobry's dispersal of body parts around London's animal and human waste sites defiled her husband's body, confused species boundaries, and polluted the city. Such contamination could only be cleansed by fire. Both *An Account of the Manner* and *A Cabinet of Grief* reminded readers that Hobry would "be burnt with Fire till she be Dead" (A1v; *Cabinet*, A5r), the implication being that she would not be mercifully strangled before the pyre was lit. *A Warning-Piece* claimed she would be "burnt alive." And like many earlier execution reports, *An Account*'s title page reported she was "Burnt to Ashes."[84] These notices reassured readers of the city and state's moral and legal obligations and re-established violated gender hierarchies. According to *An Account*, Hobry remained severely depressed after sentencing and sorrowfully penitent at her execution "in her manner of Carriage and Gesture as was Evident to Spectators." In fact she was not burnt alive, but hanged at the stake for a quarter hour while the faggots were piled around her, and was dead before they were lit. Her body was consumed "in about half an hour more to Ashes, *etc*." The final "*etc*" left readers to imagine the details of her otherworldly torments or deliverance.

L'Estrange recognized that Hobry's murder story carried inflammatory religious associations. At the end of her testimony, she was asked:

> How it came to pass that she, this Examinate, being of the Communion of the Church of *Rome*, came to throw the Quarters of her Husband into a House of Office at the *Savoy*, which was a way to bring so great a Scandal upon the Religion she professed . . . ? (F2v)

During the autumn and winter of 1687–88 James II had been trying to reimpose Catholicism on a largely unreceptive public by replacing Church of England officials with Catholics and dissenters.[85] L'Estrange was a loyalist, however, having been knighted by James in March 1685 and reappointed press censor when the Licensing Act was reinstated that May. For years his political enemies had accused him of being a crypto-Catholic, and he was one of the MPs James forced on electors to pack the Commons and repeal the Penal Laws.[86] One reason why Hobry's confession had not circulated publicly even by word of mouth before publication of *A Hellish Murder* was that her examination, uniquely among all the other witnesses, had taken place in private. According to L'Estrange, this was "for fear of any unseasonable Discovery of what she might declare" (F3v). His oblique statement probably referred to fears of the crime being exploited by anti-Jacobite propagandists. (The private interviews might also have served L'Estrange's own publication interests.) His explanation would not have prevented the public, alarmed by James's romanizing agenda, from reading the worst into Hobry's crime. Yet her religion remained marginal to *An Account*, which reported that she "held some Discourse or Conference with a certain Person there attending." As there is no report of public prayers or the presence of the Newgate visitor (who usually accompanied the condemned prisoner to execution), this sounds like a final confession to a Catholic priest, possibly the Fr. Gasper mentioned in *A Warning-Piece* who had tried to reconcile Mary and her husband.

Perhaps more than any other news document discussed in this book, *A Hellish Murder* highlighted the influential but often nebulously represented role of neighbors and third parties in prosecuting and defending local women suspected of murder. Testimony by nineteen French and English witnesses revealed variable sources and contexts of information and multiple paths of enquiry that L'Estrange and his fellow examiners had to sift to establish a justifiable story about the Hobrys' marital troubles and Mary's motives. Like a murder mystery writer (although perhaps less admired ones nowadays), L'Estrange edited this process to clarify the journey from initial obscurity to full knowledge, and thereby maximize the power of his and his colleagues' forensic expertise. Yet *A Hellish Murder*'s explanatory control could never be absolute, and given L'Estrange's long-established reputation as a combative royalist suspected of Catholic sympathies, it was unlikely to be read neutrally in the year of the Glorious Revolution. Less partisan-minded readers, however, could have evaluated Hobry's motives and actions differently, as the contemporary news accounts derived from it demonstrated.

Just as importantly, L'Estrange's compilation named the examinees and allowed readers to see distinct gender differences when evaluating testimony.[87] It confirmed the implicit evidence of earlier news reports that early modern women were highly aware of one another's activities in their parish, and beyond it as well. This is unsurprising given the actual mobility of city women in carrying out their occupational and domestic duties. *A Hellish Murder* confirmed that women routinely possessed uniquely intimate information about accused female neighbors because of their interconnected community roles, Mary's career as a midwife being one of these. Although a little less than half of the examinees were women, their information was far more detailed and relevant than the men's. Mary Hope and Marie-Anne Rippault were familiar enough with Hobry's daily routine to notice quickly that her husband had disappeared, and they immediately connected it to prior awareness of her marital troubles. This did not mean their testimony was infallible, but it sounded more accurate and credible than that of the men, whose knowledge of women's day-to-day lives was impressionistic and conceptually naive or misogynist. Many of the men seem to have been called on to testify for little reason other than that they were *male* neighbors or officials. Culturally and legally, their information was axiomatically more authoritative. Yet as readers proceeded through L'Estrange's volume and the murder story emerged, some would surely have recognized that Julian Coze was merely a friend of a friend of Denis Hobry's. Henry Fuller's involvement as constable was limited to escorting the suspect to the Gatehouse prison. John Desermeau's testimony, though he was Hobry's son, proved to be the most evasive and self-contradictory of all, as L'Estrange himself pointed out, although emotional shock obviously troubled his responses.

The contextual depth and moral viewpoint of L'Estrange's gathered testimony may have had an influence on the court at the February 1688 Old Bailey sessions even before it was published. Hobry appeared sorrowful and with a "much dejected Countenance and Behaviour" according to David and Elizabeth Mallet's half broadside *Account Of the Manner, Behaviour, and Execution of Mary Aubry*. The arraignment report tried to play down Hobry's dismemberment and removal as aggravated homicide by explaining to readers that Hobry had cut her husband in pieces "for the more private and convenient disposal of him, thereby to prevent discovery," not out of vengeful spite as Settle's *Epilogue* and *A Cabinet of Grief* later represented it. *Account Of the Manner* briefly noted the indictment's charge ("for Murthering her said Husband, by Strangling, &c"),[88] to which the gravely depressed Hobry pleaded guilty. "Yet," it continued,

> The Court was so favourable to tell her, that she might, seeing it was a case that rendered her Dead in Law by her pleading Guilty, Retract that Plea, and put her self upon the Country for her Tryal, if she thought it [ ] or convenient; but she still persisting to plead Guilty, her Confession was Recorded. (A1v)

The lacuna [ ] caused by faulty inking can be supplied by *A Hellish Murder*, which originally stated that the "Court with all possible tenderness . . . offer'd her yet the Liberty to depart from her Plea, and take her Tryal, if she thought fit."[89] "Convenient" in the Mallets' *Account* means both "suitable" and "morally proper" (*OED, sb.*, 5–6). It underlined the court's apparent hint that a trial might exhibit the moral equity of her case and thereby open up a possible route to a reprieve or a pardon should the jury not acquit her. On the other hand the court might have been hoping for a trial to give "Public Notification of the Foulness of the Cause" and its aftermath to justify a capital sentence. Not-guilty pleas leading to jury trials were preferred by the court if grand juries found true bills.[90] In all events, for reasons that remain speculative, Hobry declined to change her plea. The judge's offer authorized L'Estrange to publish the testimony that would have supported her defense and which represented the court's compassionate handling of the case. By presenting Hobry's story in such ideologically destabilizing detail from a range of adversarial perspectives, L'Estrange and his contemporaries demonstrated with unusual clarity how early modern writers and readers could vigorously contest a battered wife's criminal identity from both legal and socially equitable perspectives.

In this chapter I have tried to show that such perspectives were normative throughout the period, even though the dominance of religious and confessional news narratives—on which my next chapter focuses—reduced their legibility before the mid seventeenth century. Practices of comparative reading and contextual representation built up a diversified public memory of mitigating explanations for women accused of homicide. Jurors and judges brought their knowledge of these disputed cases with them to early modern examinations and assizes.

3   Confession, Conversion, and Tactical Resistance

Sixteenth- and seventeenth-century readers were just as fascinated by murder and its involving passions as modern TV viewers and film goers. Their basic questions were the same: Why did she kill? How did she do it? What will her sentence be? Does she deserve it? Yet early modern news about female homicides also had specific cultural origins in Reformation theology, traditional concepts of natural law and divinely devolved human justice, and nascent commercial journalism. Forensic perspectives became predominant as crime reporting expanded into serialized print formats after the Restoration. Before then, news writers sought to give meaning to shocking crimes primarily by considering their ontological and metaphysical implications: How is the murder to be understood in terms of human nature, sin, and divine law? How does it reveal God's will communicating through a shocking event and the criminal's punishment? What signs of providential judgment is it giving the wider community? These contexts distinguish the period's murder narratives from the pop psychological and hyperadversarial frameworks of today's mass-media crime news.

Although not all murder pamphlets were shaped by theological concerns, many of the period's news writers were anonymous clergymen and/or puritan-inclined authors with strong commitments to public godliness. They reconstructed murderers' lives as allegorical narratives of transgression and redemption to advance a Calvinist agenda of spiritual and social reform. In attempting to evangelize a broad readership, their didactic accounts shared some of the aims of cheap books of popular Protestant piety.[1] As we shall see from Arthur Golding's paradigm-making decision to focus on Anne Saunders's posttrial confession, female subjects were especially useful to this Calvinist project because they slipped easily into binarized stereotypes of good and bad women familiar from classical and biblically derived assumptions about female nature.[2] Homicide news also had civic justifications of deterring crime and inculcating moral discipline in concert with the state's desire to maintain order. It re-affirmed the public boundaries of acceptable and deviant behavior while seeking to produce criminal-law principles discursively for public consumption. The flexible media of the printed news ballad and pamphlet, accessible to a broad spectrum of consumers, effectively communicated these instrumental and ideological goals. Murder news thus participated in the wider cultural project of imagining early modern England as an orderly God-fearing nation. But since this agenda was highly politicized, appropriations of murderesses in confession-and-conversion narratives were subject to public debate by readers whose legal opinions, moral reasoning, and sectarian beliefs differed from those of the author and his implied audience. In these diverse contexts of reception lay possibilities for equitable re-interpretation or mitigation of individual women's crimes.

ANNE SAUNDERS AND THE REPRESENTATION OF THE REPENTANT FEMALE MURDERER

Arthur Golding was the first English writer to seize the opportunity of writing about a domestic murder that had aroused extraordinary interest in non-aristocratic criminal subjects. His thirty-two-page quarto pamphlet, *A briefe discourse of the late murther of master George Saunders* (1573, reprinted in 1577), sold well because of Golding's prominent reputation as translator of major classical and Reformation texts, including Ovid's *Metamorphoses* (1565) and Calvin's *Sermons* (1577). These associations endowed the narrative voice of *A briefe discourse* with exceptional cultural authority.

Golding's approach to reporting the controversial murder in *A briefe discourse* was anything but sensationalizing. He announced straight away his refusal "to feede the fond humor of such curious appetites as are more inquisitiue of other folkes offences than hastie to redresse their owne" (A2v). Ostensibly this meant suppressing details that might gratify prurient curiosity. However it also foreclosed evidence that readers might have considered independently to evaluate the prisoners' guilt, or that might have militated against prosecution arguments, as a certain segment of public opinion clearly had already done. Having received information from a neighbor, Anne Drewrie, that George Saunders would be staying overnight in Woolwich and visiting a local church the next morning, Anne Saunder's lover George Browne intercepted her husband and his servant John Beane on their way and fatally wounded both men with a sword. Saunders died almost instantly, but Beane managed to crawl some distance until he was found by passers-by and carried to Woolwich, where he gave information that led to Browne's arrest. While readily admitting his guilt at the trial before King's Bench at Westminster Hall on 17 April, Browne maintained that Anne knew nothing about the plan to murder her husband, and "he laboured by al meanes to cleare mistresse Saunders, of committing evill of hir body with him"—claims that Golding derided. Browne was executed three days later and hanged up in chains, the public degradation meted out to especially vicious or notorious criminals.[3]

One of Golding's most significant narrative decisions was to shift attention away from the principal male murderer to the female accessories, Anne

A briefe difcourfe

of the late murther of ma-

fter George Saunders, a worship-
full Citizen of London : and
of the apprehenfion , arreignement,
and execution of the princi-
pall and acceffaries of
the fame:

(∵)

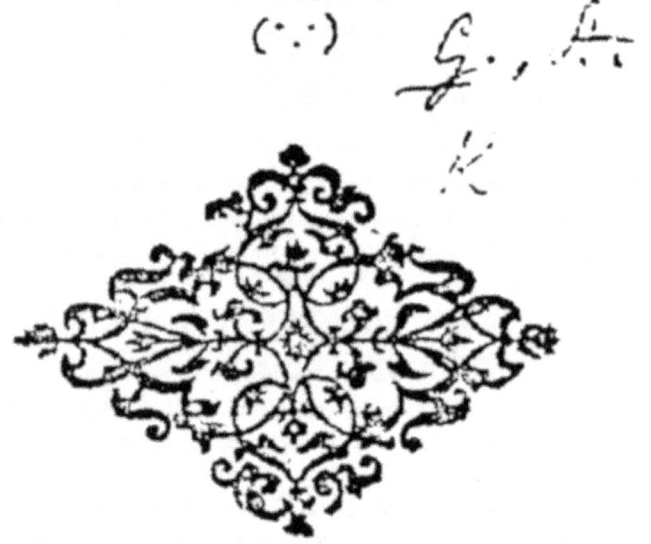

¶ *Jmprinted at London by*
Henry Bvnneman, dwelling in Knight-
riders ſtreete , at the ſigne
of the Mermayde.

ANNO. 1573.

Figure 3.1 A briefe discourse of the late murther of master George Saunders (1573).
Reproduced by permission of the British Library.

Saunders and Anne Drewrie, who were tried for aiding Browne's murder.[4] Golding supplied only a bare outline of Browne's killing, apprehension, and trial, and said almost nothing about the personal relationship between him and Anne Saunders. Whether Browne's execution in Smithfields actually attracted much attention—and it seems unlikely not to have done, given the high ranking people who had a stake in seeing George Saunders's death avenged—it received no comment from Golding. When the two women were executed, however, he claimed that the event drew

> so great a number of people as the lyke hath not bene seene there tog-ither in any mans remembrance[;] for almost the whole fields, and all the way from Newgate, was as full of folke as could well stande one by another.[5]

The question of Anne's guilt bred "much diversitie of reports & opinions." While allegedly reflecting the truth of historical events and developments, Golding at the same time selected them to fashion female exempla of devi-ant behavior and pious contrition that would suit his wider agenda of pro-moting godly reform.

In terms of narrative construction, Golding's most immediate challenge was, respectively, to unify and discredit prosecution and defense arguments associated with a contested murder trial. Even though she was only an alleged accessory after the fact, Golding represented Anne as a malicious reprobate who stubbornly refused to confess her complicity and tried in vain to thwart God's will in exposing the crime.[6] From the beginning, editorial jabs at her bad faith led readers to anticipate Anne reversing herself and vindicating both the judicial verdicts and the wisdom of the Privy Council (who appointed the magistrates and assize judge). Unusually, the Council had intervened directly in this case because of George Saunders's personal relationships with govern-ment officials.[7] They also oversaw examination of suspects and management of the trial, assigned senior London clergymen to extract confessions from Anne and her associates, and arranged for abject speeches of repentance from the scaffold to justify their handling of the case.

After their trials and sentencing at the Guildhall on 6 May, Anne Saun-ders and Anne Drewrie gained a bit of hope when their executions were put off because Saunders was just about to give birth (whether to Browne's child or her husband's, Golding does not venture to say). In this interval an unap-pointed minister named Mell took up Anne's cause and independently tried to defend her. Unfortunately he discussed his plans with "an honest Gen-tleman" whom he mistakenly believed was sympathetic to Anne and who revealed his intentions to the Council. This person may have been Golding.[8] The Council was able to sabotage Mell's efforts and had him publicly pil-loried at Anne and Mrs. Drewrie's place of execution.

When Anne's reversal eventually came about, it may have been the result of deliberately orchestrated pressure—or a bolt of divine grace, depending on the reader's beliefs. The Council had granted her a further stay of execution, which Anne understood was meant to allow her husband's executors to settle their children's inheritances and to give her friends time to obtain a royal pardon on her behalf.[9] She was then ambushed in this temporary state of hope. On the day set originally for her execution, men passed through the courtyard of Newgate prison talking in loud voices "of the gallowes that was set vp" for her. Their words "did so pierce vnto the watchfull eares of mistresse Saunders" that she was "striken to the heart with the horror of the present death whiche she loked for that day" (B4r-v). Thinking her stay had been revoked and that she was suddenly facing imminent death, Anne panicked when ministers returned to work on her. "[B]eing striken both with feare and remorse," she confessed to giving consent to Mrs. Drewrie and George Browne to kill her husband, and submitted to a penitent display in prison before her husband's brothers and relations, "kneeling mildely on hir knees, with abundance of sorrowful teares" (C1v). These allegedly spontaneous gestures preceded her carefully rehearsed performance of prayers and confessions on the gallows, written collaboratively with her clergymen visitors and presented as separate documents in Golding's pamphlet (C4r–D2r). Cumulatively these events reconstituted Anne's public identity as a redeemed sinner while encouraging all readers to an "inward consideration" that God "rayseth [the reprobate] by their ouerthrow, amendeth them by their wickednesse, and reuiueth them by their death" (C4r-v). Both the narrative structure and didactic emphases of Golding's *A briefe discourse* dominated clerically authored murder pamphlets and the popular image of the adulterous female husband-killer for decades until the advent of trial-reports and newspapers.

Golding further justified his rather unlikely foray into topical murder news by contextualizing the Saunders murder within several common Reformation discourses. The most prominent of these was providentialism, a bundle of pre- and post-Reformation concepts positing the reality of divine intervention in everyday human affairs. In terms of popular notions of detecting and punishing homicide, providentialism secured the currency of the proverb "murder will out."[10] The absence of local police and the period's rudimentary development of forensic science necessitated faith in providential retribution to assure the public that crimes of blood would inevitably be exposed and revenged.[11] In the news pamphlets that followed Golding's model, homicide and personal sin were equated, while social, economic, and mental conditions which readers might have considered reasons for legal mitigation were suppressed or excluded.

Protestant theology had also reinvigorated the Augustinian paradigm of divine will working within guilty consciences to bring about life-changing confessions and conversions. The focus of early modern murder news on spiritual interiority mirrored Reformation initiatives dematerializing hell and rubbishing medieval practices associated with gaining salvation through traditional works of penance.[12] *A briefe discourse* instead highlighted the

Protestant doctrine of omnipotent divine grace by alleging that after killing Saunders, Browne suffered "terrour and agonie of hart," swooning at the sight of one of Saunders's children: "a notable example of the secret woorking of Gods terrible wrath in a guiltie and bluddie conscience" (A3v–4r). Anne Saunders was "stricken both with fear and remorse," although in her case this happened after her hopes of a pardon were dashed. Anne Drewrie's resistance to confession also collapsed suddenly, and she became "fully determined not to dissemble any longer, nor to hazarde hir owne soule eternally" (B4v). These representations of natural law throwing prisoners' psyches into intolerable mental torment was as much as an aesthetic as an ideological principle, as we shall see in a moment when examining the theory and mechanics of gallows conversion.[13]

WONDERFUL MURDER

Golding also drew on the conventions of a second providentialist discourse, wonder news: popular reports of prodigies, monsters, and natural disasters betokening divine displeasure at lax national morals, and intended as warnings to bolster public and private discipline.[14] Before the arrival of news books about foreign and political events in 1620s, stories about "strange and wonderful" events largely defined the popular profile of topical news in ballads and cheap pamphlets.[15] Sixteenth-century digests of monsters and (un)natural marvels first appeared on the Continent and then spread to England. Konrad Lykosthenes's *Prodigiorum ac ostentorum chronicom* (1557), for example, was translated by Stephen Bateman as *The Doome warning all men to the Iudgemente* (1581). *The Doome* catalogues spectacles of rampaging human sin linked to natural portents of divine wrath. As Mark Thornton Burnett also observes, the early modern term "monster" was a topically and perceptually constructed category built on two Latin verbforms: *monstro* meaning to show, whence *monstrum*, a portent, prodigy, or "unnatural thing;" and *monere* meaning to warn or presage.[16] Whereas earlier wonder books had linked the appearance of monsters to personal violations of the traditional deadly sins, Lykosthenes connected them to social sins: rebellion, sedition, heresy, conspiracy, and so forth. His volume was preoccupied with monsters as reflections of sixteenth-century sectarian violence and institutional upheaval.[17] A conceptual kinship between natural disasters and civil turmoil explains the surges in crime news in England during periods of national instability such as the 1580s and 90s, and the 1630s to 40s. The symptomatic theory underlying belief in wonders was also recognized by more ambitious genres such as Raphael Holinshed's *Chronicles* (1577, reissued in a censored and politically moralized edition in 1587), which included many seemingly tangential or incongruous reports of marvels, including the murder conspiracies of both Anne Saunders and Alice Arden (of whom more anon).[18]

Yet while prodigy collections such as Lykosthenes's and Bateman's contained all kinds of monsters and horrors, bloody murders were not among them. Golding's innovation, it seems, was to add notorious homicides to the familiar repertoire of newsworthy wonders and to link them to official anxieties about public disorder. Golding strengthened the discursive associations between natural and imminent human calamity through publication of a second, similarly titled, pamphlet three years after the 1577 reissue of the Saunders report: *A discourse vpon the earthquake that hapned through this Realme of Englande ... the sixt of Aprill. 1580*. Both his *discourses* framed their reported events eschatologically as portents of divine wrath. Golding argued that the earthquake was an urgent warning that the disorder-and-repentance model he had represented through the Saunders case had been ignored, and that the truly cataclysmic judgments were imminent. Peter Lake has argued that news stories of crimes that inevitably bring down divine retribution in the form of state-sanctioned judicial punishment were an approved means of terrifying potential murderers and promoting a reformist agenda.[19] Both goals are visible in Golding's two *discourses*, which posited murder and earthquakes as public risks, defined as socially reflexive conditions that were calculable and preventable.[20] This linkage may seem odd because earthquakes, unlike murders, were widely recognized as having explicable physical causes.[21] In Shakespeare's *1 Henry IV*, for example, Hotspur used such arguments (possibly alluding to the 1580 quake) to refute the portent-obsessed Glendower:

> ... oft the teeming earth
> Is with a kind of colic pinched and vexed
> By the imprisoning of unruly wind
> Within her womb, which, for enlargement striving,
> Shakes the old beldam earth and topples down
> Steeples and moss-grown towers. (3.1.26–31)[22]

From this viewpoint, earthquakes normally fell into the category of unavoidable natural risks. Golding had in mind the moralizing origins of the modern insurance phrase, "act of God," in arguing that because this particular earthquake was *not* preceded by warning tremors, its causes were human sin. For him and other puritan news writers, the deeper origins of murder and sudden earthquakes were ultimately the same:

> Their faults came into the open Theater, & therefore seemed the greater to our eyes, and surely they were great in deede; neyther are ours the lesse, bycause they lye hidden in the couert of oure heart. God the searcher of al secretes seeth them, and if he list he can also discouer them. (D1r)

Golding's fellow Calvinist and Ramist William Perkins argued in his influential taxonomy of sin, *The Whole Treatise of the Cases of Conscience* (1608,

C1r–v) that all humans are potential criminals because of their shared intrinsic sinfulness. Only personal vigilance and state discipline would keep these impulses at bay. Golding's discursive linkage between the Saunder's murder and the 1580 earthquake implicitly urged the government to punish crime more vigorously to avoid the manmade causes of both calamities.

Golding's two *discourses* differ, of course, because the legal drama of trial, confession, and scaffold-speech allowed the stories of Anne Saunders and others to be represented as positive examples of ameliorating conversion, whereas the rhetorical mode of the earthquake pamphlet remained admonitory. Nonetheless, Golding's pamphlets encouraged other writers to exploit the prophetic potential of printed crime news, and some advertised their debt to him.[23] Anthony Munday's *A View of sundry Examples* (1580) included not only "*many straunge murthers, sundry persons periured, Signes and token of Gods anger towards us . . . since the murther of Maister Saunders by George Browne to this present,*" but "*Also a short discourse of the late Earthquake.*" His collection opened with an account of the "George Brown, who murthered maister George Saunders . . . by the consent of maister Saunders wife" (the principal murderer is not Anne Saunders, as she is in Golding). Munday continued with modern swearers, perjurers, blasphemers, suicides, murderers, blazing stars, monstrous births, and earthquakes. One of his two brief records of female murderers referred to an unnamed woman in Kilbourn who brained her two children with a "peece of billet," "the summe wherof is at large described in a book imprinted" (Div).[24] This last remark indicated his source was a news pamphlet of the crime that is now lost. Of the murder stories catalogued by Munday, only the Saunders case is recounted in a now extant news ballad. Most of the other murders would have been first reported separately in ballads and/or pamphlets, and these were Munday's sources for crimes he had not heard about directly, just as the anonymous author of the domestic tragedy, *A Warning for Faire Women* (written *ca.* 1585–99, printed 1599), drew on *A briefe discourse* and other contemporary news accounts of the Saunders murder.[25]

Golding's other Elizabethan epigones included T. I., whose Preface to *A World of wonders. A Masse of Murthers. A Covie of Cosonages* (1595) observed that contemporaries now lived "in that same iron worlde whereof *Ouid* speaketh in which is small store of good frutes but such as barren soyles do buy" (A2r).[26] He claimed that recent murders, perjuries, adulteries, and so forth were "euident and manifest signes, that that finall . . . shutting vp of these transitories and vanities of this mortall world are at hand." Thomas Beard's *Theatre of Gods Iudgements* (1597) contained half a dozen "home-bred examples" among its hundreds of illustrations drawn from an original French text by Jean de Chassanion. The English crimes were derived from chronicle histories by Foxe, Holinshed, and Stowe as well as sixteenth-century wonder ballads and pamphlets.[27] Yet now it was Alice Arden who was prominent among female murderers, not Anne Saunders.[28]

As local crimes involving adultery, go-between neighbors, husband-murder, and repentant female homicides, the Saunders and Arden stories mirrored each other. The Kentish setting of Thomas Arden's murder provided a provincial counterpart to the metropolitan Saunders crime and formed the core of a national anti-history of female petty traitors represented in ballads, murder pamphlets, and crime compilations well into the seventeenth century. Both women's stories also helped to spawn two plays in the briefly fashionable genre of domestic tragedy: *A Warning for Faire Women* and *The Tragedy of Master Arden of Faversham*.[29]

The Saunders and Arden murders were also appropriated by Raphael Holinshed's *Chronicles of England, Scotland, and Ireland* (1577), at which point their cultural meanings began to change. When Golding's pamphlet was re-issued in the same year (with his new edition of Calvins's sermons),[30] he may have intended the work to complement the *Chronicles*. Both items were published by Henry Bynneman, one of a circle of godly London printers.[31] Holinshed redacted Golding's account, and Stowe repeated Holinshed's version virtually verbatim several years later.[32] But Holinshed and Stowe cut Golding's posttrial story of the prisoners' confessions and execution performances, which were the religious heart of his pamphlet.

On the basis of its familiar story of illicit sex and domestic violence and its numerous critical and artistic offshoots, Richard Helgerson has argued that Alice Arden's narrative represents "the first 'modern' crime" displaying the state's power over secular nonaristocratic criminals.[33] Yet the Saunders case not only illustrated the operations of such power in greater detail but also inaugurated the post-Reformation history of notorious female criminals. Anthony Munday's digest of contemporary crimes began with Anne Saunders, and both it and the Arden case, as Helgerson noted, appeared in Thomas Heywood's *Troia Britannica* (1609) as well as *A World of Wonders* and other manuscript and printed sources.[34] In terms of the sub-genre of English domestic tragedy, *Arden of Faversham* was indeed the generic model, as Lena Cowen Orlin has demonstrated in illuminating detail.[35] It fortuitously achieved minor classic status in the later canon of Renaissance drama because of a contentious eighteenth-century attribution to Shakespeare, and its psychologically acute script was also favored by the emergent fashions of theatrical naturalism. But if "the religious dimension of early modern crime news is what separates it from modern journalism," as Sandra Clark has rightly argued,[36] then Golding's presentation of the murder story as a conversion narrative was far more culturally productive as a crime news prototype.

PREACHING GIBBETS:
CONFESSION AND EVANGELICAL CONVERSION

Golding fashioned Anne Saundersand her fellow prisoners as exemplary justified sinners: "The parties conuicted were to be reformed to Godwarde," he reported, "and to be broughte to the willing confessing of the things for whiche they had bene iustly condemned" (B2v). These combined forensic and spiritual goals were typical of the new roles played by Protestant prison chaplains, and they emerged as a characteristic narrative focus of murder news during the first half of the seventeenth century:

> [T]hrough Gods good working with their labour, they recouered them out of Sathans kingdome vnto Christ, insomuch that besides their vol-untary acknowledging of their late heinous fact, they also detested the former sinfulnesse of their life, and willingly yelded to the death which they had shunned, vttering such certaine tokens of theyr vnfayned re-pentance by all kinde of modestie & meekenesse. (C1r)

Given his theoretical resistance to differentiating criminals from ordinary sinners, the collective redemption of Saunders, Drewrie, her servant Roger Clement, and Browne represented an ideal microcosm of a spiritually mobi-lized nation. Before they went to work on the prisoners, the ministers alleg-edly found all three "very rawe and ignorant in all things perteyning to God & to their soule [*sic*] health, yea and euen in the very principles of the Christen religion" (C1r). The prisoners emblematized the under-Reformed condition of England lamented by many godly commentators. For cleri-cal and lay Protestants such as Golding, remedying this situation became perhaps the most urgent social project in early modern England. At the popular level it consisted of encouraging ordinary men and women to embrace the lived immediacy of Christian grace and salvation, manifested in conspicuous personal acts of confession, belief, and allegiance. Such val-ues were acutely constituted by the experience of conversion, in which a passively derived "reprobate" identity was exchanged for a new spiritu-ally reborn one.[37] Golding used Browne to showcase the results of visitors' edification:

> [D]uring the time of his imprisonment, [Browne] cōming to a better minde than he had bene of in time paste, cunfessed that he had not heeretofore frequēted sermous, nor receiued the holy sacrament, nor vsed any calling vpon God, priuate or publike, nor giuē him selfe to reading of holy Scripture, or any bookes of godlynesse ... Neuerthe-lesse God was so good vnto him, and schooled him so well in that short time of imprisonment, as he cloased vp his life with a maruellous ap-parance of heartie repentance, constant trust in Gods mercy ... and willingnesse to forsake this miserable worlde. (C3r)

Having published a translation of the martyrdoms of Martin Bucer and Paul Phagius in 1562,[38] Golding was aware that inner subjectivity was dis-played in especially intensive yet malleable states by condemned felons on the gallows. *A briefe discourse* introduced Anne Drewrie's surprise denials of poisoning her late husband to the Earl of Bedford, and of causing a rift between the Earl and Countess of Derby, as spontaneous revelations to "prompt" her servant Roger's exemplary confession performance (C2r–v). Drewrie was less forthcoming about the Saunders conspiracy and may have failed ultimately to match her servant's newborn zeal.

Golding's pamphlet concluded with two documents that were to become iconic features of seventeenth-century murder news: Anne Saunders's gallows confession and prayers. They were surprisingly eloquent given that Golding had earlier described Anne and her friends as utterly ignorant of Christian principles (a discrepancy that recurs in later confession-and-conversion pamphlets). These artifacts were intended not only to transform the lives of English readers and auditors,[39] but also as professional advertisements of proselytizing expertise. Well over a hundred years later, the self-promoting clerical reporter of Mary Goodenough's trial and execution in 1692 assumed that God who caused the "Gibbets to preach, [would] make the most Refractory of Rebels hear" (Mr. Birch [?], *Fair Warning to Murderers of Infants*, A4v). Conversion became a negotiable skill in the keen competition for civic and clerical preaching appointments, as well as a lucrative commodity in the market for popular printed news.

As Michael Questier has shown, the inward regeneration signalled by the theatrics and symbolism of gallows conversion was manipulated in overlapping ways by both Protestant and Catholic cultures of martyrdom to ambiguous political effect.[40] For Protestant ministers in charge of prisoners, and puritan minded ones in particular, public conversions provided prime opportunities to publicize Calvinist ideology. Ideally the scenario called for a sudden, emotionally staggering, dissolution and reconstitution of the self by divine grace.[41] The inward nature of this transformation was embodied by the subject's gestures and speeches before execution crowds, who in turn confirmed the subject's reformed identity with their verbal and physical reactions. Ministering clerics or lay reporters then represented this emotional and gestural interaction in popular printed reports. Their appropriations attempted to extend the signifying power of the interior event into the public sphere for the conversion of general readers.

News writers used the trope of last-moment conversion as a retrospective narrative tool, working back, as Golding had done, to rearrange the woman life's so as to heighten details that supported the Crown's arguments, confirm the criminal's spiritual redemption, and magnify the awesome potency of divine grace. The anonymous clerical author of *A Warning for Bad Wives: or, The Manner of the Burning of Sarah Elston* (1678), cited in the previous chapter, succinctly expressed this theologically inflected formula: "The rashness of a wicked Fury drew her into Affliction, that Affliction humbled her, and God took the advantage of her Humiliation for her Conversion" (A3r). Packaging murder news as prison confessions and gallows speeches served the interests of judicial and state authorities by legitimating court verdicts. The deterrent value of publicizing convicted criminals received symbolic affirmation when framed in terms of evangelical conversion because it vindicated the criminal law as an authentic forerunner of ultimate divine judgment.

Most early modern murder pamphlets supplied few details about the interpersonal negotiations that led to these highly visible and, in theory, culturally reforming outcomes. Interpreting the appropriated lives and actions of female homicides thus invites closer attention to their mediated subjectivity in prosecution-dominated news narratives. To unpack greater meaning from pamphlets' often elliptical accounts, exemplary or otherwise, it will be useful to examine the public role and practices of ministers charged with obtaining their confessions in greater detail.

EARLY MODERN PRISON VISITORS AND
THE CULTURE OF GALLOWS CONVERSION

Securing the repentance and conversion of condemned felons was the responsibility of clerical visitors (or "ordinaries") who attended prisoners in jail from trial to execution. Visitors were appointed to preach and lead services in London or county prisons and to care for prisoners' spiritual welfare. Although this ministry predated the Reformation, institutional and theological changes in sixteenth-century England as well as the century's intensely fraught culture of martyrdom radically transformed the kind of experience sought after, its range of political and sectarian resonances, and the visitor's professional interests. In the case of the condemned, visitors were employed by city or county authorities to coach and stage manage— the theatrical terms describe the process exactly—their confessions, prayers, and pious exhortations to assembled spectators from the gallows ladder or execution pyre. Confessions were especially valuable to legal authorities to validate court judgments after the verdict, since the rapid pace of early modern assizes and absence of defense counsel precluded any elaborate airing of circumstantial evidence. The pre- and/or posttrial period also provided an opportunity for the condemned prisoner to unburden herself to a visiting minister—although by no means, as we saw in Goodcole's account of Alice Clarke (Introduction, p. 15) without institutional pressure and psychological duress.

The most prominent figure exercising these roles in early modern England was the visitor of Newgate Prison. Newgate was infamous as a filthy, overcrowded, and raucous jail in which prisoners of both sexes accused of committing the most serious felonies were held before their trials at London and Middlesex sessions at the Old Bailey.[42] Women received the same treatment as men except for being housed in a separate ward, though both sexes intermingled freely because the whole prison was open to public traffic.[43] With the exception of the Newgate visitor, news pamphlets and city records published before the seventeenth century indicate that preachers or ministers were assigned to prisons by local church authorities on a case-by-case or short-term basis, usually but not invariably as part of their regular duties elsewhere.[44]

The visitor of Newgate's relatively well-documented role thus illuminates the under-noticed work of many visitor news writers before the Restoration.[45] As a clergyman, his main responsibilities were spiritual, although the ideological thrust of his work changed significantly between the mid-sixteenth and early seventeenth centuries. Post-Reformation reconstitution of the Newgate visitorship occurred when the Mayor and Aldermen of London took over the administration of St. Bartholomew's Hospital in 1552 (not co-incidentally the year the second, more Protestant *Book of Common Prayer* was issued).[46] They laid out the visitor's new duties in *The ordre of the Hospital of .S. Bartholomewes in Westsmythfielde*:

> Your charge is faithfully and diligētly to visite all the poore and miserable captiues within the pryson of Newgate, and minister vnto them suche ordinary seruice at times conuenient, as is appointed by the kynges maiesties booke for ordinary praier. Also that ye learne without booke the moste wholsome sentences of holie Scripture, that may comforte a desperate man, that redilie ye may minister thē to suche persones as ye shal perceyue them moste nedefull to be ministred vnto ... And in al their extremes and sickenesses ye shal be diligent and redy to comforte them with the moste pitthie and frutefull sentences of Goddes moste holy worde. (E8r–F1r)

These rubrics re-aligned the visitor's ministry with the Reformation's Bible-centered theology, while continuing the traditional emphasis on pastoral care and maintaining order within the prison. Early in Elizabeth's reign the London Court of Alderman replaced John Philpot, a Marian and presumably Catholic visitor and vicar of St. Christopher's, with "Mathewe Yonge minister." Yonge was charged with giving "good and godly advice" to "the cast men of Newgate when they are goinge to their deathes."[47] He was Visitor of Newgate from 1562–75.[48] Golding's *briefe discourse* identified him as one of several clerics who worked on Anne Saunders but did not mention his connection with Newgate. The omission was probably explained by the fact that a team of visitors had been specially appointed by the Privy Council under the direction of the puritan dean of St. Paul's, Alexander Nowell.[49]

Yonge was mentioned earlier by the anonymous writer of the first printed execution report now extant: *Of the endes and deathes of two Prisoners / lately pressed to death in Newgate* (1569). A serious broadside filled with realistic details, it was entered in the Stationer's Register in 1568–69 and published by John Audley.[50] The writer inaugurated a structural contrast between two condemned prisoners, one unnamed and other called Watson, designed to put a favorable spin on the disputed trials. This dichotomy was symbolically related to the different responses of the two criminals executed with Christ in Luke 23:39 to 43. Calvin and his followers had interpreted this passage as a revelation of the doctrine of election, with one felon's exemplary conversion counterbalancing the other's reprobation. In *Of the endes and deathes of two Prisoners* the unnamed penitent spends his last night tearfully singing psalms and dining humbly on bread and cheese. His conversion was initiated the day before by a lay-visitor, alderman Sir Christopher Draper, and followed up by Yonge (who does not seem synonymous with the narrator). As one might expect, Watson comes across as the livelier of the two, partly because he rails against the cruelty of his keeper in Limbo, the lowest dungeon in Newgate,[51] and partly because of his fearless jesting: "even if I boil in lead."[52] The narrator's intended readership included other godly clerics, whom he exhorted to follow Mr Yonge's example of converting the condemned and deterring crime rather than preaching to the faithful. As we saw in Goodcole's *The Adultresses Funerall Day* and will encounter again, many news accounts imitated the pattern of contrasting exemplarity and reprobation.[53]

By the early seventeenth century the Calvinist-inspired goals of bringing about conspicuously edifying personal conversions and (if a prisoner was facing death) of encouraging zealous declarations before execution crowds had further redefined the post-Reformation duties of prison visitors. In 1615, the Mayor of London briefly summarized his employee's duties thus:

> ... sayinge divine service, and ... Preachinge twice, or thrice everie weeke vnto the prisoners in the Goale [*sic*] ... his greate paynes in goinge with the condempned Prisoners, to the place of Execution, to exhorte them to prepare themselves to God.[54]

The visitor was now a gallows choreographer and proselytizer charged with guiding the condemned person to perform his conversion before spectators.[55]

The first depiction of these new duties after Golding's *A briefe discourse* occurred in the play it inspired, *A Warning for Faire Women*. In the closing scenes a clerical Doctor (perhaps representing Yonge) who has "seriously instructed" Anne Saunders and Mrs Drewrie in Newgate but only been able to convert the latter, prompts Saunders a final time at her execution to confess. To this point she has resisted in order "to escape / The worlds reproach" (2604–05). Having been urged by Drewrie and presumably recognizing that her hopes for a pardon have failed,[56] Anne admits her guilt and performs a tearful farewell to her children, bequeathing them copies of *Godly Meditations on the Lordes Prayer* by Reformation martyr John Bradford (published in 1562, the same year as Golding's account of Bucer and Phagius).

The visitor's new public role was exemplified more powerfully by William Perkins (1558–1602), possibly the most widely read Elizabethan divine, and, as we saw in the first chapter, a popular exponent of legal and social equity. Before securing his first church appointment, Perkins launched his clerical career in 1581 to 84 by conducting services in Cambridge Castle (i.e. gaol), "preaching deliverance to the Captives."[57] He quickly became famous for converting many condemned prisoners, as Samuel Clarke recalled in a well-known anecdote (which bears citing at length):

> A young lusty fellow going up the Ladder discovered an extraordinary lumpishness and dejection of spirit, and when he turned himself at the upper round to speak to the people, he looked with a rueful and heavy countenance, as if he had been half dead already: whereupon Master *Perkins* labored to chear up his spirits, and finding him still in Agony, and distresse of mind, he said unto him, *What man? what is the matter with thee? art though afraid of death?* Ah no (said the Prisoner, shaking his head) but of a worser thing: Saist thou so? (said Master *Perkins*) come down again man, and thou shalt see what Gods grace will do to strengthen thee: Whereupon the prisoner coming down, Master *Perkins* took him by the hand, and made him kneel down with himself at the ladder foot, hand in hand, when that blessed man of God made such an effectual prayer in confession of sins, and aggravating thereof in all circumstances, with the horrible and eternal punishment due to the same by Gods justice, as made the poor prisoner burst out into abundance of tears; and Master *Perkins* finding that he had brought him low enough, even to Hell gates, he proceeded to the second part of his prayer, and therein to shew him the Lord *Jesus* … which [Perkins] did so sweetly press with such Heavenly art, and powerful words of Grace upon the soul of the prisoner, as cheared him up again to look beyond death … as made him break out into new showres of tears for joy of the inward consolation which he found, and gave such expression of it to the beholders, as made them lift up their hands, and praise God to see such a blessed change in him; who (the prayer being ended) rose from his knees chearfully, and went up the Ladder again, so comforted, and took his death with such patience, and alacrity, as if he actually saw himself delivered from the Hell which he feared before.[58]

This story recorded an idealized template for encounters between condemned prisoners and the godly divine. In it the visitor became a heroic figure infusing spiritual energy into the felon, jointly transforming both into agents of providential grace. Theologically, the emphasis on the young man's ontological negation and mental anguish, the efficacy of Perkins's "Heavenly art" in pressing him with words from Scripture, and the man's sudden seizure by grace, were distinctly Calvinist, as was Perkins's aim to dramatize his subject's labor of re-imagining his physical pain into a controlled artifact to edify the unreformed.[59] Perkins's intervention actualized the English puritan preference that the subject should experience conversion as a progression of inner states—here highly compressed—synchronized by a sharp mental and emotional reversal.[60] The "worser thing" feared by the young man presumably referred to the sufferings of eternal damnation. His "agony" and "distress," signifying emotional despondency and impotence of human will, were presumed to be necessary conditions for the reception of grace.[61] His kneeling and return to the ladder encoded a spiritual descent and ascent, as did Perkins's taking him hand in hand "even to Hell gates" before proffering the hope of salvation, a gesture that distantly emblematized the traditional image of Christ handing the redeemed out of Hell's mouth. The young man's tears signalled his newly internalized subjectivity, which spectators objectively validated in their vocal and gestural salutations. His final embracing of death with "chearfulness" and "patient alacrity" manifested the psychological benefits of conversion in the form of charismatic self-confidence and potency of will.[62]

Visitor authors rehearsed details of the Perkins scenario in their appropriations of female murder stories for at least the next 150 years. Henry Goodcole, for instance, contrasted the responses of multiple-murderers Thomas Shearwood and Elizabeth Evans in *Heavens Speedie Hue and Cry* (1635). He represented Shearwood (a.k.a. "Country Tom") offering a visually arresting scaffold performance: "[I]*n the* Posture *of his* Body, *he expressed true* Humility, *for all the time of Prayer, he prayed kneeling.*" Execrating his former life "as a kinde of Hell unto him," Shearwood voiced his new godly subjectivity with equal fervor:

> *his death he ioyfully embraced, and mortall life cheerfully did surrender up, and sent his soule out of his Body flying, calling on the name of the Lord Iesus to receive him. And all the people speaking to God for him, likewise with their lowd voyces, and strong acclamations, Lord Jesu take mercy on him.* (C3r)

Shearwood's flamboyant gestures were the obverse of his spectacular violence, which *Heavens Speedie Hue and Cry*'s publishers Nicholas and John Okes conjured sensationally by displaying an oversize image of the murder weapon—a massive club with sharp metal barbs—in the frontispiece illustration and the margins beside Goodcole's account of the murders.[63]

Goodcole's work on Evans ("Canberry Bess"), on the other hand, accomplished little, and her behavior conveyed very different messages to spectators and readers:

> I found her with the feares of Death very much perplexed and amazed, distractedly casting her eyes here, and there[;] at last shee espies the high Elmes neere which place Master *Claxton* [one of the murder victims] was slaine, and fetcht a deep sigh and said, would to God I had never seene that place. (C4r)

Goodcole's rationale for publishing this account was presumably not to advertise his professional failure but to verify Evans's gender-marked

IF one fmite another with an Inftrument of Iron, that hee Dye, hee is a *Murderer*, and the *Murderer* fhall dye the Death. Or if hee fmite him with an hand-weapon of wood whereby hee may be flayne, if hee dye, hee is a *Murderer*, and the Murderer fhall dye the Death. *Numb.*35.*v.*16.

Countrey-Tom.   *Canberry Beſſe.*

he forme of the inftrument of wood and iron that he ufed to hurt with.

Figure 3.2 Heavens Speedie Hue and Cry sent after Lust and Murther (frontispiece, 2nd edn, 1635). Reproduced by permission of the British Library.

reprobation, as she refused to abandon her criminal identity. As Michael Questier observes of such cases, the wider implication is that "God [was] distinguishing . . . between the saved and the damned. Those who did not repent were those who were not called effectually."[64] In theory such exclusions allowed Goodcole, like other visitors faced with recalcitrant charges, to dismiss absolutely Evans's denials of guilt and her "base aspersions on the

Dead" (i.e., the murder victims' complicity in meeting Evans for clandestine sex in covert rural–suburban spaces, where the lurking Shearwood coshed them with his fearsome weapon [A1r]).

The visitor author of "*A Relation of what passed in the Imprisonment, and at the Execution of* Hannah Blay," appended to the twelfth and thirteenth editions of Richard Alleine and Robert Franklin's *A Murderer Punished, and Pardoned* (1668), also contrasted negative and positive prisoner responses to convince readers of the effectiveness of their vocation. They located Blay's deepest core of reprobation on the morning of her execution, Friday 26 February. Striking a total contrast with the "*Shameful-Happy death*" of Blay's fellow convict and model convert Thomas Savage, the authors asserted that she

> ended her wicked life by a shameful death, without the least sign of sorrow or Repentance for her abominable whoredome and wickedness. (C8v)

In the thirteenth edition they felt it necessary to add:

> ... wickednesses: So that howsoever notoriously wicked she had been in her life, answerable thereunto was she in her shameful end, in impenitency and hardness of heart. (C8v)

Appealing to readers' beliefs in eternal truth and the social utility of evangelical conversion, the late-Restoration visitor of Newgate, Samuel Smith, issued a stream of self-congratulatory pamphlets about penitent and unregenerate felons. *The Behaviour of the Condemned Criminals in Newgate, Who were Executed On Wednesday, the Sixth of May, 1685*, published by George Croom, typified Smith's semi-official format: a short account of the latest Old Bailey sessions; a thematic summary of his pre-execution Newgate sermon; and brief individualized reports "of such who Voluntarily offered themselves to be directed by the Ordinary, as unto the better clearing up of their fitness for Death and a future Judgment" (2). On this occasion, however, twelve of twenty-three prisoners stubbornly rejected his exhortations to confess "with greater Obstinacy, than ever any did for nine years past, as desperate and hardned in Wickedness, or being bold to venture into an Eternal State, without any desire to be Instructed or prepared for it" (2). As later sections of this chapter will show, such resistance was by no means an unusual response, and was related in the minds of both the condemned and readers to popular ideas of equity.

PATRONAGE

The Reformation project of proselytizing execution crowds had mandated godly ministers to extend their labors from inside prisons to public sites such as Tyburn, Smithfield, or the local common.[65] The burden on individual visitors to deliver consistently edifying and state-approved performances grew, and included the necessity of proving to pious civic employers that their annual stipends were being well-earned. Representing such performances as morally uplifting also ostensibly justified exploiting the same gruesome murders for profit as commercial printed news. After being regarded as a rather lowly profession for much of the sixteenth century, church and preaching positions were becoming more socially prestigious owing to intense competition for positions, despite often poor financial prospects.[66] Murder news provided an opportunity for prison visitors with insider knowledge of criminals' lives to publicize their serviceability, godly orthodoxy, and ambitions in an increasingly professionalized market.[67]

Yet there were plenty of skeptical or anticlerical readers in early modern England who could bring the heavenly ideal of gallows conversion down to earth by focusing on direct or implied evidence of writers using their criminal subjects to court potential patrons and advance their worldly careers. Some readers judged these goals to be in conflict with the legally and socially justifying aims of obtaining prison confessions. Such perceptions opened alternative interpretations of an alleged criminal's trial and punishment.

Before Samuel Smith and the highly lucrative Newgate *Accounts* of his eighteenth-century successors, the most conspicuous example of a metropolitan crime-writer using murder news to advance his career was Henry Goodcole.[68] Starting as a prison preacher, he progressed to become visitor of Ludgate and Newgate prisons, chaplain to one of the Inns of Court, and finally the beneficed clergyman of St. James Clerkenwell, the parish in which he lived his entire life.[69] In his named publications and official documents he is styled "preacher," "minister," or "clerk" rather than "master."[70] These titles as well as the Latin quotations in many of his pamphlets suggest that he received a grammar-school education but was not a university graduate.[71] He would thus have lacked the personal contacts and institutional opportunities for ecclesiastical preferment provided by attendance at Oxford or Cambridge. For men intent on a clerical career, this background was becoming a disadvantage in the early seventeenth century as more and more candidates for both beneficed and non-beneficed appointments were graduates or had spent some time at the universities.

The Mayor and Aldermen of London first appointed Goodcole as a weekly "lecturer" or preacher to the prisoners of Ludgate prison in 1613.[72] His salary was a meagre 33s 4d a quarter, or £6 13s 4d annually. In February 1616 he successfully petitioned his employers for a rise to £10 after demonstrating his competence, and on the expectation that his work would continue to be satisfactory.[73] These and later records indicate that Goodcole's effectiveness as a visitor was continually being evaluated by his civic employers, and that further promotions were dependent on achieving conspicuously edifying outcomes with condemned prisoners at Tyburn.

Seeking to build on his success in securing the visitorship of Ludgate, Goodcole published *A True Declaration of the happy Conuersion, contrition, and Christian preparation of Francis Robinson, Gentleman* (1618) to draw public attention to his skills. In the dedicatory epistle, he explained that he sought out Robinson to raise his visibility among legal and government officials involved in this high-profile treason trial, and he openly solicited the patronage of his dedicatee, Sir Henry Montague, Lord Chief Justice (A2v). Goodcole's ministrations to Robinson were not officially authorized, however, since another chaplain, Robert Pricket, had been appointed by Montague to attend Robinson while in custody. But he avoided Mell's mistake in the Saunders trials of antagonizing his superiors by working on-side with Pricket to re-convert Robinson from Roman Catholicism. His pamphlet unabashedly claimed credit for obtaining an exemplary confession of loyalty with maximum propaganda value for the government, and for prompting Robinson's abject performance on the gallows.

As a result of this and other prison work, the Mayor and Court of Alderman appointed Goodcole visitor of Newgate in 1619 and increased his stipend. A little more than a year later the trial of Elizabeth Sawyer for witchcraft and murder erupted to test his handling of a sensational case and display his expertise to his employers. Part of the trial's notoriety lay in its rarity, since doubts about the validity of charging local women or men with practising witchcraft (at least among the educated) had led to a sharp drop in indictments.[74] The public's curiosity was also stirred by rumors of transgressive sexual acts alleged against Sawyer, to which publisher William Butler's title page alluded (*"Together with the relation of the Diuels accesse to her, and their conference together"*). This potential revelation was not so subtly coded by the title page image of a phallically distended and snake-shaped cloud pointed directly at a large, open-topped hat worn by an old woman.

The story centered on Sawyer allowing a dog-devil named Tom to have the pleasure of sucking blood from a "teat" discovered on her backside, after which she would "stroake him . . . and then he would becke vnto me, and wagge his tayle as being therewith contented" (D1r). After Tom had been satisfied, he would allegedly do Sawyer's malign bidding, which included bewitching to death several infants, some cattle, and a neighbor, Agnes Ratcliff, with whom she had quarrelled. Sawyer was charged with these deaths in three indictments. The jury acquitted her of the first charges but convicted her of killing Ratcliff.

Goodcole arranged his account in three sections: a preface; a brisk description of Sawyer, the charges, trial, and verdicts; and Sawyer's confession, consisting of a question-and-answer dialogue read aloud at her execution on the orders of the Recorder of London, Robert Heath (one of Goodcole's dedicatees in *The Prodigals Teares* [1620] and a member of the Court of Aldermen). Given the public interest aroused by Sawyer's alleged crimes and trial, Goodcole presented a remarkably restrained account that might have disappointed certain readers anticipating salacious details implied by the pamphlet's (ultimately misleading) title, *The wonderfull discouerie*. Goodcole's refusal to satisfy these desires was not aimed at foregrounding the story's morals, however, as it had been for Golding's *A brief discourse*, but at defending his professional conduct and maintaining his superiors's good opinions. Citing external pressures that "by importunitie extorted" his account, Goodcole largely avoided "discuss[ing], or disput[ing]" the actuality of witchcraft. He was more concerned to verify both Sawyers' confessions and his professional relationship with her in Newgate to "free mee from all censorious mindes and mouthes" (A3r). His propriety had been called into question when "ridiculous fictions" had been sung by balladmongers on the way back from Tyburn that Sawyer had "communed" with devilish spirits (or Goodcole himself) while she was in his charge (A3v). Later during the interrogation he pinpointed the source of his anxiety by asking her: "Did the Diuell neuer come vnto you since you were in prison?" (D1r). His marginal note explained that "I asked this question because it was rumoured that the diuel came to her since her conuiction[,] and [that rumour] shamelesly printed and openly sung in a ballad, to which many giue too much credite" (D1r). These (now lost) allegations would have been taken seriously because they followed an official crackdown three years earlier on "lewd and shamefull comforts" enjoyed illicitly by prisoners in Newgate.[75] Coming soon after his appointment as visitor, both his expertise and authority were effectively put on trial. He entered his pamphlet in the Stationers' Register just eight days after Sawyer's execution on 19 April 1621, and presumably it was issued very shortly thereafter.

Goodcole's attempts to restore his credit explained his relatively brief account of the crime and trial in contrast to the longer quasi-legal confession. There he presented an impeccable display of examining skill which he claimed was verifiable by several witnesses. It was also not surprising that Goodcole expressed little personal feeling towards or imaginative engagement with Sawyer, though he did allow humane compassion to emerge from her own words:

Quest[ioner]:

What moues you now to make this confession? did any urge you to it, or bid you doe it, is it for any hope of life you doe it?

Answ[er]:

No: I doe it to cleere my conscience, and now hauing done it, I am the more quiet, and the better prepared, and willing thereby to suffer death; for I haue no hope at all of my life, although I must confesse, I would liue longer if I might. (D1v)

Allowing Sawyer's responses to speak largely for themselves (or presenting them as if they did) countered the negative rumors about her time in his care and bolstered his reputation for forensic dexterity. Her plain descriptions of past encounters with Tom authenticated (and perhaps aesthetically height-ened) their imaginative impact for readers while discounting the impression that Goodcole was exploiting the story for personal profit. The mild moral of Goodcole's Conclusion (D3r–v) was that readers should avoid "cursing, swearing, and blaspheming," which lay one open to the devil's subverting wiles. Otherwise he mentioned nothing further about witchcraft or murder.

When Goodcole returned to writing crime news in 1635 after a fourteen-year gap, he drew attention to the intervening silence: "I Have resumed my Pen which I resolved in this Nature for ever to be silent: But the Common good, preservation of my Countries welfare, incites me unto this officious service" (*Heavens Speedie Hue and Cry*, A2v). With the benefit of hind-sight we can perceive a double-meaning in "officious" in the older sense of "being concerned with an office," because Goodcole was to receive his first church appointment and its long-desired higher status and income the fol-lowing year. His two 1635 pamphlets—*Heavens Speedie Hue and Cry* and *The Adultresses Funerall Day*—were therefore in part fresh bids for patron-age, this time to ecclesiastical news readers in particular. And again they may have represented justifications to his civic employers. For in March 1633 the Court of Aldermen had appointed a commission of lay visitors to inspect conditions in Newgate. Not surprisingly, they found them to be appalling. Although not naming Goodcole explicitly, they made a number of potentially damaging observations that touched on his professional respon-sibilities, such as keepers' and prisoners' absenteeism from chapel. They also emphasized the visitor's responsibility for maintaining spiritual discipline and certifying penalties for offenses.[76] In view of these unflattering reports, Goodcole may have felt the need to re-advertise the effectiveness of his prison ministry as he had done in the Elizabeth Sawyer case.

I shall return to Goodcole's *Heavens Speedie Hue and Cry* in the next section. Before then let's look at one further illustration of a clerical news author using his insider knowledge to advance his career, but in this case one that clearly created ambiguous effects for lay-readers evaluating the culpability of his criminal subjects.

Thomas Cooper was chaplain of Fleet Street prison and a zealous puritan author. He dedicated *The Cry and Reuenge of Blood* (1620) to same pow-erful patron as Goodcole's *A True Declaration*, Henry Montague, as well as to Sir Henry North, High Sheriff of Suffolk, and several other county magistrates and JPs. Internal evidence indicates he obtained his informa-tion about the crime from Montague and North, although he also claimed to have attended the Bury assize, presided over by Montague, in person. Regardless of his exact sources, he blatantly reconstructed them to serve his personal interests and those of his regular publisher John Wright, who may have prompted him to seize this opportunity. Like Henry Goodcole and other seventeenth-century pamphlet writers, Cooper justified his publication partly on the grounds of correcting false reports by "flying and suspitious pamphlets" (i.e., Wright's commercial rivals). Wright also commissioned the printer publisher, Nicholas Okes, to design an eye-catching woodcut showing a man being vigorously brained at the devil's bidding, naked bodies being staked deep in a pond, and skeletal corpses being exhumed.

The fact that the homicide remained largely unsolved did not deter Cooper from expansively "*Expressing the Nature and haynous*nesse of wilfull Murther." Readers who anticipated a juicy crime story must have been quickly disappointed. Cooper deferred talking about the murder until page twenty-nine, preceding it with an exegesis of sin and murder. His narrative crept forward for sixty-three pages, continually digressing into biblical analogies and homiletic commentary inspired by William Perkins.[77] Given that one of Cooper's main themes was the omniscience of a vengeful providence, the murder narrative inevitably fell apart when he was forced to admit that none of the principal suspects had been apprehended. Only two accessories, Land and Worlich, were brought to trial. Cooper tried to solve his narrative dilemma by imposing the now-familiar model of contrasting confessions and execution behavior. Land's obstinate refusals became a foil for Worlich's contrition. Cooper claimed their opposite responses confirmed the justice of both verdicts and the wisdom of the judges because they reflected the eternal truth of the biblical archetype: "A notable image of God's righteous decree, in the hardening of ye one & softning of the other, and a wise item to obstinate sinners, that what they haue beene in their liues, they likely prooue in their deathes" (F3r). Yet readers could plainly recognize that local magistrates and jurors had made Land and Worlich scapegoats for the real but missing culprits. The expediency of this outcome explained Cooper's strained rhetorical efforts to contain local controversy over the crimes ("to the stopping of all gain-saying lippes," G4r–H1v), which also implicitly anticipated objections of disaffected or skeptical readers. Even godly ones might have recalled Arthur Golding's far more skilfully managed presentation of prosecution arguments and moral expostulation.

FURTHER MIXED MESSAGES

Samuel Smith's *The True Account of the Behaviour and Confessions Of the Criminals Condemned, on Saturday the 16th of October, 1686* directed readers' attention to a single recalcitrant charge, Anne Philmore, who was condemned for killing her nine-week-old child. Smith explained that despite his efforts he could not get her to confess what he regarded as any genuine motives for the crime. Asked whether poverty was a factor, she replied no: she worked hard with her husband to support her four children. The recent fifth arrival had made things difficult, however, by hindering her employment as a linen washer. Smith remarked that Philmore showed few signs of sorrow and remained of a "sullen, reserved temper." Incorrigibility presumably wrote her off.

Women who heard or read about Anne Philmore from the perspective of working mothers might have been able to imagine Philmore's desperate remedy as something more than motiveless malignity. In general, readers' responses to Smith's, Cooper's, and Goodcole's obvious personal interests and their conventionally contrasted subjects must have varied. Cooper's implied audience were readers who presumably shared his strong predestinarian views and might have felt edified by his sermonizing commentary. Those who did not, including more detached local magistrates and jurors in neighboring counties, must have wondered at the palpable imbalance between his pamphlet's absolute claims for the consolations of divine grace and justice, and its defective narrative and legal outcomes, both of which failed to secure the truth of "murder will out" implied by the pamphlet's title.

Goodcole, partly because of his ambitions for advancement within London institutions, targeted a much broader London readership and seems to have been more conscious of their ideological diversity. Their responses to Elizabeth Evans's fear of death and resistance to conversion might also have been influenced by the unexpectedly gendered perspective of his account. Goodcole sympathetically assessed her slide into crime as a series of remediable social problems, such as a loss of kinship support owing to the sexual nature of her offences, community abandonment, and female poverty. Initiating an approach very different from Cooper's or Smith's, Goodcole shifted normative assumptions about the origins of homicide from internal moral values to disparities of economic power and social justice. He opened a new horizon on future discussions of female criminal motives that anticipated the increasingly realistic details and contexts of later seventeenth-century journalism and narrative fiction.[78]

Furthermore, documented anti-puritan attitudes towards evangelical conversion suggest that the gallows behavior of Shearwood and Evans in *Heavens Speedie Hue and Cry* would have been open to contested interpretations by certain spectators and readers.[79] Thomas Laqueur and Susan Dwyer Amussen have shown in different ways that the emotional and semantic effects of public executions were neither certain nor stable. Rather, when they were not treated merely as a backdrop to local festivity, penal violence was always being judged by onlookers for its legitimate—or equitable—relationship to the character of the criminal and the contextual circumstances of the crime.[80] The second edition of *Heavens Speedie Hue and Cry* provided direct evidence of delegitimizing reactions by public spectators who refused to read Shearwood's behavior in terms of reprobation and salvation. These protesters may have included readers of Goodcole's first edition. He originally concluded the report of Shearwood's repentance with an advertisement: "Here endeth the Narration of Thomas Sherwood, who now hangeth in chaines near Pancras Church" (C3v). After a "A generall Admonition," the second edition continued Shearwood's story in an appendix: "*The* Habeas corpus, *or Remove of* Countrey Tom *into the Countrey*" (C4r–v). Whereas

Evans's body was taken to Barber Surgeons' Hall to be anatomized, Tom's was removed to a gibbet in the suburbs of St. Pancras, symbolically marking the City's expulsion of provincial contagion (Shearwood had migrated from Staffordshire).[81] Coming that way at night, a butcher allegedly remarked on seeing Tom, "it was no matter if all such rogues were serv'd so" (C4r). At that moment two gentlemen eyewitnessed the butcher being ambushed by "lurking villaines" who "presently seized on him, and tooke his cloathes, and bound him naked to the Gibbet with a gagge in his mouth, bidding him watch the Coar[p]se." In what looks like a calculated replay of Shearwood and Evans's assault on Claxton (B3r and frontispiece), the party of rogues revenged the honor of their mate, turning the display of criminal deterrence into a defiant counter-spectacle by the London criminal community. Meanwhile the two eyewitnesses retreated into typical urban anonymity, failing to aid the butcher until after it was safe to do so. Their cowardice wryly undercut Goodcole's proto-modern assumptions throughout the rest of the pamphlet that neighborhood surveillance and the presence of casual passers-by would promote urban safety.

This was not the end of Shearwood's story. The appendix continued with a Not-In-My-Backyard sequel that further revealed how the execution and possibly its appropriation by Goodcole generated further protests. True suburbanites, the St. Pancras residents were "much damnified and annoyed" to learn of Tom's officially sponsored intrusion into their neighborhood. They complained of the "spoile and depopulating the growing fields there abouts, stript of all fences, and the grasse trodden downe, and made levell, by the infinite confluence of all sexes from all parts" who had heard or read about the murders and came to view Tom's body, as well as the sight's "confusion" of spectators' reactions (C4v, alluding to the butcher's attackers). The disgruntled citizens petitioned the king and council to have the "hated spectacle" taken away at night to "the Ring-crosse beyond Islington," where "those that are not yet satisfied, may see *Country Tom* got farther into the Countrey." Goodcole's complacent pursuit of Tom's post-execution peregrinations kept alive Shearwood's memory with his *confrères* and contributed to an after-life celebrity that rallied their opposition to his gallows humiliations as well as the appropriation of his criminal identity by the state institution of evangelical conversion.

HEAVENLY BLACKMAIL

Goodcole's *Heavens Speedie Hue and Cry* and *The Adultresses Funerall Day* were unusually candid about the strenuous personal and institutional coercion exerted by keepers, visitors, sheriffs and other officials on the condemned. They also revealed that such treatment could provoke destabilizing responses to the state's legal and moral authority. The Perkins conversion model benignly referred to such strategies as "Heavenly art." Calvinist divines theorized that sinners were most receptive to divine grace when their "hard hearts" had been "broken" (i.e., when they were in a state of extreme abjection verging on suicidal despair). Driving prisoners into this condition was obviously regarded by some as a legitimate path to salvation. But such practices could look different from the perspective of non-godly readers who did not share puritan beliefs or approve of its social or political agenda.

Arthur Golding's explanation of why Anne Saunders's resistance to confession suddenly collapsed indicated that, in the eyes of godly readers, exercising or representing such pressure-strategies was unexceptionable. In *The trueth of the most wicked and secret murthering of Iohn Brewen ... committed by his owne wife* (1592), Anne Welles had been reluctant to admit poisoning her husband at the instigation of her lover John Parker until examiners led her "to beleeue that Parker had bewrayed the matter" (even though he hadn't) and that her own denials were hopeless (A4v). An unnamed maidservant who tried to poison her mistresses in 1677 at first denied the charges, but after "some suggestions of pardon"—which the writer implied were never genuine—she admitted not only this attempt but also poisoning her mother and another maidservant several years before (*Horrid News from St. Martins* [1677]). Such ruses seem to have been routinely employed by civic and clerical authorities to break the resistance of stubborn suspects. Writers generally represented such feints as morally unproblematic on the assumption that readers would regard the prisoner as unquestionably guilty and her resistance as damnable (e.g., Elizabeth Abbot, chapter 2). But if readers had any doubts about the personal circumstances of the crime, trial, or officials' personal motives, they could have regarded such deceptions as morally doubtful and instead reconstructed the suspects's resistance according to alternative principles.

The danger of creating negative public impressions was clearly recognized by later visitor-writers such as John Quick, who in 1676 worried openly about readers misinterpreting his actions. His own professional confidence in his thirteen-year career as an Exeter prison visitor was severely—even agonizingly—tested by his failure to persuade Philippa Cary and Anne Evans to confess their alleged poisoning-murder of the Weeks household in 1675. The case related by *Hell Open'd* (1676)—at 92 octavo pages the longest seventeenth-century murder "pamphlet" I have come across—was shot through with Quick's self-conscious anxieties about his limited success, often addressed as self-exculpating questions and answers to skeptical readers. At other moments Quick seemed to lose rhetorical control, becoming unaware of the unsympathetic impressions conveyed by his violent language in interviews with his two condemned charges. Midway through the pamphlet, frustrated by Cary's steadfast refusal to confess, Quick turned his attention to the younger and more malleable Evans, threatening

That as she had by her envy, malice, Instigation, and Correspondence with the Devil Murdered her two Mistresses ... And that as they were dead and Buried, so would she also shortly die a very horrible death, and without wonderful mercy be swallowed up of everlasting wrath. That the fire which was to consume her in *Plymouth* would be very painful, but the Fire of Hell in which she must live and lye for ever would be insupportable. (D4v)

Yet Quick later admitted that Evans's involvement in the poisoning of her two mistresses was inadvertent (E5r), as indeed the testimonies by neighbors he presented earlier had confirmed. For these people as well as other readers of Quick's account, his terror tactics must have appeared victimizing (possibly reminding them of similar abuses of official power that W. Burdet and others writers had criticized in the prosecution of Anne Greene; see chapter 5). Given the pamphlet's date and locale, they may also have stirred anti-clerical reactions to Quick's self-promoting ministrations. For in 1660 he had been publicly ejected from his Plymouth curacy. Readers familiar with his controversial reputation might have wondered at his presumption in judging and attempting to convert possibly innocent suspects. (Local supporters of Thomas Caldwell expressed similar objections to his wife's prison evangelism; see *A True Discourse*, B3v.) In late 1663 Quick was arrested and convicted at the western-circuit assizes for preaching illegally and jailed for three months. Neither the events described in *Hell Open'd* nor its original publication or re-issue in 1679 seem to have improved Quick's public credentials, because by 1680 he had left England to become a pastor in The Netherlands. When he returned to London the following year, he was again fined and imprisoned for inflammatory illegal preaching. Quick's combative career as a nonconformist preacher only settled down after James II's declaration of indulgence in 1687.[82]

During the climactic executions reported by *Hell Open'd*, Philippa Cary proclaimed her innocence even while suffering excruciating fear on the gallows ladder. Quick reported that she "did howl and yell," "the very terrors of death [were] upon her, she crie[d] as if her Heart would break." Being asked whether she wished anyone to pray for her, Cary allegedly gestured to Quick. He refused to comfort her without an admission of guilt. In turn "She tells us. *She cannot Confess that whereof she is not Guilty*" (F5v–8v). After Cary's death her suffering—and perhaps Quick's own conduct—continued to haunt him. Anticipating a hostile readership, he ended *Hell Open'd* by plaintively defending the reasonableness of his methods and denouncing Cary's highly public repudiation of his efforts (G1r–G2v).

THE PANGS OF DEATH

As many news reports examined thus far demonstrate, condemned women and men submitted to their enforced roles in the state-sponsored drama of gallows conversion with varying degrees of enthusiasm. Visitors' "pains" with prisoners could be understood in conflicting ways depending on readers' personal values, communal identities, and imaginative empathy. The Perkins scenario revealed that satisfactory performances required strenuous self-transformation within brief intervals. The prisoner had to reconstitute her memory-identity as a guilty sinner and doomed criminal and to control her body so absolutely so as to appear to die without fear of approaching pain or death. Anne Welles's steadily raised arms and hands clasped piously together amid the engulfing flames in the title page illustration of *The trueth of the most wicked and secret murthering of Iohn Brewen* (1592) seemed to project the perfect icon of redeemed criminality. Yet when readers came to end of the pamphlet, the report implicitly cast doubts on this idealized image by failing to mention anything about her execution behavior. The paradigm memorably established twenty years earlier by Arthur Golding's portraits of Anne Saunders and Anne Drewrie suggested that, optimally, adulterous homicides such as Welles should have been represented expressing their repentance in exemplary words and actions that validated the trial verdict. In this pamphlet, however, like those about the criminally caricatured Mrs. Beast (*A Briefe Discovrse of Two most cruell and bloudie murthers, committed bothe in Worcestershire* [1583]), Mrs. Browne (*Two most vnnaturall and bloodie Murthers* [1605]), and others, there are only silences.

Exemplary public confessions by women in fact appear infrequently in seventeenth-century news of female homicide and infanticide, notwithstanding the tremendous institutional pressures on women to admit their guilt. Partly because trials were swift and normally followed rather than preceded by demands for full confessions, most news reports suggested the condemned felt the most acute internal pressures to behave penitently immediately before death.[83] The rigors of imprisonment and the terrors of having to perform correctly before large crowds of spectators (who often had their own expectations or agendas) were extremely challenging, and prisoners met them in a variety of ways ranging from catatonic passivity to carnivalesque insouciance. In popular news about female homicides, responses were much closer to the former than the latter.

The conversion script called for significant oral/aural participation in the form of recitations of speeches, prayers, and dialogue with attending clergymen and spectators. For Arthur Golding and Henry Goodcole, Anne Saunders's and Thomas Shearwood's practised kneeling movements and imploring gestures authenticated their final performances for spectators and readers, including assize officials who expected to see their decisions publicly vindicated. Gilbert Dugdale found it easier in 1604 to reposition Elizabeth Caldwell as a momentarily lapsed member of the elect deserving of a royal pardon because of the remarkable—and long-rehearsed—fluency with which she conversed with attending officials and execution crowds (see chapter 2). Caldwell's verbal bravado validated the transcendent closure of Dugdale's converted-offender biography, constructed as a morally "truthful" narrative of fall and redemption, and encoded with biblical references and allegorical signs to prompt its correct interpretation by readers.

Like the textually mute Welles, Beast, Browne, *et al.*, Elizabeth Evans's inability to mimic similar gestures illustrated the incapacity or reluctance of some prisoners to adopt the customary speeches or movements, let alone improvised ones signifying a sudden rapture of divine grace. Evans's fears of pain, isolation, and shameful death nullified Goodcole's spiritual therapy and propelled her regressively towards despair. The horrifying realities facing her and other condemned women indicated that co-ordinating the tricky variables of the conversion scenario into coherent performances was difficult. Relationships between the prisoner and visitors, sheriffs, executioners, and mounted or standing spectators required controlled negotiations of action, submission, and participation in volatile public conditions. The many news readers who had personally witnessed executions at Tyburn or elsewhere recognized such physical and human contingencies as the reality behind idealizing confession and execution reports. (Spectators' motives for attending executions were more often curiosity about unexpected or improvised deviations from the official script, rather than willing conformity to it, though godly pamphlet writers suggested the opposite.) The condemned felon's self-transformations required her to cross wide social and educational boundaries because she was usually sub- or nonliterate, whereas visitors and legal officials were educated professionals. Women criminals also had to endure the casually ingrained misogyny of male officers.

In her groundbreaking study of the mental mechanics of physical pain and abjection under torture, Elaine Scarry has shown that, in persons facing death, the "edges of the self [become] coterminous with the edges of the body."[84] Early modern murder news frequently represented this psycho-somatically shrunken state in their reports of the "deadness" and "silence" of condemned prisoners on the gallows, who were unable to transform the intensity of physical dread into feelings of emotional comfort or metaphysically empowered agency. When in 1670 Mary Cook killed her daughter to revenge her husband's and relations' alleged unkindness and neglect, she rejected efforts by her husband to obtain a pardon and remained "dejected in spirit and deeply afflicted with melancholy," "her intellects being much impaired," and "unheeding of ministers advice." Presented with the usual repertoire of ghost-written speeches and prayers to perform, "[s]he told us she could only word it and not heart it" (*The Cruel Mother* [1670]).

A more extensively reported case of "deadness" on the scaffold occurred in 1680 when Margaret Osgood was executed for bludgeoning her terminally drunken and abusive husband to death with a hatchet. According to one of the related trial and execution reports, when Osgood appeared before assembled spectators on 16 March dressed in white, she seemed already "half dead" (*The True Narrative of the Confession and Execution Of the Prisoners at Kingstone-upon-Thames, on Wednesday the 16th of this Instant March, 1681*). An article in *The True Protestant Mercury*, Number

24, for Wednesday 16 March to Saturday 19 March confirmed this reaction, briefly reporting that she "seem'd very little concern'd at her Tragical end" (A2r). *The True Narrative* further observed that she managed to speak just a few words (presumably by rote) asking spectators to pray for her and to take warning from her sad end. The absence of active agency might have reinforced readers' questions about the ambiguous legal evidence used at her trial (see chapter 2).

Other Restoration news reports qualified conversion optimism by depicting the prisoner approaching death through barely controlled resignation, as he or she struggled to inhabit the visitor-induced ideal of fearlessly justified salvation. Two revealing instances appear in *A True Account of the Behaviour, Confessions, and Last Dying Words, Of . . . Jane Langworth, and Elizabeth Stoaks . . . On Wednesday the 21th. [sic] of December, 1684,* which related the executions of Langworth and Stoaks for killing their newborn children. With "loud Laments" Langworth "bewailed her misfortune[,] declaring that she had been a loose Liver, and a neglecter of Gods Holly [sic] worship" (A2v). When the ordinary invited her to pray,

> she did it as well as she could, though with many abrupt stamerings, the abnndance [sic] of her Grief and Terror of Approaching Death, not suffering her to express her self freely in her Devotion, to help which, she desired the Prayers of the spectators[,] admonishing them with a low Voice to take warning by her unhappy end. (A2v)

During her time in Newgate, Stoaks also "greatly bewailed her self, and would not for some days be comforted as being extreamly terrified at the approach of a certain Death." She became more resigned after being worked on by several divines. But at her execution she reverted to distress, "lament[ing] greatly" and "seeming very desirous of a longer Life, although she confesse[d] she had deserved to dye." The visitor tried to re-assert control over the situation, singing parts of the 51st psalm, "in which the Prisoners and Spectators ioyned." Stoaks seemed to regain her self-possession, "and that ended, the Cart soon after drove away" (A2v).

TACTICAL PRACTICES ON THE GALLOWS

The human and instrumental contingencies of public executions repeatedly compromised the symbolic power of conversion as a divinely inspired triumph of early modern legal and religious ideology. They also raised questions about the ability of news representations to sustain the internalization of domestic and civil obedience on which early modern authorities relied to maintain order, deter crime, and assure English men and women about their personal security.[85] The prevailing view of modern historians has been that the reported behavior of condemned felons generally supported the normative values and procedures of the criminal law, and that men and women convicted of murder usually co-operated with judicial and clerical authorities after (if not before) their trials.[86] Trial and execution news ostensibly provided an important indication that the common people accepted the criminal justice system as having moral legitimacy when it interrogated local suspects, prosecuted felons, and dispensed punitive justice.

This interpretation of English public executions was first theorized by J. A. Sharpe, who in a seminal article argued that unforced confessions and willing collaboration were common among condemned early modern men and women, whilst active defiance on the gallows was rare, and rarely recorded.[87] Sharpe's conclusions were based on a fairly small body of later seventeenth-century murder pamphlets and left room—as he readily acknowledged—for modifications in the light of future research.[88] He also expressed skepticism about the effectiveness of punitive deterrence and the rationale of upholding civic order claimed or implied by most news writers. Thomas Laqueur took up this alternative perspective to argue that public interactions between authorities, crowds, and the condemned were typically disruptive and semiotically confused as expressions of hegemonic ideology. His work was based mainly on late-seventeenth and eighteenth-century documents and left the bulk of printed crime news up to 1700 under explored and female subjects, in particular, under represented.[89]

Peter Lake and Michael Questier's recent work has tried to explore a middle ground between Sharpe and Laqueur while also expanding our understanding of the semantic and cultural complexities of murder and execution news. Lake's position has evolved from two earlier articles: "Deeds Against Nature" (1994) and "Popular Form, Puritan Content?" (1994). The first of these demonstrated how clerical and elite writers appropriated murder stories to advance a range of religious positions for consumption by a heterogenous popular readership, with ambiguous political and social effects. The second situated such texts within a public dialectic of puritan and popular ideologies. In both cases, Lake claimed, the competing rhetorical frameworks "crowded out" meaningful forensic details.[90] These conclusions were based on selected texts and sometimes hasty readings. Assigning primary importance to crime news as a vehicle for sectarian agendas, they underestimated the historical contributions of legal, gender, and reader perspectives to the production of cultural meanings. In "Agency, Appropriation and Rhetoric Under the Gallows" (1996) and their introduction to *The Antichrist's Lewd Hat* (2002), Lake and Questier revised these conclusions by rightly emphasizing the varied topical and polemical uses to which gallows and conversion events could be put and through which they were understood. Their analysis shifted dominant attention away from officials (and implicitly, state and prosecution interests) to the often contentious interactions of spectators that destabilized the legal and/or sectarian power ostensibly manifested by such occasions. The result was a "whole range of gestures and counter-gestures, a serious set of exchanges between state, victim and audience."[91] I would argue that the vital generation of social and political energies that Lake and Questier identified in spectators' participation at public executions found a corresponding lease in the discursive construction of legal knowledge by news writers and readers in their varied interpretations of individual murder trials and executions.

Sandra Clark's recent study *Women and Crime in the Street Literature of Early Modern England* (2003) moves in similar directions as Lake and Questier by demonstrating the semantic ambiguities and contextual diversity of many popular pamphlets about serious female crime, especially from the neglected perspective of gender. Her work takes a slightly more sanguine view of their discursive effects than Frances E. Dolan's ground-breaking study of early modern domestic crime, *Dangerous Familiars* (1994). Focused on the construction of transgressive female subjects, Dolan argues that popular news and drama framed women's public agency predominantly in negative terms. Like Lake's earlier work, both Dolan and Clark rely on a limited number of cases and texts, mainly from the first half of the century. This prematurely forecloses the scope of historical evidence of female agency that was actually available to early modern news readers. The present study is concerned with enlarging this horizon by relating the large number of news reports about women accused of homicide or child murder to evolving cultures of commercial journalism and news readership that mobilized popular legal opinion. It also complements Hal Gladfelder's work on criminal narratives in the long eighteenth century (*Criminality and Narrative* [2001]) by connecting the growth of secular forensic knowledge and public evaluation of disputable judgments to female homicide as a dynamic category of social and (in Gladfelder's study) fictional identity.

The full range of sixteenth- and seventeenth-century popular news about women murderers indicates that, when they did not simply go unreported, confession and conversion scenarios were routinely disrupted or only imperfectly displayed, thus making official claims about the legal and social effectiveness of gallows representations tenuous. Of the 123 legible news accounts of female homicide and infanticide trials and executions between 1573 and 1697 considered by this study, a majority (65 or more; 53%) do not tell readers anything about the condemned woman's acceptance of her guilt or her behavior at the gallows. (The pretrial situation is different; many women, especially those charged with infanticide, denied the charges and/or defended their innocence.[92]) Of those accounts reporting details about verdicts and gallows demeanor (58), a minority (20; 34%) described women who ultimately accepted the court's verdict and actively submitted to pressure to make edifying speeches from the gallows ladder. A combined majority (38 out of 58; 66%), however, described either limited or coerced co-operation with legal officers and prison clergy (23; 40%), or complete rejection of the court verdict and open or passive defiance to the very end (15; 26%). Overall, early modern news about female murder indicated that, although submissive or terrorized co-operation between the condemned and state authorities was not uncommon, active defiance was not unusual either. Conscientious—that is to say, equitable—resistance in some form of reserved personal memory and agency was the norm. These findings agree with Hal Gladfelder's examination of late-seventeenth and eighteenth-century *Accounts* of the Visitor of Newgate, which frequently recorded acts of "resistance within submission" that were a "source of vexation" to office holders such as Samuel Smith.[93] The various news genres recording such outcomes and the circumstances leading up to them, combined with the increasing literacy of local officers and assize personnel, circulated legal and social knowledge that informed juror and judicial mitigation of accused women felons.

On the broader question of the internalization of deference on which early modern authorities relied to control disorder,[94] these texts likewise suggest such hopes were precariously founded. The interests served by having ordinary condemned women publicly endorse legal judgments and punishments went far beyond simply affirming or denying government and church authority. As we have seen so far, those interests included advancing civic and clerical careers, profiting from selected publication of notorious trials and executions from among the hundreds processed on regular assize circuits, and defending the professional reputations of prison visitors, jurors, and judges. Early modern news portrayed condemned women from the exemplary to the ambivalent to the obstinate. This diversity reflected an equally broad spectrum of competing ideological positions among readers.

The condemned and their families often had personal reasons for not co-operating—or being represented as not co-operating—with authorities. Husband-murderer Eulalia (Glanfield) Page's anti-heroic message in several news accounts (and possibly a lost play by Ben Jonson and Thomas Dekker) was that "she had rather dye with [her lover] Strangwidge, then to liue with [her elderly husband] Padge," whom her covetous parents had forced her to marry. When the equally adulterous and defiant Mrs. Beast was imprisoned with her lover Christopher Thomson, they reportedly remained fearlessly besotted with each other (*A Briefe Discovrse of Two most cruell and bloudie murthers, committed bothe in Worcestershire*). Mrs. Beast solicited "her sweet Christopher, with mony, hand kerchers, nosegaies, and such like amorous and loouing tokens" (B4r). Thomson doted on a lock of her hair, and allegedly asked the jailer to rip his heart from his body after he was executed, "& cleauing the same in sunder, he should there beholde the liuely Image of his sweet mistresse, to whom (as the cheefest Iewell he had) hee desired him to make a present of that precious token" (B4r–v). However romanticized, these stories are consistent with the absence of any report of confessions or repentance when Mrs. Beast was burnt outside Evesham and Thomson hanged in chains at Cothridge.

The conceptual model of gallows conversion as a discourse of state power has derived from Michel Foucault's *Discipline and Punish: The Birth of the Prison* (1977). Foucault argued that the early modern state used execution spectacles to construct its ideological hegemony, triumphantly inscribing its centralizing authority on the pacified bodies of its most powerless subjects.[95] This dichotomized narrative failed to account for the actual diversity of public and private interests and conflicted execution events documented by seventeenth-century English news. As Susan Dwyer Amussen has also observed, forms of legitimate correction which manifested political and juridical structures of power in early modern England were "far more diffuse than the 'monarchical superpower' of early modern France."[96]

A more accurate model to explain the social effects of gallows performances might be the agency reserving paradigm of tactical resistance developed by Michel de Certeau in *The Practice of Everyday Life* (1984). Partly concerned with problematizing Foucault's over-schematic narrative by drawing attention to forms of "antidiscipline" that evade and undermine hegemonic systems without overthrowing them, de Certeau proposed an alternative "ethics of tenacity" to define such behavior.[97] In his view marginalized individuals—whether modern office workers or condemned criminals—appropriate public events, spaces, and codes of behavior in divagating ways to express ruses of creative protest, conscientious resistance, or private memory. By recourse to subjective desires and alternative popular values, these mundane and often seemingly incoherent or limited gestures challenge, in fleeting public ways, institutionalized systems of power, as Elizabeth Evans and Alice Clarke, for instance, seem to have demonstrated on the mornings of their respective executions in 1635. The heated protests of local residents and the criminal community to Shearwood's execution likewise suggested that tactical interventions materialized out of subversive impulses of re-interpretation and re-appropriation. De Certeau's flexible and non-totalizing "ethics of tenacity" articulates the desire for equitable justice in the personal behavior of many early modern women who were under compulsion to confess but defended their innocence or mitigated their official culpability in improvised repertoires of autonomous remarks and gestures. His concept of practice also illuminates the reading habits of early modern newsbuyers who imaginatively or orally rewrote judicially authorized narratives of accused women.

The cardinal points of diffusion and reception in the confession and conversion process—trial, prison, gallows, and printed news—were programmed public shows. Foucault's *Discipline and Punish* characterized early modern executions as a "theatre of punishment." Pamphlets such as Thomas Cooper's *The Cry and Reuenge of Blood* (1620), or *Blood for Blood* (1670) endorse Foucault's portrayal insofar as they made use of theatrical metaphors, dividing their "Tragedies" into "parts," "acts," and "scenes." Judicial punishment conceived as a dramatic performance also made sense in relation to the common early modern image of the world as a stage populated by player-subjects acting out phases of life, now perhaps best known through examples in Shakespeare. However as *Heavens Speedie Hue and Cry* (1635), *The Cruel Mother* (1670), and many other reports revealed, and as Questier and Lake have emphasized in their later work, any "scene" in the public conversion drama was open to a virtually infinite range of pressures, slippages, and redirections by individual and collective "players." Foucault's theatrical conceit was in fact far more rhetorically and phenomenologically apt than he himself seemed willing to recognize in (English) historical evidence. Like any live show, gallows conversion was a highly mediated but uncertain event. It relied on interactive physical timing and imaginative cooperation without any guarantee of semiotic stability or repeatability as a cultural script. To a degree far greater than hitherto recognized, sixteenth- and seventeenth-century printed news about women murderers made such contingency increasingly visible. It could not avoid raising doubts about state conversion and punishment both as public rituals for asserting iconic differences between the governing elite and its subjects, and as symbolic representations of divine justice.

FAUX CONVERSION

If prison visitors sometimes used offers of sacramental reconciliation or other spiritual benefits to induce or trick prisoners into confessing, with a possible loss of integrity for some readers, women and men charged with murder could use a show of contrite behavior to try to persuade officials to grant their requests for mercy. Like many wives convicted of murdering their violent husbands, Sarah Elstone displayed deep repentance for her past shortcomings as a wife, even though she denied any wilful intent to murder her husband. She chose to dress in white at her execution, where she publicly reiterated distinctions between her moral and legal culpability. Her gallows performance represented a final effort to convince public authorities to delay or mitigate her punishment on the grounds that she was demonstrably not a reprobate criminal. The nonclerical reporter of *The Last Dying Speeches, Confession, and Execution of . . . Mary Williamson . . . Executed at Tyburn, the 5th. of March, 1684* presumably had no professional stake in the conversion process and therefore contrasted the practical uses felons made of it to obtain reprieves or pardons, albeit in these cases for felonies other than murder. Among the twelve persons condemned at these assizes, eight succeeded in obtaining clemency and four were executed. One convict, Edward Conyers, represented the fortunate majority. He made a point of appearing strenuously sorrowful after his trial and was rewarded with a pardon just before his execution. Another prisoner, John Stokes, remained obstinate after sentencing and was denied a pardon; he became receptive to repentance only after his petition had been turned down. A woman named Mary Williamson, convicted for grand larceny and named on the pamphlet's title page, was singled out as an example of how not to go about obtaining a pardon. She rebuffed visitors' efforts to persuade her to confess or convert, first trying unsuccessfully to plead her belly. She then begged for mercy, but not the right kind, since she remained "very desirous to Live, and earnestly praying for Pardon, more temporal" than spiritual. On the gallows she pleaded a final time for mercy, but denied the charges on which she had been convicted. She also allegedly appeared self-righteous, forgiving those people who had testified against her and refusing to make "any publick speech to the People, as also to Joyn in singing the Psalm to the last" (A2r).

Hope of reprieves or pardons created an alternative dramatic scenario that competed with the utter closure of gallows conversion—expectant comedy, as it were, versus tragedy. The latter was premised on the subject abandoning this life to clear a pain-free path to heaven, while the former was an imaginative investment in procrastination and, in some cases, dissembling. As Peter Lake observed

> There must be no prospect of pardon . . . or else the condemned would remain in the thrall of this world, rendered unable to confront the enormity and consequences of his or her own sin by lingering hopes of reprieve. Only when death was finally certain would felons really and finally confront the extremity of their spiritual condition . . . and throw themselves on the mercy and grace of God.[98]

These tensions were related to wider debates about proper degrees of separation or collaboration between civil magistrates and clerics, and the hierarchical priority of powers and jurisdictions—divine, natural, and monarchical.[99] When Jane Hattersley was charged with killing several of the children she had had with her long-time married lover Adam Adamson, he provided for her material welfare in prison and encouraged her to deny the charges in hope of obtaining a royal pardon (and of deflecting attention away from his own complicity, which seems to have been successful as he was not charged as an accessory). Hattersley accordingly rejected authorities' efforts to persuade her to confess or convert all the way to her execution in the (ultimately mistaken) belief that a pardon would arrive to save her (Brewer, *The Bloudy Mother* [1610]).[100] When Elizabeth Tymon was charged with murdering her daughter-in-law in 1684, the jury acquitted her of murder but found her of guilty of manslaughter; her fate was execution all the same because women could not claim benefit of clergy for manslaughter. Then on the night before she was to be executed, she received a reprieve that was probably tantamount to clemency (*A True Account of the Proceedings on the Crown-Side at this Lent Assize Held for the County of Surrey . . . on Thursday the 13th of March, 1683* [1684]); *The Last Dying Speeches, Confession, and Execution of Rice Evans . . . The 19th of March 1683/4* [1684]; both published by George Croom).

Visitors knew that their professional interests could be threatened by friends or relations working to obtain reprieves. To return for a moment to

Hell Open'd, John Quick complained that resistance to confession based on the possibility of climactic pardons put unwelcome pressure on officiating clergy to achieve last-minute breakthroughs in shattering the condemned felon's resolve and pushing her towards reimagining the approaching death as a spiritual rebirth (*Hell Open'd*, E5r, E8v–F1v). Spectators and news readers were equally aware that reprieves or pardons could arrive suddenly. If the prisoner continued to deny the verdict or if the trial had caused local debate or controversy, expectations of a dramatic reversal tended to swell crowds hoping to see what might happen, thereby creating an atmosphere of suspense that could distract civic and clerical officials. Quick explained that one of the reasons spectators numbering 10 to 20,000 came to watch the execution of Philippa Cary and Anne Evans was that the people of Plymouth had sharply divided opinions about their guilt. While most allegedly viewed the women as "Monsters," some strongly defended them. The imaginative investment by individual citizens in hearing, arguing, and possibly reading about the trial in topical ballads (none now extant) heightened the public's desire to participate directly in affirming the final outcome or witnessing silently or tactically against it.

THE WANING OF CONVERSION

As the regular publication of assize-trial reports and competitive journalism began to challenge the dominance of the single-authored news pamphlet from the 1670s onward, stories of partial repentance or resistance to confession by condemned felons increased and tended to be recounted at face value by nonclerical reporters. By contrast, sermon and execution narratives by salaried ordinaries of Newgate such as Samuel Smith became rhetorically fossilized as state propaganda and/or didactic publications for personal profit. Publisher David Mallet's account of Margaret Spicer's trial and gallows behavior in 1677 was typical of the greater neutrality marking regular assize and execution reports after the Restoration. *The Confession and Execution Of the Seven Prisoners suffering at Tyburn On Fryday the 4th of May, 1677* followed the London and Middlesex sessions for 25 to 26 April. Spicer killed her newborn child and hid it in her bed for some time before it was discovered. At her trial she denied the murder, and "she persisted in that negative to Master Ordinary and other Ministers since she received Sentence, alleadging that [her child] was Still-born; or at least, contracted its death as soon as ever it saluted the light, by an accidental fall" (A2v). The anonymous reporter reminded readers that the infanticide statute of 1624 obliged women to call for help if they went into labor alone. Spicer not having done so, the court concluded she had killed her child. She was executed at Tyburn after the usual prayers but, like others executed with her, "without any considerable or remarkable Speeches" (A4v).

Such statements began to appear more often in Restoration news sheets, implying that visitors' attempts to persuade condemned felons to perform their conversions had failed, thereby weakening the impression of ritual closure and leaving readers to wonder about the condemned woman's guilt and the fairness of her trial. Two accounts that reveal a discursive battle to persuade public opinion about the truth of prisoners' behavior related to the controversial robbery and murder of John Talbot in 1669. He was an Essex minister who had fled to London to avoid being sued by some of his parishioners. He was pursued there and set on—apparently unrelatedly—by four to six men and one woman, Sarah Swift, whom Talbot was alleged to have met previously for a sexual encounter. His attackers cut his throat and robbed him. Two of them, Eaton and Swift, hid in a garden before being discovered by bricklayers who had returned to cover their bricks during a shower. Talbot survived long enough to identify several of the men and deny ever seeing Swift or the men before. *An Exact Narrative of the Bloody Murder, and Robbery Committed, By Stephen Eaton, Sarah Swift . . . upon the Person of Mr. John Talbot* (1669) reported that several persons tried for this crime as well as others condemned at the same assizes were "much wrought upon while they were in *Newgate*" and "died very cheerfully," including two unnamed women (probably not Swift; see below). Others "seemed not at all concerned, though they had not many minutes to live" (B1v–B2r). The mixed results of the clergy's efforts were highly visible, because along the way as the execution procession passed

> the streets were thronged with Spectators, and at *Tyburn* they were in such numbers that the Carts could not get up to the place of Execution, the Prisoners being led thither on foot, where being placed in Carts, Mr. *Partridge* a Minister made an Exhortation to them, and [other ministers] prayed with them. (B1v)

Partly owing to the prisoners' unsatisfactory responses and persistent rumors of Talbot's assignation with Swift, a second thirty-eight page pamphlet was issued immediately afterwards by a different but unnamed printer. *A Perfect Narrative of the Robbery and Murder Vpon the Person of Mr. John Talbot* (1669) sought to defend the visitors' efforts, refute allegations of Talbot's impropriety, correct the "notorious mistakes and falsities" of other printed accounts (i.e., *An Exact Narrative*), and defend the court's judgment in a murder that had aroused spirited public debate. Partly anticipating the format of court transcriptions used by Roger L'Estrange in *A Hellish Murder* (1688; see chapter 2), *A Perfect Narrative* sought to impose interpretive closure by selectively reproducing written testimonies from Talbot, constables, witnesses, and a coroner (but not indictments, the coroner's inquest, or court documents that might otherwise have suggested the pamphlet's authorship by a legal official). The co-ordinating author, almost certainly one of the visitors, countered rumors that Talbot "had been naught with

Sarah Swift; and so by that means was surprized with her, and fell into the hand of his barbarous and bloody enemies" (D1v) by describing Swift as "so pitiful a scrubbed, lowsie creature, that I think it should have loathed [Talbot] or any man to come near to her" (D2r). The author also claimed she had stated "she would burn in hell before she would confess anything" (D4v). An "*Attestation of the Ordnarie [sic] of Newgate*" by Henry Gerrard appeared towards the end declaring that, despite efforts by him and his colleagues to persuade the resistant prisoners, "they would confess nothing of [the murder]," and therefore they made no effort to convert them at the gallows, simply reciting formal prayers instead (E2r). The author concluded by praising the magistrates, church-Wardens, constables, physicians, and surgeons who cared for Talbot.

Similar ambiguities marked the ending of *A Full and True Account Of A Most Barbarous and Bloody Murther, Committed By Esther Ives . . . on the Body of William Ives, her Husband* (1686). Noyse reportedly made conventional visitor-induced scaffold speeches against sabbath-breaking, drunkenness, and lust. However Ives (or Ivyleafe[101]) said virtually nothing before being strangled and burnt, and the comparison with Noyse, as in earlier accounts of felonious duos, suggested the woman's rejection of co-operation with authorities. The anonymous reporter of Mary Goodenough's execution at six in the morning on Monday 7 March 1692 stated that "she said, or did little there but dy'd; only beg'd of the People to be warn'd against her Sins, by her shameful and untimely End" (Mr Birch [?], *Fair Warning to Murderers of Infants*, B1r). Any reader familiar with late-seventeenth century murder news would recognize these claims as utterly conventional and possibly suspect. The author of *Fair Warning* might have decided to include these glimpses of inconsistent outcomes because of what Tyburn spectators had actually witnessed, and because it had another document attesting to Goodenough's godly contrition to offer readers: a letter of moral advice to her children, "Sign'd by her own Hand the Night before she was Executed" (title page). This letter was demonstrably written by the prison visitor who attended her.[102] In the context of growing public awareness of, or skepticism about, clerical, civic, and commercial interests involved in publishing exemplary conversions, nongodly or independently minded readers could have reinterpreted *Fair Warning* to understand that Goodenough had managed to speak a few formulaic phrases supplied by the minister. He went on to admit as much by acknowledging that she "seem[ed] never to have had any great Faculty or Freedom of Speech" (B1r).

More detached approaches by writers who were not professional visitors were also becoming apparent in reports such as *Horrid News from St. Martins: or, Vnheard-of Murder and Poyson* (1677), a pre-execution account published by David Mallet. The anonymous writer appealed to a broad, nonsectarian readership by declaring that, although murder-news preambles—often in the form of little homilies—were usually dispensable as "the Excrescencie of a Pamphlet," in this case one was needed because "the

matter being so very strange and impresidented as requires some prepara-
tory Address to recommend it to the sober Readers belief" (A2r). The preamble offered a personally contextualizing account that must have emerged
after the suspect's trial and conviction. It told of how several years earlier
she had poisoned a fellow maidservant "that was sick of the Small-pox, and
afterwards gave some of the same [ratsbane] to her own Mother" (A3v).
Asked why she should want to murder her mother, her reply was not clear,
but the gist was that "she was very sickly and troublesome, and she did it
to be rid of her: and some such sorry reason she gave for poysoning the
Maid" (A3v). Although not actively sympathetic to the girl, this relatively
restrained account allowed readers to draw their own conclusions about the
deaths, possibly as some confused form of mercy-killing and/or as evidence
that the girl was mentally unstable.

Varied reports of Joan Peterson, a herbalist and physician convicted in
1652 of using witchcraft to murder her mistress, revealed how the absence
of exemplary confession reports might indicate that public controversy had
dominated a trial. It also showed how the outcome of a contrasting case
might be used to defend the Crown's arguments. The anonymous author of
The Witch of Wapping (1652) said nothing about Peterson's posttrial behavior, even though most of the pamphlet presented a damning account of her
life and alleged crimes, which would lead one to expect that he would have
pressed his advantage if she had converted. A second source, however, stated
that Peterson strenuously denied the charges and remained unrepentant after
her contentious trial and conviction (*The Tryall and Examination of Mrs.
Joan Peterson . . . for her supposed Witchcraft , and poysoning of the Lady
Powel at Chelsey* [1652]). When urged at the gallows to show some sign of
contrition, Bernard Alsop's *A Perfect Account of The daily Intelligence* also
reported that she still refused, saying "she had confessed before the honourable Bench, as much as she would acknowledge" (Number 67, April 7–14).
In the context of these opposing reports, *The Witch of Wapping*'s omission
of Peterson's refusal to confess looks strategic, as does its decision to include
a brief and much less lively report about Prudence Lee, who was condemned
at the same assize for stabbing her husband after she discovered him with
a lover in a nearby alehouse. *The Witch of Wapping* summarized Lee's formulaic confession of her past sins and jealous outbursts of violence as well
as her warnings to female spectators and pious expressions before the pyre
was lit. The author seems to have included this report of Lee's correct but
undistinguished gallows performance to fill the void created by Peterson's
lack of co-operation.

Greater realism among Restoration news writers led to questions about
the absolute deterrent value of publishing crime news. Notwithstanding the tentative conversions wrought upon Langworth and Stoaks, the
visitor-writer of *A True Account of the Behaviour, Confessions, and Last
Dying Words, Of . . . Jane Langworth, and Elizabeth Stoaks* (1684, published by R. Turner) candidly admitted:

Strange it is, that the Fatal and untimely Ends of such as suffer for Crimes Notorious, should not deter others from running into the like Extravagances thereby, to reender [*sic*] themselves obnoxious to the to the [*sic*] Law; or that the expiring Confessions of such as have made their Exits by untimely Death, should not be a sufficient Warning. (A1r)

With the traditional rationales for criminal deterrence and conversion faltering, the writer justified the continuing publication of yet another execution report with a "softer" argument: that it publicized normative moral and behavioral boundaries. His honesty about the limited repentance of condemned prisoners indicated that he anticipated readers would judge the truth value or impartiality of his report based on their comparative knowledge of earlier news stories. The implication was also that trial and gallows news continued to serve the professional and commercial interests of prison visitors and publishers but now needed to be marketed with more self-aware approaches, including a progressive sense of journalistic objectivity.

As their intertextual resonances with the sixteenth-century culture of martyrdom grew more distant, idealized conversion stories strained the credulity of independently minded news readers. Educated laymen and women were also growing more critical of providentialist rhetoric, whose legitimacy had always been in the eye of the beholder.[103] Certain writers and publishers were eager to capitalize on the greater skepticism (if not cynicism) of newsreaders, with the pieties of evangelical conversion becoming a commercial liability for some classes of potential buyers and a satirical butt for others.[104] Changing attitudes are evident in two reports in 1684 about Elizabeth Ridgeway, a "religious Maid" and serial poisoner. Her last victim was her husband William, to whom she served mercury-laced broth two weeks after they had been married against her will by her father. At her trial she pleaded not guilty, and the jury was divided in its decision, ultimately recommending a reprieve. The judge overruled their recommendation, however, and sentenced her to death. Perhaps as a result of these controversies and the lingering hope of an extra-judicial pardon, Ridgeway resisted confessing anything until the day of her execution, and she refused to co-operate in displaying any signs of repentance. All this was narrated in mostly factual but sometimes amused tones by the writer of *A True Relation Of Four most Barbarous and Cruel Murders Committed in Leicester-shire by Elizabeth Ridgway* (1684). He was a journalist employed by the prominent London crime publisher George Croom.[105] At the end of his pamphlet he focused attention on Ridgeway's combative response to two divines' offers to assist her at the gallows. She told them "she could Read and Pray as well as they could. Neither would she add any thing more at the Stake, or repeat what she had before confess'd; telling the People she had made a Confession before she came out" (A4r).

In the face of Ridgeway's recalcitrance, one of the attending divines (who had probably been appointed by the mayor of Leicester) issued an alternative version of events. John Newton's *The Penitent Recognition of Joseph's Brethren: A Sermon Occasion'd by Elizabeth Ridgeway* (1684, published by Richard Chiswel) added circumstantial details to her life story but remained defensive about the trial's outcome and his own failure to convert her. Putting his professional credit to the fore, Newton claimed that Ridgeway partially confessed details of the previous poisonings after several visits to her in prison. She allegedly revealed further information after hearing a sermon he delivered on the Sunday before her execution, finally admitting to killing her husband. Newton was aware that arguments in Ridgeway's defense had circulated publicly. So he could only present readers with a response of wondering incredulity at her lack of co-operation: "All this obstinacy and reservedness amazed me" (B4r). He apologized to readers for giving what he called an uncertain and contradictory account—by which he seems to mean its lack of a familiar conversion plot rather than factual opacity—but asserted it was sufficient to vindicate the presiding assize judge and refute local claims that Ridgeway had been treated unfairly. Newton's persistent anxieties about the lack of legitimate moral and legal closure are evident in his decision to omit an account of her execution and substitute a sermon exhorting parents and children to obedience.

These two pamphlets demonstrated that rival clerical and secular accounts of the same trial or execution, as well as competition amongst reporters and publishers with different implied readerships, could lead to open contradictions about whether a condemned person had been justly tried or legitimately converted, and cast skeptical glances back to their alleged lives. This potential scrutiny compelled later seventeenth-century accounts to became more transparent about what the condemned person actually said on the gallows ladder, and what was spoken on her behalf by attendant clerics—a distinction many earlier writer writers fictionalized or edited. Despite their proselytizing aims, the visitors Partridge and Sharpe felt obliged to tell readers that Mary Cook expressed "a mixture of fear and hope" at her execution in 1670 (*Blood for Blood*, C6r). Mounting the ladder and being prompted to make her rehearsed speech, Cook, "wanting strength," was unable to do so. She allegedly signalled to them to speak on her behalf, which cued Partridge and Sharpe to substitute their own infinitely more controlled words. They did not seem to think this ventriloquism would belittle the conversion event or its edifying message to readers; their rationale seemed to be that reporting Cook's silences honestly would enhance the event's credibility and the pamphlet's moral truths. In 1692, however, to return to Mary Goodenough's story, the writer acknowledged that the cultural memory of wonderful gallows-conversions had become discredited. Resignedly, he explained Goodenough's failure to make an even passable conversion as the natural reaction to the shock of being criminalized:

And indeed, without a Miracle almost, it could not be expected she should say much [than she did at her execution]; for she must needs by in great Confusion and Surprize, who in less *than Two Months time*, was Committed, Try'd, Condemn'd and Executed for her Crime. (B1r, original italics)

* * * * *

In this chapter I have explored the development of early modern gallows conversion as a social and represented practice in the light of women or men who denied charges against them, disputed the court verdict, or responded to visitors' agendas with reactions ranging from less than full co-operation to outright resistance. The live theatrics of gallows conversion were continuously open to evasion or disruption. Spectators and readers could interpret the news stories that preceded and followed these events in ways that challenged prosecution viewpoints or the career and commercial interests aligned with them. Gender differentiated or locally particularized accounts fed alternative opinions of individual convicts and loosened moral and legal concepts of homicide. Just as spectators responded in multiple ways to the volatile theater of state punishment, so they formed independent judgments about the motives and circumstances of individual women. The chapters that follow will examine further cases and also return to some of the ones discussed above in greater detail. Chapter four on poison will show how even the most unmitigable form of homicide was open to public debate and equitable re-interpretation by early modern news buyers.

4 Women and Poison

Murder by poison provided early modern English readers with some of the most gruesome news of deadly crimes. Although reported more intermittently than other forms of homicide, accounts of the effect of arsenic or mercury on victims' agonized bodies aggravated popular assumptions about female cruelty in passionate conflicts. While some writers could be partially sympathetic to women's motives, as Henry Goodcole's story of the unnamed wife in *The Adultresses Funerall Day* (1635) demonstrated,[1] juries and judges were less equivocal: indictments for homicide by poisoning were rarely turned back, and convictions almost never mitigated or reprieved because the felony by definition was premeditated.[2] From the viewpoint of the criminal law, poisoning was a form of murder least amenable to equitable discretion or flexibility.

What kind of cultural work, then, in terms of equity, did news of poisoning homicides do? Setting aside legal outcomes, the publication and reception of such news showed that practices of differential reading and interpretation did not fail to generate vigorous public debate about certain defendants' motives. Perspectives often diverged because of contextually related associations. The alignment of poisoners or victims with nonconforming religious beliefs, for example, could lead to varied explanations of guilt. The usual medium for poison was food, and common ideas about what constituted healthful food and physic were intertwined with ambiguous uses of herbal and mineral poisons. These uncertain practices made alleged murders open to arguments about the causes of death and suspects' precise intentions. Cookery and household physic were women's domains in this period, but they involved wider economic, gender, and domestic-service relationships, as well as contentious theories of female conduct and moral responsibility. As in other forms of homicide, circumstantial factors shaped alternative versions of the event among interested parties and officials, and competitive journalism exploited these divergences profitably. Beyond assize trials, this range of contexts led some readers to resist reducing defendants' motives to simple premeditation or atavistic female impulses.

In certain respects, moreover, murder by poison was more open to equitable re-assessments than other forms of homicide. The unique chemical and physiological aspects of killing by poison attracted reader interest in an age when scientific knowledge in these areas was expanding rapidly. (The same holds true for disputed cases of newborn child murder, as we shall see in the next chapter.) As early modern homicide news moved away from moral didacticism towards more material and secular forms of criminal analysis and trial-reporting, and as coroners' duties became professionalized, physical evidence of poisoning became subject to skeptical and/or scientific appraisal that often clashed with long-standing legal and moral verities. So although popular accounts of female poisoners remained heavily weighted towards prosecution frameworks and traditionally gendered attitudes, increasingly they also reflected new standards of forensic enquiry, and were evaluated according to the same standards of narrative consistency, ethical fairness, and public order that prompted early modern readers' diverse responses to other forms of homicide news.

"A WILD ANIMAL EVEN MORE POLLUTED THAN AN ASP IS THE WOMAN WHO DABBLES IN POISONS." (AELIAN[3])

Motives for poisoning spanned the same range of conflicts and emotions as other forms of murder. Most often it was used to get rid of an undesired spouse in an age when divorce was impossible and legal separation, particularly for women, was difficult.[4] For these and other reasons to be explored in this chapter, such as the contagious associations between poison and women's knowledge of food, medicine, cosmetics, and witchcraft, it was widely believed that female killers turned to poison more readily than men. T. I.'s *A World of wonders. A Masse of Murthers. A Covie of Cosonages* (1595) implied that the history of murder in England began with female poisoners. It opened with a brief account of the legendary king Bithricus, poisoned by his wife (F1r). Reginald Scot's widely read treatise *The Discouerie of witchcraft* (1584), while critical of popular views on the subject, otherwise expressed the unremarkable claim "That women haue vsed poisoning in all ages more than men."[5] Popular news continually reproduced these assumptions even though they were contradicted by some of period's most high profile poisoning conspiracies by men.[6] The stereotype of the woman homicide poisoner was also later belied by eighteenth- and nineteenth-century statistics showing poisoning homicides to be evenly divided by gender.[7]

In her study of seventeenth-century Cheshire homicide records, Garthine Walker observes that poison was the method alleged to have been used by women in eight out of twelve cases involving adults, whereas nine of 161 men charged with homicide were suspected of poisoning. In the male cases this included mitigated forms of murder (e.g., manslaughter) from which women were virtually excluded. If only cases of wilful murder are counted, the percentage of women and men who used poison was 31% and 17%.[8] Furthermore, there were methods of murder that women never used but men did (e.g., sword, cudgel, tool). By comparing women's use of poison with equivalent male cases, "the gender differential all but disappears," Walker concludes. Although poisoning was one of the nonconfrontational methods of killing preferred by women, it was "less an *a priori* feminine method of killing . . . [than] the mark of lethal and treacherous intimacy, the most extreme violation of domestic order."[9]

Actual cases of poisoning homicide were physically complicated by the fact that individual reactions to poison varied enormously and treatments were uncertain. Correctly judging a fatal dosage was difficult and often proceeded by trial and error, as the repeated efforts of Frances Howard and Anne Turner to poison Thomas Overbury in 1613 demonstrated (see below). Details of antidotes used to counter the effects of poison that often appeared in early modern news seemed partly intended to inform the public about what to do if faced with similar situations. Neighbors administered "Sack and Oyl" to William Weeks and his household in 1676, for instance, after Phillippa Cary had allegedly poisoned them with yellow arsenic (Diarsenic trisulfide, As_2S_3). The remedy worked for most of the family but unfortunately not for Mrs. Weeks and her daughter-in-law (*Hell Open'd* [1676]).

Poisoning symptoms could also be temporarily overlooked (and presumably sometimes go permanently undetected, making it one area of unrecorded crime[10]). They could be innocently confused with the presence of prior illness, or defensively refuted by such linkages, as Gilbert Dugdale tried to do in the case of the little girl who died after eating Elizabeth Caldwell's poisoned oatcakes (see chapter 2, p. 50). Garthine Walker observes in her analysis of Chester records that in none of the cases of poisoning homicide was the body examined beforehand by a coroner. The deaths were not initially believed to be unnatural. And because many poisonings were not discovered or revealed until long after the death, they were often tried after equally lengthy intervals. This made gathering evidence for successful prosecutions more difficult, and it allowed time for *post-facto* evidence of the defendant's good conduct and credit to be established that might challenge her alleged criminality, thus more making juries more open to dismissals or acquittals.[11] As in most cases of suspected female homicide not resulting in guilty verdicts, these were rarely reported by early modern news.

Alternatively, poisoning could easily be mistaken for other kinds of gastrointestinal illnesses. When Elizabeth Powle tried to poison her brother-in-law Hugh and his twelve-year-old son in 1662, she served them milk spiked with a large dose of ratsbane (arsenic trioxide, As_2O_3) after they had returned for refreshment from plowing. The tainted milk produced a "high distemper," which Hugh Powle tried to alleviate by drinking "twice very plentifully" and his son attempted to expel by riding hard "up and down the fields."[12] When these methods failed, friends sent to Hereford for a doctor. Although he diagnosed the symptoms as poisoning, he initially had difficulty persuading his patients that this was the cause of their illness, "so insensible were these poor innocent creatures of the mischief" in the trusting context of their own home and the care of their sister-in-law and aunt. The boy died four days later. This pretrial report's only explanation for Mrs. Powle's actions was that she was a Quaker.

"PHYSICAL" POISON

Poisons doubled as medicine in early modern households. Mercury compounds were used as laxatives, treatments for syphilis, and contraceptives.[13] White arsenic (arsenic trioxide) was introduced into twelfth-century Europe as a treatment for "tertiary fever" and became widespread.[14] Because it was soluble, virtually tasteless, and odorless, it was also an apt poison. Women were aware that such minerals could have beneficial or destructive effects because of the integration of early modern medical and culinary knowledge for care of the Galenic humoral body, which required continual balancing through ingestion, purging, and cleansing.[15] Manuscript and printed books of housewifery freely mingled cookery and "physical" receipts,[16] some of which called for potential poisons. Gervase Markham's first chapter on physic and surgery in *The English Housewife* (1615) included treatments for "the itch" (i.e., scabies) and "the French or Spanish pox" that employed white mercury, or mercury sublimate, and quicksilver respectively.[17] Sir Hugh Plat's *The Jewel House of Art and Nature ... with Sundry New Experiments in the Art of Husbandry, Distillation, and Moulding* (1594) preceded and added receipts to his equally popular *Delightes for Ladies* (1602). *The Jewel House* was later edited by a D. B., who from 1653 onwards added an appendix, *A rare and excellent Discourse of Minerals, Stones, Gums and Resins; with the vertues and use thereof*. He began with quicksilver, describing it as

> a cold poison, yet being prepared according to Art, it is of Soueraign use in Physick, and sometimes it is giuen in its natural body, an ounce and a half, or 2 ounces at a time, inwardly, for a stoppage of the guts, and some take it in milk to kill worms, but let them be sure that the quantity giuen be ponderous enough to make its way clean through the body (*The Jewel House of Art and Nature* [1653], Ff1r).

However, the domestic expertise and cultural authority ceded to women as medical and food providers generated anxieties about unauthorized combinations of domestic and "secret" knowledge. This epistemological promiscuity was reflected structurally in the heterogeneous authorship and categories of traditional receipt books themselves.[18] In his chapter's opening remarks, Markham attempted to restrict female medical education to "approved medicines," "old doctrines," and elementary practices using common herbal and household substances: "Indeed we must confess that the depth and secrets of this most excellent art of physic is far beyond the capacity of the most skilful woman, as lodging only in the breast of the learned professors" (8). Yet later in the chapter his credit as a well-informed author evidently obliged him to publish the mercury-based receipts mentioned above as well as others requiring mineral compounds available only through apothecaries and dependant on specialized knowledge of their hidden "virtues."[19] Poisons such as mercury and arsenic were purchasable in many affordable forms, and their sales were not legally restricted until 1851. As Lynnette Hunter has demonstrated, fears of women (mis-)practising medicine, including the use of chemical-based receipts, prompted a gradual separation of such "deep" physic from cookery, with the former increasingly being cordoned off as the exclusive domain of male professionals.[20]

Popular news accounts mirrored the same cultural reflex wherein traditional knowledge of cookery, physic, herbal remedies, and/or white magic cultivated by daughters, mothers, servants, and cunning-women could quickly turn into accusations of poisoning and witchcraft in suspicious contexts. John Quick and the witnesses whose testimony he recorded in *Hell Open'd* (1676) used such associations against Anne Evans when she was reported to have found Philippa Cary's poison "among the Marygolds" as she gathered herbs in the garden. Henry Goodcole declared in his "Short Tract Vpon The *hainousnesse of Poysoning*" that poison was often administered secretly "under the shadow of some Physicke, or other medicine, colored with an outward shew of an honest intent" (*The Adultresses Funerall Day*, B3v). A patient's death could supply a pretext for charges of murder or witchcraft against women who were disliked or feared in the community, as the account of Elizabeth Sawyer demonstrated (*The wonderfull discouerie of Elizabeth Sawyer* [1621]). Because women were primary health care providers or physicians in early modern England, especially in rural areas, they were at greater risk of being accused of murder if a patient died in unexpected or suspicious circumstances. As Goodcole further observed in his "Short Tract," the Latin word for poison and witchcraft, dating back to ancient Rome, was the same: *veneficium* (A2r). Semantically it was associated with a Latin synonym, *maleficium*. Since early modern legal indictments were written mainly in Latin, a woman formally charged with poisoning was in some sense simultaneously defending herself against witchcraft.

Joan Peterson's trial in 1652 illustrated these kinds of semiotic and cultural slippages while also showing how the commonly presumed link between poisoning and female physicians could be strongly—if in this case ultimately unsuccessfully—contested. Peterson's identity as a witch was publicized by several news reports after she was charged with killing her patient by poison. Besides two brief newspaper entries,[21] the main representation of this view appeared in *The Witch of Wapping* (1652). It was published after Peterson's trial and conviction on 11 April but possibly before her execution at Tyburn. Like other cases linking murder, poisoning, and witchcraft, this report relied heavily on hearsay from neighbors who disliked Peterson and read into her behavior diabolical motives. *The Witch of Wapping* may have been deliberately published in opposition to a more skeptical and sympathetic pamphlet published the day after Peterson's examination and indictment before a grand jury on 8 April: *The Tryall and Examination of Mrs. Joan Peterson . . . for her supposed Witchcraft , and poysoning of the Lady Powel at Chelsey* (1652). As a report of a grand jury trial, *The Tryall and Examination* is rare among crime news. Its publication attested to the controversial nature of the charges against Peterson, and is probably also attributable to her gentle status. The reporter described her as a "practitioner in Physick" who was charged for conspiring with another gentlewoman "to administer a potion, or posset" to Lady Powel, who died shortly afterwards. Peterson denied any malicious intent or dealings in witchcraft, claiming that she had only given the 80-year-old woman "what was comfortable and nourishing" (A4v). Many people believed Peterson, opining that the elderly Lady Powel had died from natural causes, but others disagreed. The grand jury trial lasted most of the day—highly unusual—as "very many Witnesses, of good reputation, [were] examined on both sides." Tantalizingly, the reporter promised readers a further account of the testimony in the *Faithfull Scout* the following Friday. Unfortunately neither this nor later reports about this case have apparently survived, and we must assume that Peterson was executed after her sentencing on 11 April.

Murder or assassination by poison had particular legal antecedents in England as a political crime. It had been declared high treason by Henry VIII in 1530 after a cook in the bishop of Rochester's household named Richard Roose poisoned a batch of gruel. Roose's punishment—boiling to death in oil—answered the inversion of both domestic and patriarchal authority.[22] The statute remained in force only until 1547 before poison was reclassified as homicide. But it left conceptual traces of *lèse-majesté* that influenced the cultural construction of murder-by-poison for decades to come. T. I.'s second of three entries about women murderers before his discussion of the Saunders case in *A World of wonders* (1595) was Margaret Davie in the reign of Henry VIII, "a mayde seruant boyled in Smithfeeld for poysoning of three seruerall housholders with whome she had dwelled" (F1r–v). The third entry referred to Rebecca Clifford, executed by burning in 1571 for killing her husband (F1v). T. I.'s associations were publicly reinforced by several attempts to poison Elizabeth in the 1590s, including the notorious Lopez conspiracy in 1594, and later by the even more sensational murder of Sir Thomas Overbury in 1613.

A SACRED TRUST

Poison's early modern associations with female petty treason were also readily explained by its symbolic transgressions of social and gender boundaries in everyday domestic settings associated with maternal nourishment, safety, and comfort. Its potential for rewriting individual acts of female violence as manifestations of deviant maternity was closely related to wider assumptions about women's natural instincts and wifely duties within a well-ordered patriarchal family. During the Overbury trials, Sir Francis Bacon argued that poison violated rituals of the table that constituted family and community hierarchies, and it negated traditional obligations of hospitality that were widely (if increasingly nostalgically) celebrated in early modern England.[23] Gilbert Dugdale's pamphlet about the attempted murder of Thomas Caldwell, *A True Discourse* (1604), focused on both kinds of transgressions. Domestically, the main enabling figure of the conspiracy was a neighbor, Isabel Hall, "an ancient motherly woman" who seemed to project benevolent impulses. She became the perfect go-between for Elizabeth Caldwell and her lover, Jeffrey Bownd. Because Dugdale's larger aim was retroactively to validate the pardon that local gentry had tried unsuccessfully to obtain on Caldwell's behalf,[24] he downplayed her responsibility for the poisoning, deflecting it onto Bownd and Hall. Hall recommended disguising ratsbane in oatcakes because she knew that Thomas "much affected them." But Elizabeth allegedly neither bought the poison nor prepared the cakes nor actively served them. Bownd first purchased ratsbane in a nearby town and brought it to Elizabeth. Under the cover of exchanging culinary knowledge, Hall then sent to her for some of the "spice" and baked it into oatcakes that she sent to the Caldwell household as a present. Elizabeth set them in a bedchamber window before going to bed. The next morning Thomas noticed the cakes and asked if he could have some, to which Elizabeth cheerfully agreed. He shared several cakes with a little girl, who had been sent to their house for fire, as well as the extended Caldwell household, "children and all" (B1r–v).

Notwithstanding his deliberate sidestepping of Elizabeth's direct guilt, Dugdale did not try to shield her from responsibility for inverting the household hierarchy. Neglecting her wifely duties, Elizabeth remained in bed while her husband and the rest of their family rose to start the day's work. Her self-indulgence might have reminded readers of the sexual liaison with Bownd that partly motivated the murder. The reversal of domestic roles continued as Thomas took over Elizabeth's abandoned duty of feeding the household. Elizabeth's slackness and duplicity also betrayed the wider community, here extended to two dogs and a cat who died by eating Caldwell's vomit, as well as the neighboring girl. Dugdale raised doubts as to whether her death was caused by the poisoned cakes or a longstanding illness. But for readers focused on the poisoning homicide, this forensic ambiguity probably carried little weight, since Elizabeth's protective relationship with the sick girl had been double crossed by the polluted food and her repudiated duty of trust. The surviving Cheshire gaol book states that Elizabeth, Bownd, and Hall were examined on suspicion of committing "murdre omu[?] venem." Elizabeth and Bound were simply accused of homicide but Hall was charged with murder "for poysoninge a Childe." All three were tried and sentenced "for suspicion of murder by poyson."[25]

One indication of the power of cultural assumptions linking discontented women, petty treason, and poison was that allegations of poisoning were frequently made in female homicide cases in which it was not the actual or ultimate cause of death. In reconstructing narratives of domestic murder from the Crown's viewpoint, news writers assumed poison to be the first means of resort after a wife made the mental decision to get rid of her husband. It represented a stage of premeditated aggression that transformed the woman into a legally culpable subject even before her direct or deputed violence.

News accounts of the three most notorious murderesses of the sixteenth century—Alice Arden, Anne Saunders, and Eulalia Page—included claims of attempted poisoning as precursors to their homicides. Both Holinshed's *Chronicle* and *The Tragedy of Master Arden of Faversham* reported that Alice Arden turned unsuccessfully to poisoning after her hired killers Blackwill and Shakebag had bungled their initial attempts to murder her husband. The only surviving ballad account described Alice first trying poison immediately after she and her lover Mosby decided to kill Arden. All accounts reported that Alice or her servants failed to mix poison in food with enough subtlety to allow it to pass undetected. As the ballad put it:

> To London faire my Husband was to ride,
> But ere he went I poyson did prouide,
> Got of a Painter which I promised
> That Mosbies sister Susan he should wed.
> Into his Broth I then did put the same,
> He lik't it not when to the boord it came,
> Saying, There's something in it is not sound,
> At which inrag'd, I flung it on the ground.

(*[The] complaint and lamentation of Mistresse Arden [ca. 1633]*)

Broth was used as both food and physic; hence common allegations of poisoned broth against suspected women such as Margaret Ferneseede (1608), Frances Howard (1616), Elizabeth Ridgeway (1641), and Margaret Osgood (1680)—to cite four representative examples.

News writers included these incriminating scenarios in pretrial reports to influence jury decisions. Or they were retroactively projected onto past behavior after a woman had been tried and condemned to justify the capital verdict. In both cases, writers sought to construct a personal history of sinful deviance that would mark the murderess as constitutionally criminal and/or reprobate, rather than being merely a momentary offender.[26] Some convicted women recognized these implicating constructions. Although Anne Saunders was not linked to poison, her co-conspirator Anne Drewrie was rumored to have killed her late husband by that means. In her gallows speech Anne Drewrie admitted her guilt in the death of George Saunders but vehemently denied the charge of poisoning, as well as other posttrial accusations that she had practised witchcraft and fomented a jealous rift between the Earl of Derby and his wife (C2r–v). Arthur Golding does not contradict Drewrie's denials of these charges (which possibly provided further motives for official involvement by the Privy Council in the Saunders case). His silence suggested that the gravity of Drewrie's transition between life and death as well as her affective performance of repentance should have led readers to give these protestations the benefit of the doubt.

After Alice Arden and Anne Saunders, the third most notorious woman murderer of the late sixteenth century was Eulalia Page of Plymouth, who in 1591 conspired with her lover George Strangwidge to kill her husband after her parents had married her to Thomas Page over her strenuous objections. Her story was the subject of several ballads by Thomas Deloney as well as a play by Ben Jonson and Thomas Dekker performed at the Globe in August 1599, but now lost.[27] The ballads contained no murder details, but they did express sympathy for Mrs. Page's enforced marriage and her domestic resistance. Most information about the case derived from an anonymous pamphlet about this and another unrelated provincial crime: *Sundrye strange and inhumaine Murthers* (1591). Following her arrest and/or trial, Eulalia Page allegedly confessed that she had tried for more than a year to poison her husband in doses that proved to be too small to kill him. The pamphlet writer claimed he was saved by God's protection, "yet was he compelled to vomit blood and much corruption" and would in all likelihood have soon died had not Mrs. Page and her lover Strangwidge grown impatient and moved on to hiring killers (B2v). The writer does not explain why God stopped protecting Page, but he does hint that Eualia initially expressed dissatisfaction with her marriage by also killing, or creating circumstances leading to the fatally premature delivery, of two children she had had by him (B3r).

The chains of sin and transgression presented by *Sundrye strange and inhumaine Murthers* were typical of early modern murder news, as writers unified the crime's elliptical events within cohesive narratives of deviance and repentance. Such patterns transformed random acts of local violence into familiar plots with stereotypical characters and symbolic ornamentation borrowed from other genres.[28] Yet while this particular pamphlet pieced together Eulalia Page's use of poison and possible infanticide to magnify her criminal identity, the writer separated the two crime events causally. This dissociation was also characteristic of early modern news and hints at latent differences in attitude towards female poisoners and infanticides, and thus at their varying potential for equitable mitigation.[29] Mothers or other female caregivers intending to kill their children never use poison, even when they have ready means to do so. Newborn or small children are always killed by physical violence or fatal neglect, whereas poison is reserved exclusively for adults.

Henry Goodcole's account of Elizabeth Barnes in *Natures Cruell Step-Dames* (1637) raised the prospect of poisoning a child only to deflect it. According to Goodcole's reconstruction of Barnes's prison confession, she had fallen into debt after inheriting a small estate as a widow but wasting it on a lover who deserted her (A4r). Growing desperate and suicidal at the prospect of poverty and perhaps never marrying again, she was tormented for over a month with thoughts of killing her daughter. Finally she decided to use the pretense of going on a country picnic. After preparing "alluring junkets" such as "an Apple Pye, a Herring Pye, Raisins of the Sun, and other fruits" (A2r–v), Barnes and her daughter journeyed four miles from home on the last evening of the old calendar year, 24 March, into the fatefully named Wormwall Wood near Fulham. Given Goodcole's attention to Barnes's menu and the location, readers familiar with the literary and dramatic scenario of the fatal banquet might have expected a revelation about poisoned food. Yet "having eaten of such things formerly provided for it," Goodcole continues, the daughter fell asleep, and between the hours of eleven and twelve Barnes cut her throat.[30] Why did she not slip some poison into the food she had prepared? And why did Goodcole seem to lead readers in this direction by focusing detailed attention on the dishes? The effect in both cases was to present Barnes's actions in an ambiguous light. The carefully prepared picnic represented both a compassionate treat and a trap. As a form of culinary display, it masked a violation of the primary bond of nourishing and protective motherhood.[31] Barnes may have found it easier in this way to work herself up imaginatively into the role of a momentary child killer rather than passively watch her daughter suffer from poisoned food.

Whatever her reasons for avoiding poison, Barnes retained the physical and charismatic control of a mother over her young child. It was these powers, by contrast, that were absent in critical situations in which women poisoned their husbands, masters, or mistresses. Poison represented a unique opportunity for wives or servants under physical and legal authority to correct perceived abuses of power or debilitating dependency. The economic and class imbalances of such cases opened women's motives to equitable dispute among neighbors and friends of defendants, and subsequently readers, even if the law disallowed accused or convicted women any formal means of mitigation.

Extreme if not extenuating circumstances characterize many wives' resort to poison in popular news ballads and pamphlets. All three extant accounts of Eulalia Page, to return to her case for a moment, focus considerable attention on her lack of rights or equitable remedies in the face of patriarchal tyranny. The author of *Sundrye strange and inhumaine Murthers* emphasized her father's implacable dominance and greed, and made him morally responsible for his son-in-law's death.[32] Although Thomas Deloney's *The Lamentation of Mr. Pages Wife of Plimouth* sentimentalized the conflict as true love destroyed by mercenary parents and generational arrogance, Eulalia's disgust at being married off to the elderly Page created an

Natures
Cruell Step-Dames :
O R,
Matchleſſe Monſters of the Female
Sex; *Elizabeth Barnes*, and *Anne Willis*.
Who were executed the 26. day of *April*,
1637. at Tyburne, for the unnaturall murthe-
ring of their owne Children.

Alſo, herein is contained their ſeverall Confeſſions,
and the Courts juſt proceedings againſt other notorious
Malefactors, with their ſeverall offences
this Seſſions.

Further, a Relation of the wicked Life and
impenitent Death of *Iohn Flood*, who raped
his own Childe.

Printed at London for *Francis Coules*, dwelling in
the Old-Baily. 1637.

Figure 4.1 Natures Cruell Step-Dames (1637). Reproduced by permission of the
Folger Shakespeare Library.

individualized voice of distress: "Scant could I taste the meat whereon I fed, / My legs did loath to lodge within his bed." The vigor of Deloney's physical details strengthened the impression of personal advocacy for his subject and vivified his popular critique of early modern marriage negotiations. As modern scholars have shown, these practices were a contentious topic in conduct books about proper female behavior. The new Protestant ideal of companionate marriage challenged but largely failed to overturn the traditional power of parental decision-making in marriages and their paramount importance (at least among the nonindigent) as property transactions between families.[33] At the time Deloney's ballad was issued in 1609 (although his and other versions may have appeared before then), enforced marriage was being dramatized as a social tragedy in several plays, possibly including the lost one by Jonson and Dekker.[34]

The cultural power of the news trope of aggrieved wives resorting to poison was further illustrated by a telling slip in *The Adultresses Funerall Day*. Goodcole, who was well-acquainted with earlier crime news, states incorrectly that Eulalia Page killed her husband with poison rather than by hiring servants to do the deed (B1r). The author of *Sundrye strange and inhumaine Murthers* had suggested that Mrs. Page's use of poison was her initial reaction to the devil inspiring *her parents'* capricious decision to reject the previously highly favored Strangwidge. Satan, the writer says, "crept so farre into the dealinges of these persons, that he procured the parents to mislike of Strangewich." They insisted on the widowed Page, "one of the cheefest inhabitants of that town," not only for his wealth but also because Eulalia's father preferred her daughter to remain nearby rather than leaving for London with Strangwidge (B2r). Yet Goodcole suppressed or misremembered this version of events, defaulting instead to the conventional link between discontented wives and poison.

CARNIVAL POISON

The anonymous author of *The trueth of the most wicked and secret murthering of Iohn Brewen . . . committed by his owne wife* (1592) presented a more complex tale of poison to illustrate gender oppression and marital rebellion. This pamphlet is the lone survivor among six accounts (four ballads and two pamphlets) of the case recorded in the Stationers' Register within a month of the Page murder, on whose notoriety it probably aimed to capitalize with fresh news of a sensational crime.[35] The title page image of a woman dressed in a thin shift, hands half raised in an attitude of prayer, being dispassionately burned at a stake amid ferocious flames, drew readers' attention to the punishment for petty treason but also resembled better-known images of female martyrs from Foxe's *Actes and Monuments*, where this image in fact originally appeared.[36] Readers may also have noticed that the woman's neck was open and free. Ostensibly this indicated that she was not mercifully strangled before the fire was kindled, and was therefore guilty of a barbarically aggravated husband-murder. Yet neither the title page nor head title named Anne Welles. The head title repeated information about Brewen and Parker, but added that the former "was poysoned of his owne wife in eating a measse of sugar sops" (A2r). The anonymous writer focused Welles's transgression—although she is not yet named—on a wife's trusted role as a provider of food, and specifically the pollution of holiday dishes. "Sugar sops" or pancakes were tradition-ally served during Shrovetide, and the writer later confirms that the crime took place in this season. His title therefore anticipated Anne overreaching Carnival freedom in the form of lethal domestic sedition. Anne's transgres-sion of these still resonant (if increasingly evaded) cultural boundaries was also signalled by her feigned desire for herring rather than pancakes, a food that customarily defined Lenten self-discipline but here seems uncannily to denote an unconscious gesture of penitence for the murder she is going to commit.

Anne Welles was "a proper young woman" courted by two goldsmiths, Brewen and Parker.[37] Parker was not "in estate to marrie," presumably because he was still apprenticing, while Brewen was free to do so. Welles nonetheless rejected Brewen after a long suit and many presents of gold and jewels, which he then demanded back. When she refused, Brewen tried to blackmail her into marrying him. Welles was so alarmed at the prospect of being arrested that she submitted. She was reproached furiously by Parker, who had got her pregnant and pressured her to get rid of Brewen. Eventu-ally she agreed if Parker promised to marry her. She lay with Brewen only on their first night, refused to take his name, and lived independently in a house close to Parker's (A2v–A3r). She still cooked his meals, however, and tried using poison three days after they were married, but the dosage was too small and simply made him sick. In this section one recalls the pamphlet's initial avoidance of naming Welles. Although the writer or publisher could have identified her using her married name, they chose not to, and through-out the pamphlet she always is referred to by her natal name. They presum-ably intended this wilful identity to be understood as a sign of reprobate criminality, and Welles herself as an everywoman husband-killer, which the generic ambiguity of title page illustration reinforced. Unlike Eulalia Page, moreover, there were no parents or relations to share the blame; and despite Parker's control, Welles played a larger part in her own undoing. Yet if some readers recognized the Foxeian associations of martyrdom from the title page they might have read her actions more equitably as a form of social protest, in this case against being demeaned as the prize in an unseemly bid-ding war between two men. That some readers could have read her situation this way is indicated later in the pamphlet when the writer revealed that cer-tain neighbors did not object to Welles's behavior because they thought she was too young to know yet how to "behave . . . to her husband so kindly as she ought, which they imputed to her ignorance, rather than to any mallice

The trueth of the moſt wicked and ſecret murthering of Iohn Brewen, Goldſmith of London, committed by his owne wife,

through the prouocation ot one Iohn Parker
whom ſhe loued : for which faƈt ſhe was burned,
and he hanged in Smithfield, on wedneſday, the 28 of Iune, 1592. two yeares after the murther was committed.

Imprinted at London for Iohn Kid, and are to be ſold
by Edward White, dwelling at the little North doore
of Paules, at the ſigne of the Gun. 1592.

Figure 4.2 The trueth of the most wicked and secret murthering of Iohn Brewen
(1592). Reproduced by permission of Lambeth Palace Library.

conceaued against her husband" (A4r). The writer undercut this naturalistic explanation, however, by also claiming that these or other neighbors chose to believe her pregnancy was attributable to Brewen (A4r).

Parker bought strong poison for Welles, "whose working was to make speedy haste to the heart, without any swelling of the body" (A3r). The substance was probably mercury sublimate or chloride (HG_2Cl_2), which in some persons can cause death from heart failure and would be consistent with Brewen's symptoms (A3v).[38] While administering it in the sugar sops, she accidentally spilt the dish before serving them. She was quick-witted enough to send Brewen out on the pretense of craving some red herrings, which allowed her to ready another batch. After eating them Brewen began "to vomit exceedingly, with such straines as if his lungs would burst in peeces." He begged Welles to stay with him, but she returned to her own house, leaving him to a night of excruciating pain. Her desertion hardened the image of compassionless and unnatural femininity and thus drew the writer's harshest condemnation. These impressions seemed to be fortuitously (or providentially) confirmed by the fact that when she gave birth to the child that was assumed to be Brewen's, it did not survive.

When Welles returned next morning, Brewen reproached her for abandoning him but she feigned surprise at the gravity of his illness. He died that day and was buried with no-one suspecting what had happened. Parker began to abuse Welles physically for two years but refused to wed her, even after she again became pregnant. Presumably the pamphlet writer makes this domestic violence visible to suggest Welles was now reaping what she sowed; but it also highlighted her underlying manipulation by Parker and personal powerlessness from the beginning. During a fiery row dramatized in first-person dialogue, their hot reproaches were overheard by neighbors who reported them to magistrates. When Welles was examined, she confessed only after she was tricked into believing Parker had already done so. Her trial was put off until after she had given birth. She was condemned with Parker and they were executed at Smithfield on 28 June 1592.[39] Like the title page illustration of *The Adulteresses Funerall Day*, the site's associations with martyrdom possibly explain printer-publisher John Kid's recycling of a woodcut from Foxe. But here the image is not obviously incongruous and sends more ambiguous signals about Welles's criminal identity to buyers and readers.

"CAST OUT THOSE SEVEN DEVILS": THE OVERBURY MURDER TRIALS

The most infamous and widely publicized case of poisoning related to women's iconic roles as preparers of food and medicines occurred in the case of Sir Thomas Overbury, who died on 15 September 1613 after being repeatedly poisoned while he was imprisoned in the Tower. Overbury was

the powerful and widely disliked secretary of Robert Carr, Viscount Rochester and favorite of James I. He vehemently opposed the divorce of Frances
Howard from her husband the Earl of Essex after nurturing a love affair
between her and Carr. Like Eulalia Page, Howard had married Essex only
reluctantly under parental pressure, and like Anne Welles she refused to live
with him or consummate their marriage, partly because she was only fifteen when they were betrothed.[40] Overbury's opposition to her plans for
divorce and remarriage enraged Howard, who plotted to kill him after he
was imprisoned for refusing James's offer to lead an embassy to Moscow.
When the Lieutenant of the Tower Sir William Wood rebuffed Howard's
proposal to kill Overbury, she arranged to have Wood replaced with the
complacent Sir Gervase Elwes, and she had Richard Weston, a servant of
her confidante, fellow Roman Catholic, and dressmaker, Anne Turner (née
Norton), appointed to be Overbury's servant.[41] In hindsight Overbury's
death seems to have been caused by an incrementally debilitating sequence
of syphilis, legitimate remedies, poisoned food, fake medicines, and a lethal
enema.[42] During the sensational trials of Autumn 1615, beginning with that
of Weston, eyewitnesses and later readers learnt how Howard paid Turner,
Weston, and others to poison Overbury.[43] She was almost certainly acting
partly under Carr's direction.[44]

Overbury was poisoned three times before being finished off with the
enema. The means were homely. Howard first tried putting realgar or red
arsenic (tetraarsenic tetrasulfide, As_4S_4) in Overbury's broth. He became very
ill but recovered.[45] Overbury believed that by making this most recent illness appear more critical he might convince the Privy Council to release him
from the Tower. He therefore wrote to Carr asking for an emetic. With it,
Howard and Turner included some white arsenic (arsenic trioxide). Turner
had learnt about both medicines and poisons (partly?) from her husband,
who had been a fashionable physician, and she and Howard bought them
from a disgruntled apothecary named James Franklin. Initially he sold them
a "languishing" drug in aqua fortis (nitric acid) that they tested on an unfortunate cat. Dissatisfied with the results, they tried the white arsenic. After
five days of violent purging and unslakable thirst, Overbury again recovered. Howard and allegedly Turner then made pies, jellies, and tarts under
the guise of comfort food sent from well-wishers but that had been spiked
with mercury sublimate.[46] These brought Overbury close to death, but again
he survived. Suspecting what was happening, he wrote to Carr in a shaky
hand threatening to publish details of his private life that he claimed to have
written down. Carr bribed William Reeve, an assistant to Elwes's official
apothecary, to put mercury sublimate in an enema administered to Overbury by his servant Richard Weston on 14 September. By next morning he
was dead.

The murder was not discovered until nearly two years later when Reeve
confessed on his death bed at Flushing, and Elwes inadvertently revealed
his collusion while drunk. After Elwes was examined, James appointed a

commission headed by Sir Edward Coke to investigate the murder. They implicated Carr (newly elevated Earl of Somerset) and Howard, who had married him after her divorce to Essex had been approved, though both ultimately received a controversial pardon from James in May 1616 after Howard had pleaded guilty at her state trial. As the lead-up, Weston, Turner, Franklin, Elwes and their associates were individually tried, convicted, and executed.

Turner's sensational trial on 7 November followed Weston's on 19 October. He had confessed little and revealed nothing further at his execution on 25 October, and there was no printed news about him or the other alleged conspirators published to this point.[47] Turner was charged with abetting his poisoning but was unaware that Weston had already been tried and executed. She, her relations, and supporters therefore entered the courtroom confident of acquittal. Certain eyewitnesses noted her apparel. She wore a black baize dress with a starched yellow collar and a fancy hat, a sartorial combination that ambiguously coded aristocratic self-display and decorous modesty. Turner had introduced the fashion of stiffening of collars with yellow starch to the court from France in 1603. Its popularity as an expensive accessory grew, and Turner patented and successfully sold a receipt of her own.[48] But like other upper-class foreign fashions it was widely derided. Spotting the ruff and deciding to shake Turner's confidence, Coke compelled her to remove her hat in court, leaving her hair dishevelled as she tried to regain her dignity by covering her head with a handkerchief.[49] Her forced change in appearance is depicted a stage further in one of two images on the broadside *Mistris Turners Farewell to all women* (1615). There she holds the handkerchief in her left hand while her head appears covered with a black veil.

Turner was also unaware that the prosecution had amassed a battery of circumstantial evidence against her. Their strategy was character assassination in the face of little solid proof of her involvement in the poisonings. Rather, poison, as David Lindley has observed, became the imaginative catalyst for an array of stereotypical female vices that damned Turner by implication, beginning with witchcraft.[50] The chief prosecutor Lawrence Hyde accused her of acting as a go-between for Howard several years earlier when she employed the notorious physician and necromancer Simon Forman to bewitch Carr and her own lover George Mainwaring, whom Hyde implied was the real father of Turner's three children. Hyde then exhibited a bizarre collection of love philtres, cabalistic writings, occult tokens, and dolls that had been raided from the recently deceased Forman's house, including a wax figurine of a copulating woman and man that electrified court spectators.[51] None of these objects or allegations had any legal relevance to the indictment, as more detached observers must have noted. Coke summed up their persuasive effect in his charge to the jury by accusing Turner of embodying the seven deadly sins: "a whore, a bawd, a sorcerer, a witch, a papist, a felon, and a murderer, the daughter of the devil Forman." He exhorted her

Figure 4.3 Mistris Turners Farewell to all women (1615). Reproduced by permission of the Society of Antiquaries, London.

"to repent, and to become a servant of Jesus Christ, to pray to him to cast out those devils."[52]

Turner reportedly followed Coke's advice in exemplary fashion both in prison and on the scaffold after being too shattered to defend herself in court and subsequently convicted of murder. Witnessed by "an infinite number" of spectators at Tyburn, her gallows conversion to Protestantism, recorded in manuscript accounts, was orchestrated by a government-appointed chaplain, Dr Whiting.[53] Although her prison confession added little information to what was already known about the poisoning and could not strictly be used as evidence, it strengthened the prosecution's hand against Elwes, Franklin, and others.[54] Politically it validated Coke's master narratives throughout the trials that the Overbury conspiracy was part of a wider Catholic conspiracy against the state and that royal justice operated infallibly as the human arm of divine justice.[55] On 14 November the executioner bound Turner's hands with black silk ribbon and pulled a black veil over her face before the cart pulled away, leaving her hanging, "in whom there was no motion at all perceived." She was buried by her brother that evening.[56]

Despite the predominance of prosecution oriented accounts of the Overbury trials, the alleged wicked motives, bad character, and class privileges of some defendants were publicly contested. From a detailed study of manuscript and printed reports of Anne Turner's trial and later representations, Alastair Bellany has shown that skeptical or mitigating reports circulated amongst a wide readership representing diverse religious, political, and professional interests. This spectrum of opinion reflected extensive public debate about her case, including equitable (re)considerations of her alleged motives and guilt.[57] Richard Niccols's *Sir Thomas Overbvries Vision* (1616) attested to this now largely obscured dialogue by criticizing unnamed contemporary commentators for "excus[ing] that which was most amisse" (2). Niccols revised Thomas Baldwin's older collection of moralizing verse tragedies, *The Mirror for Magistrates*, in 1610, replacing James VI of Scotland with perennial scapegoats Edward II, Richard II, and Richard III. *Sir Thomas Overbvries Vision* topicalizes Baldwin's *de casibus* complaints and historical analogies by arguing that the Overbury murder was a systematic outcome of the corrupt ideology and culture of the Jacobean court.[58] Framed by the stone portal of Traitors' Gate, Weston's theatricalized ghost appears to Overbury's shade and the narrator to correct vulgar opinions questioning his guilt. Distressfully agitated and standing naked from the waist up in the Thames except for a severed rope around his neck, Weston confesses mixing poison in Overbury's food after being seduced by "The doctrine of that *Whoore*, that would dispence / With subiects for the murther of a Prince," learnt in the Turners' household (21). Anne Turner's ghost follows equally naked and neck-roped but with long dishevelled hair, one hand raised in lamentation and the other clutching her signature handkerchief. Still physically beautiful—Turner was famous before the Overbury scandal for her blonde hair—but now deathly pale, she confesses suborning Weston with gold to please her friends at court and to support her "state." Her descriptions anticipated the sexual and cosmetic gauds of Lady Pride in *Mistris Turners Farewell*, including the "that phantasticke vgly fall and ruffe, / Daub'd o're with that base starch of yellow stuffe / . . . Whose very sight doth murder modestie" (31; see below). Niccols then added his own historical twist, citing Holinshed's account of Lady Alfrith, painted wife of Earl

Ethelwald, who refused to follow her husband's advice to dress modestly when King Edgar visited their house. The young king became so inflamed with lust for Alfrith that he murdered Ethelwald (31).

In addition to reports in contemporary correspondence and *Thomas Overbvries Vision*, Turner's posttrial piety was represented in two extant broadsides and a verse complaint. These publications extended Turner's defamed status by portraying her as an evil widow motivated by vanity, greed, class ambition, vicarious sexual pleasure, and witchcraft, thereby constructing a powerful composite image of female disorder.[59] Like manuscript accounts of the trial, the popular printed representations of Turner, Diane Purkiss observes, generated "competing and conflicting constructions of wayward femininity" based on subjective interpretation of her words and actions by variously interested interlocutors and news writers.[60]

Thomas Brewer's *Mistres Turners Repentance* (1615) was issued by Henry Gosson, who specialized in godly ballads, broadsides, and pamphlets and had published the reports of Margaret Ferneseede and Elizabeth Abbot in 1608 that defended the trial-juries and judiciary, including Coke.[61] Brewer's double column of rhyming couplets appeared within an eye-catching stylized classical frame with pillars at each side. The poem purports to describe Mrs. Turner's mind and conduct during her prison conversion and execution. Its narrator travels the justified sinner's usual journey from tearfully lamenting her misspent life of "lust, gawdy pride, / And wanton painted pleasures," to embracing "Heauen's pleasure" in her terrorized guilt: "Fire, Water, Torture, any way: 'tis well / *To goe to Heau'n, eu'n by the Gates of Hell.*"

Mistris Turners Farewell to all women (1615) connected Anne's use of poison with every early modern cliché of the sexually transgressive widow. Like *Mistres Turners Repentance*, it was a large and striking broadside, published by John Trundle, well known as "a hawker of popular news" to a wide readership.[62] It depicted Turner transformed into a repentant widow holding a prayer book in her right hand, formerly corrupted by "phantastick Tires, / Paintings, and Poysonings." She appeared symbolically in both guises within a strapwork oval frame decorated with putti and garland clusters of fruit and flowers. On left side she is represented by the figure of Lady Pride, flamboyantly coiffed and bejewelled, wearing a sumptuous gown with fully exposed breasts and admiring a feather fan. Her attributes of vanity and lust are conventional except for a brief reference to "yellowed ruffes" (which Lady Pride does not actually wear; her image is generic). As Alastair Bellany notes, the "unusual color and its oversized, starch-assisted dimensions made [yellowed collars] typical of a fashion sense more concerned with novelty, sensuality, and profligacy than with the ideal, modest use of clothing recommended by moralists."[63] During her trial, yellow ruffs had become an emblem of Turner's spiritual and political corruption as a recusant, a relationship mocked at her execution when Coke insisted that Turner should wear yellow ruffs when delivering her gallows speech renouncing Catholicism (Tuke, *A Discovrse Against Painting and Tincturing of Women* [1616], I2v, K2r). Readers recalling her initial court appearance might also have found her confident dismissal of Lady Pride to divine judgment while reserving justified salvation for herself a little ironic: "To the last Barre Tribunall, thee I summon, / Where I shall stand all white, thou black and foule."

The "sorcerous Drugges" mentioned by Mistress Turner in this broadside referred not only to poison but also to Lady Pride's "Paintings." Cosmetics were another gendered attribute of the socially disordered widow projected onto Turner. Both were materially connected to substances supplied by apothecaries such as Franklin, who boasted about his noble clients.[64] The cultural associations of crime and cosmetics extended far wider than court circles, however, and partly explained why they were so easily mobilized against Turner. Books of housewifery typically included beauty receipts, and some of these relied on mineral poisons. Mercury, arsenic, and lead provided the main ingredients for a large variety of early modern cosmetics. Plat's *Delightes for Ladies* (1602) included a receipt for a "fucus for the face" made from "foure ounces of [mercury] sublimate [the deadliest form], and one ounce of crude Mercury," "dulcified" with water and applied with "oyle of white poppey" (G11v). His volume ended with a recipe for chestnut hair-coloring using "one part of lead calcined with sulphur, and one parte of quicke lime," and water (H11r). The most common ingredient—and one of the most lethal—in early modern cosmetics was white lead, or ceruse, a combination of lead carbonate and lead hydroxide $(2PbCO_3.Pb(OH)_2)$.[65] It was highly favored as a skin whitener and color base. Frances Howard almost certainly used it to achieve her fashionably clear and pale complexion.[66] Because of their material affinities with poison and because they enabled suspect modes of female concealment and/or assertion, cosmetics were widely denounced by contemporary moralists and playwrights as inventions of the devil and a threat to social order.[67] John Quick prepared readers of *Hell Open'd* for the full malice of Philippa Cary's crime by reporting that when the chunk of yellow arsenic she had ordered was first found, her fellow servant Anne Evans assumed it was Cary's "Painting" (B4r).

Thomas Tuke's *A Discourse Against Painting and Tincturing of Women* (1616) cited white lead and mercury sublimate, another popular skin whitener, as moral and physical dangers to both the user and the public.[68] Tuke seems to have begun writing a historical polemic against cosmetics. He then shifted his focus to poisoning and murder as news emerged from the Overbury trials, since this exemplified his theme that "this sinne [painting] goeth not alone." His volume grew into a meta-commentary on the Overbury affair by exploiting the cultural nexus between cosmetics and female poisoners. Although painting and other vicious vanities shared ontological origins in human pride and ambition, they were not only rarer in men than women, Tuke claimed (citing St. John Chrysostom), but also more likely to lead to murder (F1v). Alluding to the common political analogy between the household and commonwealth, Tuke argued that it was the husband's or master's duty to forbid women from using cosmetics before they slid into the deeper crimes of whoredom, witchcraft, and poisoning (F1v–F2r). Tuke also repeated Coke's observation at Turner's trial that poisoning was an Italian vice especially reviled in England:

> But among all the deuises of murderers, which are many, these Italian deuises by poisoning are most vile and diuelish, and they say, *An Englishman italianated is a diuell incarnated.* If these arts should come in once amongst vs, who shal be secure? (I1r)

These proverbial assumptions became politicized from the sixteenth century onwards as English travel to Catholic Europe increased fears of cultural contamination. Richard Bexley for example wrote to Lord Burghley on 25 June 1572 warning him to avoid Dr Gifford's physic because he had "recently come from Rome, lest he be Italianated."[69] Allegations that the Earl of Leicester had tried to murder Sir Nicholas Throgmorton with a poisoned salad were based on the observation that he had Italian physicians in his household.[70] Schools for poisoners did indeed operate in Italy during the early modern period and the rate of poisonings in Rome reached fourteen a day by the late fifteenth century. In part this was due to the cheapness and local availability of mineral forms of arsenic such as realgar and orpiment, which were naturally abundant around the Mediterranean basin.[71] But such arts had of course long been cultivated at home, as T. I'.s references to Bithricus's wife and Margaret Davie in *A World of wonders* paradoxically affirmed. Two recent notorious instances were attempts by Lopez and Squire against Elizabeth in 1594 and 1598 respectively that Coke cited in sentencing Weston.[72] Seventeenth-century murder-by-poison news writers alluded to these cases time and again. Yet contemporary writers and readers also recognized the contradictory claims of poison's foreign yet immemorially English origins, which problematized the application of such assumptions as self-evident truths when assessing women's motives and guilt.

Henry Goodcole's *The Adultresses Funerall Day* was one of these. Its "Short Tract Vpon The *hainousnesse of Poysoning*" (B3v–B4v) summarized many common attitudes expressed sporadically in reports and publications about Turner and the other Overbury conspirators. On the one hand Goodcole echoed the opinions of Coke, Bacon, and others during the Overbury trials that poisoning was the most hateful form of murder, and that murder was the first and worst of all crimes.[73] He endorsed William Perkins's views in *A Golden Chaine* (H6r) and *The Whole Treatise of the Cases of Conscience* (25–6) that poisoning is a premeditated and unpardonable sin that demands capital justice. Goodcole listed four arguments to support these claims, with appropriate Latin tags to add an air of quasi-legal authority: (1) poison is a premeditated and deliberate act done in cold blood; (2) its secrecy makes it particularly odious, especially if it is offered under the cover of medicine; (3)

it destroys the human body made in god's image and takes away the victim's opportunity to repent his sins; and (4) it inevitably makes others knowing or unwitting accessories to the crime and therefore implicates both the community and the perpetrators (B3v–B4v; as the efforts of Cheshire gentry simultaneously to individualize and differentiate culpability in the Caldwell murder conspiracy had demonstrated [*A True Discourse,* 1604]).

Although Goodcole does not allude to this case specifically, the last of these four points seems to have made a particularly strong impression on him, perhaps because of his career-long involvement with condemned prisoners and their personal histories. The alterity and cultural revisionism of Goodcole's brief chronicle of poison was reflected in his departures from earlier authorities, most notably Perkins, whose life and work were otherwise models for his entire career.[74] Goodcole first argued that scriptural examples of poisoning illustrated its aggravated sinfulness. His evidence corrected Francis Bacon's claim during the trial of Frances Howard that the Bible contained no instances of poisoning at all.[75] Second and more significantly, Goodcole dissented from traditional (or more puritan) views of Perkins, Coke, and others about poisoning's origins as the devil's invention. He argued pragmatically that its historical origins lay in human power struggles of the classical world and Renaissance Italy, a view that modern historians have largely confirmed.[76] He began with ancient history, citing Ovid's description of the iron age in *Metamorphoses* (I.144–8) when "mortiferous drugs" came into existence. They were first "tempered" by "The [unnamed] rough-brow'd Step-dame" who deceived "her yong step-son" (A3r). This allusion validated the early modern association of poison with matrons, wise-women, and widows. However Goodcole also cited the Cornelian laws of ancient Rome making the use of poison as well as "abhorrid Arts ... magicke spells and wisperings" capital offenses, with three main categories of male or female offenders: poisoners, sorcerers, and apothecaries or empirics (A4r–v). His "Tract" thereby broadened the causes of domestic poisoning beyond gender-specific deviance to social and economic relationships for which the wider community bore some responsibility and that were opened to public debate by print journalism. Like other innovative features of Goodcole's 1630s crime pamphlets, this more equitable focus on socially dispersed but rationally analyzable agencies provided influential models for later news reports of poisoning homicides.

The historical perspectives of Goodcole's "Short Tract" and Niccols's *Sir Thomas Overbvries Vision* took a popular religious turn in *The Bloody downfall of Adultery* (1615). As in Brewer's *Mistris Turners Repentance*, Turner laments her misbegotten life as a traditional exemplum of the repentant widow. Thirty-four stanzas of couplet quatrains construct a conventional biography of female sin, followed by a tearful prayer mimicking the penitent Magdalen.[77] The anonymous work was reprinted multiple times with the variant title *The iust Downefall of Ambition,. [sic] Adultery, Murder* (1615). All editions presented readers with same woodcut of Turner, again draped in black, and Weston, both kneeling and incanting "*Mercy Sweet Jesus*." The volume's popularity was undoubtedly partly due to its prose Preface, which presented a thinly veiled attack on Howard and Carr for procuring Overbury's murder after it had railed against corrupt courtiers who keep company with "witches and charmers" (e.g., Anne Turner and Simon Forman) in order to learn "to be excellent at poysons, to kill lingringly, like the *Italian*" (B1r).

COMPANIONS IN MISCHIEF

Later seventeenth-century accounts of husband murders involving poison reconstructed random personal details as symbolic inversions of household roles and betrayals of maternal trust. Such stories supported prosecution charges by infusing individual crimes with iconic significance as social and moral transgressions associated with unruly female desires and nonconformist political and religious communities. Hardworking male husbandry destroyed by negligent housewifery was a theme of several news pamphlets such as *Murther, Murther* (1641). This pretrial report was probably issued to whip up public opinion—including the views of jurors and judges—against the prisoners.[78] It was a hyperbolic account in every sense. The author characterized Anne Hamton and her husband as the exemplary dysfunctional couple of contemporary conduct books: she the vainglorious and wasteful wife and he the long suffering and patiently forbearing husband.[79] The author upped the ante of transgression by hinting that Anne had female as well as male lovers. Earlier he described Anne gossiping "with one young fellow or other, or else with such women as were like to herselfe: never was she more joyfull then when she was out of her good husbands company" (A3r). Eventually her widowed landlady, Margaret Harwood, suggested Anne should do something about her situation:

> for shee [Harwood] hearing her Ningles unjust [i.e. justified] complaint, she cryed out that it was [Anne's] own fault, for letting such an abject villaine to live; hang him, cut his throat, or poyson him, for he is not fit to live upon the earth amongst good fellowes (A3v).

"Ningle" or "ingle" was the term for a catamite or boy prostitute, from the verb "ingle" meaning to fondle or caress (*OED*).[80] As Sandra Clark has observed, Harwood has no practical or obvious motive for her involvement in Anne's affairs other than personal loyalty. Her role may generically reprise that of widows in earlier crime pamphlets who collaborate with a friend's male lover to persuade the discontented wife to accept him and kill her husband, such as Anne Drurie, Isabel Hall, and Anne Turner.[81] Alternatively the author could be using the term "Ningle" metaphorically to describe Anne's promiscuous social "lusts." Whether a same-sex relationship is being hinted

The Bloody downfall

Of $\left\{ \begin{array}{l} \mathcal{A}\,dultery. \\ \mathcal{M}urder, \\ \mathcal{A}mbition, \end{array} \right\}$

At the end of which are added *Weſtons*,
and Miſtris *Turners* laſt Teares, ſhed for the
Murder of Sir Thomas Ouerbury *poyſoned in the*
Tower; who for the fact, ſuffered deſerued
execution at Tiburne the 14. *of*
Nouember laſt. 1615.

Mercy Sweet Jeſus.

Printed at London for *R. H.* and are to be ſold at his
ſhop at the Cardinalls Hat without Newgate.

Figure 4.4 The Bloody downfall Of Adultery. Murder, Ambition (1615). Reproduced by permission of the Huntington Library.

Murther, Murther:

Or,

A bloody Relation how *Anne Hamton,*

dwelling in Westminster nigh London, by
poyson murthered her deare husband. Sept.
1641. being affisted and counselled
thereunto by *Margeret Harwood.*

For which they were both committed

to Gaole, and at this tyme wait
for a tryall.

Women love your owne husbands, as Christ doth the Church.

Printed at London for *Tho. Bates,* 1641.

Figure 4.5 Murther, Murther (1641). Reproduced by permission of the Huntington Library.

at, the writer could only grasp at an analogous word to describe Anne's unnatural desires. Her inner discontent, as well as Harwood's interests, remained in some sense unspeakable.[82]

Like other women involved in adulterous relationships such as Anne Welles, Elizabeth Caldwell, and Mrs. Beast, Anne initially resisted Harwood's motions to get rid of her preachy husband. Once persuaded, however, Anne allegedly went overboard by buying five drams of poison, "enough to have destroyed ten men," and mixed it in her husband's food. After he began to swell in pain, Anne left him to his agony to report her deed to Harwood. When they returned the man was "burst." The writer emphasized that the breakdown of domestic order was not merely a private matter but one that sent shock waves into the community. Anne and Harwood both dissembled a lamentable cry that attracted the neighbors to view the body (and perhaps is obliquely linked to the title page image of two women (the two Marys?) discovering what looks like an empty tomb[83]). Merging their reactions with his own, the writer anticipated (or perhaps drew on) the coroner's inquest by anatomizing the corpse in grotesque detail:

> there did see his nayles quite pulled of, his hands did seeme onely like two great boyles, his belly seemed as if hot irons had been thrust into it, his visage was so much defaced by the quicke operation of the scalding poyson, that had they not well knowne the body, they would have sworne it not to have beene the man. (A4r)

Confirming this voyeuristic account with a touch of forensic analysis characteristic of murder news from the midcentury onwards, he then reported that the coroner opened the body to find poison "lying round about his heart" and tested it in a Venice glass, which shattered.[84] Susan C. Staub observes that the double explosions of the husband's body and the vessel through which the community measured the effects of female poisoning "literalizes the explosion of the household" that prescriptive conduct books, and in turn the author of this pamphlet, warn against.[85]

When Philippa Cary poisoned the family of her master William Weeks in 1676, the fare was oatmeal and beer laced with orpiment or yellow arsenic. It was served by a young maidservant, Anne Evans, as the first course of a Sunday lunch of boiled beef and neck of veal with cabbage and carrots. Much of the individual testimony recorded by John Quick's *Hell Open'd, Or, The Infernal Sin of Murther Punished, Being A True Relation of the Poysoning of a whole Family in Plymouth* (1676) focused on the household economy and cuisine, how Cary obtained and administered the poison, and whether Evans was aware of her intentions when she served the fatal meal, although both women were convicted and hanged. Two of the three panels in the title page illustration set the main scenes of this domestic tragedy with theatricalized flourishes. In the top panel, a family sits at table beneath large mullioned windows while a woman stirs a pot over a smoking fire at the left side of the room. On the right a curtain which appears attached to the image frame rather than part of the room itself is drawn back. The suggestion of stage play recurs in the middle image. Two persons lie in a postered bed with the curtains pulled back on either side while one woman is walking towards them holding what appears to be a cup and another woman sits sadly at a table. Ominously, a dog eats something at her feet.

Quick feminized his narrative by including an abundance of domestic details and quaint provincial vocabulary, occasionally providing translations into standard southern English. The animosity between Cary and Mrs. Weeks had been longstanding but reached a crisis when they quarrelled about the "the Frying of Pilchards." Cary resolved on revenge against "the old *Gypson*" (i.e., gypsy) but decided not to buy ratsbane from a nearby apothecary because "he would take her name." She instead purchased orpiment from one further away who did not know her and employed a local delivery boy who tossed the poison wrapped in a paper over the garden wall. Evans discovered it "among the Marygolds" when she was gathering herbs and brought it to Cary, assuming, as noted above, that it was her painting. Cary stored the yellow arsenic out of sight in the kitchen salt cellar, later grinding it up "between two tiles into Powder" and steeping it in beer in a "cloam-dish" overnight ("cloam" is south-west dialect for clay or earthenware [*OED*]). Her treatment indicates expertise. Arsenic minerals such as orpiment are normally insoluble, but when mixed with carbonated substances such as beer they form the soluble salt, sodium arsenate, which is very poisonous.[86] She instructed Evans the next day to put some of it into the dishes when she served the pottage and bread. Mr. Weeks later alleged it "crushed in his Teeth" (C1r), which suggests the mineral had not fully dissolved. When the Weekses became thirsty and called for beer, Cary slipped a bit of poison into it, which caused the drink to taste "keamy" and Mr. Weeks to complain that the beer had "keam" on it (words not recorded by *OED*).

Evans claimed that she was a poor "*Ingrant*" soul who simply bought the "Girts" from a local vendor on Cary's instruction. One wonders whether Quick really needed to gloss her vocabulary (as "Ignorant" and "Oatmeal," "girts" being a dialectical variant of "grits"; *OED*, n.2) to aid his readers. His implicit aim seemed to be to create a rhetoric of authorial mastery over his resistant subjects.[87] Reflecting the greater medical and forensic interests of later seventeenth-century readers, Quick meticulously described symptoms and antidotes. The victims began to feel pains in the "Stomack, Head and Belly" and then to suffer "Griping in the Guts" and "Violent Purging and Vomiting, and cold Sweats, and Faintings, with great drought" (B2v, B4v). The "Sack and Oyl" antidote saved Mr. Weeks, his son-in-law, and some neighbors but not, as noted earlier, his wife or daughter-in-law. Acknowledging the wider community's injury by and involvement in the crime, several neighbors set themselves the forensic task of isolating the poison. They boiled a spoonful of the "Girts" in a pint of water and tested it on the dog, who became sick after half an hour. When they examined the "bottom of the

Skillet" they found some "Yellow Gravel," which was sent to a local male physician, Dr. Holland, who identified the substance as yellow arsenic. They also noticed that a chemical reaction had occurred in the bottom of Mrs. Weeks's silver tankard, which was "black, yellow, and discolored, as though it was Cankered" (B7r). Drawing on this evidence, a coroner's jury later officially confirmed that Mrs. Weeks and her daughter-in-law had been poisoned (B8r). Quick presented readers with these lengthy reports to authenticate and approve his actions with the aura of science. He seemed unaware that the same medical and forensic details could serve independent or skeptical evaluations by contemporary readers, who on the same evidence might have reached quite different conclusions about Cary's and Evans's guilt.

SERIAL POISON

The Weeks murders raised a related question I have occasionally been asked when writing this book: Were there any early modern instances of female serial killers? To my knowledge the only ones represented in popular news are poisoners. A comparison of the two surviving pamphlets about Elizabeth Ridgeway shows how the association between poisoning and female serial murder was popularly constructed in later seventeenth-century printed news. John Newton's *The Penitent Recognition of Joseph's Brethren: A Sermon Occasion'd by Elizabeth Ridgeway* (1684) was, in his own words, a "confused tedious story" (C2r). As noted in the previous chapter, Newton was Ridgeway's prison visitor, and much of his interest in writing about the case lay in defending his professional dealings with her to civic officials. Newton accordingly presented her as an exasperating prisoner who may have been mentally unstable. His narrative also deliberately mimicked her allegedly spasmodic, often contradictory, and sometimes fabricated confession of details about various murders, without trying to smooth or re-order the sequence to make the salient facts clearer to readers. A rough form of expressionism reflecting the woman's subjective version of events replaced the rhetorically tendentious conversion model as a narrative strategy.

Elizabeth's activities came to light with the latest murder of her husband, Thomas Ridgeway, whom she poisoned with a large dose of white arsenic in broth. After dying in great torment that night, he was buried without any suspicions being aroused until one of their apprentices, Richard Tilley, told his master's relations that he had seen *"something like to Gritt or Lime"* in the bottom of his master's dish, which Elizabeth had hastily taken away (B1v). A coroner's inquest concluded that Thomas had been poisoned, but Elizabeth protested her innocence. As Newton observed, the trial's outcome hinged on the testimony of the sixteen-year-old Tilley, and at first the jury was divided about its validity. After further debate they found Elizabeth guilty. The jury's initial lack of agreement reflected wider differences of opinion in the community, some of whom actively involved themselves in Elizabeth's defense by petitioning the trial judge on her behalf for a reprieve. But he rejected their request. The lingering public controversy made it imperative to substantiate the court's verdict by pressuring Elizabeth into admitting her guilt; and at this point Newton's main account of his efforts to do so began (B2r). Gradually it emerged that she previously poisoned her mother, a former suitor, and more recently her husband's rival for her hand in marriage. She at last killed Thomas after being "frustrated of *her expectations in her marriage*," because she "could not *love her Husband as she ought*" (a complaint similar to that of Anne Welles in 1592), and because her sister-in-law called in a £20 debt that would have bankrupted them (C1v).

The full title of the second pamphlet announced a thoroughly digested account that reconstructed these events as a criminal biography: *A True Relation Of Four most Barbarous and Cruel Murders Committed in Leicester-shire by Elizabeth Ridgway* (1684). Whereas Newton described Ridgeway killing her victims randomly according to varying circumstances and motives, *A True Relation* re-presented her as an instinctive killer with a coolly deployed *modus operandi*: "her way of Poysoning was, by mixing *White Mercury*, or other Powder, in [her victims'] Broath, or Drink." Ridgeway's homicidal history unfolded victim by victim, arriving finally at the death of Thomas, and her unsuccessful attempt to murder two apprentices, Richard Tilley and William Corbet. There was little sense of narrative uncertainty about the details, nor did the writer explain Elizabeth's motives; rather, he reduced them to a malicious urge to assert her will in the face of minor provocations or differences of opinion—streamlining typical of certain prosecution-oriented metropolitan journalism. Ridgeway seemed to kill for petty reasons and almost for the pleasure of exercising her own devious power. The amoral triviality of her motives redefined female criminality in a way hitherto unseen in popular murder news about women murderers.

The anonymous writer's tone was also metropolitan in being slightly detached and amused, as opposed to Newton's self-absorption. Certain key details were changed, such as Ridgeway's preference for mercury rather than arsenic and the fact that her husband was named William, not Thomas. The writer not only seemed aware of these discrepancies, however, but used them to win the reader's confidence over Newton's account. To this end he specifically identified two alternative and seemingly authentic sources of information: William Corbet, newly come up to London, and George Ridgeway, the dead husband's brother. On the other hand the writer was not above adding a few folkloric titbits, such as the fact that Thomas's corpse allegedly bled at the nose and mouth when Elizabeth was forced to undergo the medieval test of cruentation by touching it.[88] She also allegedly confessed that "for eight years past she had lain with a Familiar Spirit" (A3v) who first tempted her to poison not only herself but anybody who offended her. Seeking to elevate Elizabeth into a near-mythical figure of urban danger, the writer concluded his insinuations of witchcraft by claiming she "constantly concealed Poyson in her Hair," buying a fresh supply at local markets whenever necessary (A3v). Her uncooperative behavior at the stake made her mercyless execution seem fitting.

A True Relation's publisher was George Croom, whose story of a serial female poisoner may have been issued partly in response to a similar account published several years earlier by his keen commercial rivals, David and Elizabeth Mallet. The Mallets were crime news innovators, and it would not be surprising if theirs proved to be the first unequivocal account of a female serial killer. *Horrid News from St. Martins: Or, Vnheard-of Murder and Poyson* (1677) is a pre-execution report, probably written by a prison visitor. Its claim that the case was "Vnheard-of" is not quite the usual puff, at least as far as surviving early modern murder news is concerned. This unnamed fifteen-year-old girl anticipated Elizabeth Ridgeway's frightening tendency to poison people on slight pretexts, albeit perhaps in a more naïve or childish way. As in the Ridgeway case, the girl's poisoning career emerged only after several victims had already died without arousing suspicions among neighbors. Unlike puritan Thomas Cooper, who claimed in *The Cry and Reuenge of Blood* (1620) that this kind of delayed and/or fortuitous discovery of murder *proved* the operation of vengeful providence, the writer of *Horrid News from St. Martins* did not regard these as comforting revelations but ones that "might render the Relation suspicious" to readers were the facts now not legally documented and the crime openly confessed (A2r). He felt obliged to present discrepancies in the story openly, and then to persuade readers that prosecution claims were consistent with them and really proved the accused woman's guilt. His arguments acknowledged that readers could interpret the narrative independently, in ways that questioned or mitigated the Crown's case. Equitable reasoning and discursive negotiation were, at this date, normal expectations of news writers and buyers.

The girl had been taken in a year and a half earlier after the death of her mother by a charitable widow living with another gentlewoman. One day they chid her for some small fault and the girl mixed poison in their food, causing them to become exceedingly sick. They recovered, however, after being given "Alexipharmacks" (i.e., medical remedies or antidotes to poison). Yet as so often in these stories a poor cat who licked up part of their vomit "fell into a strange fit of trembling and swelling" and shortly died. Tracing the origins of the women's illness to the girl, she at first denied any wrongdoing. After being offered "some suggestions of pardon" (possibly genuine, for at this stage she seemed to be guilty only of attempted homicide), she began volunteering details of her history. She had tried to kill the women previously but given them too small a dose that had made them mildly ill. She also confessed that she had poisoned a maidservant who was suffering from small-pox and then her mother, who she said was "very sickly and troublesome" (A3v). Possibly the girl believed her actions were merciful. But the writer did not suggest this. Unusually, he was more baffled than morally outraged by the girl's casual amorality. While regarding her as young and childish, he did not present her as merely naïve, nor did he attribute her malice to the catch-all agency of the devil. Rather he implied that someone "so well skill'd and detestably practised in the mysteries of Poysoning" (A2r) must have learned her behavior, and he linked this inference to the girl's cryptic admission that her actions were partially instigated "by a certain Woman" who had since fled. In the absence of further information or material evidence that might have emerged at a later stage, *Horrid News from St. Martins* implied that behind the girl's homicidal tendencies lay a secret legacy of female knowledge that subverted its gendered origins by victimizing other women.

Similar cultural fears and ambiguities surrounded women's knowledge of and responsibility for childbirth, and these became associated with news representations of infanticide and child murder, the subject of the next chapter. Unlike poison, however, which was less associated with equity in legal practice than with public debate over related social values and cultural assumptions, the application of seventeenth-century infanticide laws was materially affected by concepts of equity circulated by printed news.

5 Changing Representations of Infanticide and Child Murder

Early modern news seemed to present readers with the same story of women who killed their newborn infants or young children, over and over:

- *The Bloudy Mother* (1610)
- *A pittilesse Mother* (1616)
- *No naturall mother, but a monster* (1634)
- *Natures Cruell Step-Dames* (1637)
- *The Unnatural Grand Mother* (1659)
- *The Cruel Mother* (1670)
- *The Unnatural Mother* (1697)

Yet beyond these repeated titles—normally supplied by publishers rather than writers—lie a wide range of rhetorical styles, narrative plots, and individual experiences of troubled motherhood. Then as now, it was not just sensational headlines and Medea stereotypes that stirred readers to buy news of the latest female child killer, but interest in the lives of individual women who were partially reconstructed as recurring figures of violent mothers. When analyzing modern media representations of female killers, Kathleen Daly and Lisa Maher observe that the "real woman" cannot be understood outside historical discourses that represent her. Conversely, news reports can never fully capture the depth and complexity of individual subjects, who in certain ways remain beyond representation.[1] Similar epistemological challenges characterized early modern news of infanticide, which framed the private actions of obscure local women in terms of both mythical images of monstrous mothers and shifting public ideas about the crime's meaning and appropriate punishment. Religious associations transformed some accused women into powerful symbols of political and sectarian ideology, especially during times of heightened conflict such as the Civil War and the Popish Plot.[2] News readers and auditors routinely compared and debated these multiple layers of actuality and representation.[3] As with other categories of female homicide news, they included neighbors, local authorities, and assize officials whose fluctuating attitudes of legal rigor and equitable leniency resulted in variable levels of prosecution and conviction.[4]

Infanticide is the loose but defensibly useful term to describe parents who kill their recently born children.[5] Unlike homicide, it was associated almost exclusively with women during the early modern period, both in law and popular news. The majority of printed reports, especially after the Restoration, concern unmarried maidservants who became pregnant and were alleged to have murdered their newborn children immediately or very soon after giving birth. This scenario became deeply entrenched in seventeenth-century and later English culture, as the prose fiction of those periods attests.[6] Yet the stereotype of the bastard-killing single mother was anchored in real material conditions of early modern employment and domestic hierarchies. Continually refashioned by emerging markets for popular news and new desires for scientific knowledge about pregnancy and birth, infanticide stories tended to be more assimilable to changing cultural attitudes and historical contexts than, say, the female poisoner or husband killer, who represented relatively deeper violations of social order.[7]

Over sixty cases of infanticide survive in news accounts to the end of the seventeenth century. Most derive from a surge in commercial journalism that occurred from the late 1670s to the early 1690s. "Stories" or "cases" range in length from a few lines in newspaper columns, to brief summaries in assize-trial reports, to relatively substantial biographies in pamphlets. This chapter will take into account all these accounts to explore their diverse contexts of production and reception. Proceeding simply by date of publication might imply a steady development in progressive thinking, however, and would tend to flatten the significance of changing circumstances. The historical arc of early modern infanticide and child-murder news was not linear, but periodically contingent and increasingly ambiguous. Like regular female homicide news, it exhibited both continuity of traditional attitudes and increasing openness of equitable representation. So while keeping loosely to chronology, I shall focus attention on crime genres, material formats, and political conditions that altered legal and social concepts of infanticide over the century. Newspaper and trial-reports published after the Restoration, in particular, made the legal criteria of the 1624 infanticide statute (discussed below) highly visible and contested. Their accounts generated long-term trends to limit and ultimately rewrite the 1624 law, as did the public's increasing familiarity with the irreducibly unique lives—however mediated by textual representations—of individual women. In law, this elusive human element (noted by Daly and Maher) that lies beyond, or exceeds, discursive constructions of personal identity is related to equity, insofar as the singularity of local women presented material and ethical challenges to the general principles of human (mis)conduct established by universalizing statutes and precedents. Equity sought to recognize differences between conservative legal constructions and present criminal identities, sometimes managing to mitigate the law's severity.

WOMEN ARE MILD, SOFT, PITIFUL, AND FLEXIBLE,
THOU STERN, OBDURATE, FLINTY, ROUGH, REMORSELESS.

(Henry VI Part Three, 1.4.141–42)

In law, infanticide was not differentiated from homicide before the statute of 1624. Before that date, county records of prosecutions and convictions for infant and child murder remain limited and obscure.[8] The small body of popular infanticide news from the late sixteenth and early seventeenth centuries thus constitutes important evidence of contemporary attitudes and practices. As in the case of domestic murder by commoners, because no conventional genre for female infanticide or child murder existed before the late sixteenth century,[9] writers turned to post-Reformation reports of monsters and prodigies, allegorized within a framework of Calvinist providentialism, for rhetorical and epistemological models.[10] They also drew on proverbial animal lore, folk history, and iconic literary and dramatic figures of bad mothers.[11] Placed in these discursive contexts, infanticide became a trope of the wonder-ful—metonymic signs of human reprobation portending divine vengeance.

Anthony Munday deployed this tropical figuring of infanticide in his downmarket miscellany *A View of sundry Examples* (1580). He reported that one unnamed woman recently buried alive her illegitimate infant, "casting all motherly and naturall affection" (Ciir). Another Kilbourn woman brained her two small children with a "peece of billet" and died in Newgate after being arrested (D1v). Similarly, T. I.'s *A World of wonders. A Masse of Murthers. A Covie of Cosonages* (1595) mentioned one story of a Whitechapel maidservant made pregnant by the son of her mistress. She concealed the pregnancy and gave birth alone on the day her mistress was being buried after having lately died. She cut the child's throat and threw it in a privy, but a boy in the room below heard the infant's cries and raised suspicions, whereupon the maid was examined and the child's body recovered. The woman was tried for murder and executed at Tyburn (F2r). Stated thus, the coincidental details suggest some kind of vicarious revenge killing.[12] T. I. deflects this explanation by adding that "vnnatural" local wives believed "the diuell was with her" (whether referring to the infant or maid is unclear) and helped the pregnant woman "dispatch it in that manner" (T2v). If true, it made them legal accessories. T. I. merely concluded tangentially that whoredom and adultery lead to murder, thus corralling the incident into another of the volume's illustrations of "wonders" presaging divine wrath.

These opaque entries confirm infanticide's cultural status as an ungendered form of murder, unlike petty treason in Munday's more extensive account of Anne Saunders. As a prodigy phenomenon, infanticide was also connected to human physical deformities: both were errors of nature against which normative human behavior and social values could be differentiated.[13] Just as Shakespeare or Middleton and Rowley counted on "ill-featured" characters such as Gloucester and DeFlores being immediately recognized as potential villains (and played against those reflexes), so the monstrous maternal became a trope that early printed news represented and problematized by situating it in ideologically unstable contexts. Dehumanizing animal imagery implied that infanticidal mothers lacked even the natural parenting instincts of beasts. Thus Thomas Brewer described Jane Hattersley in *The Bloudy Mother* (1610) as a "Chimera, with a Lions upper-part in bouldnesse: a Goates middle part in lust, and a Serpents lower part in sting and poyson" (B3r).[14] This pamphlet's focus on the lustful and suffering bodies of Hattersley and her lover Adam Adamson also heightened the contrast between the providential gaze that triumphantly uncovered and punished their secret crimes, and the equitably calculated—or relativizing—responses of the West Sussex community of East Grinstead.

Hattersley was Adamson's servant for ten years or more, in which time they allegedly managed to conceal an unknown number of pregnancies from Adamson's wife and neighbors while killing and secretly burying the off-spring (C4r–v). Brewer's narrative concentrated on the three infant victims and one lucky survivor to which Hattersley confessed in prison and on which she was presumably indicted (A4v). While staying in the house of a goodwife King, Hattersley kept her first pregnancy secret "with loose lacing, tucking, and other odde tricks" (A4v). Although King discovered her in labor, Hattersley covered up the murder by making it look as if she had "ignorantly ouer laid the baby[15] and by outswearing King's claims that she had originally noticed signs of violence on it. When King and her husband tried to withhold some of Hattersley's possessions for unpaid rent, Adamson aggressively sued them. His superior wealth and public reputation allowed him to maximize the law's vexations to "vtterly undoe this poore couple" and bear down all rumors that increasingly dogged his long-running affair (B1v–B2r). Adamson's active defense of his relationship with Hattersley (sentimentalized by Brewer) represents an unusual twist among narratives of secret infant births and deaths, in which fathers of illegitimate children typically remained absent and unnamed.

Adamson played against this role after Jane's second "priuie offending." He buried the corpse at night beside a box tree in his orchard that was later sold to a neighbor, Edward Duffield. During her third secret childbirth, again in Adamson's house, Hattersley was spied through a chamber-door keyhole by goodwife Frances Ford. With an experienced eye she observed "a bole-dish, in which was the after birth of a child, and other perspicuous and euident tokens of a childe borne at that instant" (B2v). But Hattersley had locked the door, and by the time Ford gained entry Hattersley had cleared away tell-tale evidence—including, it seems, the baby, whom Brewer presumed was murdered and also buried by Adamson. In the absence of material proof, Adamson managed to silence Ford's wife (B2r). Local suspicions were now keenly raised, however, so Hattersley went to her sister's house when her next "swelling" appeared. This child survived to be raised by her brother-in-law. He supplied the wonted nurturing parent of the story not only by hiring a wetnurse but also providing her with "a good cow to giue her milk, that the allowance of the child might be better" (B3v). Hattersley meanwhile returned to Adamson.

At this point Brewer drew attention to the unelaborated history of Hattersley's "great bellies," obscuring the question of whether these occurred before, during, or after the narrative presented thus far. The ambiguity might have intensified readers' curiosity about a further, and hardly veiled, narrative deflection: that the community evidently knew much more about Hattersley and Adamson's relationship than Brewer's paradoxical descriptions of King's and Ford's ability to be deceived and yet remain weakly—or willingly—undeceived. Whether this represented East Grinstead's implicit mitigation of the couple's conduct, their hesitancy in dealing with a community scandal, or the force of Adamson's legal and personal bullying, remained open to interpretation. Brewer noted that Adamson turned away local searchers and opposed "all such as mutterd in suspicion" (B2r) against his lover (whom, again unusually, he never abandoned, although he ultimately avoided prosecution and preserved his masculine credit by doing so). Similarly, "many eies" watched to see the outcome of Hattersley's later pregnancy/ies, indicating some winking by neighbors at the crimes when they passed "undetected." Early modern neighbors often played ambidextrous roles in the local regulation of illegitimate pregnancies and births, choosing whether to initiate or avert prosecutions of alleged offenders partly on the grounds of moral and social equity.[16] (Locally negotiated interventions become transparent in later accounts of Abigail Hill and Mary Compton; see below.) Brewer's pamphlet confirmed this situation while attempting to shut down any impression of the community's ethical relativism in his Preface to the Reader (A2r) and by publicizing the names of five male and five female witnesses (including King and Ford) at the end of his pamphlet.

Neighbors bided their time, waiting to act until Adamson and Hattersley had incriminated themselves during a "windie battaile." Their row prompted Duffield to recall and/or investigate Adamson's warnings to avoid digging near the box tree. He and a party of neighbors exhumed the bones of a child, verified by a "cunning and very expert Anathomist" (B3v). Hattersley and Adamson were charged and released on bail. The latter provided money for their welfare in prison. Using these means, he pressured her into denying the accusations she had made against him, reassuring her that if she co-operated, he would obtain her pardon. Hattersley remained astoundingly loyal and credulous. She perjured herself to secure her master's acquittal by jury (which, given the usual composition of assize juries, probably consisted of local freeholders known to Adamson, who welcomed the opportunity to maintain *their* positive image of a member of their class). Hattersley behaved fearlessly at the gallows, "as if she had bin but (like a stage player) to act the part in ieast" (B4v). Sensing that her savior was cutting things a bit close, she gave the hangman sixpence to cut her down quickly after she had been turned off to allow the pardon to materialize while she was still gasping for breath. The hangman pocketed the money.

Notwithstanding Brewer's disavowal of farfetched wonders (Preface, A2r), his pamphlet ended on a strongly providentialist note that sought further to counter any impression of community compromise or compassion. A section set in larger black-letter type gloatingly informed readers that Adamson was soon attacked by flesh-eating worms and lice that putrefied his body for over half a year. The right panel of a double original woodcut on the title page depicted him propped up in bed being devoured by vermin. These creatures had also been colored red by double inking along with the large main title.[17] Adamson died in quarantine behind a locked door in a well-furnished room, which warned readers that even wealthy offenders could not buy their way out of divine justice (C1r–v). Sandra Clark also notes that the prominent well-shaped keyhole in the door recalled the one through which Frances Ford spied Hattersley's crime, yet in vain, and contrasted God's unerring vision.[18]

"[A] CREATURE MORE SAUAGE THEN A SHEE WOOLFE, MORE VNNATURALL THEN EITHER BIRD OR BEAST"

Deeds Against Natvre, and Monsters by kinde (1614) aligned negative stereotypes of moral and physical abnormality with those of the unmarried mother in more complex ways than *The Bloudy Mother* by paralleling the story of a crippled male murderer. Arthur James was a London beggar who allegedly strangled his recently estranged lover after she insisted on his keeping a promise to marry her. He supposedly found his own bad faith intolerable. Scambler was an alleged prostitute who became pregnant and threw her newborn male child down a privy. It was joined there by an unfortunate dog thrust in by an "vntoward ladd" from an adjoining house. After enduring the dog's yelping for three nights, the goodman of the house, "greeued to see a dumbe beast so starued," had the privy opened (A4v), whereupon "by Gods justice" the dog was rescued and the murdered child discovered. Women searchers interrogated Scambler, who confessed to killing the child after it was born alive.

The story's formulaic providentialism (e.g., the "miracle" brought about by human and nonhuman agents, the three-day subterranean "harrowing" before the dead infant's recovery, the householder's empathetic impulses contrasted with Scambler's maternal indifference) points to a heavily conventionalized narrative of the crime. Yet the titillation and moral lessons offered to readers in *Deeds Against Natvre* differed from other allegorized news of early seventeenth-century murders. The title page illustrations juxtaposed images of a man being hanged on the left and a woman on the right. An identically clothed executioner appears in both images straddling the gibbet's crossbar with a foot on the ladder, adjusting the noose. This

DEEDS AGAINST NATVRE,
and Monſters by kinde:

Tryed at the Goale deliuerie of Newgate, *at the Seſ-*
ſions in the Old Bayly, the 18. and 19. of *Iuly* laſt, 1614. the one
of a London Cripple named *Iohn Arthur*, that to hide his ſhame and luſt,
ſtrangled his betrothed wife. The other of a laſciuious yong Damſell named
Martha Scambler, which made away the fruit of her own womb, that the world
might not ſee the ſeed of her owne ſhame: Which two perſons with diuers others
were executed at Tyburne the 11. o Iuly following.

With two ſorrowfull Ditties of theſe two aforeſaid perſons, made by them-
ſelues in Newgate, the night before their execution.

At London printed for *Edward Wright.* 1614. 7

Figure 5.1 Deeds Against Natvre (1614). Reproduced by permission of the Bodleian Library.

suggested (falsely, in fact, but emblematically) that Arthur and Scambler were hanged together and shared criminal identities. The hanging man is missing his lower right leg. This may have been due to faulty inking of the woodcut and/or damage to a corner of the single extant copy. But it fortuitously anticipated the writer's revulsion towards Arthur's physical disabilities, which he understood as traditional signs of reprobation against which readers could measure their moral superiority. "Scambler" is being observed by a group of guards armed with pikes and halberds projecting a reassuring image of state security. The one closest to her points up, as the guard next to him also points while conversing with his mates. Their gestures indicated these were objects of public notoriety, and invited prospective buyers to find out more about them.

The author denounced Arthur's existence prior to the murder on two counts: his "waste" of ordinary people's charity on drink and sensual pleasure; and that sex between cripples is unnatural because it results in deformed births. Shame in the guise of outrage at the complicity of alms-givers was matched by horror at the prospect of "loues pleasures" (A2v). The perceived scandal of confused categories precluded any possibility that affections between Arthur and his lover could be other than "base wicked-ness: yea more then [sic] base in that a deformed lumpe of flesh and no perfect creature should thus abuse the seed of generation, and now and then in the fields and high-waies commit such beastly offences" (A2v). Their dan-ger in fact lay in too little ontological or spatial distance from their fellow Londoners. The writer marveled that "a deformed creature, an vnperfect wretch wanting the right shape and limbes of a man" could nonetheless be "in forme and visage like vnto one of us" (A2r).

Julia Kristeva has observed that both disabled persons and physically stigmatized criminals threaten normative social values by contaminating acculturated boundaries that define the ordinary person's corporal integ-rity and safety. The abject body refuses to be absolutely othered;[19] and what disturbed and fascinated the pamphlet writer was a similar slippage between Arthur's deformity and his life as a person like "vs in this Cittie." He solicited alms for being pitifully "subhuman," and yet he had regular capacities for pleasurable sex and explosive violence ("In this my life much wonder lies: / That borne a lame deformed wight, / Should thus take pride in loues delight;" "The Cripples complaint," B1v). Moreover, Arthur alleg-edly expressed his own awareness of abjection as unbounded otherness, but believed it could manipulated to his advantage. After he killed his lover: "he thought the world too simple to looke into his life, and his decreped car-riage would keep away all suspition, and that no man could thinke a lame creature could be able to doe so wicked a deede" (A3r). Arthur assumed that cripples would be thought incapable of criminal violence because of the infantilized status projected on to them by ordinary people. Or as his balladized persona put it in the concluding verse-lament, "Though limbes I want and could not go, / Yet was my mind not pleased so: / But had my faults, as others haue" ("The Cripples complaint," B1r).[20] The pamphlet writer deflected this paradox by attributing Arthur's unsuspected physical strength to demonic inspiration:

> The Cripple perceiuing all secure and silent, and now thinking to be rid of the shame thus daily following him, tooke the womans owne girdle,

and putting the same slyly about her necke, where though nature had denied him strength and limbes, yet by the help of the diuell, which alwaies adds force to villany, he made meanes in her sleep to strangle her ... who would haue thought such an out cast of the world, such a lame deformed creature, not able of his own strength to help himselfe, should haue power to take away another's life. (A3r)

Demonism also shaped Martha Scambler's identity, which was constructed from ambiguous metaphors and comparisons drawn from natural history that characterized maternal power as both fructifying and self-sacrificing (A3v). She allegedly possessed a lustful and cannibalistic animality that dispossessed her human body, allowing her pregnancy to pass unnoticed amongst her fellow lodgers, and for her to give birth alone.[21] The writer also claimed that "by a divilish practice [she] sought to consume [her child] in her body before the birth," as a harlot makes "no conscience to be the butcher of her owne seed" (A3v). This claim made the legal point that Scambler intended to kill her baby and was therefore guilty of wilful murder. It also introduced a controversial distinction between infanticide as prenatal termination and postnatal killing. For the writer, however, Scambler's confusion of guilt and self-preservation produced a defiled womb and a monstrous outcast: a creature of "lust & shame" (A2v), and a "sweet Babe ... all besmeared with the filth of that loathsome place" (A4v). "I did exceed the deeds of men" concluded the ballad narrator of "The Cripple's Complaint" (B1r); "I full soone thereto agreed, / To act more then womans deede" echoed the voice of *Martha Scambler's Repentance* (B2r).

Deeds Against Natvre departed from the usual narrative of isolated female infanticides first instanced by T. I.'s account of the Whitechapel maidservant in *A World of wonders* and repeatedly confirmed by seventeenth-century legal records.[22] By manifesting the moral and physical contradictions and transgressions perceived in cripples, the image of the infanticidal mother could not be contained by the myth of prostituted female sexuality. The conduct of Arthur and Scambler bodied forth an irrepressible human agency that outstripped the cultural tropes of natural female weakness, subhuman maternal savagery, and spiritual reprobation. For readers who recognized or were skeptical about these rhetorical constructions, the meaning of Scambler's "deformed" energies might have resolved partially into extenuating categories of broken humanity.

By contrast, the good mother was characterized by the ideal of unconditional and self-consuming love: "for a woman esteemes the fruit of her owne womb, the pretious and dearest Jewell of the world, and for the cherishing of the same will (as it were) spend her liues purest blood" (*Deeds Against Natvre*, A3v). A pamphlet published two years later used a traditional emblem from animal folklore to illustrate this instinct: "as the Pellican that pecks her owne breast to feed her young ones with her blood" (*A pittilesse Mother* [1616]). The anti-mother of this account was Margaret Vincent, who "purposed to become a Tygerous Mother," behaving more cruelly than "the Viper, the inuenomed Serpent, the Snake, or any Beast whatsoeuer . . . [taking] away those liues to whom she first gaue life" (A3v). Yet despite these conventional (and inconsistent) analogies from natural history, Vincent's criminal identity could not be easily elided with that of the harlot. She was a well-educated gentlewoman of impeccable modesty who had married into a middle-class family, and, according to the writer of *A pittilesse Mother*, had lived in harmony with her husband Jarvis Vincent for more than twelve years and given birth to three children. Her story necessitated a shift in rhetorical presentation from the hypersexualized unmarried mother to the fanatical convert. This new image would elicit a more contentious range of reader reactions.

THE RELIGIOUS REVENGE KILLER

The Vincents' troubles began over religion. Margaret was "seduced" to Catholicism and tried to persuade her husband to join her, which he refused to do. She decided to avenge her frustration by killing their three children. Taking advantage of her husband's and maidservant's absence from the house on Ascension Day, 9 May 1616, Margaret strangled the eldest two. The youngest escaped because he was being nursed away from home. She then tried to kill herself but was prevented by the nurse returning home unexpectedly. Hearing the nurse's calls for help, neighbors and Margaret's husband rushed in to find the children murdered, at which point the pamphlet writer reported their climactic exchange:

> Oh, Margret, Marget, how often haue I perswaded thee from this damned Opinion, this damned Opinion, that hath vndone vs all.

> Oh Iarvis, this had neuer beene done, if thou hadst beene ruld, and by mee conuerted, but what is done, is past, for they are Saints in heauen, and I nothing at all repent it. (A4v)

Under pressure from clergymen after her arrest and imprisonment, Margaret allegedly came to acknowledge and regret her deeds, although reports of her trial, execution, and gallows speeches are conspicuous by their absence. The pamphlet writer's aim was to focus disapproval on Margaret's religious motives, which he related to contemporary conflicts of political ideology.

Vincent's crime would be classified by social workers today as a revenge killing, in which a parent uses violence against natal children to inflict harm on a partner. The majority of revenge killers are men trying to stop women from leaving abusive relationships. They are motivated partly by the perception that the children are the woman's property, insofar as modern

A pittileſſe Mother.

That moſt vnnaturally at one time, murthered
two of her owne Children at Aĉton within ſixe miles from
London vppon holy thurſday laſt 1 6 1 6. *The ninth of May.*
Beeing a Gentlewonan named *Margret Vincent*, wife of
M^r. *Iaruis Vincent*, of the fame Towne.

With her Examination, Confeſſion and true diſcouery of all the
proceedings in the ſaid bloody accident.

Whereunto is added *Anderſons* Repentance, who
was executed at Tiburne the 18. of May being Whitſon-Eue. 1 6 16.
Written in the time of his priſonment in Newgate.

Printed at London for I, T, and are to be ſold by Iohn Wright,

Figure 5.2 A pittilesse Mother (1616). Reproduced by permission of the Bodleian Library.

courts tend to award custody of children to mothers rather than fathers.[23] In the early modern period, however, this perception was reversed. A wife's lack of autonomous property rights and the legal custom of primogeniture made children the property and symbolic capital of the patriarchal householder.

Contemporary readers recognized these dimensions of the Vincent case, although the pamphlet writer revealed some directly and coded others. For example he mentioned that the occasion of the maidservant's absence was a dispute over the use of a commons claimed jointly by the town of Acton, where the Vincents lived, and Willesdon. On the day of the murders, Acton women had been delegated to defend the commons from Willesdon cattle. Margaret excused herself from participating and sent her maidservant on her behalf. The writer parallels her refusal to defend community property rights with the domestic violation of her husband's "property" in her desire for revenge (A3v).

Jarvis Vincent's patriarchal authority was also connected to institutionalized structures of religious and political power. The dramatized first person exchange quoted above represented Margaret's ambitions to rule the household, while earlier in the pamphlet Jarvis accused her of being "undutifull to make so fond an attempt, many times snubing her with some few vnkinde speeches" (A3r). Betty S. Travitsky observes that these passages not only related Margaret's interior integrity to tenuous and shifting early modern subject positions for women, but also conveyed the patriarchal theory that "the good rule of the home depended on the subordination of the wife and represented in microcosm the good rule of the nation."[24] Obedience to male authority was also essential because women were deemed more susceptible than men to Catholic conversion. This weakness resulted from a combination of powerful Catholic insinuation and inferior female reasoning and control of unruly passions. *A pittilesse Mother*'s view that papists "haue such charming perswasions that hardly the female kinde can escape their inticements, of which weake sex they continually make prize of and by them lay plots to insnare others" (A2v) anticipated the opinions of William Gouge and other writers of female conduct books. Disobedient wives are incipient amazons, Gouge claimed, because

> being seduced by Iesuites, Priests, or Friers, [they] take the Sacrament, and thereupon by solemne vow and oath binde themselues neuer to read an English Bible, nor any Protestant bookes, no nor to goe to any of their Churches, or to heare any of their Sermons: and such most of all as enter into some Popish Nunnery, and vow neuer to returne to their husbands againe.[25]

Reflecting these prejudices, the writer claimed that before Protestant neighbors and ministers prevailed, Margaret threw away "with great stubbornesse" an English Bible given to her while in custody, and in Newgate she "refused to looke vpon any Protestant booke . . . affirming them dangerous for any Romish Catholique to looke in" (B1r–v).

Two other contemporary references politicized the crime in different ways. A letter by Sir Edward Sherburne, secretary to the East India Company, to Sir Dudley Carleton, ambassador to The Hague, dated 18 May[26] stated that the murdered children were both boys, and that Margaret was not mentally unstable at the time. She was thus striking consciously at both her husband and his heirs, and therefore subverting the legal rights and class privileges enshrined by primogeniture. A second shorter letter by John Chamberlain addressed to Carleton on the 17th shifted the origins the Vincents' conflict. Chamberlain claimed that Margaret was "a violent recusant[,] and urged by her husband to conforme her self, and to have her children other-wise educated, she tooke this course to rid them out of the world rather then to have them brought up in our religion."[27] In *A pittilesse Mother* the issue of boys being educated as Catholics or Protestants came *after* the dispute over Jarvis's personal conversion; in Chamberlain's account it was central and raised further questions about Margaret's suspect identity as a female Catholic. From Chamberlain's perspective and the pamphlet writer's, Margaret's attempt to control her children's education against the wishes of her husband subverted his patriarchal obligations to his household and his country's official religion. Her child murder was domesticated treason.

Early modern Catholic readers, however, might have read the Vincents' situation in other ways. Margaret's loyalty to her faith and possibly to the priests who instructed her (though distorted by the writer and obviously pushed to wrongful ends) represented a dilemma of divided allegiance between her outlawed religion and her socially prescribed duties as an English wife and citizen (A3r). Devout Catholics, for instance, might have agreed with her that reading "Protestant booke[s]" could imperil one's soul. These contexts also complicated Margaret's criminal identity in different ways from Martha Scambler's in *Deeds Against Natvre*. The latter's murder was represented as an extreme sign of a universally flawed female nature. Margaret's motives and actions manifested public clashes over legitimate attitudes to competing religions, state sovereignty, and moral conscience that were intensifying throughout this period. For some readers, these factors could have created equitable shadings in what was otherwise absolutely culpable behavior.

Sectarian perspectives would also have been in people's minds because they were hearing and buying an unprecedented stream of reports about the Overbury poison and murder trials that were circulating in 1615 to 1616. Providentialist assumptions about God's justice intervening through his authorized agents shaped the multiple narratives of hidden treasons that emerged during the Overbury trials and in the gallows speeches of penitent convicts such as Anne Turner (see chapter 4). *A pittilesse Mother* drew attention to these intertextual associations in its description of the maidservant's fortuitous return, which deflected Margaret's spiral into suicide towards godly repentance (A4r). The centrality of poison to the Overbury trials had mobilized popular associations of Catholic zealots with secret murders, and these created further cultural lenses through which to read the Vincent case. Sir Edward Coke had hinted publicly that the heir to the throne, Prince Henry, had been murdered in 1612 by poisoned grapes, and implicitly linked the Overbury case with earlier Catholic plots against the monarch in 1605 and the 1580s.[28] *A pittilesse Mother* adopted the same strategy of authenticating Margaret's criminality by associating it with previous Catholic conspiracies against the Crown. The writer claimed that Margaret "deemed it a merritorious deede to charge [her husband's] conscience with that infectious burthen of Romish oppinions." She also rationalized her decision to kill her children because "their Religion [claims] that it was merritorious yea and pardonable to take away the lives of any opposing Protestants were it of any degree whatsoeuer" (A3r). The word "merritorious" (also A4r, B1r) coded Protestant outrage (or Catholic dismay) towards the 1570 papal bull *Regnans in excelsis,* which was popularly understood to declare it "meritorious" for English Catholics to assassinate Elizabeth, and to absolve them of guilt in using violence to send Protestants to heaven or elsewhere.

Publisher John Trundle extended these associations by appending a conventional verse lament in the second half of the pamphlet: "Andersons Repentance who, was executed at Tiburne the 18. of May being Whitson euen. 1616" (B3r). The concluding signature *"William Anderson"* (C4r) is curious, because this was the well-known alias of William Richardson, the last Catholic priest to be executed under Elizabeth, on 17 February 1603. Trundle may have recycled this text from an unidentified source to cover the execution of another priest that took place around the same time as Margaret's condemnation. John Chamberlain noted in a letter to Dudley Carleton on 6 July 1616 that "a seminarie priest [was] hanged at Tiborn on Monday that was banished before, and beeing taken again offered to breake prison."[29] Whether this was the same person signified by "Andersons Repentance"—the discrepancy might not have mattered to contemporaries, because the analogy was clear—the lament supplied the Protestant closure missing in the account of Margaret Vincent, which ended without any gallows confession or conversion but symbolically merged her domestic identity with that of an enemy of the state.

Or for Catholic readers, was Vincent, more ambiguously, some kind of martyr? *A pittilesse Mother* seemed aware of readers opting for this perspective, since it used polemical language to ridicule contemporary religious positions that might resignify murder in special circumstances as valid or beneficial, while at the same time relying on normative criminal law assumptions that child killing is a statutory felony and unequivocally wrong. Such assumptions derive authority from an idea of the law as a timeless and objective moral authority. The modern legal theorist Bernard Jackson describes this relationship as "co-referentiality," in which trials invoke arguments and statutes appropriate to judging the event and determining guilt or innocence according to the law's putatively neutral and transhistorical ideals of justice. These concepts supposedly remain unchallengeable, even though the law's applications may be disputed at lesser levels of circumstantial evidence.[30]

Writers of early seventeenth-century news pamphlets such as *A pittilesse Mother* relied on similar assumptions about absolute legal principles and their impersonal application by the courts. These appeared to leave little formal room for equitable counter arguments, or nonnormative cultural positions. Yet as Coke's musings about past and present Catholic poisoners during the Overbury trials indicated, early modern law did not strive for value-neutral judgments or classify evidence "objectively" in ways that modern jurisprudence attempts to do. For Coke, the law's authority was grounded in English legal and political history, in which certain interpretive positions had gained ascendancy over, or temporarily erased, others. As Stanley Fish has argued, while the courts draw their power and legitimacy from an apparent situation of completeness and self-sufficiency, the fact that interpretation always has a history means it is never permanently closed and can be re-opened by new discursive reasoning and social energies.[31] Like Coke, early modern readers and officials valorized Margaret Vincent's crime within historically contested fields of religious belief and legal interpretation. They continued to do so in other cases with varying degrees of intensity over the course of the century. To contain interpretive or material ambiguities and affirm their own narrative viewpoint—in effect to impose closure on "history"—news writers sought to construct rhetorical and ideological compacts with imagined readers. But the latter were far from culturally unified or immune to changing perspectives, and were capable of re-interpreting cases from their own independent perceptions of equitable differences.

Religious discourses in other early modern news pamphlets relativized normative legal and social interpretations of infanticide. The detailed but probably almost entirely fictional *Horrible Murther of a young Boy of three yeres of age, whose Sister had her tongue cut out* (1606) strikingly demonstrated this ambivalence. The unnamed boy had been killed by robbers after they viciously murdered his parents. They allowed his older sister to live after cutting out her tongue. She survived as a vagrant and village orphan until one day identifying one of killers and her son when they visited the community. The pamphlet's title had advertised its providentialist credentials to readers: "and how it pleased God to reueale the offendors, by giuing speech to the tongueles Childe." Yet the conclusion turned the anticipated interpretation inside out (B3r–v). The writer claimed the story's deeper moral was that it was desirable to rejoice in children's early deaths—even by murder—because by outliving their offspring, parents would avoid improper self-love (or perhaps love that turned their children into negotiable property in marriage alliances). One wonders what this writer would have made of Margaret Vincent's actions—if she had not been Catholic.

Child murders motivated by religious fanaticism—or opposition to it—continued to complicate legal and cultural reception of their representations in popular news. The title page illustration of a grim little pamphlet entitled *Bloody Newes from Dover. Being A True Relation Of The great and bloudy Murder, committed by Mary Champion* (1646/47) depicted a man with arms raised in surprise facing a woman holding out a bleeding infant's head in the palm of one hand, while she points behind her with the other to a headless naked corpse. A knife lies at her feet. The man is labelled "Presbyterian" and the woman "Anabaptist," thus situating the story within the highly charged sectarian conflicts of the 1640s. An anonymous publisher's line at the bottom of the page, "Printed in the Yeare of Discovery, *Feb*, 13. 1647," informed buyers of the pamphlet's point of view. "The Yeare of Discovery" alluded to a publishing sensation the year before: Thomas Edwards's *Gangraena* (1646), an 800-page catalogue of alleged dissenting religious practices and beliefs (or, as the Preface to the Third Part put it, a "Discovery of the Errours, Heresies, and Insolencies of the Sectaries;" Preface to the Reader, A1v).[32] The slight discrepancy between the "Yeare of Discovery" and the different publication dates of *Bloody Newes from Dover* and *Gangraena* was noted by a contemporary annotator of the British Library copy, who marked "1646" beside the pamphlet's publication date.[33] This punctiliousness usefully confirms the intertextual relationship between the two publications.

Gangraena was Edwards's (*ca.*1599–1647) chief work. He was a clergyman who published several vociferous polemics to support reorganizing the Church of England along presbyterian lines. Despite its length, *Gangraena* sold spectacularly well in multiple editions, which testified to the emotional urgency of the propaganda wars between presbyterians and independents for public support.[34] The independents included the loosely defined Anabaptists, a sect of radical religious and social separatists. Edwards drew on information supplied by a vast body of informants to compile his "discoveries" or "Relations" of sectarian outrages. These generic labels created another intertextual link with *Bloody Newes from Dover*. Aside from the illustration, the second most prominent feature of its title page was typographical: the oversize word RELATION, which crowded out *Bloody Newes* in much smaller print at the top of the page. The visual connection between "Relation" and the labelled image drew the attention of buyers—even ones with limited reading skills—to the religiously motivated nature of the crime, and implied that the pamphlet would supplement Edwards's parent volume of discoveries. Later seventeenth-century news pamphlets recycled these typographic and sectarian associations when describing themselves as "Relations." The title page of *The Unnatural Grand Mother* (1659, discussed below), for example, printed "Relation" and "Murther" in extra-large type and denounced Jesuits and Quakers who allegedly contested the normative definition of murder (A3r).[35]

Bloody Newes from Dover prefaced its main story by reporting an earlier revenge killing that might have reminded some readers of the Margaret Vincent case. Because this was a pretrial account, it was intended partly to remind readers, including jurors and judges, of legal precedents. The previous murder took place in Yorkshire at the beginning of Charles I's reign when national religious conflicts were intensifying. A Protestant husband and his Catholic wife quarrelled over the upbringing of their four-year-old son. The unnamed woman vowed to have the boy brought up a Catholic "or else he should be of no Religion at all" (A2v). The wife grimly literalized her threat by murdering her son, for which she was tried and executed.

Bloody Newes from Dover updated infanticide's relationship to discourses of religious controversy from Protestant–Catholic conflicts in the first decades of the seventeenth century to Protestant factions during the Civil War, while repeating a similar plotline. Divisions between Mary and John Champion of Dover arose over the christening of their first newborn child. As an Anabaptist, Mary would have favored adult rather than infant baptism, and she temporarily prevailed over her "much perplexed" husband. But her victory failed to resolve the domestic stand-off, which reached a climax six or seven weeks later when Mary took advantage of John's absence from home and "took a great knife and cut off the Childs head" (A3r).

On one level the legal and moral values of the story again seemed straightforward. Yet Mary Champion's representation as a fanatical infanticide might have been read more equivocally by non-presbyterian readers. *Gangraena* illustrated the raised stakes on both sides by relating a story about an antinomian woman who claimed "*That if a child of God should commit murther, he ought not to repent of it.*"[36] From Edward's point of view, the woman's claim was evidence of irrational wickedness. It might not have been understood the same way by Edwards's opponents, such as John Goodwin, author of *Cretensis, or, A Briefe Answer To an ulcerous Treatise* (1646). If independent or Anabaptist readers did not simply dismiss *Bloody Newes from Dover* as propaganda, they might have interpreted Mary Champion's motives with varying degrees of skepticism. For example, they might have seized on the pamphlet's concluding report that she was both conventionally penitent and

> distracted, by beholding strange Visions. For, shee can no wayes fixe her eyes upon any thing, but presently (she conceives) the poore Babe to appear before her without a head. (A3v)

Edward Sherburne had carefully affirmed that Margaret Vincent was not suffering from "distemper or distracion" at the time she killed her children. He meant to forestall John Chamberlain wondering about the possibility of insanity to explain her actions. Early modern persons found *non compos mentis* were often held not responsible for their actions and were legally acquitted. Because *Bloody Newes from Dover* was a pre-assize account, the writer's description might have raised the possibility of equitable mitigation. According to Garthine Walker, this defense began to have an impact on trial juries and judges by mid-seventeenth century and became "an increasingly common means of interpreting and mitigating new-born child-murder."[37] Given *Bloody Newes*'s reports of Mary Champion's "distraction" after the killing, contemporary readers might have wondered not only whether it explained her violence beforehand but also undercut the religious premise of the whole account.

THE PRICE OF MOTHERHOOD

The stories of female child-killers examined so far have attempted to control the narrative slippages and contextual ambiguities of individual women's lives by reducing their subjects to monstrous types of natural or religious disorder, and by reconstructing their actions within axiomatic legal and ethical positions. One of the obstacles to more equitable understanding of women's circumstances was an absence of perspectives other than those based on deductive or traditional categories. Early modern assizes did not allow defendants legal counsel except in the most important state cases, such as the Overbury or Castlehaven trials. Yet then as now, juries or readers could inductively challenge prosecution arguments found in indictments, or popular news reports derived from them, by identifying internal inconsistencies in the criminal narrative or material evidence that created doubts about the defendant's motives or the law's legitimate application.[38] Besides the grounds of insanity (to which I shall return later), female infanticides could escape punishment through judicial pardons, informal or indefinite reprieves, and by pleading pregnancy.[39] Yet these recourses made little attempt to understand the woman's actions from her own perspective. Rather they employed mitigating remedies to soften or divert normative judgments.

Constructing gender differentiated defense narratives for nonaristocratic women that would shift public opinions about "excusable" infanticide and ultimately rewrite criminal laws required finding alternative material and social discourses that would "talk" new categories of knowledge and interpretation into being.[40] *Natures Cruell Step-Dames: Or, Matchlesse Monsters of the Female Sex* (1637) took some tentative steps in these directions, not from theoretical principles, but by virtue of Henry Goodcole's empirical experiences of condemned felons over twenty years that highlighted systemic as well as personal causes of female violence. These encounters led him to introduce real social analysis and defense perspectives into his story of Elizabeth Barnes, a widow who murdered her young daughter in 1637.

When he first met Barnes in prison, Goodcole's impressions seem to have been influenced by earlier seventeenth-century reports about female child murderers, possibly including Martha Scambler and Jane Hattersley. As we saw in *Deeds Against Natvre,* such stories titillated readers' imaginations by describing the "lusty body [and] strong nature" (i.e., hypersexualized femininity) that supposedly allowed such woman to give birth unassisted.[41] Goodcole's curiosity about Barnes seemed to have been similarly piqued by her physical appearance and its relationship to the received image of murderous mothers:

> [Barnes's crimes] being rumoured abroad, I went unto Newgate to visit this mizerbale delinquent, who at my first view of her matronly aspect, induced me to enter into present discourse with her, to prevaile if I could possibly, to find out the cause that moved her unto such unheard of cruelty. (A3v)[42]

Even after three interviews, Goodcole never found an answer that satisfied him. Yet it was significant that he told readers about his attempts and limited success, rather than trying to project an image of professional mastery through consummate narrative closure. The element of doubt was also legally meaningful, as Goodcole was aware. The pamphlet opened without any special pleading for broaching such low subjects, or any potted history of biblical sin and murder. Instead Goodcole presented the crime's events in order of their occurrence, beginning with Elizabeth Barnes's tormented thoughts of killing her daughter a month before the deed. He deferred realistic explanations of her motives to later in the narrative, however, and drew readers in by reconstructing Barnes's crime as a domestic version of the Fall, centering on a fatal picnic in Wormewall Wood near Fulham (discussed in chapter 4, p. 132). The shrouded secrecy of the location, conventionally associated with criminal violence, had been boldly anticipated by the original title page illustration showing a kneeling woman in petticoats vigorously cutting the throat of a child lying on the ground with her left hand. The alternating light and shadow of the densely clustered trees conveyed active darkness, while the somewhat undulating tree-trunks suggested a disturbing energy in rhythm with the human violence. The absence of people, animals, or any distant town signalled a deserted location far from the protections of civilization.[43]

"[H]aving eaten of such things formerly provided for it," the daughter fell asleep, and between the hours of eleven and twelve Barnes cut her throat. Soon afterward "[Barnes's] eyes were opened," but her attempts at suicide failed (A3r). She fled to Kensington and was discovered hiding in a barn, a site symbolic of her life turning full circle. In Newgate, Goodcole discovered during the course of his three interviews that Barnes had fallen into desperate poverty after inheriting a small estate as a widow but wasting it on a faithless lover (A4r). Growing mentally overwrought and suicidal, she thought about killing her daughter for over a month, but hesitated from discussing her dilemma with anyone out of shame and female modesty. Goodcole had heard and written about similar stories of abandonment and poverty before (see his pamphlets about Elizabeth Evans and Alice Clarke, above pp. 95, 14). But he was also still a prison visitor demanding a confession. Without one forthcoming, he inserted a homily relating the causes of Barnes's tragedy to her failure to embrace traditional spiritual disciplines such as fasting or prayer and to seek counsel from clergy (while mentioning nothing about the acculturated feelings of shame that inhibited public disclosure of her situation). More unusually, he accused parish neighbors of neglecting to support a woman at risk:

> If this womans house had beene set on fire, doubtlesse she would have made such an out-crie in the streets, that all her neighbours must of necessity rise, and adde unto her all help possible to quench the fire. Her heart was here set on fire by hell, musing to perpetrate mischiefe. (A4v)

His comments anticipated later news writers who opposed strictly legal and moral interpretations of a woman's guilt with humanitarian ones and assumed communities had responsibilities to protect their most vulnerable or wayward members (e.g., *A Particular account of Mary Compton*; see below).[44] Goodcole's authorial voice and speaking position in *Natures Cruell Step-Dames* were arguably the most self-assured of any of his half-dozen crime reports. This may have been partly due to receiving his first church appointment the year before, possibly on the strength of his two very successful crime publications in 1635. In his intervening homily he presented a passionate defense of his work as a prison chaplain and articulated a vision of Christian social justice that his personal experiences had gradually built up through knowledge of individual women and men.

When he resumed Barnes's story briefly before her execution, Goodcole revealed that she had become pregnant by her lover, Richard Evans, who had spent all the estate she inherited from her dead husband and then abandoned her, "upon whose conscience lieth very heavie, his false dealing with the poore woman" (C1v). Goodcole boldly lay partial responsibility for Barnes's crime on Evans's personal abdication of masculine credit and responsibility, by "whose deceits and flatteries, this poore creatures ruine was occasioned' (C1v). His naming of Evans in print was unprecedented and opened the possibility of him being eventually disciplined by the church courts. By shifting responsibility for Barnes's behavior partly on to a disordered male offender, Goodcole re-imagined the female criminal subject not simply as an autonomous victim of her own moral weakness, but constrained by hostile social agencies. His focus on poverty and gender called attention to imbalances of power that became new epistemological categories for explaining the origins of child murder. When Mr Birch (?) the nonconformist clergyman author of *Fair Warning to Murderers of Infants* (1692) began his account of Mary Goodenough, the first thing he mentioned was her "Great Poverty and Straits." This situation left her vulnerable to financial as well as emotional manipulation by a neighboring baker, whom the author accused of causing the mother and child's tragedy—despite the pamphlet's otherwise conventional moralizing about female wickedness.

Several mid-century child-murder pamphlets followed the new orientation toward material and gendered contexts taken by *Natures Cruell Step-Dames*. In *The Unnatural Grand Mother* (1659) Elizabeth Hazard drowned her two-year-old grandchild in a tub of water. If the case was not simply a misreported accident built on conjecture or hearsay because it was a pre-trial account, her motives nonetheless remained unclear. Like Goodcole, the anonymous author combined moralizing and socially discerning commentary, relating the grandmother's actions to the devil's seducements and her unnamed daughter's financial hardships. Her daughter had just given birth to yet another child that threatened to push the family over the edge. After the mother left to take her newborn into the country to be nursed, Hazard inveigled her two-year old granddaughter away from its nurse at home into bed with her. There the narrator dramatized Hazard wrestling with her conscience about getting rid of the girl. Eventually she considered "the charge her daughter had of children, and a bad husband that would not endeavor to maintain them; and how that she [presumably, her daughter] was in debt, and like to run her self more in debt towards the maintaining them" (A3v–A4r). Overall, the writer indicated that a desire to improve the older children's chances of survival prompted Hazard to murder the child.[45]

In her discussion of this pamphlet, Toni Bowers argues that the writer revised the normal explanations for child murder as exceptional female deviancy by highlighting circumstances similar to those that affected Elizabeth Barnes's behavior:

> material circumstances can make motherhood untenable … there are times when a mother will be forced to choose between her own survival and the survival of her child. Elizabeth Hazard defines her daughter's motherhood as an economic problem; she presumes to place both financial and moral responsibility on her daughter's "bad husband."[46]

Hazard punished both the husband and her daughter, whom the writer praised for her self-sacrificing care and diligence, by killing the child. The daughter was "almost destroyed." Hazard thus became the pamphlet's scapegoat, defining transgressive motherhood as the choice of economic security and female independence over "natural" maternal affection and duty.[47]

This reading is perceptive, but other narrative details complicated the pamphlet's moral dichotomy. The writer stated that the morning after the murder, Hazard dressed in her best clothes, put £6 in her pocket, and left the house. Her neighbors immediately noticed something was up: "good Morrow Gammer *Hazzard*, you are very fine this morning" (A4r). Hazard allegedly invited one neighbor to see the tub with the drowned child, where-upon she fled to the window crying "Murder, Murder." Hazard not only denied the murder before the examining alderman but also "either madly or impudently affirm[ed] that if it were to do again she would do it" (A4r-v). Following this outburst, rumors circulated that she had also thought of murdering her daughter before she was married.

Hazard's unappeased anger after the murder (which contradicts the title page claim that she lay "in a sad condition," implying contrition) was not uncommon in early modern homicide news. Rhetorically it may have been added to verify the report that she willingly displayed the dead child to neighbors. More incongruous was the discovery that £6 in ready money was lying around a household that was supposedly very hard up, and that Haz-ard could still dress in fine clothes. Perhaps these were Hazard's personal possessions. But they also raised questions about insupportable poverty as the catalyst for murder.

One other possibility—as tentative as other readings—was suggested by the prominence given to the mother and daughter's work. Both the title page and inner title heading identified precisely where Hazard and her daughter sold fruit: "in *Cheap side*, neer *Soper* lane end." Repeating this information a third time, the writer further specified: "under the signe of the Golden-key" (A3v). He stated that they sold "all manner of fruit in a remarkable place." These details indicated the writer and his publisher, Thomas Higgins, wanted London readers to recognize the mother and daughter personally. Presum-ably they ran a flourishing business and were well known to local custom-ers. Hazard may have felt her son-in-law's indolence was "killing" both her daughter and their thriving trade. From this perspective, Hazard's infan-ticidal identity begins to resemble Margaret Vincent's and Mary Champi-on's, although here the revenge motives are financial and matrilineal rather than religious. Hazard felt driven to destroy the only "property" that the (nearly invisible but still biologically capable) son-in-law legally possessed. The writer prefaced his story with accounts of several other recent revenge murders,[48] and he lectured readers about the wickedness of private revenge (A2v-A3r), comparisons aimed at defining the case legally before it came to trial. These intertextual references also seemed to confirm that Hazard wished to punish her delinquent son-in-law by killing one of his children. Their stereotypical enmity was also suggested by the final hearsay report that she was willing to consider killing her daughter rather than allowing her to marry him.

SECRET BIRTHS

The more socially contextualized representations of child murder in these mid-century news pamphlets partly reflected conceptual changes that accom-panied a new law. A 1624 statute made newborn child murder a distinctly female crime, targeting poor unmarried women.[49] It remained on the books until 1803, although prosecutions and convictions started to decline from initially high levels in the mid-seventeenth century. Recent studies of legal records indicate that public attitudes towards its peculiar definition of murder became more skeptical and negotiable than those reported in pre-1624 pamphlets. Paradoxically, the growth of new forms of crime journalism in an increasingly competitive market created the opposite impression.

Earlier efforts to legislate an infanticide bill in 1607 and 1610 may have been partly instigated by the sensational revelations of London brothels employing neighborhood married women in *The Araignement & burning of Margaret Ferne-seede* (whose name carried the implication of "by-blows" of the trade being surreptitiously disposed of), or of serial adultery and multiple-infant murders revealed by *The Bloudy Mother*.[50] The 1624 act aimed to deter and punish illicit sexual behavior and to reduce the financial burden of illegitimate children, labelled "chargeable bastards," on parish relief paid for by male householders after the passage of the Elizabethan poor laws.[51] Framers of the act assumed unmarried "lewd Women" regularly killed their newborn children by secretly drowning or burying them to avoid being prosecuted by the church courts and/or sent to the house of correction, as a 1610 law had already provided for.[52] Women in these situations would also almost certainly lose their places in service and become respectably unemployable. The 1624 statue therefore made concealment of birth without any witnesses or assistance presumptive proof of murder, regardless of whether the child was born alive or dead. It also eased the forensic difficulty of proving infanticide under common law, which required evidence that the child had been born alive and then deliberately killed. Such evidence and corroborating witnesses were hard to produce.[53]

Martin Parker's gallows ballad, *No natural mother*, licensed for publication on 16 July 1634, is the first extant publication bearing signs of the statute's new definition of infanticide.[54] Its anonymous maidservant narrator lamented that after she had become pregnant and the "father on't was fled," she ran into the yard when she went into labor. Despite being in public view, she claimed that no-one was available to assist her delivery. Parker probably added this incongruous detail to "prove" his subject had given birth alone and violated the new 1624 law. The narrator's confession focused attention on what became the main physical issue of many early modern infanticide trials—material evidence of intent to conceal a birth—and foreshadowed scores of similar claims by women charged under the act.

In the ballad's second part the narrator says she hid her newborn baby "in the straw, where it was smother'd," yet a few lines later she calls it "my strangled infant." This alteration led listeners or readers to understand the death as homicide. In their research into seventeenth-century infanticide trials at Chester, J. R. Dickinson and J. A. Sharpe observed that coroners' inquests increasingly included charges of both infanticide and murder on indictments to enable prosecutors to select the second charge if the first was considered unlikely to stick.[55] This equivocating practice answered juries' increasing reluctance to accept newborn infant murder as concealment alone, or to attribute dishonest or malicious motives exclusively to solitary births.[56] Strong doubts about these key aspects of the 1624 statute were sown by the most famous infanticide case of the century involving a twenty-two-year old Oxford maidservant named Anne Greene.

STRANGE WENCH! WHAT CHARACTER MAY FIT [THEE] BEST, THAT STILL CANST LIVE, THOUGH THOU ART HANG'D AND PREST?[57]

On 14 December 1650 Greene caused a sensation among Oxford dons by reviving just before she was about to be dissected in an anatomy lecture. Only hours before she had been hanged for infanticide. As the news spread, the public quickly understood Greene's resuscitation as a divine rebuke of her trial and verdict, and, more gradually, a critique of the 1624 law. In terms of early modern infanticide news, Greene's story was exceptional owing to the multiple accounts that reassessed her "crime" and its spectacular aftermath from innovative legal, scientific, and cultural perspectives. They also illustrated the new social functions of emergent printed-news formats.[58]

Penny pamphlets presented the crime from traditional providentialist perspectives. W. Burdet's eye-witness report of Greene's trial and recovery in fact served as the basis for two published reports: *A Wonder of Wonders. Being A faithful Narrative and true Relation, of one Anne Green* (1651), and *A Declaration from Oxford, of Anne Green, A young woman that was lately, and unjustly hanged in the Castle-yard; but since recovered* (1651). Only *A Declaration* identified the place of publication and publisher on its title page: "*LONDON, Printed* by J. Clowes." Clowes must have issued both pamphlets, because they used the same illustration interpreting the story's key moments: Greene praying on her knees beneath the gallows ladder; hanging hooded from the gibbet while her cousin (mercifully) pulls on her feet and a soldier hits her chest with the butt of his musket to hasten her death; Greene starting awake in bed beside a (somewhat bemused looking) woman and declaring "Behold Gods providence;" and an empty coffin with a shroud inside. The extended title page wording of *A Wonder of Wonders* suggested it was intended for a local readership because it referred familiarly to "*Mr. Clarkes* house" where the dissection was to take place and to "*Dr. Petty*," the Oxford reader in anatomy and professor of medicine whose treatments revived Greene.[59] *A Declaration* omitted certain local details while contextualizing Petty's involvement for non-Oxford readers by identifying him as one of the "Colledge of Physitions" who gathered to dissect Greene's body.

Although identical in most sections, the pamphlets' contrasting styles of presentation and degrees of embellishment were tied to distinct news readerships, and perhaps different markets, in Oxford and London.[60]

A Wonder of Wonders.

BEING

A faithful *Narrative* and true *Relation*, of one *Anne Green*, Servant to Sir *Tho. Reed* in *Oxfordshire*, who being got with Child by a Gentleman, her Child falling from her in the houfe or Office, being but a fpan long, and dead born, was condemned on the 14. of *December* laft, and hanged in the Caftle-yard in *Oxford*, for the fpace of half an hour, receiving many great and heavy blowes on the brefts, by the but end of the Souldiers Muskets, and being pul'd down by the leggs, and was afterwards beg'd for an Anatomy, by the Phyficians, and carried to Mr. *Clarkes* houfe, an Apothecary, where in the prefence of many learned Chyrurgions, fhe breathed, and began to ftir; infomuch, that Dr. *Petty* caufed a warm bed to be prepared for her, let her blood, and applyed Oyls to her, fo that in 14 hours fhe recovered, and the firft words fhe fpake were thefe; *Behold Gods Providence* ! *Behold his miraculous and loving kindnefs* ! With the manner of her Tryal, her Speech and Confeffion at the Gallowes; and a Declaration of the Souldiery touching her recovery. *Witneffed by Dr. Petty, and Licenfed according to Order.*

Figure 5.3 A Wonder of Wonders (1651). Reproduced by permission of the British Library.

Notwithstanding its title and woodcut image, *Wonder of Wonders* was more factually neutral. It took the form of a letter with anti-royalist overtones, dated "*Oxford* Jan. 13. 1651," briefly reporting the crime and Greene's conventional gallows speech. Burdet stated from the beginning that Greene's "delivery" was a miscarriage and that the child's father was an Oxford "Gentleman of good birth, and kinsman to a justice of the Peace" (2). Local readers could have identified this person as Jeffrey Read, the sixteen- or seventeen-year-old grandson of Sir Thomas Read JP, in whose household Greene served and who aggressively prosecuted her for infanticide.[61] Burdet further stated that Greene was "clear and innocent of the crime of murdering" the child, which was "dead-born," although she confessed under examination (possibly by Thomas Read himself, among others) of being "guilty of the [1624] Act." He briskly characterized Greene's revival as a wonder in an age that no longer believed in miracles. His main interest became clear at the end where he presented Greene's trial as an example of ruling authority and class interests overbearing justice and equity. William Perkins anticipated Burdet's more popular observations in *E'ΠΙΕΙΈΙA* [*Hepieíkeia*]: *or, A Treatise of Christian Equitie and moderation* (1604, Cbv–B1r) by arguing that judges were responsible for tempering criminal statues, which favored the powerful, with natural law and justice: "he is but halfe a Iudge, who can do nothing but vrge the lawe, and is not able also, to mittigate the rigor of the lawe, when neede so requireth" (A5v). Burdet likewise warned magistrates and judges "to take a special care in denounsing of sentence, without a due and legal process," and to employ "an impartial and uncorrupted Jury, either of men or women." His comments may have implied that Read had pressured or bribed the jurors who tried Greene. Read was also undoubtedly the "great man" who attempted to have her re-hanged after she revived, "contrary to all Law, reason and justice."

Criminal law technically sentenced condemned felons to be hanged until they were dead. Occasional survivors of seventeenth-century executions (a not uncommon occurrence before introduction of the drop, which killed by snapping the neck rather than strangling; hence efforts by Greene's relations to shorten her agony by pulling on her legs) were sometimes re-hanged by officious sheriffs.[62] But according to *A Wonder of Wonders*, New Model Army soldiers garrisoned in Oxford had their own ideas of justice, declaring

> That there was a great hand of God in it, and having suffered the Law, it was contrary to all right and reason, that any further punishment should be inflicted upon her, which words brought a final end and period to [the legal] dispute and controversie. (5–6)

Cynthia B. Herrup and J. A. Sharpe have each shown how involvement in litigation by ordinary people at many levels led them to formulate independent ideas about the law, which were often different from those of the elite.[63] Burdet provided an example of this consciousness in action, as Oxford's soldiers and the public used local structures of authority to impose ideas of equitable justice while deflecting the strict application of a legal statute. Just as importantly, his pamphlet and other reports preserved the memory of this dispute for readers involved in future cases of infanticide.

Burdet's critique of judicial power reverberated through other reports of Greene's case, though sometimes in ambiguous ways. *A Declaration from Oxford* repackaged his story in Calvinist eschatology. An opening preface presented Greene's story as a latter-day example of heaven's "All seeing" judgement against the "corrupting juglings" of the reprobate (here referring to court officers). The final report of local soldiers' opposition to re-hanging Greene was replaced, however, with a tearful prayer in which "she" compared herself to Mary Magdalene. This ending reinstalled her as a daughter of Eve and shifted the event's meaning towards the apocalyptic, verified by Greene's alleged "death-trance:"

> being (as it were) in a Garden of Paradice, there appeared to her 4. little boyes with wings, being four Angels, saying, *Woe unto them that decree unrighteous Decrees, and take away the right from the Judges, that the innocent may be their prey.* Upon which words they vanished, *&c.* . . . . And being further asked . . . she saw her chief enemy [i.e. Thomas Read] dead before her. (A3v)

Prophecies by women such as Lady Eleanor Davis and Anna Trapnel represented notable interventions by women in the religious politics of the civil-war years.[64] This attempt to enlist Greene among them seemed to be confirmed *post hoc* by the elder Read's death three days after she was granted a pardon.[65]

Other news versions of the story avoided such metaphysical claims, however, and continued legal and politicized debates about the trial itself. The earliest account appeared in Marchmont Nedham's newsbook *Mercurius Politicus*, which filed two reports. The first dated 18 December 1650 (Number 28, 12–19 December) distinguished two sorts of readers, the "ordinary sort" amazed by such "remarkable act[s] of providence," and "discreet and reasonable men;" that is, skeptical or rationally minded readers. *Politicus* appealed to this educated class by emphasizing forensic evidence for the defense; for example, Greene's miscarried foetus was "not above a span long, and of whether sexe scarce distinginguished." It chose some details to impart a wryly ironic tone: for example, Greene was tried at the Oxford assizes "by one 'Mr. *Crook*.'" And after Greene was first seen to be breathing, "a lusty fellow standing by, thinking to do an act of charity, stamped upon her breast and belly" before Dr. Petty and his colleagues arrived to spare her.[66]

On the other hand Nedham anticipated *Wonder of Wonder*'s endorsement of natural law and popular justice by reporting that "thousands of people" came to visit Greene after her recovery:

all seem to be satisfied of the wenches innocency to the murther, which she doth now, as on the Gallowes she did assert and stand in: so that 'tis apprehended to be such a contrary verdict from heaven that may strike terror to the consciences of those who have been any way faulty in this businesse.

A later issue of *Politicus* (Number 32, 9–16 January 1651) refuted *A Declaration*'s "angel vision," characterizing it as an old wives's tale. Dr. Petty noticed that some "Women about [Greene]" had begun insinuating "unto her to relate of strange Visions and apparitions to have been seen by her in that time wherein she seem'd Dead." To prevent this, Petty ejected everybody but male physicians from the recovery room. When Greene became conscious she remembered nothing between the morning of her execution and her revival (184).[67]

Dr. Ralph Bathurst, president of Trinity College, Oxford, chose not to include this debunking explanation in his substantial and otherwise far more scientific account, *Newes from the Dead. Or A True and Exact Narration of the miraculous deliverance of Anne Greene* (1651). It was a synthesis of Dr. Petty's notes about Greene's daily examinations and medical treatments, as well as earlier news reports (e.g., *Politicus*, whose details and wording Bathurst occasionally recalls; or was Bathurst the Oxford-educated Nedham's correspondent?). Although publisher Leonard Lichfield's title page advertised Greene's story as a "miraculous deliverance," Bathurst described it as a "very rare and remarkable accident . . . being variously and falsely reported amongst the vulgar" (A2r). His attitude towards Thomas Read's death, which occurred only three days after Greene was pardoned, reflected the professional restraint in judgment and privileging of verifiable data that were slowly transforming jurors' evaluation of legal evidence and standards of journalistic reporting: "because [Read] was an old man, and such Events are not too rashly to be commented on, I shall not make use of that observation" (B1r).[68]

Bathurst's refusal to venture into metaphysical speculation respected a line that national (i.e., London-based) crime writers such as Henry Goodcole had hitherto used to distinguish pamphlet news from ballad news *buyers*, but that in all events continued to be blurred in popular journalism well into the future. Nonetheless, Oxford's substantially divided town and gown markets (*pace* cross-over buyers such as Anthony à Wood) prompted Bathurst to define his readership by demanding a high level of literacy, as he presented lengthy, technically precise explanations to clear Greene of the two legal charges against her and to validate her original claim of being unaware of being pregnant. Medical examination of the foetus by midwives and physicians proved that Greene's pregnancy had not gone beyond seventeen weeks and that she had had "continual Issues" a month before the miscarriage, "which [was] of that nature (Physicians say) as are not consistent with the vitality of a child" (B1r). Until this point, moreover, she had gone ten weeks "without the usual Courses of women." So when Greene claimed the child "fell from her unawares," this "long and great Evacuation might make her judge, that it was nothing else but a flux of those humors which for ten weeks before had been suppressed" (B1r). By medicalizing Greene's body functions as miscarriage and premature stillbirth, *Newes from the Dead* decriminalized Greene's allegedly immoral behavior, reconstituting her public identity as a servant woman victimized by her "Grand Prosecutor" Thomas Read (B1r) and his gentry family, and, in a wider sense, by cultural ignorance of female physiology. For the first time among infanticide news reports, Bathurst formulated a positive legal defense based on gynaecological and socially contextual evidence (*viz.* "a Review of the Cause ... as a matter of fact for which she suffered" [A4v]). His pamphlet initiated the cultural work of challenging the puritan ideology of the 1624 statute by educating readers about medical explanations for alleged cases of infanticide. Bathurst's report was reproduced in William Derham's *Physico-Theology* (1713, and reissued in twelve editions over the eighteenth century), which used Greene's case to illustrate the "more than ordinary Strength of the Wind-pipe" ("Of Respiration," 157), and in Joseph Morgan's popular *Phoenix Britannicus* (1731).

Later writers disseminated Burdet's and Bathurst's redefinition of Greene's "crime" as malicious prosecution and judicial misinterpretation. *Britains Triumphs* (1656) defended her "innocence and integrity" while impugning the "prejudice" and "unadvised actings of men" who condemned her (67–9). Denis Petau's entry in *The History of the World* (1659) stated:

> *Anne Green*, innocently condemned to dye, as for murder of an abortive Infant, at *Oxford* Assizes in 1650, through a too harsh prosecution of her potent Master Sir *Tho. Reed*, by one of whose men or friends in that house she affirmed to be with child: the overstraining of whose body by working, caused this abortion to be made in a house of easement. (502)

Petau's volume continued to shift the determining criterion of infanticide back to the common-law's requirement of material evidence to prove murder. Like Burdet in *A Wonder of Wonders*, James Heath read the case as a warning to judges and juries in *A Brief Chronicle Of the Late Intestine Warr In the Three Kingdoms of England, Scotland, and Ireland* (1663). His entry headed "A memorable accideut [*sic*] at Oxford" was recycled (with acknowledgement) for somewhat different purposes by Robert Plot's *The Natural History of Oxfordshire* (1677). Plot used the case to explore Pliny's belief that women revive more often than men after being apparently killed.[69] Echoing earlier commentators, Plot attributed Greene's resuscitation to providential justice making use of natural and human means to produce seemingly supernatural effects (197–99). He also concluded Greene's biography, reporting that Anne went to live with friends in Steeple Barton, married and had three children, and lived there until her death in 1659.

Questions about Greene's legal, sexual, and/or ontological status after her legally unauthorized—or providential—survival remained open to discursive speculation. Oxford dons played with her identity in a collection of waggish poems written in Latin, English, and French appended to the main prose report of *Newes from the Dead*:

> The Womans *Case* put to the Lawyers
> Mother, or Maid, I pray you whether?
> One, or both, or am I neither?
> The mother dyed: may't not be said
> That the survivor is a Maid?
> Here, take you Fee, declare your sense;
> And free me from this New Suspense.
>
> (John Watkins, Queen's College, B2r)

Not surprisingly, many poems praised the skills of Dr. Petty and his colleagues, which demonstrated the rational superiority of forensic science and secular medicine:

> Some rigid ones perhaps this act will spell
> With the strange letters of a Miracle:
> But know, *Physitians* have a larger Call,
> *Apollo*'and *Physick* are colaterall.
>
> (J. Hutton, New College, B4v)

Sympathy for Greene did not exclude dashes of traditional humor:

> Women in this with Cats agree, I think,
> Both Live and Scratch after they'have *tip't the Wink*. (B4v)

1624 REVIVED

The 1624 statute exhibited feline longevity as well. Historians have demonstrated that, in terms of prosecution and convictions, seventeenth-century infanticide was always an unusual crime in comparison with other felonies committed by women, though not as rare as witchcraft.[70] Successful prosecutions and convictions under the 1624 statute started at relatively high levels in the 1630s and 40s and then began to fall at variable rates from the mid-to-late seventeenth century into the eighteenth.[71] Analyzing the unusually full records of the Court of Great Sessions at Chester, Garthine Walker finds the execution rate was correspondingly lower because the 1624 act inadvertently created unique opportunities for female defendants to obtain acquittals and pardons on the basis of gender-differentiated evidence, such as signs of violence against newborn infants. She reports that thirty-three Cheshire women were executed for infanticide between 1560 and 1709. The law was never severely enforced even immediately after its introduction and gradually became evaded and discredited.[72] The full explanation for these outcomes, however, lies not just in technical strategies for mitigation created inadvertently by the 1624 law. Ideas of social and moral equity represented in popular news also gave the possibility of mitigation at arraignments or trials the necessary cultural legitimacy in the eyes of jurors, judges, and the public. Celebrated cases such as Anne Greene's, as well as contextual recognition of legal and religious controversies and economic and social disadvantages facing isolated single mothers, encouraged later seventeenth-century juries and judges to hesitate to convict on the grounds of concealment alone. In Surrey between 1660 to 1800, seven of twenty-three indictments for infanticide were dismissed by the grand jury. Of the remaining sixteen women who were tried, nine were acquitted and six were convicted (one case is unknown, as is the number ultimately executed—almost certainly lower).[73]

The 1624 act undoubtedly had negative cultural effects, such as the labelling of unmarried mothers "bastard-bearers." The term became common from mid-century, and it deepened presumptions that single mothers would kill their children.[74] The statute thus hardened the judgmental link between illegitimacy and culpability, though as Mark Jackson has shown, the primary impetus for such attitudes remained financial: "women who threatened to burden parishes with chargeable bastards."[75] A significant anomaly in the historical trend of prosecutions occurred in the years 1680 to 81, and to a lesser extent for the remainder of that decade. Chester records indicate that prosecutions temporarily spiked upwards from initially elevated numbers that had passed into a declining trend. Dickinson and Sharpe observed that "[s]urviving [court] documentation leaves no indication why this ["local infanticide wave"] obtained."[76]

Popular news may suggest an answer: politicized and markedly increased publishing activity that influenced public officers and the courts. Infanticide was a highly marketable story at a time when crime journalism was expanding rapidly. The growth of printed news in the late 1670s and 80s revived the threatening image of the unmarried and incipiently murderous mother of bastard offspring, and thereby restricted equitable perspectives (except, perhaps, in readers who were skeptical about, or opposed to, particular ideologies or parties). Although the picture from legal records does not support the idea of "an obsession with the classic crimes of horror—infanticide and petty treason" and ruthless prosecution throughout most of the century, popular printed news after the Restoration does.[77]

NEWPAPER ACCOUNTS

Indications of the new competitive market for stories of infanticide was provided by *Domestick Intelligence. Or, News both from the City and Country* (later *The Protestant (Domestick) Intelligence* from 16 January 1679), published by Benjamin Harris in half-broadsheet format from Monday 17 July 1679 until Friday 14 April 1681. As the later title suggests, the paper specialized in polemical items about treason-conspiracies that gave life to the Popish Plot, particularly those involving the soon-to-be infamous Titus Oates. Harris also squeezed in stories about natural disasters, medical remedies, elections and appointments, and assize-trial summaries featuring the occasional sensational murder.[78] The first female criminal appeared in Number 5, Tuesday 22 July 1679. An unnamed woman of Kingston "lately delivered of a Bastard-Child," "for fear of discovery most barbarously threw the Innocent Babe into the fire, and burnt it to Ashes." Exemplifying the way serial news publication could expand crime stories and keep a felon's image before the public, the *Domestick Intelligence* followed this pretrial report with news of the trial itself in Number 9 for Tuesday 5 August:

> There having been mention made of a woman lately committed to the *White Lyon* Prison in *Southwark* about burning her Child, when she came to be heard at the last Assizes held at *Kingston* . . . it rather appeared to be a business of Malice or Cheating, than Reality; for the Woman at first accused her Brother in Law for having burnt a Child, which she said she had lately been delivered of; whereupon the Person accused was Committed to Prison, as well as her self, but when she came to the *Assizes*, she denied all she had said, affirming that she had not had a Child these four years, and that she was advised by some Persons to do it.

Although her brother-in-law was released, the women remained in prison "for her false Accusation."

While readers were waiting to learn of this outcome, *Domestick Intelligence* picked up the execution story of Katherine Tumince in Number 6, Thursday 24 July. Reporting the most recent Old Bailey sessions and Tyburn executions, it noted that

> There were also seven more carryed to Execution yesterday at Tyburn; a young woman for murdering her Bastard Child, and afterwards hiding it in a Garret near to the place where she lay under some Tiles and Rubbish, she alleaged it was Stillborn, but could not make it appear.

Domestick Intelligence was competing with two other trial publications. *The Tryals and Condemnation of Several Persons for Murders, Felonies and Buglaries . . . which began on the 16th of this instant July 1679. and ended on Fryday the 18th* (publisher unknown) briefly reported that Tumince was found guilty for murdering her bastard male infant. Though several witnesses were called, "[s]he made little defence." *The Proceedings at the Sessions for London & Middlesex ... Beginning on Wednesday the Sixteenth of July, 1679* (publisher unnamed) vilified the transgression of natural maternal instincts by female child killers. It claimed the crime was endemic, with at least one person being charged every session for the past six years. Tumince, it reported, was maidservant to a gentlewoman, of good credit and affections with her worthy family. She disposed of her privately delivered child in an empty garret under tiles and rubbish. When neighbors noticed some "Feminine Symptomes," a midwife was called to examine Tumince and found her newly delivered. Tumince alleged the baby was still-born. The midwife was unable positively to affirm the child had reached full term, but testified it had both hair and nails. Unmarried and lacking witnesses, Tumince was convicted and condemned.

During these years London news buyers were routinely presented with multiple reports of infanticide that created the impression of an alarming increase in offences. Although this looks like a media-constructed panic, evidence from the Chester records during this period indicates that public images and legal reality were complexly related. Newspapers and other print formats represented violent women as emblems of wider social and political turmoil during the Popish Plot, just as they had appeared in news books during the Civil War. As Joad Raymond has argued, since the early modern family was the essential model for relations between subjects and the state, *parti pris* news reports transcoded religious and political conflicts onto the bodies of accused women, who became othered as sectarian fantasies of state and community subversion.[79] Reactions to Margaret Vincent's crimes in the context of the Overbury trials, as we have seen, attested to this kind of discursive appropriation prior to the sectarian clashes of the Civil War. In the similarly rancorous context of the Popish Plot, secret massacres of innocents by sexually deviant women became a perfect symbol for clandestine Catholic treason. The ominous cultural linkages between religious controversy and infanticide created by popular news may explain why prosecutions for infanticide rose temporarily during this period, while afterwards continuing their statistical decline.

The strongest evidence for such associations comes not from newspapers, however, whose publication was spasmodic and short lived before 1695, but from a more powerful news genre dedicated exclusively to crime: the assize-trial report.

PROCEEDINGS FROM THE OLD BAILEY

The intrinsic interest of trial-reports in motive and culpability, as well as infanticide's marketability in the hierarchy of felony journalism, made the 1624 law more publicly visible than ever before. *A Continuation of the Inquest after Blood, and Goal-Delivery [sic] of Newgate, April 13. 1670,* reporting the Old Bailey trial of Hannah Whitford, displayed the kind of informed questions the reporter anticipated his readers asking about the relationship between statutory concealment and mitigating "virtual proofs."[80] Whitford, an unmarried maidservant, covered up her pregnancy by alleging she was suffering from scurvy and dropsy. When she had given birth, she wrapped her male infant in a petticoat and stowed it in a cupboard. It was discovered after a visiting nurse had raised suspicions about Whitford's condition, her body was searched, and she confessed. She pleaded not guilty, claiming that her child had been born dead. Whitford knew or had been advised what material evidence was required to validate her claim. She accordingly "produced one Witness to prove she cryed out [during her delivery]," who may have been a friend or compassionate neighbor (verso). Her testimony caused the judge to direct the jury to find a "Special Verdict" (i.e. mitigated conviction), though Whitford's evidence was disputed. The verdict was "to be Controverted before the Judges, and as they shall determine in that point of the Statute which concerns this present Case, so it must fare with her either as to Life or Death" (verso). Because the trial judge appears to have been in a merciful mood, reprieving several other felons, this pre-execution trial-report ends by expressing the hope that Whitford's version of events will be endorsed and the "special verdict" sustained.

Not all trial reporters were so generous, even though their normal attitude tended to be worldweariness rather than moralizing outrage. An unnamed female servant indicted in August 1673 for murdering her illegitimate male child was not as well prepared or legally informed as Hannah Whitford had been: "she having not any thing to say for her self sufficient to make her just Defence, the Jury found her guilty of Murder" (*News from Newgate . . . on Wednesday the third of September* [1673], A2r). The same pamphlet also made it clear that virtual proofs and positive testimony were sometimes not enough to trump concealment if that was what jurors and judges decided to focus on. Another anonymous maidservant allegedly managed to cover up her pregnancy until she gave birth while sleeping in the same room as her master and mistress. Hinting that she had turned a blind eye to this point, the mistress prompted her servant with possible shielding explanations, asking if "she had not lately miscarried of a Child, or if she had not a Child born" (A2v–A3r). If the maidservant had answered yes, her mistress might have vouched for hearing her "cry out," since the latter's household reputation was touched in the matter, given that all three persons shared the same bedroom (who was the father?). But the maidservant denied any knowledge of a child, and then confessed it was still-born. "Her Master with the advice of his Neighbours sent for a Chyrurgion and Midwife" who confirmed the woman's claim. The trial jury did not accept their testimony, however, which the reporter explained by citing the "Statute of the 21*th* of King *James,* That if any Child be unlawfully begotten, and born dead, without one witness at the least, and concealing the same to hide their shame ... it shall be accounted as Murder" (A3r). Both women subjects in *News from Newgate* also failed to obtain mercy at their sentencing. They pleaded their bellies "notwithstanding they were so lately delivered, which was not above 6 weeks" (A4v). A jury of matrons found neither pregnant and they were executed several weeks later on 17 September.

Illicit sex, secret pregnancy, and clandestine birth became the main features of infanticide cases covered by assize-reports in 1670s and 80s. When Elizabeth Simmons was charged with murdering her newborn child in April 1676, she found two or three witnesses to testify it was still-born and that she had thrown it into a pond because the ground was too hard to dig a grave. Perhaps because of the rough disposal, the jury focused on the concealment of her pregnancy and delivery and found her guilty "according to an Act of Parliament in King *Edward's* [sic] time."[81] Simmons's execution was reported in another pamphlet issued by David and Elizabeth Mallet. Given the genre, the narrative focused on Simmons's repentance, first noting that she was not among the lucky persons reprieved in order to sue for a pardon:

> *Elizabeth Simmond's* Crime was yet of a deeper dye and more horrid nature than any of these [male robbers and burglars] ... but as her sin was the most heinous and unnatural, so likewise has her Penitence (since sentence) been in the highest degree, expressing the sense of her wicked Act in continual tears and Lamentations, and desiring in very Pathetick Language, all young Maidens to take warning by her shameful death ... [and to resist] the temptations of *Satan* to adde Murther to Uncleanness.[82]

Margaret Spicer's killing of her newborn child was reported in the same combination of news formats later that month. After being "privately delivered of a Bastard-childe," she hid it "above a week under her Pillow." At her trial she alleged it died by falling "to the floor as she was getting up to go to the door." Her story changed slightly after the trial in conversation with visiting ministers, Spicer "alleadging that it was Still-born; or at least, contracted its death as soon as ever it saluted the light, by an accidental fall."[83] Perhaps because of the wobbles in her story, or because she was very young ("A woman, whose age might have promised more Chastity and prudence," as *A true Narrative* put it), the reporter invoked the criteria of the 1624 statute to deny her the benefit of the doubt: "But the law obliging women in such cases to cry out, it is supposed she killed it." Unsurprisingly, he also concluded that she died unrepentant, "without any considerable or remarkable Speeches."

Garthine Walker has argued that signs of violence inflicted on an infant's body was perhaps the most crucial evidence used to distinguish cases of deliberate killing from inadvertent homicide or passive killing in mitigating interpretations of the 1624 law.[84] This forensic criterion was rapidly disseminated by popular news, and indeed reporters could economically code guilt by the briefest mentions of indirect violence, such as the unnamed maid servant who wrapped her bastard child in an apron, "flinging it up over the Bedsteaster" where it was later found by her mistress ([A] *Relation of The most Remarkable Proceedings at the late Assizes at Northampton* [1674]). The reporter said nothing further about the child or mother and presumably did not have to. When Susan Emery was charged with infanticide in early 1670, her defense of still-birth was fatally undermined by the discovery that the child had been strangled before being hid behind a wall, to which she later allegedly confessed on the gallows (*Inquest after Blood* [1670]). A blind woman, Mary Line, was not spared execution because there was evidence she had choked her bastard infant "by thrusting a Cloth down its mouth" (*A Continuation of the Inquest after Blood* [1670]).

PLOTS UNDER COVER

During the frenzied years of the Popish Plot and its aftermath, however, bastardy and illicit birth became the characterizing marks of infanticidal identity in popular news. Presumably both kinds of conspiracy scenario suppressed the likelihood of many readers interpreting individual cases equitably. Publishers also intensified public feeling by placing illegitimacy and secrecy in discursive dialogue, thereby capitalizing on the related upturn in prosecutions under the 1624 law. The result was the century's greatest concentration of news reports about newborn child murder, and the first media-created infanticide panic. Between 1679 and 1681 more than twenty (now extant) cases appeared in printed news. The corresponding low proportion of mitigated trials or acquittals was attributable not only to their limited marketability but also to the danger of undermining the symbolic logic between secret births and treasonous plots. The *Domestick Intelligence* for Thursday 24 July 1679 connected Katherine Tumince's prosecution for infanticide with her suspect status as a foreign Catholic:

> She was it seems a *French*-Woman born, and bred up a *Protestant*, and came to live with a Gentlewoman who was a *Papist*: who persuaded her to go to *Mass*, which she for fear of losing her service was forced to do, though, as she says, much against her Conscience; for while she was there she used *Protestant* Prayers to her self, yet this troubled her very much, and being debauched in her Religion, she soon became so in her life also.

Later that October *A True Relation of the Names and Suspected Crimes Of Prisoners now in Newgate, to be Tryed … this 15 of October 1679* highlighted two women charged with infanticide, Jane Blackwell and Elizabeth

Dyke, in its extended title and opening accounts, and included an unusual third account about Rebecca Rudd, charged with the same felony, on the verso of its restricted half-broadside format. *Domestic Intelligence* likewise continued to include infanticide cases while it covered the Plot's vicissitudes. It selected Blackwell's crime as well as the murder of a bailiff for brief entries in Number 31 for Tuesday 21 October 1679. Again in Number 40 for Friday 21 November 1679, it reported that "Susanna Parslow, alias Nasby, [was] committed to Newgate for murdering her child" two days before.

Despite the banal predictably of such cases, news publishers kept devoting precious space to them, presumably because they validated larger suspicions of Catholic conspiracies. To cite one prominent example, a flurry of reports about Mary Bucknell the following year built up a criminal biography of serial concealment leading to murder. When she found she was pregnant, Bucknell left her position and moved to lodgings shared with another woman. She hid her newborn illegitimate child "between the Bed and the Mat" while her room-mate allegedly slept.[85] At the trial the servant denied suspecting or perceiving anything suspicious, reinforcing the implication of Bucknell's capacity for dangerously effective secrecy. Like most women charged with infanticide, she claimed the child was still-born; but this "availed her not; for on the reading of the Act of Parliament made to prevent such Cruelties, she having none to justifie that i[t] Still-born, was found guilty of the Murther."[86] The second account about Bucknell illustrated another notable feature of infanticide news during the Popish Plot years: explicit reference to the 1624 statute being read out at trials to affirm concealment as evidence of intent to murder, and thus strict deference to the law's literal interpretation. Similar links between secrecy and evil intentions were at the heart of testimony made by Oates and his supporters in the press.[87]

Infanticide reports during the Plot also focused unprecedented attention on women's bodies being searched by mistresses, midwives, and neighbors to detect signs of unlawful pregnancy and/or birth. Earlier news pamphlets and reports had occasionally mentioned this common feature of infanticide cases,[88] but both the frequency and contextual associations with contemporary politics would have heightened their topical significance for readers, as infanticide trials became domestic analogies for uncovering and punishing national subversion. Katherine Tumince was first suspected when she betrayed some "Feminine Symptomes" of pregnancy (e.g., milky breasts). A midwife (presumably English) called to examine her body accused Tumince of recently giving birth and provided grounds for prosecution.[89] News about Mary Clark the following year highlighted physical detection by female neighbors. Clark had passed for a widow in the community (i.e., was presumed to be beyond child-bearing years). She was nonetheless questioned when a newborn infant was discovered in a local privy. After she denied any knowledge, searchers were authorized to take "view of her Breasts" and investigate "other symptoms," from which they certified "she had lately had a Child." Without witnesses to her delivery, she was found guilty and condemned.[90] One trial and two newspaper reports about Anne Price, a maidservant living in Woolstable, mentioned that her mistress first became suspicious that she had given birth to an illegitimate child after she complained of a "Griping of the Guts" yet was remarkably recovered by the next morning. The mistress called in a midwife to examine Price, who was found guilty of concealment and murder "upon the reciting the Statute."[91] Similarly, the account of Elizabeth Messenger in *The Tryal and Condemnation of Several Notorious Malefactors ... Beginning May 20. 1681* credited Price's mistress and a midwife with discovering her crime, and again informed readers that the "Statute of King James" was read against her in court to prove her guilt.

Equally notable from 1681 onwards was the shift away from concealment towards malicious violence as the most commonly explained motive in infanticide stories, and thus a return to the more traditional image of the savage mother. There had been several accounts of violent child-killing, some contestable, in the prior period when agitation over the Plot was at it height. A pamphlet about the provincial case of Elizabeth B., for example, alleged that she had stabbed her newborn under the left arm with her bodkin and suffocated it, before burying the corpse with the help of an old woman who afterwards helped her to wash the sheets and linen.[92]

But the 1682 story of Elizabeth Neal, who murdered her male infant "by *choaking* and *strangling*," signalled a clearer shift in the journalistic image of the female infanticide for the remainder of the decade and beyond.[93] Many news reports re-constituted the woman child-killer's identity in terms of active maternal violence rather than illicit sex and concealed pregnancy and birth. The result, in terms of leaving readers imaginative space for, or pointing them towards, equitable interpretations of alleged crimes, was the same, however: the negative image tended to overwhelm mitigating explanations that supported defendants' counterarguments. Toni Bowers has argued that this period marks the beginning of a cultural redefinition of privatized and transhistorical virtuous motherhood set against mythical antitypes that extended into the next century. Changes in popular news seemed to confirm this development, while also ceasing to refer explicitly to the 1624 statute.[94] In early 1684, readers learnt that while suffering from small pox Jane Langworth strangled her illegitimate female child with an apron before stashing it in a trunk where it was later discovered. She said she had done it to stop the child from crying. The same pamphlet reported that Elizabeth Stooks murdered her male bastard infant on 28 December (Holy Innocents' Day) by throwing it out the window of her garret. The baby was not dead when it was found, but presumably it did not survive. The writer did not mention its fate and might have felt the information was superfluous, because Stooks's violence confirmed her maternal wickedness for readers.[95] In one of three news reports covering the Southwark Lent assizes that year, Margaret Corbet, "a very Young Woman of *Wandsworth*," admitted cutting her infant's throat, although she allegedly waited until she was on the gallows ladder before confessing.[96]

News reports for the remainder of the century continued to represent the female infanticide chiefly in terms of malicious maternal neglect or brutality. Samuel Smith, Visitor of Newgate, briefly reported Katherine Brown's drowning of her infant in a brook in the context of her conventional gallows speeches.[97] In the same generic mode Smith recounted Anne Trahern's disposal of her newborn child "into the Bog-house."[98] Mary Mott was less discrete in 1691. In a report that foreshadowed the common eighteenth-century image of the bastard foundling, Mott was charged with wilful murder after abandoning her newborn infant in a street gutter, where it was found dead.[99] The anonymously published *Concealed murther reveild* (1696) recounted the (possibly apocryphal) story of a mother who was haunted by the ghost of her mother after drowning her infant girl.

The last infanticide news of the century seemed to return to a pre-1624 image both in its sensationalizing title and the folkloric aspects of its narrative: *The Unnatural Mother: Being a Full and True Account of One Elizabeth Kennet . . . who, on Tuesday the 6th of April, 1697, privately Delivered her self, and afterwards flung her Infant in the Fire, and Burnt it all to Ashes*. Because this was a pre-assize account written by the "Minister who prayed with her," it anticipated the Crown's efforts to prove wilful guilt in a defendant who may, in fact, have been legally insane. The story began with the honest Mr. Kennet, who innocently asked his full-term wife why she seemed not to be preparing for her lying-in. Elizabeth assured him she was, and he went for a stroll. When he returned, he found "a Hubbard [i.e. hubbub] about his house." Elizabeth told him a neighbor had stolen the child and drowned it in the Thames. When questioned, the neighbor vehemently denied her accusation. After small bones were found in the fireplace, Elizabeth claimed they were the remains of a lamb's head. Asked why the head was wrapped in a cloth, she was speechless. She later confessed by way of explaining that the child was a monster born with two heads.

To modern eyes this looks like a case of mental illness, which, as we observed earlier, provided legal grounds for mitigation for some women charged with infanticide, and constituted another variant in news constructions of the unnatural mother. In pamphlets earlier in the century, subjects who might be *non compos mentis* were nearly always veiled by the narrative presence of the devil's seductions (e.g. Margaret Vincent 1616, Elizabeth Barnes 1637). Like other forms of mitigation for women felons, mental and emotional disturbance became more recognized by juries and visible in court records after the Restoration, and were covered proportionately in popular news.[100] The report of an unnamed woman who burnt her newborn child to death in *A True and Perfect Account of the Proceedings . . . for London and Middlesex, Upon the 15. and 16. of January Instant* (1674) was transitional in offering several explanations (which would not necessarily have been seen as mutually incompatible). It began by stating the common rumour that the woman had been seized by the devil. The reporter went on to summarize neighbors' trial testimony that they had "observed for some time before [she was] some what discomposed and distempered in her mind . . . [and] that those were about her were fearful at any time to leave her alone" (A2v–3r). The trial jury accepted this testimony in deciding the woman was not of sound mind before or at the time of the crime, and she was found not guilty. Charity Philpot's explanation for murdering her mistress's young child was reported in 1681 with even greater detachment:[101] "she told them That a Man in an High-crown'd Hat bid her to do it, and that he had wheted the Knife and put it into her hand, and also told her she should fire the House."[102] An early trial-report recorded an unnamed married women of St. Martins-in-the-Fields being found not guilty after she killed her newborn infant in a fireplace as Elizabeth Kennet had done. (Had the fireplace scenario become a conventional news trope for cases of suspected mental disturbance? Compare Elizabeth Abbot in chapter 2.) The narrative began similarly to Kennet's with the good reputation of her husband, but it differed in noting that after her labor the woman

> was observed for some time before to be some what discomposed and distempered in her mind; the ground of which is Variously reported but not certainly known, but was so far taken notice off [*sic*], that those that were about her were fearful at any time to leave her alone.[103]

The woman bought time to carry out the deed by sending the nurse on an errand, who returned to spy "some of the child's clothes on the fire" and "some part of the Child that was not then consumed." Crucial to the jury's evaluation of the case was evidence of the woman's mental disturbance before and during the crime. Such evidence was apparently lacking several years later when an unnamed widow of about forty with six children gave birth alone to an illegitimate child and then crushed and mutilated its head "with a pair of Sizzors." She put the body "into a Platter and [set] it upon a shelf," where it was found by a lodger after she had observed some "symptoms" in the widow (of birth or insanity or both is unclear). At her trial she claimed she was distracted, but the jury convicted her for having "sense enough to endeavour to conceal it."[104]

Guided by the prosecution's arguments and the jury's verdict, the reporter constructed this case along conventional lines as a story of sexual lust deforming natural maternal instincts, rejecting any suggestion of distraction as spurious. Regardless, the account probably struck some readers as a familiar instance of a woman overwhelmed by too many mouths to feed. A minority of infanticide reports from the 1670s onwards drew readers' attention to the economic hardship, social isolation, and physiological imbalances associated with pregnancy and birth in deprived circumstances (factors compassionately analyzed by Henry Goodcole's *Natures Cruell Step-Dames*). These were in fact increasingly recognized community and legal grounds for equitable mitigation.[105] When writing the brief biographical preface to Sarah Dent's conventional gallows conversion, for example, Samuel Smith placed his usual emphasis on personal sinfulness, but he also felt obliged to acknowledge Dent's financial straits by noting that the fellow servant who had fathered her child had died before it was born. Not knowing "how to maintain it," she "made away with it."[106]

Smith's handling of Anne Philmore's execution preparations in 1686 was more empathetic, although the well-recognized self-interest of his publications would have given some readers cause to be skeptical.[107] Anne was condemned for drowning her nine-week-old child in a pail of water, but would not reveal what Smith regarded as any genuine motives (again, compare Henry Goodcole's conclusions about Elizabeth Barnes's reticence in *Natures Cruell Step-Dames*). When asked whether she did it out of need, Anne replied that she and her husband worked hard to support their four children, but that the new child was demanding and hindered her work as a linen washer. Smith implied that Philmore put greed ahead of her child's life, but the two factors could have been connected. A trial-report offered more conflicting testimony about Anne's motives: "The Prisoner being a very Covetous woman, and fearing she should be Poor, and having lost a small parcel of Bottles that she used to sell Small-Beer in, she grew into an ill Humour." She allegedly killed her child when her husband and children were asleep, but later revealed the deed to the child's godmother. At the trial her defense was that she was distracted, but the jury rejected this claim.[108]

In other cases juries recognized not only (perhaps less equivocal) evidence of economic hardship but also the negative impact of what we would now call employer discrimination. *The Narrative Of the Proceedings at the Sessions . . . on Wednesday the 10th of December* (1679) described an Islington maidservant who was put out of service after confessing to be seven months pregnant. She stayed with her mother in Chiswick for twelve days and then returned to her mistress and asked to be taken on again since she was no longer pregnant. Her mistress had her charged with murder along with her mother, who "had buryed [the child], &c." The always evocative "etc." leaves the early modern reader to wonder whether the child was aborted, miscarried, or still-born. The grand jury probably judged the indictment on an absence of material evidence that undermined the moral presumptions of the prosecution (compare the account of Mrs. G.B. below), and perhaps also from the economic perspective of the maidservant, and acquitted both women.

Earlier that autumn the more extreme betrayal of Joan Blackwell attracted exceptional public and journalistic sympathy that influenced the mitigation of her sentence. According to *The True Narrative Of The Sessions Begun at the Old Bayley On Wednesday the Fifteenth of October, 1679*, Blackwell was "an object of Compassion to most People present . . . a poor young Wench . . . betrayed (as she alleadged) by a promise of marriage" and made pregnant (A1v).[109] When she went into labor, a fellow lodger, to whom

Blackwell had revealed her condition and who until then had concealed it, had a change of mind:

> this barberous Woman, fearing some charge or trouble might happen to her, who had so entertain'd [Blackwell], cruelly turned her out of doors, an[d sent her into] another Parish, and there left her in pains, telling her that now the said Parish were bound to provide for her. (A1v)

According to the reporter, Blackwell gave birth alone and was found lying half dead in the street by the watch. A midwife was summoned and discovered the child dead "but not seperated from her Body." This detail affirmed that Blackwell could not be charged with murder, because full parturition was required to do so.[110] The reporter also presented readers with reasonable alternative testimony. Blackwell

> heard [the child] cry, but denied that she intended or used any wilful means to make away the Life of it[,] nor did there any sign of Violence appear, save only some littel spots or marks of a Bruse or Pinch on the Throat, which some conceive might be occasion'd Involuntarily in struggling to Promote its birth; by an ignorant Woman in her circumstances. (A1v)

Blackwell's treatment caused public opinion to judge her case outside the frame of the 1624 law from a position of rational fairness and humane compassion. Yet because her child was technically a bastard and she allegedly delivered it without calling for help, the jury accepted the claims of the indictment. The judge formally sentenced her to death, but also supported her request for a pardon, as she ultimately escaped execution. The *Domestic Intelligence*, which had been following the case, reported in Number 33 for Tuesday 28 October 1679: "There being about one or two and thirty Persons condemned to dye the last [Old Bailey] Sessions; several of them obtained their Reprieves, and among the rest the woman who was Tryed for killing her Bastard Child, upon consideration of her Circumstances." The judge arrived at the same equitable conclusions represented by news reports and popular debate, and his decision was possibly influenced by them.

THE "TRADE OF KAINE"

The roles played by neighbors and third-parties in child-murder news became especially visible in cases involving the disposal of unwanted infants, often by midwives and nurses hired quietly for this purpose with varying degrees of acceptance by the community. This kind of news story drew further attention to conflicting ethical and socioeconomic factors that reshaped early modern cultural conceptions of infanticide. It also tended to shift moral, if not always legal, culpability off the grounds of personal deviance or concealment and onto shared local responsibility. The scope of equitable scrutiny expanded from rationally explaining or mitigating the actions of individual defendants, to publicizing the community's sins of omission and commission.

Serial infanticide involved coded negotiations or tacit compromises at various levels among parents, neighbors, parish authorities, and legal officers. References in *The Unnatural Grand Mother* to such situations included a "cruell Foster mother" reported the previous year in *A true Relation Of the most Horrid and Barbarous murders committed by Abigall [sic] Hill* (1658). This old-fashioned black-letter pamphlet began with a providentialist introduction tracing murder's pedigree from Cain and citing examples of undetected murders revealed by divine agents such as birds and dogs. Hill entered this history having the local reputation of a compassionate woman who took in children "in distresse" to nurse. The writer did not define "distresse," but his reference to "wicked mothers" who abandoned their children made it clear that these were bastards left on the parish. Over the years Hill returned some children to the parish's keeping while others vanished, though no-one seemed to mind, least of all parish ratepayers. Somewhat lamely the author explained that the community assumed the missing ones had died of sickness or that Hill had given them to poor women to look after (A7r).[111] In a scenario reminiscent of *The Bloudy Mother* (see above), suspicions and "jealousie" (i.e., angry indignation, apprehension or mistrust of evil [*OED* 1, 5]) about "the sodnnesse of the removall of the [children], without any noise of Sickness or discontent" (A7v), indicated that many neighbors knew what was going on but neglected to take action.

One day a neighbor overheard Hill's husband reproach her for getting rid of certain children. Once her activities had become publicly "acknowledged," neighbors felt free to scapegoat Hill by prosecuting her for murder. At her trial on 15 December she allegedly said little and was unable or unwilling to say where the children had been buried, confessing only to a single mercy-killing of a dying child. The court found her guilty of four murders, of making a trade of killing parish children, and of defrauding the parish by borrowing children from her poor friends to present on quarter days as "chargeable bastards" she was paid to raise, but afterwards returning the children to their families.

Regardless of these allegations, which cannot be verified, the trial effectively whitewashed the community as ignorant victims of Hill's activities. But the pamphlet's reports about the circulation of local knowledge and financial dealings over orphaned and illegitimate children implied that arrangements had benefited many parties for some time. The writer's concluding emphasis on Hill's personal deviance attempted to deflect responsibility away from the parish, as did his report of her reprobate behavior on the gallows. After rejecting exhortations to confess or repent, Hill allegedly complained as the executioner placed the rope around her neck: "What!

Doe you make account to choake me?" This outburst (noted on the title page) consummated Hill's symbolic role as a maternal antitype and bore out publisher Francis Cole's advertisement: "a Caveat to all other Women that are suspected for the like unnaturall and most unmericifull Practices." Yet if readers were wondering about the rarity of Hill's case, rumors of women engaging in similar practices in Shoreditch and Shoe Lane reported near the end of the pamphlet (*A true Relation*, A8v) disabused them of this notion.

Two accounts of baby disposal services that appeared in the last decade of the century illustrated the growing problem of infanticide as a neighborhood cost-saving measure created by parish outsourcing of poor relief. In both cases it involved women of varied social ranks and was abetted by metropolitan anonymity. Unlike most infanticide news, which re-constructed the lives of poor maidservants as an illicit sexual history proceeding through secret birth, the infant's death, and the crime's inevitable discovery, the writer of *The Proceedings on the King and Queens Commissions of the Peace . . . the 9th, 10th, and 11th. Days of December* (1691) created a rudimentary murder mystery by opening with the object of discovery: "[T]he Child was found Dead, lying in a Vault, in some Old Ruined Houses, in *Park Street* at *Westminster*, being a most amazing Spectacle, having no Covering about it; and its Tongue forced out of the Mouth, which was done by great Violence." An investigation led to "a person of Quality" testifying that a woman identified only as G. B. with whom she lodged had "complained of the Gripes" and travelled to the house of Anne Richardson and Jane Bromley in Westminster where she gave birth.[112] Bromley and Richardson later disposed of the child in the abandoned house. When it was found and traced, Mrs. B confessed the child was hers, and she, Richardson, and Bromley were charged with murder, as principal and accessories respectively. The trial's outcome matched the account's fictional structure:

> But there was no Evidence that could Charge [Mrs. B] to have offered any Violence to the Child, and *Richardson* and *Bromley* came to see her after she was Delivered, and found the Child Dead, but whether born alive or no, could not be found; and the Prisoner Mrs *B*– had made provision for her lying in; so in the End they were all Acquitted. (A1r–v)

The verdict exposed the factitious relationship of the 1624 law to illicit practices of infant disposal that had long existed even if they had only lately become more frequently reported in popular news.

The law's difficulties in prosecuting infanticide when practised collectively in spatially dispersed and locally depersonalized urban settings also explains the enigmatic pretrial ending of *The Cruel Midwife* (1693). A second unusually detailed publication about the trial, however, reported a judgment which apportioned blame personally and communally, thus publicly circulating arguments for both justice and equity.

The public reputation of midwives for morally ambiguous activities had long been established in folklore and printed news. Knowledge of the mysteries (in both seventeenth-century and modern senses) of birth, life, and death gave them considerable symbolic capital. This combination of suspicion and respect was legally acknowledged when midwives were called on to examine women accused of infanticide or who had pleaded their bellies after conviction and sentencing.[113] But the same knowledge, outside male experience and control except among a small but growing class of professional physicians, also gave midwives social power that was routinely demonized, doubly so if the midwife was foreign (e.g. Mary Hobry [1688]; or the Parisian example of *The Murderous Midwife, with her Roasted Punishment* [1673], in whose house were discovered 62 infant corpses in various states of putrefaction, and who was burnt to death in an iron cage with 16 wild cats hung over an intense fire).

The anonymous writer of *The Cruel Midwife* described Mary Compton (or Crompton) as a fifty-to-sixty-year-old woman who for the previous two years had lived "very privately" in a grand house with a maidservant and regularly paid government taxes and parish rates. Neighbors' maintained continual surveillance but implicit acceptance of Compton's business. They observed numerous children living intermittently in the house, Mrs. Compton's frequent departures by coach for several days at a time, and visits by "some Gentlemen and others often in the Evening or Night" (3). As in the case of Abigail Hill, they intervened only after a circumstantial event brought the system into open disrepute. For reasons unexplained here, Compton and her maid had suddenly decamped, leaving a seven-year-old boy and six-year-old girl in charge of an infant, whose unattended cries attracted attention. The boy directed constables to two dead infants in a hand basket, another in the cellar, and one buried in the garden. Some of the bodies were decomposed and partially eaten by vermin. A coroner's inquest discovered six more children's skeletons buried in the cellar. Following exhumations, "Many of the Spectators took several of the Bones and carried them away, some of which are now to be seen at the *Ben-Johnson's* Head, near St. *Brides* Church by *Fleetstreet*" (6). Almost superfluously, the writer explained that the dead infants were "*By-blows*, or *Bastards*" whose unknown parents paid Compton to keep them as long as they lived. She was charged with murder on 22 August. Recalling the account of Mrs. G.B.'s trial, the writer reports that she "carr[ied] herself with a great deal of Confidence, not seeming in the least concerned, or much denying the Fact" (8). Several gentlemen, meanwhile, were also observed enquiring in alehouses adjacent to the Ben Jonson's Head about certain children.

The main details of this account were recycled in three ballads issued that autumn: one by T. Moore (*The Injured Children, Or, The Bloudy Midwife*), and two by J. Bissel, respectively before and after Compton's trial and execution on 23 October (*The Bloody minded Midwife*, and *The Midwife of Poplar's Sorrowful Confession and Lamentation in Newgate*). Assimilating

Compton's identity with the mythical figure of the monstrous midwife, all three ballads erased any hint of parents' and neighbours' complicity. Instead they emphasized the secrecy and isolation of Compton's alleged thirty-three-year career and the parish's innocent astonishment at the discovery of starved and dead children in her house ("For 'tis supposed a turn for good / she with a *Child* take" [*The Injured Children*]). The implicit paradoxes in this version of her life were challenged by *A Particular and Exact Account of the Trial of Mary Compton ... also of her Maid ... who were both Arraigned in one Indictment for Felony and Murder ... also Ann Davis as Accessary* (1693), which lives up to its lengthy billing as a legally detailed account. The half-broadsheet trial-report quoted the indictment and summarized the testimony of individually named witnesses, although as a prosecution-oriented document it cited the names only of those called for the defense.[114]

Compton was so lame she had to be brought to court and set before the bar in a chair. She and her daughter pleaded not guilty to killing four children—perhaps incidentally, the same number for which Abigail Hill and Jane Hattersley had been indicted—by starvation. The principal witness, Richard Drake, testified entering Compton's house around Whitsuntide.[115] He found Compton drunk, the children famished, and an "Infant in the Cradle, tearing, rending, and yawning its Mouth to and from for lack of Nourishment" (recto). The local church-wardens' solution was to tell her to leave the parish; "for which they had no thanks from the Court, being told, That it was their Duty to have taken particular care of poor Children" (recto). On 20 August following further complaints, a minister charged a local nurse with removing three children from Compton's house. One died three days later, possibly from intolerance to food in a state of extreme starvation. When the nurse returned to the house to arrange for the child's burial, the boy informed her that there was another dead child in the cellar and that she should "*bury them both together.*" This raised a "mightly Jealousy" among the neighbors and prompted a search of the house, where variously rotten infant corpses were discovered in a hand basket and the cellar. A maid, Anne Davis, impassively claimed no knowledge of them. Eight neighbors testified to the starved and neglected condition of the surviving children and the maggoty bodies. Churchwardens of three Poplar parishes also admitted lately placing eleven children with Compton at £5 a child. She was paid a further £3 to take them "wholly off the parish," but the churchwardens admitted they had kept no account of what happened to any of the eleven children:

> which matter was very ill resented by the Court. For all the Ends and Designs of Church-wardens and Overeseers now-adays was to secure their Parishes, and had but little respect to the Life and well-being of the Infants. Yea, the Court did not spare to tell them who are Masters of Parishes; That by such Indiscreet Actions as these, they made themselves Accessaries to the Murther of such poor Children, in selling their Lives (as it were) for 5 *l.* and 3 *l.* a Child. (verso)

Only Compton *mère* was found guilty by the jury. Her daughter was acquitted and Davis escaped with being burnt in the hand. Although Compton's exclusive conviction turned her into a legal scapegoat for the community, in terms of moral and social equity the parish authorities stood equally convicted of infanticide.

The negative moral assumptions and malleable criteria of either incriminating or mitigating evidence that framed the 1624 infanticide law created opportunities that were variously exploited by crown prosecutors, grand and petty juries, judges, and defendants over the century. Popular news reflected the ebb and flow of the statute's applications and cultural legitimacy. Perhaps more importantly, it drew attention to wider discursive appropriations of the crime, in which immoral and patriarchally unregulated women were used to symbolize wider threats of Catholic subversion and political disorder. In terms of equity, popular news stirred public debate about the facts of miscarriage, childbirth, and maternal violence in the light of expanding scientific knowledge and economic misfortune. As reports circulated more accurate information about these contexts, they became reasonable choices to temper or deflect judgmental reflexes. Multiple reports with commercially competing details also created public debates that substantiated a range of attitudes about female infanticide among neighbors, juries, and judges. Such stories exposed narratives of endemic female whorishness or religious fanaticism as journalistic tropes. Increasingly they were confined to ballad or patently didactic accounts, and discounted by educated and/or secular-minded readers. Yet universalizing moral perspectives remained culturally potent. The anonymous author of *The Unnatural Grand Mother* expressed the regularly affirmed position that child murder was unacceptable in any circumstances, and that weak governing authority and a lack of categorical rigor permitted it to be tolerated: "the cruelty and bloodiness of this Age we live in, where some Jesuits or rather divils, stick not to affirm that *killing is no Murther*" (A3r). On the other hand, later seventeenth-century news of Abigail Hill and Mary Compton revealed that local complicity with, or pragmatic negotiation of, infanticide was neither as socially constrained as *The Bloudy Mother* (1610) implicitly alleged, nor as morally focused on uniquely wicked individuals as the author of *The Unnatural Grand Mother* and many other popular accounts believed the crime deserved to be regarded.

6 Conclusion

The growth of early modern printed news opened the realities of female homicide and child murder to forensic and ethical scrutiny by a diverse readership outside the courtroom. In this book I have tried to show that, even though the higher volume of news stories about women murderers than men misrepresented lower proportional rates of female prosecutions and convictions, these trends were related at a deeper level. The publication of accused women's lives and circumstances disseminated knowledge of social differences and human vicissitudes that explained their motives and justified legal officials in mitigating charges and sentences selectively. Popular news and its reception created the imaginative liberty and temporal re-orientation from closed interpretation to innovative reasoning that could accommodate equitable flexibility. Culturally, this dialogue also gradually redefined public images of female criminality as complex constructions of socially heterogenous discourses.

Equitable values were formally conceptualized by historically oriented theories of statute interpretation and theological principles of moral fairness. Their overall aim was to achieve truer or more authentic justice by questioning standard criminal-law verdicts and punishments in the light of unique personal considerations. Equitable reasoning tended to be based on recognition of contentious or ambiguous material evidence, subordinated legal or social rights, and compassionate leniency towards women of good character who committed violent acts in response to extreme abuse. Crime news circulated these perceptions explicitly or implicitly in the course of reporting the varying circumstances of female homicides, mainly in prosecution-dominated narratives that were sometimes highly caricatured. Printed news also tapped into and helped build up a robust culture of popular legal opinion that was often at variance with established interests. Early modern readers possessed high levels of independent legal awareness from their personal experiences as civil and criminal litigants. English men and women, it has long been noted, were remarkably litigious, especially earlier in the period when a variety of national and county courts of equity were in operation.[1] In terms of criminal law, they also experienced the dramatic increase in felony convictions and public executions that took place over the sixteenth century. This trend reached a peak between the 1590s and 1630s, after which it declined gradually into the 1700s (with exceptions, as we have seen, such as the temporary rise in infanticide prosecutions in the late 1670s). Decreases in guilty verdicts and hangings coincided with an expansion in the ways criminal behavior was formally defined or mitigated by trial evidence and procedures, and with the pragmatic evaluation of local suspects by a wide range of civic and legal officials. As early modern criminal historians have demonstrated, seventeenth-century prosecutions and punishments became increasingly discretionary and exemplary. The motivation for these choices was partly jurisprudential, and partly to safeguard the law's authority to preserve economic and class privileges of governing elites.[2] However as this study has shown, decisions or challenges were also based on broader cultural issues of sectarian conflict, gender disparities, and advances in forensic and scientific knowledge.[3] All these contexts diversified the emplotment and metaphors of commercial murder narratives and readers' interpretive horizons. Magistrates, jurors, and judges were presumably attuned to these perspectives through printed reports of the latest Old Bailey proceedings or Southwark assizes, in addition to professional commentaries and their personal experiences. Court records in these jurisdictions and elsewhere (from which assizes were rarely reported but where news of London sessions regularly circulated) attest that jurors and judges in all counties put this discursive awareness into practice by dismissing, acquitting, or reprieving accused women relatively more often than men. Rather than enshrining the criminal law as oracular knowledge that transcended mundane contingencies, popular printed news made legal- and lay-readers aware that its authority was inescapably entwined with the shifting forces of ideology, history, and local memory. These relationships loosened its resistance to change and made it receptive to conceptual and institutional improvisation from within and without.[4]

Public knowledge of mitigating or defensible circumstances increased quantitatively as newsgenres multiplied. The early print media of occasional ballads and pamphlets expanded into serialized newspapers, news pamphlets, and broadside reports. Rhetorically fossilized ballads and godly pamphlets became less credited as the century advanced, at least among discerning and/ or nonsectarian readers. Topically less responsive, they tended to subsume individual women within traditional roles and moral assumptions secured by narrative manipulations and invented dialogue. Emerging formats, on the other hand, intensified competition among publishers and introduced innovations of content and presentation that ramified into new hierarchies of evidence. Newspaper and trial- and execution-reports charted the stories of individual women diachronically over successive numbers, rather than epitomizing their lives as metaphysical portents. They stimulated the public's desire for semi-weekly or daily installments of fresh information and rival interpretations. These discursively produced expectations contributed to longer-term changes in temporal and attitudinal reflexes: being socially well-informed outweighed affirming eternal verities, and openness to rational argument replaced criminal eschatology.[5] Pretrial news pamphlets, being concerned with influencing judicial decisions, were important forerunners of these cultural changes. They valorized public opinion about, and approval towards, future trial decisions, and therefore solicited the involvement of empowered readers. Perhaps not incidentally, their appearance (at least in terms of surviving accounts) from mid-century onwards (beginning with *Murther, Murther* in 1641) coincided with the introduction of regularly serialized news books during the Civil War.

Emergent news-forms lengthened the spectrum of moral and ideological positions represented by writers, publishers, and readers. Heterogeneity significantly redefined female criminal identities as discursive intersections of competing social values and vernacular interests. The content profile of murder news also profoundly affected readers' abilities to evaluate women's motives and actions independently. The dominantly secular details—however manipulated rhetorically to support prosecution claims—that made the Margaret Ferneseede and Elizabeth Abbot pamphlets relatively unusual in 1608 became more common as the century progressed. Readers' abilities to sift legal arguments also depended to some degree on the volume of reported information. Hal Gladfelder has argued that the rise of transgressive yet often sympathetic individualism characteristic of eighteenth-century criminal fiction was partly owing to the substantial accumulation of facts that could count (or not) as imaginatively persuasive evidence for readers. The "circumstantial realism" of Defoe, Fielding, and other novelists, and the news reports that inspired them, enriched both kinds of texts with countercurrents of "recalcitrant singularity." Their presence tended to unsettle conventional patterns of narrative and legal closure and stimulated readers to think beyond cultural norms.[6] This kind of discursive and ideological polyphony has been theorized in later contexts by Mikhail Bakhtin's concept of "heteroglossia."[7] Bakhtin argued that nineteenth-century novelists such as Dostoevsky "orchestrated" dialogues between official and popular discourses of human and social knowledge that commented critically or ironically on one another. Out of this dynamic interplay, readers were at liberty to affirm images and identities as real or invalid. Such "orchestration" was not invented by nineteenth-century writers, however. It can be traced back to eighteenth-century fiction, as Gladfelder showed, or (less globally) to competing prosecution and defence claims represented by substantial or multiple early modern news reports.

Partly because of its emphasis on personal sin and social (dis)order, sixteenth- and seventeenth-century news rarely sympathized with, let alone romanticized, women accused of fatal violence. But narrative details of social and personal circumstances, such as those Henry Goodcole began to put before readers, could engage readers' critical imaginations and humane responses. The numerous reports of tenacious principled resistance at the gallows, whether passive or active, also seriously challenged the state-sponsored regime of exemplary confession and conversion, as well as assumptions about internalizing public deference on which early modern authorities relied to maintain order. The circulation of such outcomes and their back-stories mobilized social and legal knowledge that informed the strategic calculations of juries and judges. Salient forensic or medical facts could confirm positive detection of premeditated malice, or—as the several reports about Anne Greene in 1651 demonstrated—undermine it in ways that prompted readers to construct alternative explanations of alleged crimes. As news reports focused on empirically reliable evidence and procedural technicalities, and less on patterning crime-events after godly trajectories, trial and gallows news exchanged real individual profiles for allegorical ones.

The greater realism of such profiles was also constituted by representations of legitimate female rights within patriarchal laws and penal discipline. These could be jurisprudential rights, based on the evaluation of mitigating legal evidence and personal testimony—categories that Garthine Walker has meticulously clarified in *Crime, Gender and Social Order*. Or they could be socially negotiated rights, such as the degrees of extreme violence women were forced to bear at the hands of abusive husbands, and the point at which they could legitimately defend their lives, either personally or with the community's assistance.[8] Here again seventeenth-century news representations of women such as Elizabeth Lillyman, Sarah Elestone, or Margaret Osgood partly anticipated but also contrasted with later discourses. Margaret Doody's studies of Old Bailey depositions from the 1720s onward have demonstrated how the latter gave individual women unprecedented scope to defend their actions publicly in their own voices.[9] Before then, women's legal defences were more limited in terms of normal trial procedures and usually summarized rather than reported verbatim (exceptions were Elizabeth Caldwell in 1604, Leticia Wigington in 1681, and Margaret Hobry in 1688). Their motives had to be reconstructed in the minds and conversations of readers, notably male jurors and judges. They decided whether women's legal rights and mitigating considerations exceeded prosecution claims and whatever testimony—usually minimal—female defendants could muster to explain themselves.

All ordinary readers, however, were positioned by popular printed news, and especially trial- and execution-reports, as rational judges of forensic arguments. Writers normally did so in the expectation that they would share the Crown's point of view, but never with any absolute assurance of approving it. Even the most didactic and biased accounts left room for counter-interpretations of controversial cases, beginning with Anne Saunders's contested conviction in 1573. The 1615–16 Overbury murder trials of Anne Turner and other defendants established a new threshold for discursive debate about personal crime even though the charges of murder-by-poison were least amenable to formal mitigation.[10] Anne Greene's revival and popular re-trial in 1651 accomplished a cultural and legal breakthrough for women accused of infanticide. Post-Restoration trial reports recorded dismissals, acquittals, reprieves, and pardons in addition to convictions and sentencing. Writers' routine references to earlier crimes indicated that printed news created a public memory pool of personal histories and court verdicts. These could re-affirm legal decisions and traditional criminal narratives, or enable re-interpretation of the latest story according to equitable options available within the criminal law's formal boundaries.[11] Either the force of alternatives or the divergence of reasonable opinions could open pathways to mitigation in the consciences of lay-readers or news-reading officials.

Popular news also reflected the changing stature of the law. Perhaps the most important roles played by both were as agencies of secularization.[12] John Sommerville has defined this process as the gradual separation of religious faith from all functional aspects of social life and thought.[13] In terms of the law, J. A. Sharpe concludes that by the end of the period covered by this book, the law "had come to replace religion as the main ideological cement of society."[14] This process can be seen clearly in the evolution of seventeenth-century murder news. The Calvinist imperatives and (often highly ambiguous) images of martyrdom that dominated earlier news reports receded as journalist reporters overtook godly writers and publishers, and as medical and forensic investigations became laicized domains of professional coroners and JPs. On the other hand, while the Devil's appearances declined and some publishers became wary of putting off skeptical news buyers with prophetic denunciations of sin, especially after the Civil War and Commonwealth, publishers continued to value the popular appeal of providentialist assumptions. These did not so much disappear as they became softly layered into the texture of criminal commentary. And despite increasing indifference or cynicism toward the wonderful claims of "dying words," the institution of Newgate prison visitors and their regularly issued *Accounts* kept the lucrative confession-and-conversion genre of crime news going well into the eighteenth century. In other respects journalists and readers joined the law in judging accused women not only in terms of sexual and moral deviance but also as legal subjects defined by material and testimonial proof of criminal intent. These shifts in the ideology of culpability became arguments for increasing the public's stake in the criminal justice system. Secular writers and publishers felt their opinions deserved to be heard in what Malcolm Gaskill has described as the emerging "common ground" of news texts, readers, and the courts.[15] To conclude with a small but telling example, a publisher identified only by his initials, J. A., began issuing reports of Old Bailey sessions in May 1676 when his activities were temporarily shut down, probably by government censors.[16] When his reports resumed in August, he and/or the reporter argued (not without a degree of self-interest) that he was performing a public service by informing readers about crimes, and that publicizing trials and punishments would deter viciously inclined persons. Therefore, he declared confidently, "we have thought fit to continue this Narrative."[17] News buyers evidently approved. Trial- and execution-reports became recognized as productive components of effective and equitable public justice. Like crime news more generally, their representations benefitted a certain percentage of early modern women accused of homicide or child murder.

Notes

NOTES TO CHAPTER ONE

1. The title page emphasis was neither sensational nor biographical (as it usually was later in the century) but on the criminal law process and judicial punishment: *The Araignement & burning of Margaret Ferne-seede; The Apprehension, Arraignement, and execution of Elizabeth Abbot.*
2. For the historical unreliability of indictments, see Cockburn, "Early Modern Assize Records As Historical Evidence," 215–31, and the introduction to *Calendar of Assize Records* edited by Cockburn. J. A. Sharpe (*Crime in seventeenth-century England,* 8) noted, however, that some evidence from the Northern Circuit indicated that homicide indictments might be more factually accurate than those for other felonies. However the basic caveat remains that court clerks' main objective in framing indictments was to construct a narrative of the crime that validated prosecution charges according to criminal law statutes.
3. Beattie, *Crime and the Courts,* 79–80, 332, 356.
4. Bennett and Feldman *Reconstructing Reality in the Courtroom,* 94, cited in Morrissey, *When Women Kill,* 12.
5. Walker, "Demons in female form," 134–35.
6. Eden, *Poetic and Legal Fiction in the Aristotelian Tradition,* ch. 1, 7–24. Also n. 35 below.
7. Foucault, *The Order of Things,* 42–56; Shapiro, *Probability and Certainty in Seventeenth-Century England,* 167–193, on the movement away from rhetorically framed evaluations of legal evidence toward inductive and materially oriented modes, which included a role for rational conscience in assessing levels of probability and proof.
8. High ranking persons in state treason trials were the exceptions in being allowed to have defense counsel.
9. When judges occasionally took the latter course, they bolstered celebratory metanarratives about the superior fairness and mercy of the English criminal law (Beattie, *Crime and the Courts,* 345).
10. Bennett and Feldman, *Reconstructing Reality in the Courtroom,* 94.
11. Beattie, *Crime and the Courts,* 350; "The Courts in Surrey 1736–1753," 170.
12. Beattie, *Crime and the Courts,* 88–89, 490–91; Sharpe, *Crime in Early Modern England,* 95. Branding for offenses mitigated by benefit of clergy was not abolished until 1779.
13. Sharpe, *Crime in Early Modern England,* 95; Herrup, *The Common Peace,* 48. In 1624 women were allowed to plead clergy for theft of goods valued under 10s. They were not granted full benefit of clergy until 1691.

14. Walker, *Crime, Gender and Social Order*, 138.
15. Amussen, "'Being Stirred to Much Unquietness,'" 73–76; "Punishment, Discipline, and Power," 23–27; Walker, *Crime, Gender and Social Order*, 141.
16. Sharpe, "Domestic Homicide in Early Modern England," 29–48; Beattie, *Crime and the Courts*, 436–37; Cockburn, "Patterns of Violence in English Society," 70–106; Walker, *Crime, Gender and Social Order*, 112, 135–36. According to P. G. Lawson ("Lawless Juries?," 150–51), convictions for all felonies at Hertfordshire assizes between 1573 and 1624 were 52% for men and 30% for women. Acquittals and partial (i.e., mitigated) verdicts were 38% and 10% for men (48%) and 59% and 11% for women (70%). In a later study of the same assizes between 1591 to 1618, Lawson found the differential between men and women prosecuted for homicide was 88.6% versus 11.4%, respectively ("Patriarchy, Crime, and the Courts," 21–24, 33–34). As he also noted, these figures are similar to J. A. Sharpe's findings at Essex assizes, 1620 to 1680, in which women accounted for 18.7% of homicide indictments, and 59.1% of those tried were acquitted (*Crime in seventeenth-century England*, Table 12, 124).
17. Anderson and Sauer, "Current Trends in the History of Reading," *Books and Readers in Early Modern England*, 1–22, and *passim*; Chartier, "Texts, Printing, Readings," 154–75.
18. Chartier, "Texts, Printing, Readings," 165. Analyzing the changing priorities of popular morality and criminal justice in the wider context of negotiations between local agents and state authorities, Steve Hindle also concludes that the discursive accumulation of cases generated competed public interpretations of the criminal law and its applications (*The State and Social Change*, 139). Also n. 25 below.
19. White, *Natural Law in English Renaissance Literature*, xi–xii; Aristotle, *Nicomethean Ethics*, translated by H. Rackam, V.10.3, 6; Holmes, "Early English Equity," 162–74; Maitland, *Equity: A Course of Lectures*, 8. Calvinists and later Hobbes were more pessimistic about human capacities for reason and conscience. They argued that innate reprobate behavior had to be controlled by state authorities following strict laws.
20. Aristotle, *Nicomethean Ethics*, translated by H. Rackam, V.10.5.
21. Clark, *Women and Crime*, 153, citing Gaskill, *Crime and Mentalities in Early Modern England*, 224–25. As D. C. Collins, the first modern commentator on *The Apprehension, Arraignment, and execution of Elizabeth Abbot* observed, it "gives an illuminating picture of Elizabethan justice in progress" (*A Handlist of News Pamphlets*, no. 235, 87–88).
22. Vinogradoff, "Reason and Conscience in Sixteenth-Century Jurisprudence," 373–84.
23. Hill, "William Perkins and the Poor," 215–38.
24. Herrup, "Law and Morality in Seventeenth-Century England," 102–23, and in particular Perkins's Eʹ ΠΙΕΙʹ ΕΙΑ [*Hepieíkeia*], 111–12; Hay, "Property, Authority, and the Criminal Law," 35–39.
25. Herrup, *The Common Peace*, 1–2, and *passim*; Sharpe, "The People and the Law," 244–70; "Social Crime and Legitimizing Notions," *Crime in Early Modern England*, 175–203; Hindle, *The State and Social Change*, ch. 5, 116–39.
26. Cioni, *Women and Law in Elizabethan England*; Stretton, *Women Waging Law in Elizabethan England*.
27. Vinogradoff, "Reason and Conscience," 378–79.
28. White, *Natural Law in English Renaissance Literature*, 50–53.
29. "Come Parollz Sera Expounde en vn Statute, &c.," *A Discourse upon the Exposicion & Understandinge of Statutes*, ed. Thorne, 123–24.

30. "Of Interpretation of Statutes according to Equity," 31, 72; Saint German, *The Dialogues in Englysshe*, 27r–v.
31. Fish, "Force," *Doing What Comes Naturally*, 507–09, 511–15.
32. Fish, "Force," *Doing What Comes Naturally*, 505.
33. Derrida, "Force of Law," *Deconstruction and the Possibility of Justice*, 23.
34. Derrida distinguishes this positive practice from the deconstructive criticism for which he is better known: demonstrating the unavoidable gaps and slippages in textual signification that make arrival at stable final meanings theoretically impossible; that is, the "apparently ahistorical allure of logico-formal paradoxes" ("Force of Law," *Deconstruction and the Possibility of Justice*, 21).
35. Derrida, "Force of Law," *Deconstruction and the Possibility of Justice*, 14–29. Philip Sidney polemically contrasted the re-creative vigour of the poet's imagination with the (supposed) intellectual restrictions of other professions tied to the authority of past decisions and events: "The lawyer saith what men have determined; the historian what men have done" (*An Apology for Poetry*, ed. Shepherd, 100–02, 110–12). In terms of the law, Sidney had in mind exemplary methods of legal reasoning based on correspondences with traditional judgments and universalizing statutes (the prosecution's perspective, in practice). Yet the equitable challenges to finished interpretation and strict precedent proposed by Plowden and Hatton are visible elsewhere in Sidney's arguments about the power of poetic or imaginative reasoning to envisage explanations—including legal defenses—for human actions that received knowledge alone cannot:

    > And whereas a man may say, though in universal consideration of doctrine the poet prevaileth, yet that the history, in his saying such a thing was done, doth warrant a man more in that he shall follow—the answer is manifest: that if he stand upon that *was*—as if he should argue, because it rained yesterday, therefore it should rain to-day—then indeed it hath some advantage to a gross conceit; but if he know an example only informs a conjectured likelihood, and so go by reason, the poet doth so far exceed him as he is to frame his example to that which is most reasonable, be it in warlike, politic, or private matters; where the historian in his bare *was* hath many times that which we call fortune to overrule his best wisdom. Many times he must tell events whereof he can yield no cause; or, if he do, he must be poetical. (110)

    In exploring the relationship between dramatic poetry and forensic oratory, Kathy Eden argues that Sidney's celebration of the power of poetical fiction-making to represent the deep causes of human behavior is inspired partly by Aristotelian theories of legal equity and methods of defensive rhetoric (*Poetic and Legal Fiction in the Aristotelian Tradition*, 3–6, 25–61, and *passim*).
36. White, *Natural Law in English Renaissance Literature*, 47; Thorne, ed., Introduction to *A Discourse upon the Exposicion & Understandinge of Statutes*, 66–67.
37. Vinogradoff, "Reason and Conscience," 384; Sharpe, *Crime in Early Modern England*, 11–18, 98–99; Beattie, *Crime and the Courts*; "The Courts in Surrey 1736-1753," 182; Herrup, *The Common Peace*, chs. 5–6, 93–164.
38. Clark, *Women and Crime*, 152.
39. Greene, "The Jury and the English Law of Homicide," 413–99; Lawson, "Lawless Juries?," 118–19, and *passim*. Lawson observes that evidence of the extent of juror independence or activism has been underestimated because

indictments declared *ignoramus* and rejected by grand juries were normally destroyed (150).

40. *Bloody News from Clarken-well* offered readers a very brief account of "a Bloody murther committed by a Souldiers wife on her husband" (while failing to supply the examination and confession related to the wife's fatal stabbing promised on its title page), as well as a rejection of her defense, which it clearly hoped the trial would uphold: "Since which bloody murther, upon her examination she says He was not her Husband, thinking thereby to scape the better, but the Law is more just then to pardon such bloudy offenders" (A4v). The other examples cited in this paragraph will be discussed in later chapters.

41. Beattie, *Crime and the Courts*, 388; Cockburn, "Twelve Silly Men?," 158–181.

42. Lawson, "Lawless Juries?," 119, citing Dalton's *The Countrey Justice*, 229.

43. Greene, *Verdict According to Conscience*, 105–06.

44. Herrup, *The Common Peace*, ch. 4, 67–92, and *passim*; Gaskill, *Crime and Mentalities*, ch. 7, 242–80; Hindle, *The State and Social Change*, 1–36, 116–39. Ulinka Rublack finds that prosecution of local women in early modern Germany likewise depended on communal instigation and co-operation, and neighbors' assessments of the accused person's reputation—a form of symbolic capital that could be exchanged for legal credit (or demerit) in the courts (*The Crimes of Women in Early Modern Germany*, 22–35, and ch. 1, 16–42, *passim*).

45. Amussen, "'Being Stirred to Much Unquietness,'" 74.

46. Doody, "Voices of Record," 287–308.

47. Posner, *Law and Literature*, 121–22.

48. Kerrigan, "The Editor as Reader," 102–24.

49. Morrissey, *When Women Kill*, 21; Staub, "Bloody Relations," 124–28. Historical laws of uniformity, or macro-explanations, Clayton Roberts argues, do not operate in the sphere of individual human action, although teleological forms of historical explanation, concerned with personal beliefs and values, do (*The Logic of Historical Explanation*, 67–88, 157, 188, 213).

50. This account of Goodcole and his writings draws in part on my article, "Henry Goodcole, Visitor of Newgate," 153–84.

51. All recent commentators have misread this text by assuming Goodcole is writing about one woman, Clarke, rather than two (Clark, *Women and Crime*, 28, 43, 177; Dolan, *Dangerous Familiars*, 32–33, 38–39; Lake, "Deeds Against Nature," 261; Staub, "Bloody Relations," 134). Similar nontrivial reading errors are not uncommon. They justify this study's closer attention to individual texts.

52. Dolan, *Dangerous Familiars*, 11; Reynolds, *Becoming Criminal*, 18–19; Staub, "Bloody Relations," 137.

53. Misprinted as 18 in the text.

54. Herrup, "Law and Morality in Seventeenth-Century England," 109; Dolan, *Dangerous Familiars*, 38–40.

55. Sharpe, "'Last Dying Speeches,'" 153–54.

56. See, for example, Arthur Golding's *A briefe discourse* (1573). Unknown to Anne Saunders, the Council delayed her execution to extract her confession. She was led to believe, however, that the delay was to allow her to seek a pardon. She was then psychologically ambushed, perhaps deliberately, when, on the day originally set for her execution, men passed through Newgate talking in loud voices "of the gallowes that was set vp" for her. Suddenly facing the apparent prospect of imminent execution, Anne panicked: she confessed to consenting to her husband's death. For further discussion see chapter 3.

57. Amussen, "'Being Stirred to Much Unquietness,'" 84.

58. Marshall, *The Shattering of the Self*, 43. See also Marshall's fascinating discussion of the differences between witnessing an execution and reading about it. Print representation, she argues, "doubles" the condemned prisoner by distancing the actual violence exercised on her body as a nontemporal and nonhistorical object of the imagination (101).
59. Sharpe, *Crime in Early Modern England*, 82–84, 99.
60. Sharpe, *Crime in seventeenth-century England*, 108, 124; Beattie, "The Criminality of Women in Eighteenth-Century England," 80–116; Herrup, *The Common Peace*, 116–17; Lawson, "Patriarchy, Crime, and the Courts," 21–29.
61. Amussen, "Political Households and Domestic Politics," *An Ordered Society*, ch. 2, 34–66; Amussen, "Punishment, Discipline, and Power," 13–18, and *passim*.
62. Sharpe, "Domestic Homicide in Early Modern England," 29–48.
63. Goodcole, "A Short Tract Vpon the hainounesse of Poysoning," *The Adultresses Funerall Day*, B3v–4v; Harrison, "The Literary Background of Renaissance Poisons," 35–67; Lawson, "Patriarchy, Crime, and the Courts," 28–29.
64. Kaye, "The Early History of Murder and Manslaughter," 365–77, 587–601.
65. Lake, "Deeds Against Nature," 257–67.
66. Amussen, "'Being Stirred to Much Unquietness,'" 75–76; Lawson, "Patriarchy, Crime, and the Courts," 43–52; Walker, "'Demons in female form,'" 123–39.
67. Campbell, "Sentence of Death by Burning for Women," 44–59; Radzinowicz, *A History of the English Criminal Law*, 1:209–13; Reinhard, "Burning at the Stake," 186–209.
68. Chamberlain, *Letters*, ed. McClure, 2:15; Platte, *Anne Wallens Lamentation*, in *A Pepysian Garland*, ed. Rollins, no. 14, 84–8.
69. Oldham, "On Pleading the Belly," 1–64.
70. Sharpe, *Judicial Punishment*, 42, citing Cockburn, Introduction, *Calendar of Assize Records*, 117–21. Or, women were transported—the increasingly preferred judicial means of mitigating the death penalty from the end of the seventeenth century onwards. See Beattie, *Crime and the Courts*, 450–56, 470–83.
71. Wrightson, "Infanticide in Earlier Seventeenth-Century England," 10–22; Malcolmson, "Infanticide in Eighteenth-Century England," 246–69; May, "'She at first denied it,'" 19–50; Jackson, *New-Born Child Murder*.
72. Dickinson and Sharpe, "Infanticide in Early Modern England," 39. See also chapter 5 below.
73. The 1624 statute was not repealed until 1803 (Sharpe, *Crime in Early Modern England*, 158).
74. See http://www.oldbaileyonline.org.
75. Beattie, *Crime and the Courts*, 336; for example, *A True Account of the Proceedings on the Crown-Side at this Lent Assize Held for the County of Surrey* (1683/4).
76. Beattie, "Towards the Study of Crime in Eighteenth-Century England," 299–314; Lawson, "Patriarchy, Crime, and the Courts," 20–21.
77. Most county records other than for Middlesex—the county that included the City of London—do not begin until the late sixteenth or early to mid seventeenth centuries, and even then their survival rate remains sporadic into the late seventeenth century. Cockburn, "Early Modern Assize Records"; Cockburn, ed., Introduction to *Calendar of Assize Records*. In the case of contradictions, the modern impulse might be to privilege the legal artifact because its information appears to be more reliable. Nor is it practicable—although it may be tempting—when faced with two or more competing sets of reports about a crime and trial, to try to determine the "real" truth of a case by picking

and choosing amongst details. Not only is there usually too little surviving evidence to do so positively, but the re-ordered scenario would not necessarily be any more historically authoritative than any of the individual reports themselves. Setting news reports in their contemporary contexts often allows the accuracy of facts or claims to be questioned and compared to arrive at probable historical meanings, but much less satisfactorily reconstructed to arrive at absolute claims.

78. Harris, "The Structure, Ownership and Control of the Press," 83–84; Doody, "Voices of Record."
79. Dolan, *Dangerous Familiars*; Clark, *Women and Crime*; Lake, "Deeds Against Nature;" "Popular Form, Puritan Content?;" Staub, "Bloody Relations;" and her edited anthology, *Nature's Cruel Stepdames*; Walker, "Demons in female form;" Wiltenburg, *Disorderly Women and Female Power*.
80. No manuscript ballads survive from before 1476, according to Marshburn, *Murder & Witchcraft in England*, ix. Conversely, some ballads that reached print have survived but only in manuscript; for example, *Anne Saunders's lamentation*, reproduced in *Old English Ballads*, edited by H. E. Rollins, 340–48.
81. Rollins, ed., *A Pepysian Garland*, nos. 49, 50, 283–93; Watt, "Publisher, Pedlar, Pot-poet," 61; *Cheap Print and Popular Piety*, 11–14, 257.
82. Watt, *Cheap Print and Popular Piety*, 11, citing Henry Peacham, *The Worth of a Peny* (1641), D1r. Parker was the most famous ballad writer of the seventeenth century; for instance, *No naturall mother, but a monster*, entered in the Stationers' Register on 17 July 1634, and reproduced in *A Pepysian Garland*, edited by H.E. Rollins, 428. As nonessential commodities, it is difficult to say with certainty how inexpensive broadside ballads would have seemed to the semiliterate poor. But presumably this cheapest end of the book market remained relatively affordable, in contrast to pamphlets (Watt, *Cheap Print and Popular Piety*, 260–61). The latter cost two pence more, which must have made them relatively expensive for the humblest buyers, even though general inflation and steady book prices throughout the period gradually made books cheaper (except for a sharp spike in the 1630s), and more so for longer books than short ones (Johnson, "Notes on English Retail Book-prices," 84, 93).
83. Watt, "Publisher, Pedlar, Pot-poet," 66–67.
84. *The Compleat Angler*, 49, cited in Watt, "Publisher, Pedlar, Pot-poet," 67.
85. Hay, "Property, Authority, and the Criminal Law," 17–63.
86. A notable exception is Sandra Clark, whose selective but historically well-informed study *Women and Crime* elucidates the diverse semantic and contextual meanings of many of these documents.
87. Clark, *Women and Crime*, 91.
88. Harris, "Trials and Criminal Biographies," 15–16, 20–21; McKenzie, "Making Crime Pay," 250. I am indebted throughout this section to Harris's and McKenzie's articles.
89. Lake, "Popular Form, Puritan Content?," 321. Models of such prayers and speeches gradually became known in other contexts as well. Simon Patrick's book of devotions for families and "Particular Persons In Most of the concerns of Humane Life" contained a form of prayer for "a great Malefactor in Prison" (*The Devout Christian* [1673], 414–18).
90. McKenzie, "Making Crime Pay," 263, citing *The Life and Penitent Death of John Mausbridge*, 2. In the end Mausbridge's secrets were neither kept so private nor was the deity their exclusively privileged reader. As Jürgen Habermas also observes, Mausbridge chose to circulate his version of events in a space between intersecting private and officially authorized interests (*The Structural Transformation of the Public Sphere*, 27–31). Although they might ultimately become fodder for coffee house wits, their purpose would also have extended

to raising public issues and expressing opinions about them, even from beyond the grave.

91. One of the accused murderers was a woman, Sarah Swift, and some accounts of the event had already been circulating that reported Talbot met with her the day before, "as if he had been naught with *Sarah Swift*; and so by that means was surprized with her, and fell into the hands of his barbarous and bloody enemies" (D1v–2r). The main author of *A Perfect Narrative* sought to bolster his account's credibility by including written testimonies from Talbot, constables, and witnesses, as well as an attestation from the Ordinary of Newgate. See ch. 3, p. 117.

92. So do the other two pamphlets. The 1675 *News from Tybourn* advertised its inclusion of "*a true account of their deportment bfore* [sic] *several godly ministers in Newgate who came to visit them there. With allowance.*" The year after, similarly: "*a brief account of their behaviour and most material confessions in Newgate after condemnation. As also their speeches and penitent deportment at their death . . . Licensed.*"

93. Harris, "Trials and Criminal Biographies," 16, citing CLRO Rep. 89, fol. 114, May 27, 1684.

94. Harris, "Trials and Criminal Biographies," 16; McKenzie, "Making Crime Pay," 249.

95. Linebaugh, "The Ordinary of Newgate and His *Account*," 246–69; Chapman, "Smith, Samuel;" Gladfelder, *Criminality and Narrative*, 50–5. It is interesting to compare the justifications offered at this time for publishing confessions and gallows speeches with those of Henry Goodcole half a century earlier. In a petition to the Commons, Newgate ordinary Paul Lorrain claimed that his account was "for the general satisfaction of the Publick, the necessary Information of Honest People, and the Instruction and Reformation of Wicked Persons," and above all "bringing Things to Light which were before hidden in Darkness" (*The Case of Paul Lorrain, Ordinary of Newgate, most humbly offer'd to the honourable House of Commons*, n.d., before 1714, Guildhall Library Broadside, 12:107, quoted in Linebaugh, "Tyburn. A study of crime and the labouring poor in London during the first half of the eighteenth century," Ph.D. diss., Centre for the Study of Social History, University of Warwick, 184–85, cited by Harris, "Trials and Criminal Biographies," 17). An exclusive emphasis on moral reform and exhortation had yielded priority to *post hoc* legitimation of court judgments, the business of journalism, public protection from an urban criminal class, and above all, financial profitability.

96. Beattie, "The Pace of Trial," *Crime and the Courts*, 376–78.

97. Sutherland, *The Restoration Newspaper*, 49. Shorthand reporting was known but unofficial before this time and therefore limited.

98. Harris, "Trials and Criminal Biographies," citing CLRO Rep. 84, fol. 46b, January 18, 1678; Gladfelder, *Criminality and Narrative*, 59–60.

99. Harris, "The Structure, Ownership, and Control of the Press," 83; Levy, "The Decorum of News," 18. The earliest murder story in a coranto is of the fatal wounding of a man in St. Mark's Square, Venice, reported in *A True Relation of the Affaires of Europe*, 4 October 1622. In England the first newspaper story and request for information to help solve a local murder appeared in special black-letter type in *Mercurius Brittanicus*, No. 1, 31 March to 7 April 1648, cited by Foskett in her unpublished dissertation, "A survey of the first English newspapers," 212. Foskett concluded that whereas only a few murder stories eventually appeared in newspapers during the Civil War, they increased in frequency during the 1650s. Stories of robbery were more common (212, 216).

100. The printing of all news in the sixteenth and seventeenth centuries was closely regulated by the Company of Stationers and government licensers such as Sir Roger L'Estrange (see p. 32 below). Reports about foreign or political events, for example, were often printed on the continent from English translations (or purportedly from translations by continental printers). See Siebert, *Freedom of the Press in England*, 107–61; Andrews, *The History of British Journalism*, 1:25–27.
101. Raymond, "News, newspapers," 128.
102. Habermas, *The Structural Transformation of the Public Sphere*, 25–26, 37, 57, and *passim*.
103. Zaret, "Religion, Science, and Printing in the Public Spheres in Seventeenth-Century England," 212–35.
104. See also Fraser, "Rethinking the Public Sphere," 118–28. The mid seventeenth century was the first period, for instance, in which the death penalty for murder or other kinds of homicide began to be questioned by dissenters (e.g. Quakers). Although their critique of state punishments could not affect statute law after the Restoration given the outcome of political events, they did establish a cultural foothold for thinking alternatively about the origins and appropriate punishment of homicide by women.
105. Siebert, *Freedom of the Press in England*, 230–32.
106. Harris, "The Structure, Ownership, and Control of the Press," 83. The exponential growth in newspaper production after 1695 marked a significant change from earlier news culture, even though most printed formats, criminal statutes, and judicial procedures (but not sentencing) remained unchanged until later in the eighteenth century.
107. Sutherland, *The Restoration Newspaper*, vii, 67, and *passim*.
108. For instance, two women condemned at the York assizes for murdering their illegitimate children (No. 166, August 5–9, 1682). Perhaps this report was included as an antirecusant squib; it was unusual because London newspapers did not regularly report trials and executions from provincial assizes.
109. Sutherland, *The Restoration Newspaper*, 71–72.
110. Raymond, "News, Newspapers," 8; Harris, "The Structure, Ownership, and Control of the Press," 82.
111. *The Confession and Execution of Leticia Wigington*, A2r, published by Langley Curtiss. Philip D. Collington discusses Wigington's public self-construction in relation to the title page citation of Micah 7:8–9 (*Reading Early Modern Women*, 50–53).
112. *The True Relation Of The Tryals At the Sessions of Oyer and Terminer . . . in the Old-Bailey the 17th of this instant January, and ended the 18th of the same. As particularly of Elizabeth Wigenton For Whipping a Girl to Death* (1681), A1r, publisher unidentified. *The True Protestant Mercury*, January 15–18, 1680/1, 1.
113. *The Last Dying Speeches And Confessions of the Three Notorious Malefactors . . . on the 4th. of this Instant March*, 1681, A1r, published by T. B.
114. Certain accounts imply that Sadler may have been Wigington's lover: *Last Dying Speeches*, A1v; *The Tryal and Condemnation Of Several notorious Malefactors . . . And most remarkably of John Sadler, who Whipt the Child to Death at Ratcliffe* (February 28, 1680/1), A1v, published by T. Davies.
115. *The Confession and Execution of Leticia Wigington*, A2r. In this exculpatory account Wigington claimed that Sadler initiated the whipping, which she discovered in progress and challenged him about.
116. *The True Protestant Mercury*, January 15–18, 1680/1, 2. *Last Dying Speeches* presented substantially the same version of events and also named the whip a "*Cat of Nine Tails*" (A1v).

117. LMA MJ/SR/1590.
118. For further discussion about the provenance and naming of the weapon, see Martin, "'The Cat' Gets its Nine Tails," 31–35.
119. Or three days later, according to *The Tryal and Condemnation*, A1v.
120. *The Loyal Protestant and True Domestick Intelligence*, No. 1, March 19, 1681. *The True Relation Of The Tryals*, A1r.
121. *The Protestant (Domestick) Intelligence*, No. 91, Tuesday, January 25, 1680/1. "We have likewise a relation from *Ratcliff*, that a *Hue* and Cry being made after one *Sadler*, a Bailiffs Follower, for being an Assistant to *Lattice Wigington*, now condemned, and in *Newgate*, for whipping her Apprentice Girl to death, that the said *Sadler* was on the twentieth past apprehended at *Burntwood* in *Essex*, and committed to *Chelmsford* goal [*sic*]." Also *The Confession and Execution of Leticia Wigington*, A2v.
122. *The True Protestant Mercury*, February 23–26, 1681. This is the third publication about the case that names the cat-o'-nine-tails. Others describe it as a whip (or in one account, a "bundle of rods," *The True Relation Of The Tryals*, A1r).
123. *The Confession and Execution of Leticia Wigington*, A2v, stated that news ballads of the crime were also published, but none survived.
124. *The Loyal Protestant and True Domestick Intelligence*, No. 52, September 3, 1681. "*Old-Bailey, August 31* . . . The notorious Woman that whipp'd a Child to Death was called to her former Judgment, and advised to prepare for het [*sic*] now near approaching death." Also *The Domestick Intelligence*, No. 32, September 8–12, 1681.
125. *The Confession and Execution of Leticia Wigington*, A2r-v.
126. Wood also witnessed the execution and heard about the 1651 revival of Anne Greene in Oxford. See ch. 5, p. 182.
127. Raven, Small, and Taylor, eds., Introduction to *The Practice and Representation of Reading*, 8.
128. Spufford, "First Steps in Literacy," 407–35; Morgan, "The Provincial Book Trade Before the End of the Licensing Act," 32. Writing to Archbishop Laud on 29 October 1634, William Lynne reported that Thomas Cotton read out a weekly London newsletter "evry markett daye att Colcheter [*sic*]" to the same audience that gathered "as people [do] where Ballads are sunge" (Frearson, "The Distribution and Readership of London Corantos," 17, citing Stephen Foster, *Notes from the Caroline Underground: Alexander Leighton, the Puritan Triumvirate, and the Laudian Reaction to Nonconformity* [Hamden, Connecticut: Archon Books, 1978], 47).
129. Cited by Schwoerer, "Liberty of the Press and Public Opinion," 199–230. Also Raymond, "News, Newspapers," 116.
130. Raymond, "News, Newspapers," 115, citing Thomas Player in *Letters Addressed from London to Sir Joseph Williamson while Plenipotentiary at the Congress of Cologne in the Years 1673 and 1674*, edited by W.D. Christie, 2 vols. London: Camden Society. n.s. 8–9 (1874), 2:67–8. A one-penny cup of coffee gave one access to news ballads, pamphlets, and papers stocked by coffee-houses.
131. Kerrigan, "The Editor as Reader," 110.
132. Amussen, *An Ordered Society*, 168–71.
133. Thomas, "The Meaning of Literacy in Early Modern England;" Spufford, "First Steps in Literacy," 97–131.
134. Capp, "Popular Literature," 198–243. Also Adam Fox, "Popular Verses and Their Readership," 125–37.
135. Burke, "Popular Culture," 32.
136. Chartier, *The Cultural Uses of Print*, 3–10.

137. Simmons, "ABCs, almanacs," 504; Johnson, "Notes on English Retail Book-prices."

NOTES TO CHAPTER TWO

1. "Spinster" in this context does not refer to an unmarried woman but is a legal fiction meant to ensure a wife could be prosecuted independently of her husband and not claim legal immunity by virtue of being *femme couverte*. See Wiener, "Is a Spinster an Unmarried Woman?"
2. Cockburn, ed., *Calendar of Assize Records*, 32 (Southwark, February 18, 1608, 35/50/7).
3. Cockburn notes the unreliability of indictment claims, despite their official character, in "Early Modern Assize Records As Historical Evidence."
4. Ulinka Rublack discusses the powerful incriminating effect of this kind of reaction in *The Crimes of Women in Early Modern Germany*, 56–60.
5. This accusation may relate vaguely to one of the scenes on the title page woodcut, recycled from an earlier pamphlet on witchcraft, of a group of women stirring a cauldron (see p. 43).
6. *Crimes of Women in Early Modern Germany*, 59.
7. All three men were imprisoned on Saturday 13 February 1608 with Margaret Ferneseede and four other condemned felons. The pamphlet included an allocutus by Bishop taking sole responsibility for the murder and pleading with the judge to mediate to the king for mercy on behalf of the other defendants. The judge denied his request. The pamphlet reproduced Throgmorton's prayer, allegedly recited by Ferneseede.
8. Anthony Ferneseede's murder is ultimately unsolvable, but one wonders if he might have been killed by a husband of one his wife's sex workers, or one of his wife's clients, such as the ones he reportedly harangues.
9. Grieve, *A Modern Herbal*, 305–06; Hoffman, *Holistic Herbal*, 102. For fern seed see Shakespeare, *1 Henry IV*, 2.1.88n., ed. A.R. Humphreys (London: Methuen, 1960), and Ben Jonson, *The New Inn*, 1.6.16–18, ed. Michael Hattaway (Manchester: Manchester University Press, 1964). Also compare Shakespeare and Wilkins, *Pericles*, 19.90–91, ed. Roger Warren (Oxford: Oxford University Press, 2003) where Lysimachus describes the Bawd as "your herbwoman, she that sets seeds and roots of shame and iniquity."
10. I am grateful to Peter Kuling for bringing this image to my attention.
11. Besides mirroring the heightened anxiety over female witches stimulated by the publications of Reginald Scot, James I, and others, the shifts in visual and narrative focus to human agents was inevitable because, as Robert Filmer observed wryly in *An Advertisement to the Jury-Men of England, Touching Witches*, "the Devill can never be lawfully summoned according to the rules of our Common-law (B4r)." Cited by Sharpe, *Instruments of Darkness*, 221.
12. A nonextant ballad about Margaret was entered in the Stationers' Register on 7 March 1608: "The wooman that was Lately burnt in Saint Georges feildes" (Arber, ed., *Stationers' Register*, 3:371).
13. See also Anne Welles (discussed below, p. 135).
14. de Certeau, *The Practice of Everyday Life*, 26: "ethics of *tenacity*" signifies "moral resistance . . . [the] countless ways of refusing to accord to the established order the status of a law, a meaning, or a fatality." I discuss de Certeau's theory of tactical practice in greater detail in chapter 3.
15. The title page, now damaged, bears a woodcut illustration of a woman hanging from a gibbet beside a gallows ladder, while the hangman straddles the

top crossbar adjusting the rope, or perhaps prepares to cut the woman down, while a crowd of officers with halberds looks on. The image is not original and was reused in adapted form on the title page of *Deeds Against Natvre* (1614). A nonextant ballad of the murder was entered on 12 April 1608 (Arber, ed. *Stationers' Register*, 3:374), the day after Abbot's execution. The assize documents for this date also did not survive.

16. As D. C. Collins, the first modern commentator on *The Apprehension, Arraignment, and execution of Elizabeth Abbot*, observed: it "gives an illuminating picture of Elizabethan justice in progress" (*A Handlist of News Pamphlets 1590–1610*, 87–8, no. 235).

17. Loomis, "Elizabeth Abbot," 29–31.

18. Chester Gaol Book, 21/2/6r, 9r:

> 16 Mey Ao. 44 [1602]
> Elizabeth Caldwall m[ulier] Thome Caldwell y[eoman] de highleigh
> Galfrus Bounde y[eoman] de highleigh et } p[er] murdre omu [?] venem
> Isabell hall m[ulier] de John Hall de Crowley

19. Chester Gaol Book, 21/2/8v. "[Bownd] made a very penitent end" (*A True Discourse*, B3r), thereby suggesting his refusal to plead was tactical, to prevent his property passing into the hands of the state, which it would have done if he had pleaded and been convicted.

20. Dugdale states it was "a full yeare and a quarter" (D2r).

21. Wiles, *Shakespeare's Clown*, 136–44.

22. Chester Gaol Book, 21/2/6r.

23. Harris, ed., *A History of the County of Chester*, 2:36–54.

24. Chester Gaol Book, 21/2/9r. Bownd is also identified as "y[eoman]."

25. Sharpe, *Crime in seventeenth-century England*, 147.

26. She was reprieved after her trial on 4 October 1602 because she was pregnant. Within days she gave birth to a boy (B3r-v), which her husband acknowledged as his son. He nonetheless pressed the judge for Elizabeth to be executed, and a warrant was issued. But the constable of Chester Castle (who may be among the names listed in Dugdale's Preface) "conuented" the warrant (i.e. abrogated it, though "convent" does not match existing *OED* definitions in this apparent sense) by "mistaking" its delivery to the sheriff until after the date had expired, which indicates the constable's collusion with Caldwell's supporters. She was not threatened again until the spring 1603 assizes, which were delayed because of the Queen's death on 25 March 1603.

27. Walker, *Crime, Gender and Social Order*, 155.

28. Erickson, *Women and Property*, 25–26, 119–22.

29. Erickson, *Women and Property*, 85–91.

30. Dugdale again highlighted the causal link between poverty and crime when describing the motives of George Fernely, Isabel Hall's brother, whom she and Bownd originally engaged to kill Thomas Caldwell for £5 because they knew he was "slenderly furnished with meanes" (B1v). Fernely could not bring himself to do the deed, however, which gave way to Hall's plan to poison Thomas.

31. Calkins, "Cholmondeley, Mary;" Omerod, *The History of the County Palatine and City of Chester*, 1:495–96.

32. According to Amy Louise Erickson, 20% of estates were bequeathed to daughters only as heiresses. Contemporary legal documents and diaries show that these and other women were fully aware of distinctions between common law and equity in matters of marital status and property entitlement, and that they recognized the more secure benefits available to women under the latter jurisdiction (*Women and Property*, 30, 63, 113). See also Stretton, *Women Waging*

Law; Cioni, *Women and Law*; Martin, "The Autobiography of Grace, Lady Mildmay," 33–81.

33. The Exchequer followed procedures similar to Chancery in London, but was speedier and cheaper. The palatinate's legal independence diminished over the course of the seventeenth century (Omerod, *The History of . . . Chester*, 10, 36–40).

34. Walker, "Demons in female form," 133. Sandra Clark observes that this scenario partly recalls the representation of Anne Saunders's descent into homicide in *Women Beware Women* (*Women and Crime*, 157).

35. Perkins, *A Golden Chaine*, F5v–6v.

36. White, *Natural Law in English Renaissance Literature*, xiii, 9–19.

37. Ingram, *Church Courts*, 2–3.

38. These contested historical claims are examined in detail in chapter 3 below.

39. Walker, "Demons in female form," 132–33, 136.

40. Walker, *Crime, Gender, Social Order*, 156.

41. Herrup, *The Common Peace*, 93–94. As Herrup observes further, early modern grand juries were guided by cultural attitudes and local reliability of evidence. They were routinely accused of being too activist or passive in judging the validity of prosecution charges (94–5).

42. Babington, *Advice to Grand Jurors in Cases of Blood*, A4r.

43. Lawson, "Lawless Juries?," 150, 120.

44. Walker, *Crime, Gender and Social Order*, 135. Thirty-five percent of women versus 29% of men.

45. Walker, *Crime, Gender, and Social Order*, 135, Table 4.2: 38% of women versus 19% of men. Walker also cites Cynthia B. Herrup's findings from eastern Sussex records (46% of women charged with homicide were convicted versus 69% of men, *Common Peace*, 150, Table 6.4), and J. S. Cockburn's from the Home Circuit (44% of women versus 62% of men, *Calendar of Assize Records*, Introduction, 117).

46. Beattie, *Crime and the Courts*, 83, Table 3.1.

47. Beattie, *Crime and the Courts*, 388; "London Juries in the 1690s," 250–52; Cockburn, "Twelve Silly Men?," 161–64, 174.

48. Cockburn, "Twelve Silly Men?," 164, 174, 179–81.

49. Ingram, *Church Courts*, 180–83. On the other hand, neighbors routinely intervened informally when violence reached unacceptable levels (Amussen, "'Being Stirred to Much Unquietness,'" 77–82).

50. The only copy of a third account has been lost: *The Confession and Execution of Elizabeth Lillyman* (1675).

51. LMA Session Roll, MJ/SR/1489.

52. LMA Session Roll, MJ/SR/1489.

53. A gaol delivery list of Newgate prisoners for the same sessions (LMA Session Roll, MJ/SR/1489) records: "Elizabeth Lyllyman Com[ted] by Josiah Ricroft Esq[r] for Murthering William Lyllyman her husband."

54. If the detail was genuine it would support Elizabeth's assertion that she acted in an outburst of violent anger without premeditation, and it would call into question the report that her husband accused her before witnesses before he died.

55. Brittain, "Cruentation in Legal Medicine and Literature," 82–88.

56. As so often, the indictment for this case has not survived among the extant documents for these sessions (PRO ASSI 35/119/1).

57. Herrup, "Law and Morality," 110; Amussen, "'Being Stirred to Much Unquietness,'" 70–89. See also *A Warning-Piece to All Married Men and Women*, third column, and discussed below.

58. Walker, *Crime, Gender and Social Order*, 142–43.
59. *The Last Speech and Confession* tersely records "With Allowance."
60. David Mallet may have wished to make this section less conspicuous, but it is more likely that he needed to shrink the font to accommodate the added account of John Masters's and Gabriel Dean's executions for highway robbery. The pamphlet's imposition would have been rearranged after typesetting had begun, since the text begins unusually on the title page verso (with considerable bleed-through) and is erroneously signed A2 and paginated "2." None of the other leaves are signed, although the pagination continues regularly to page eight.
61. Clark, *Women and Crime*, 57.
62. Frances E. Dolan reads these shifts of voice and perspective, motivated by "sympathy for the abused wife, while keeping authority vested in the husband, however tyrannous," as "comic moments" (*Dangerous Familiars*, 35).
63. Amussen, "'Being Stirred to Much Unquietness,'" 75, 84–85.
64. Walker, *Crime, Gender and Social Order*, 142.
65. An extant indictment, PRO ASSI 35/122/5, is badly faded and unreadable in parts but otherwise conventionally worded. It names the murder weapon as "an Hatchett valor duoy denar" and claims Margaret wielded it in both hands ("in ambabus manibus") when giving Walter (formulaically) one deep and powerful mortal wound on the upper right forehead which killed him instantly. Typically, the indictment does not mention strangling or other blows.
66. The Harvard copy was annotated with a purchase date: "August: 2: 1680."
67. *Dreadful News from Southwark* was misidentified in Wing as D2153, reel 1401:19 (see below), but is now correctly listed by *ESTC* without a Wing number. The British Library (Cup21.g.32/27), the Bodleian (Godw. Pamph. 2209 [25]), and the Guildhall Library possess copies (though *ESTC* lists only BL). The confusion is owing to another pamphlet printed without a date but probably in the same year, *Dreadful News from Southwark: Or, A most true Relation How one Margaret Simpson Widow, together with Elizabeth Griffin an infant of about a year and a half old, were wonderfully struck Dead with a Thunder-Bolt in Ship-yard in Kent-Street, on Munnday the 4th of this instant August* (*ca.* 1680; Wing D2153). It has the same typeface and layout as the Osgood pamphlet, but the publisher in both cases is unknown.
68. The BL copy is annotated "17. March. 1680/1."
69. The Harvard copy is annotated "12 March 1680/1."
70. L'Estrange certified every "enformation" sworn before him with the formula "*Jurat. Die & Anno supradict. coram me*," and the first person Introduction and Postscript accord with it. It is also the only publication about the murder lacking his "allowance" on the title page, presumably because it was unnecessary.
71. Love, "L'Estrange, Sir Roger."
72. Kitchin, *Sir Roger L'Estrange*, 375–79.
73. The fact that *A Hellish Murder* does not advertise his allowance may also be taken as further evidence that he was the former's compiler and editor.
74. This disclosure was unprecedented for a seventeenth-century domestic crime by a commoner, male or female. The only comparable published accounts are those relating to state trials, such as the Overbury and Castlehaven cases.
75. Her name is spelled Hobry in three news accounts, Aubry in a fourth, Awbray in the extant indictment (LMA MJ/SR/1722), and Aubrey in a nineteenth-century depiction of the murder. A fifth contemporary account (*A Cabinet of Grief*) does not name her. In French her name would be spelled Aubray or Aubry (I am grateful to Graeme Clark for confirming this information). To

create less typographical dissonance between the text and quotations, I have kept Hobry, following the first and most substantial report, Roger L'Estrange's *A Hellish Murder*, from which all other accounts substantially derive.

76. "Bugger" in this period had two definitions: heretic and sodomite (*OED*, 1–2). The looser and less pejorative definition, "fellow," is not recorded until the late eighteenth century (*OED*, 3).

77. Dolan, *Dangerous Familiars*, 34, citing Dalton's *The Countrey Justice*, 281. Crying out was seen as equivalent to raising a public hue and cry.

78. The Harvard Library copy was bought and annotated by Narcissus Luttrell: "By Elkanah Settle. 3. March. 1687/8." Settle (1648–1742) was a playwright and city poet. He is now best known from Dryden's and Pope's scathing attacks on his limited talents, although they also envied his popular successes (Abigail Williams, "Settle, Elkanah"). Luttrell (1657–1732) was a biographer and annalist. *An Epilogue* was published by Randal Taylor and licensed by L'Estrange.

79. The title word "cabinet" is somewhat unusual; its possible meanings at this date are (1) a den, hole, or repository of a beast (last *OED* citation, 1640); (2) a museum or picture gallery; and (3) figuratively from 1, a secret receptacle, or store-house (*OED*, 1, 4, 6).

80. King, "Cellier, Elizabeth."

81. Women and men were both eligible to petition church courts for separations on the grounds of physical abuse or adultery, although this status did not allow them to remarry and women were less successful than men. See Ingram, *Church Courts*, 181–88; Amussen, "'Being Stirred to Much Unquietness.'"

82. Clark, *Women and Crime*, 161. Contrast the politically inflected moral of Thomas Deloney's *The Lamentation of Mr. Pages Wife* (*ca.* 1609, reprinted 1663–74): "Take heed you wives, let not your hands rebel."

83. Amussen, "Punishment, Discipline, and Power," 7.

84. Ruth Campbell discusses this gendered punishment in the context of its belated formal repeal in 1790 ("Sentence of Death by Burning for Women," 44–59).

85. For example, James had asked the pope to appoint four "flying" bishops to fill controversial posts such as the presidency of Magdalen College, Oxford. Speck, "James II and VII."

86. Love, "L'Estrange, Sir Roger."

87. I am indebted to Julia Wright (privately) for pointing out the different perspectives of testifying women and men in *A Hellish Murder*.

88. The indictment stated that Hobry had strangled and choked her husband to death with a piece of pack thread. It did not mention anything about the dismemberment.

89. *A Cabinet of Grief* also borrows *A Hellish Murder*'s wording to highlight the judicial offer to reverse the plea (A5r).

90. Beattie, *Crime and the Courts*, 333.

NOTES TO CHAPTER THREE

1. Spufford, *Small Books and Pleasant Histories*; Watt, *Cheap Print and Popular Piety*. As Peter Lake argued, however, the popular and material aims of each genre also diverged in significant ways ("Deeds Against Nature," 257–58 and *passim*).

2. Maclean, *The Renaissance Notion of Woman*; Woodbridge, *Women and the English Renaissance*.

3. His indictment survives: LMA MJ/SR/0179/21.

4. On Wednesday 25 March 1573, although the day Golding mentions, 24 March, was also symbolically resonant: it was the last day of the year in the old calendar.

5. Golding's description continues: "and besides that, great companies were placed bothe in the chambers neere abouts (whose windowes & walles were in many places beaten down to looke out at) & also vpon the gutters, sides, and toppes of the houses, and vpon the batlements and steeple of S. Bartholmewes [*sic*]" (B2r).

6. Either as an accessory or principal murderer she would have been hanged under sixteenth-century criminal law. *A Warning for Faire Women* extends Golding's manipulations in the same direction. See Dolan, "Gender, Moral Agency, and Dramatic Form in *A Warning for Fair Women*."

7. George Saunders was "extremely well connected." His first cousins were Sir Edward Saunders, Chief Baron of the Exchequer, and Alice Saunders, the mother of Sir Christopher Hatton, Captain of the Queen's Guard and later Lord Chancellor. He was also the half brother of Dr. Walter Haddon, the colleague of Roger Ascham and Roger Cheke. (Brooks, "A Pamphlet by Arthur Golding," 183).

8. This is Louis Thorn Golding's reasonable speculation (*An Elizabethan Puritan*, 68).

9. George's second son William was ten at the time of his father's death, and his eldest son Edward may also have not reached his majority (Brooks, "A Pamphlet by Arthur Golding," 183).

10. Walsham, *Providence in Early Modern England*, 88–89; Marshburn, *Murder & Witchcraft in England*; Lake, "Deeds Against Nature," 257–67.

11. The author was likely the clergyman who challenged Tetherton about his dissenting theological beliefs on the gallows (F2v–F3v). Also see Cooper's *The Cry and Reuenge of Blood*, ch. 4, F3r–G3v.

12. Walsham cites another conceptual illustration of "murder will out," in this case for male subjects. After Edward Wilson and Robert Tetherton had robbed the house of Wilson's former master Bowes and bludgeoned to death one of his servants, Joan Servant, they posted to Chester hoping to sail to Ireland. Contrary winds prevented them from escaping until they were captured, when, according to local reports, the winds "straight way changed." The anonymous and probably clerical author reconstructed the narrative as to reveal the "*digitus domini*" or "finger of God" actively leading to human apprehension of the murderers (*A True report of the horrible Murther, which was committed in the house of Sir Ierome Bowes*, C2r; Walsham, *Providence in Early Modern England*, 89–90).

13. Such portraits of hell-from-within, John Strachiewski argues, became a conspicuous feature of puritan didactic and imaginative literature (*The Persecutory Imagination*, 18). In *A True report of the horrible Murther*, the writer described Wilson's heart nearly bursting in agony before he finally vented his guilty conscience on the gallows: "Sorrowe was on his minde, and his minde was on sorrowe" (D4v–E1r). Even ideologically cooler news pamphlets tended to endorse common providentialist views that "God was no idle, inactive spectator upon the mechanical workings of the created world, but an assiduous energetic deity who constantly intervened in human affairs" (Walsham, *Providence in Early Modern England*, 2).

14. Lake, with Questier, *The Antichrist's Lewd Hat*, xiii–xiv.

15. Green, *Protestantism and Print*, 434; Chartier, *The Cultural Uses of Print*, 169.

16. Thornton Burnett, *Constructing 'Monsters,'* 2.

17. Daston and Park, *Wonders and the Order of Nature*, 180–83. Thornton Burnett also remarks on the tendency to extend metaphorically nonnormative events in nature to "a broader spectrum of 'unnatural' acts, peoples, and practices," including murder and treason (*Constructing 'Monsters,'* 24–25).

18. Richard Helgerson made this point in his review of Annabel Patterson's *Reading Holinshed's "Chronicles"* (Chicago: University of Chicago Press, 1994), *JEGP* 95 (1996): 239. Also Walsham, *Providence in Early Modern England*, 73–74.

19. Lake, "Ministers, Magistrates and the Production of 'Order,'" 165–66.

20. Beck, *Risk Society*, 3, 21, 41–46; Lupton, *Risk*, 5–8.

21. For example, in other contemporary pamphlets about the 1580 earthquake such as Thomas Twyne's *A Shorte and Pithie Discourse* (1580).

22. The Oxford editor, David Bevington, notes that Hotspur's views go back to Pliny (*Natural History*, 2.72) and were reiterated by Gabriel Harvey's *Discourse of the Earthquake in April Last* (1580) (*Henry IV Part One:* [Oxford: Oxford University Press (1987), 209]).

23. See also Marshburn, "'A Cruell Murder Donne in Kent' and Its Literary Manifestations."

24. Other accounts are: an unnamed woman who buried alive her illegitimate child, "casting all motherly and naturall affection" (C3r), accompanied by the proverb, "God wil not suffer wilful murder to be conceled" (C2v); Mrs. Amy Harrison (alias Middleton) a gentlewoman in St. Giles-in-the-Fields, "a very wicked liuer", "whipt, [beat], tirannically tormented, and very Jewishly intreated" her godchild when she failed to perform onerous household chores to Harrison's satisfaction, "sometime with big cudgels, sometime with a girth, so that from the crown of the hed, to the soles of the feet, was left no member vnmartired." The young girl eventually died from Harrison's abuse just before 7 March 1579/8 (C2v–3r); Margaret Dorington in Westminster, "a woman of wicked and naughty life" murdered Alice Foxe by "thrusting a knife vp vnder her clothes" (D1r).

25. Including Holinshed's *Chronicles*. Similar sources informed other compilations. The main text of *A World of wonders* constructed a pedigree of notorious English murderesses beginning with the legendary "Bithricus . . . poysoned by his owne wife." Other women mentioned are: "Margaret Dauie a mayde seruant boyled in Smithfeeld for poysoning of three seuerall housholders," Alice Arden, Rebecca Chambers, "burnt for [po]ysoning of her husband," Anne Saunders, a Dutch maidservant executed at Tyburn for killing her new-born child, and an innkeeper's wife, Mrs Thompson, hanged at Lincoln for murdering a traveller in his bed for his money (F1r–F4). T. I. ended with Rachel Merry and her brother Thomas, "being so fresh in memorie," who bludgeoned to death a man named Beech and his servant-boy Thomas Winchester in August 1594, "the male actor still hanging as a notable example to our eyes." Their story was dramatized by Robert Yarrington's *Two Lamentable Tragedies* (1601). Thomas Beard's *The Theatre of Gods Iudgements* (1597), a translation of Jean de Chassanion's original compilation and "*And Avgmented by more than three hundred Examples*," followed *A World of wonders* a couple of years later. Its classical, biblical, medieval, and early modern chronicles of notable murders and punishments ended with Alice Arden: "And thus all the murderers had their deserued dewes in this life, and what they endured in the life to come (except they obtaine mercy by true repentance) it is easie to iudge" (S3r).

26. See also Goodcole's preface to *The Adultresses Funerall Day*, A2v–3r, which cites the relevant passage from *Metamorphoses* in Latin.

27. Walsham, *Providence in Early Modern England*, 73–74.

28. Beard, *Theatre of Gods Iudgements*, 270–71.

29. *Arden of Faversham* was printed in 1592 and is thought to have been written a few years earlier. *A Warning for Faire Women* was not published until 1599, but was written earlier and may have preceded *Arden*. Its dramaturgy is more old-fashioned, closer to plays written in the mid-to-late 1580s. A modern editor suggests a time frame of 1585–1599 (Cannon, ed., *A Warning for Faire Women*, 48). Lena Cowen Orlin, on the other hand, believes *Arden* came first (*Private Matters and Public Culture*, 91).

30. This time signed "Arthur Golding." The 1573 edition printed only his initials, "A.G."

31. See W. Calderwood, "The Elizabethan Protestant Press," Ph.D. diss., University of London, 1977, 219–20, cited in Green, *Protestantism and Print*, 16–17.

32. Passages from Holinshed, Stow, *The Annales of England*, and Golding's pamphlet are reproduced in Appendices D through F of Cannon's edition of *A Warning for Faire Women*, 216–36, and discussed 64–75.

33. Helgerson, "Murder in Faversham." A shorter and different version of this article appeared in Helgerson's subsequent *Adulterous Alliances* (2000).

34. Helgerson, "Murder in Faversham," 15. For example *The wofull lamentacon of mrs. Anne Saunders, which she wrote with her own hand, being prisoner in newgate, Justly condemned to death* is a manuscript version of a printed ballad now lost and probably originally registered in the Stationers' Register between 1573–76 (BL Sloane MS, fol. 8–11, reproduced in *Old English Ballads 1553–1625*, ed. Rollins, 340–48).

35. Orlin, *Private Matters and Public Culture*, 91–98.

36. Clark, *Women and Crime*, 147.

37. Questier, *Conversion, Politics and Religion*, 58–69.

38. *A briefe treatise concerning the burnynge of Bucer and Phagius* was written two years earlier in Latin by an anonymous author. Bucer and Phagius died in 1551 and Golding may have witnessed their executions (Golding, *An Elizabethan Puritan*, 142).

39. Sharpe, "Last Dying Speeches," 148.

40. Questier, *Conversion, Politics and Religion*, 1–10, 172–202, and *passim*.

41. Marshall, *The Shattering of the Self*, 90–91.

42. Sheehan, "The London Prison System," 12–13, 29–31.

43. Dobb, "Life and Conditions in London Prisons," 207.

44. When Henry Goodcole was appointed visitor of Ludgate prison in 1613, he seems to have been the first regularly assigned preacher there since the Reformation, even though creating a salaried position had been discussed in the 1580s (CLRO, Rep. 30, fol. 339v–340r; Rep. 31, part 1, fol. 86v; Dobb, "Henry Goodcole," 17).

45. Linebaugh, "The Ordinary of Newgate and His *Account*."

46. Dobb, "Henry Goodcole," 15–16.

47. CLRO, Rep. 15, fol. 139, 92v.

48. Dobb, "Life and Conditions in London Prisons," 191. Yonge is described as "the exhorter of prisoners" in CLRO, Rep. 17, fol. 99. He also advised on the making of gallows and carts for prisoners.

49. Lehmburg, "Nowell, Alexander." Nowell was author of the government-approved *Catechisme, or First Instruction and teaching of Christian Religion*, used to inculcate an austere version of Calvinist theology in Elizabethan grammar schools. *A True report of the horrible Murther, which was committed in the house of Sir Ierome Bowes* is another instance of intervention by a specially appointed minister rather than the regular visitor. Wilson, one of the two murderers, refused to confess the crime even when he was on the gallows ladder until "pressed by one, sent vnto him, from personages of high place, vpon paine, and perill of damnation that the fault might lye on the

offēder, the faultless might go vnsuspected, iustice might be cleared ... and God might be glorified" (D3v). Wilson suddenly relented and made a speech, which prompted his partner Tetherton to do the same.

50. Arber, ed., *Stationers' Register*, 1:385. Pressing was the punishment for refusing to enter a plea to an indictment. Aside from questions of conscience, it prevented property and inheritances from being forfeited to the state if the defendant was found guilty. Enduring pressing to death was therefore an extreme tactic to protect the welfare of wives and families.

51. Dobb, "Life and Conditions in London Prisons," 543–44.

52. This was briefly the punishment for murder by poison. See ch. 4, p. 128.

53. For instance, *A Briefe Discovrse of Two most cruell and bloudie murthers, committed bothe in Worcestershire* (1583); *Two most vnnaturall and bloodie Murthers* (1605); *Three Bloodie Murders* (1613); Cooper, *The Cry and Reuenge of Blood* (1620); Goodcole, *Heavens Speedie Hue and Cry* (1635); *The Adultresses Funerall Day* (1635); Alleine and Franklin, *A Murder Punished and Pardoned* (1668); and (perhaps) *A Full and True Account Of A Most Barbarous and Bloody Murther, Committed By Esther Ives* (1686).

54. CLRO, *Remembrancia*, Letter 53, fol. 79–80; Dobb, "Henry Goodcole," 18.

55. Lake with Questier, *The Antichrist's Lewd Hat*, xix.

56. The play shows Mell's suit on Anne's behalf being dismissed (scene xix) and Anne overhearing two carpenters discussing their construction of gallows (xx), but does not suggest that she has been entrapped by false hopes, as Golding's pamphlet does.

57. Thomas Fuller, *Abel Redevivus*, liiir; Breward, *William Perkins*, 7–8.

58. Clarke, *The Marrow of Ecclesiastical History*, Eee2r–v.

59. Scarry, *The Body in Pain*, 169–71; Questier, *Conversion, Politics and Religion*, 59–68.

60. Cohen, *God's Caress*, 4–11; Lake, "Popular Form, Puritan Content?," 321.

61. Perkins's *A Reformed Catholike* (1598) discussed this point, contrasting it with the Catholic view of human will as actively co-operating with grace (A8v–B1v). See also Strachniewski, *The Persecutory Imagination*, 12–18.

62. Cohen, *God's Caress*, 5; Lake, "Popular Form, Puritan Content?," 321.

63. Goodcole calls the weapon a "truncheon" or "bastinado." Indictments against Shearwood allege he killed Rowland Holt with a "haysell batt" (i.e. hay-season flail; LMA SR 778/77) and Thomas Claxton with a "ffaggott stick" (LMA SR 778/78).

64. Questier, *Conversion, Politics and Religion*, 198; Lake, "Deeds Against Nature," 280–82.

65. When the Court of Aldermen appointed Mathew Yonge visitor of Newgate in 1562, he was to work with the assistance of deputies as necessary (CLRO, Rep. 15, fol. 139). In 1675 the Court of Alderman formally asked ministers working in other London prisons to assist the ordinary of Newgate (CLRO, Rep. 80, fol. 55). See also Pugh, "Newgate Between Two Fires," 137–63, 199–222.

66. Green, "Career Prospects and Clerical Conformity."

67. Alexandra Walsham observes that providentialist accounts of prodigies and natural disasters were sometimes written by country vicars to supplement their incomes (*Providence in Early Modern England*, 50).

68. The following account draws on portions of my article, "Henry Goodcole, Visitor of Newgate." For eighteenth-century visitors and their serialized accounts, see Linebaugh, "The Ordinary of Newgate and His *Account*."

69. Hovenden, ed., *A True Register*, 9:17; Dobb, "Henry Goodcole," 16.

70. For example, the title pages of *A True Declaration*, *The Prodigals Teares*, and *The wonderfull discouerie*. Goodcole's will is dated 23 August 1641, the day before his death, and was proved on 24 January 1642 (LMA). In the

Repertories of the minutes of the Court of Aldermen (CLRO, Rep.) he is consistently styled "clerk." In the Clerkenwell parish registers, however, from the christening of his third child Humphrey on 7 March 1610, Goodcole is occasionally styled "master." This honorific probably represents local recognition of his family's standing. His father James is recorded without any title, but he is described as a householder, and he and his wife were granted the privilege of being buried "in the body of the church" rather than in the churchyard, as eventually was Henry's first son Andrew, who died at two years of age, and Goodcole himself in 1641. His second son Humphrey and his daughter Joan predeceased him, so Goodcole died without heirs (Hovenden, ed., *A True Register*, 9:59, 60, 91, 112, 174, 248).

71. [Old] *DNB*, 8:119; Dobb, "Henry Goodcole," 16.
72. Hovenden, ed., *A True Register*, 9:116. CLRO, Rep. 30, fol. 339v–340r. The basis of the Ludgate appointment was "the pleasure of this Court and [the visitor's] diligence in preaching" (340r). Also CLRO, Rep. 31, part 1, fol. 86v; Dobb, "Henry Goodcole," 16.
73. CLRO, *City Cash Account* 1/1, fol. 41v; Rep. 32, fol. 247r. "The Court taking consideracõn of his diligence and paynes therein, and for the incouragement of his further indevo^{rs}." "Pains," which recurs in the Court's records about Goodcole, implies the goal of conversion. The word's senses of physical and mental exertion and distress are apt for both Goodcole and his subjects, as is the idea of taking trouble to secure a satisfying result (*OED*, Pain *n.*[1] 6a).
74. To one or two per assize every few years; e.g., Cockburn, J. S., ed., *Calendar of Assize Records*, 1598–1607, 16; 1608–17, 6; and 1618–27, 1. Also Rowley, Dekker, and Ford, *The Witch of Edmonton*, ed. Onat, 76, citing C.H. L'Estrange Ewen, *Witch Hunting and Witch Trials* (London: Kegan Paul & Co., 1929), 99.
75. *A Proclamation for Reformation of abuses, in the Gaole of New-gate* (1617) issued by the Mayor of London.
76. To cite an instance involving a convicted male murderer: in 1684 visitors used holy communion to bribe Rice Evans to give over his protests of innocence and admit killing his wife. The offer had the opposite effect, however. Evans told the Minister, "What, Man, do you think I will damn my own Soul to deny the truth now that I have received God's Holy Sacrament? No, I will not do it. I tell thee man I am not Guilty" (2). At the execution one of the ministers pressed Evans "at least 15 or 20 times . . . with all possible Earnestness, how necessary it was for him to Confess . . . to which he at length very passionately answered:

> What, do you think I am a Mad-man, to deny it now I am going to dye, if I was guilty? I tell you man, I am not guilty of the Blood laid to my Charge: It's true, I am a *Welchman*, and have been angry sometimes, but I have done no Murder. (2)

Evans visibly advertised his protest against the verdict—and his spiritually reconciled state—by wearing "a very white new Shirt, made of *Callico*" over his clothes, which the authors and presumably also spectators understood as being "in Token of his Innocency" (3). Also CLRO, Rep. 47, fol. 182v–186r; Dobb, "Henry Goodcole", 19.
77. Lake, "Deeds Against Nature," 277–90.
78. For example the widely reported and debated trials of Anne Greene in 1651 and Mary Hobry (or Aubrey) in 1688. For later cases in criminal fiction see Gladfelder, *Criminality and Narrative in Eighteenth-Century England*.
79. Questier, *Conversion, Politics and Religion*, 15, 192, 196–97, 200; Lake, "Popular Form, Puritan Content?," 327.

80. Laqueur, "Crowds, Carnival and the State;" Amussen, "Punishment, Discipline, and Power," 9–12, 32–33.
81. Both skeletons were displayed in 1638 in the new anatomy theater designed two years earlier by Inigo Jones in Barber Surgeons' Hall, Monkwell Street. They remained on view until 1784 when the theater was demolished (Sawday, *The Body Emblazoned,* 60–71, citing Edward Hatton, *A New View of London,* 2 vols., 2:597, itemizing the theater's human furnishings: "The skeletons of *Canberry Bess* and *Country Tom* (as they there call them,) 1638"). The skeletons were depicted within facing niches in variant states of the fourth and final scene of William Hogarth's *The Four Stages of Cruelty* ("The Reward of Cruelty"). Unfortunately Bess's and Tom's skeletons no longer survive; they seem to have been lost when the later Surgeons' Hall was destroyed by bombing during the Second World War.
82. Gordon and Wright, "Quick, John."
83. Sharpe, "Last Dying Speeches," 153–54.
84. Scarry, *The Body in Pain,* 33.
85. Sharpe, "Last Dying Speeches," 148; Questier and Lake, "Agency Appropriation and Rhetoric," 64–65.
86. Foucault, *Discipline and Punish,* 8; Spierenburg, *The Spectacle of Suffering.* 156; Clark, *The Elizabethan Pamphleteers:* "no doubt the lives of the unrepentant [criminal] might have been more interesting, but nobody wrote them" (92).
87. Sharpe, "Last Dying Speeches," 150–57.
88. Exceptions are Questier and Lake, "Agency Appropriation and Rhetoric;" Dolan, "Women on Scaffolds;" and Staub, "Bloody Relations;" all of whom reject (from different perspectives) Foucault's binary of absolute state power and abjection of the condemned. Dolan argues that women "achieve[d] public voice through the effacement of their bodies" and were "represented transcending bodily suffering and death" (159). Although I agree with her views about the fluid and relational opportunities for asserting personal agency and ethical conscience at execution events, the premise of female bodily erasure to achieve such subjectivity that she borrows from Catherine Belsey (*The Subject of Tragedy,* 190–91) is misleading both as a theory and in light of the evidence from early modern news accounts.
89. Linebaugh, "The Tyburn Riot Against the Surgeons;" Laqueur, "Crowds, Carnival and the State."
90. "Deeds Against Nature," 276; "Popular Form, Puritan Content?," 331.
91. "Agency, Appropriation and Rhetoric Under the Gallows," 65.
92. See Allyson May, "She at first denied it."
93. *Pace,* Sharpe. Gladfelder, *Criminality and Narrative,* 54.
94. Sharpe, "Last Dying Speeches," 158–59 citing Mervyn James, *English Politics and the Concept of Honour, 1485–1642,* Past and Present Supplement no. 3 (Oxford: Clarendon Press, 1978), 44. Also Lake, "Ministers, Magistrates."
95. *Discipline and Punish,* 1–80.
96. Amussen, "Punishment, Discipline, and Power," 4; Dolan, "Women on Scaffolds," 159.
97. *The Practice of Everyday Life,* 26.
98. "Ministers, Magistrates," 166.
99. "Ministers, Magistrates," 173.
100. A nonextant ballad about this case was entered in the Stationers' Register on 8 February 1610 (Arber, ed., 3:428). There is no record of Hattersley's trial in East Grinstead assizes for 17 July 1609 (ASSI 35/51/9).
101. The gaol book records her name as Hester Ivyleafe (ASSI 23, vol. 3 [of 10], fol. 63r [125]). It also marks her entry with an especially heavy asterisk.

102. The letter contains no personal details about the mother's relationship to her children and consists exclusively of moral and homiletically inflected advice. Unlike authentic and highly popular seventeenth-century mother's advice books (e.g., Elizabeth Jocelyn, *The Mother's Legacy to her Unborn Child* [1624]), it says nothing about her children's education, marriages, or vocation.
103. Raymond, "The Newspaper, Public Opinion, and the Public Sphere;" Green, *Protestantism and Print*, 434–44.
104. See Laqueur, "Crowds, Carnival and the State;" Questier and Lake, "Agency, Appropriation and Rhetoric," 96–104.
105. For example Ridgeway allegedly had earlier played off two lovers against each other: "and before she knew which she liked best, having been so free with the other as that she thought he might be some Trouble to her, she resorted to her old Trade, and continued to keep the said *John King* Company until she had an Opportunity to season him some Draught which sent him into the other World" (A2v).

NOTES TO CHAPTER FOUR

1. See Introduction, p. 12.
2. Sharpe, *Crime in seventeenth-century England*, 129; Walker, *Crime, Gender and Social Order*, 143–44.
3. Aelian, *On the Characteristics of Animals*, 1:54.
4. Farrell, *Poisons and Poisoners*, 204–05.
5. Book Six, ch. 3, 116ff.
6. Walker, *Crime, Gender and Social Order*, 144–45. J. M. Beattie similarly concludes from his analysis of Surrey assize records that the frequency of women's use of poison was comparable to other methods of killing (*Crime and the Courts*, 101). And in Essex, 1620 to 1680, the six cases of homicide by poisoning were evenly divided by gender (Sharpe, *Crime in seventeenth-century England*, 129–30).
7. Forty-nine per cent by men and 51% by women (Watson, *Poisoned Lives*, 45).
8. Walker, *Crime, Gender and Social Order*, Figure 4.8, 146.
9. Walker, *Crime, Gender and Social Order*, 145.
10. Sharpe, *Crime in Early Modern England*, 10.
11. Walker, *Crime, Gender and Social Order*, 146.
12. *Mercurius Publicus*, No. 22, Thursday May 29–June 5, 1662, p. 335, cited by Sutherland, *Restoration Newspaper*, 93.
13. Emsley, *The Elements of Murder*, 3–4, 44–45.
14. Emsley, *The Elements of Murder*, 104.
15. Paster, *The Body Embarrassed*, 1–22, 113–62; Wall, *Staging Domesticity*, 3, 163–72.
16. Hunter, "Women and Domestic Medicine," 89–107, especially 95–98; Pennell, "Perfecting Practice?," 237–55.
17. Best, ed., 49–50. Best cites John Woodall's receipt for making mercury sublimate in *The Surgeon's Mate* (1617), 299, and notes that it was used in many early modern medicines (250, n. 208).
18. Pennell, "Perfecting Practice?," 242.
19. For example, *unguentum Aegyptiacum* (whose active ingredient was realgar or red arsenic, a treatment for wounds and ulcers going back to Hippocrates [Emsley, *The Elements of Murder*, 48, 104; also *verdigris*, copper acetate, and *lapis calaminaris*, zinc sulphate, 50–1]).
20. Hunter, "Women and Domestic Medicine," 97–100; "Sweet Secrets," 36–59; Pennell, "Perfecting Practice?," 246. See also Wall, *Staging Domesticity*, 120,

165, citing John Cotta's warnings about medicines "as commeth unknowne unto them, out of Apothecaries shops" (29) in his chapter against "she-physicians" in *A Short Discouerie of the Unobserued Dangers of Several Sorts of Ignorant and Unconsiderate Practisers of Physicke in England* (1612).

21. *The Weekly Intelligencer*, No. 68, April 6–13, 1652; *A Perfect Account of The daily Intelligence*, No. 67, April 7–14, 1652.
22. Kesselring, "A Draft for the 1531 'Acte for Poysoning,'" 894–99.
23. Bacon, *Works*, 5:307–11. "[Poison] is an Italian crime, fit for the Court of Rome, where that person that intoxicateth the Kings of the earth with his cup of poison in heretical doctrine, is many times really and materially intoxicated and impoisoned himself" (309).
24. See ch. 2, p. 47.
25. PRO CHES 21/2 6r, 8v, 9r.
26. Herrup, "Law and Morality," 102–23.
27. The theatrical manager Philip Henslowe recorded a payment to Jonson and Dekker for "Page of Plymouth" (*Henslowe's Diary*, 123).
28. Clark, *Women and Crime*, 23.
29. Michael D. Kelleher and C. L. Kelleher argue that a similar cultural bias suppresses cases of female serial killers being regularly reported in the modern English-speaking media (*Murder Most Rare*, xi).
30. As depicted in the pamphlet's title page illustration, which readers may or may not have first understood as specifically related to the crime-story. Nothing in the narrative suggests that Barnes put anything in the food to make her daughter fall asleep.
31. Kristeva, *Powers of Horror*, 75–76.
32. Staub, "Bloody Relations," 135.
33. Belsey, *The Subject of Tragedy*, 130.
34. For instance, George Wilkins's *The Miseries of Enforced Marriage* (1607) or the anonymous *A Yorkshire Tragedy* (1608, long proposed by some critics to be partly by Shakespeare, who had written the classic play about parentally thwarted romantic love, *Romeo and Juliet*, around 1594–95).
35. Clark, *Women and Crime*, 59–60.
36. See ch. 3, p. 107.
37. This pamphlet survives in a single copy held by Lambeth Palace Library and is reproduced in Martin, ed., *Women and Murder*.
38. Emsley, *The Elements of Murder*, 74.
39. There is no record of their trials in the LMA Session Roll for May 9–10 or June 26, 1592.
40. McElwee, *The Murder of Sir Thomas Overbury*, 46; Somerset, *Unnatural Murder*, 5–7.
41. McElwee, *The Murder of Sir Thomas Overbury*, 77.
42. Bellany, *The Politics of Court Scandal*, 55–56, 72.
43. Wiggins, *Journeymen in Murder*, 4.
44. Somerset, *Unnatural Murder*; Emsley, *The Elements of Murder*, 89.
45. Emsley, *The Elements of Murder*, 81. I am indebted to Emsley's clear account of the sequence of murder attempts and their chemical components.
46. Bellany, *The Politics of Court Scandal*, 72, 145; McElwee, *The Murder of Sir Thomas Overbury*, 92; Emsley, *The Elements of Murder*, 83.
47. McElwee, *The Murder of Sir Thomas Overbury*, 192–93.
48. Cook, *Dr Simon Forman*, 187.
49. Somerset, *Unnatural Murder*, 270.
50. Lindley, *The Trials of Frances Howard*, 163–65; Purkiss, *The Witch in History*, 222.

51. Somerset, *Unnatural Murder*, 271; Cook, *Dr Simon Forman*, 194, 202.
52. Somerset, *Unnatural Murder*, 272.
53. Amos, *The Great Oyer of Poisoning*, 218–21; Somerset, *Unnatural Murder*, 275.
54. Somerset, *Unnatural Murder*, 272–74.
55. Bellany, "Mistress Turner's Deadly Sins," 202.
56. Amos, *The Great Oyer of Poisoning*, 224.
57. Bellany, *The Politics of Court Scandal*, 185.
58. *Court Patronage and Corruption*, 175–78. Peck observes that at some points Niccols's language recalls contemporary assize sermons (176).
59. Clark, *Women and Crime*, 66; Bellany, "Mistress Turner's Deadly Sins," 189.
60. Purkiss, *The Witch in History*, 220.
61. See ch. 2. Bellany, *The Politics of Court Scandal*, 126, cites R. B. McKerrow, *Printers' & Publishers' Devices in England & Scotland 1485–1640* (Chiswick: The Bibliographical Society, 1913), 114–15.
62. Bellany, *The Politics of Court Scandal*, 126.
63. Bellany, "Mistress Turner's Deadly Sins," 157, 189. Also Jones and Stallybrass, *Renaissance Clothing and the Materials of Memory*, ch. 3, pp. 59–85; Purkiss, *The Witch in History*, 224.
64. Wiggins, *Journeymen in Murder*, 73.
65. Emsley, *The Elements of Murder*, 278.
66. Drew-Bear, *Painted Faces*, 22. See the portrait of Howard attributed to William Larkin, now in the National Portrait Gallery, as well as the engraving by Simon van der Passe, both reproduced in Somerset, *Unnatural Murder*, between pages 212–13.
67. Drew-Bear, *Painted Faces*, 1–34; Whigham, *Ambition and Privilege*, 116; Dolan, "Taking the Pencil Out of God's Hand," 224–39.
68. B3r–B4v, cited by Drew-Bear, *Painted Faces*, 18–22.
69. Cited by McLaughlin, *The Coward's Weapon*, 53.
70. Thompson, *Poisons and Poisoners*, 132–37.
71. Thompson, *Poisons and Poisoners*, 142–44; Farrell, *Poisons and Poisoners*, 154; McLaughlin, *The Coward's Weapon*, 42, 71. McLaughlin notes that the French had the same suspicions of Italians.
72. Amos, *The Great Oyer of Poisoning*, 370.
73. Coke, *Third Part of the Institutes*, 138; Bellany, *The Politics of Court Scandal*, 144; Walker *Crime, Gender and Social Order*, 144.
74. Goodcole's conclusion that poisoning is premeditated and unpardonable and therefore demands capital justice echoed Perkins's *A Golden Chaine*, H6r, and *The Whole Treatise of the Cases of Conscience*, B5r-v.
75. Bellany, *The Politics of Court Scandal*, 146.
76. Calvert, "On Poisons," 195–98; Farrell, *Poisons and Poisoners*, 154; McLaughlin, *The Coward's Weapon*, 42; Emsley, *The Elements of Murder*, 141–42.
77. Bellany notes that a late-November entry for "Mistres Turners Teares" in the Stationers' Register indicates it might originally have been published separately ("Mistress Turner's Deadly Sins," 184).
78. The head title in the Guildhall copy reads "A bloody Relation of *Katherine Web*, who poysoned her husband at Westminster," whereas the BL and Huntington copies have "*Anne Hamton*." Similarly, the Guildhall copy identifies Hamton's landlady and conspirator companion as "*Mary Fusser*," whereas in the other two copies she is named "*Margerite Harwood*." The variant names reduce the status of the pamphlet almost to a generic story about unruly and selfish wives. Legal records, on the other hand, indicate that the name Anne Hamton (or Hampton) is correct. A surviving gaol delivery list bears the entry:

"ind[ictment]. Anne Hampton Com[mitted]: by Peter Heywood esq: ye 13th day of September, 1641 Chearged with Suspition of Murthering her husband" ("Kalendar of the Names of all Such Prisoners as hath bin Committed vnto ye Custody of Aquila Wykes Esq: Keeper of his Ma:ᵗˢ Prison of the Gatehouse in Westmʳ And are to be Tryed at the Sessions houlden for ye Sayd Citty and Liberty ye 1 day of October 1641" [LMA Session Roll 897/136]). Unfortunately the related assize roll contains very few surviving documents, all very badly damaged and mostly illegible, with apparently nothing else relating to Hamton (LMA Session Roll 900, 1 October 1641).

79. Alternatively, compare the contrasting portrait of an ideal wife in Phillip Stubbes's highly popular *A Christal Glas for christian Women* (1592), written as a memorial on the death of his wife Catherine, especially "Her demeanour toward her husband" (A3r).

80. None of the *OED* entries document the term being used to describe a female lover.

81. Clark, *Women and Crime,* 66. Besides Harwood, Hamton is accused of gossiping "with one young fellow or other, or else with such women as were like to her selfe" (A3r).

82. Henry Goodcole confronted the same challenge in *The Adultresses Funerall Day,* describing husband poisoning as akin to other unnatural transgressions, "Catamisme, Sodometry, Paracity, many-headed murders and the like" (A3v), although here he has in mind the Castlehaven case, which actually involved these particular crimes. See Herrup, *A House in Gross Disorder.*

83. See p. 148.

84. Venice glass was originally from Murano, fine and very brittle. See E. B. Browning, *Sonnets from the Portuguese,* 9:12: "Nor breathe my poison on thy Venice-glass." "[P]oison poured in Venetian glass was popularly supposed to shatter it, the quality of such glass being so fine as to feel at once the subtle element of death in the liquid" (*Complete Works,* ed. Charlotte Poster and Helen A. Clarke, 6 vols. [New York: AMS, 1973], 3.395).

85. Staub, "Bloody Relations," 132.

86. Emsley, *The Elements of Murder,* 139–41.

87. Quick also glossed the word "swapped," as in "[Cary] had swopt a Bargain with the Devil" (45) as "made," which seems hardly necessary for seventeenth-century readers, even though this meaning is technically obsolete today (*OED,* Swap *v.* 7b).

88. Brittain, "Cruentation in Legal Medicine and Literature," 82–88.

NOTES TO CHAPTER FIVE

1. Daly and Maher, "Crossroads and Intersections," 4. Daly and Maher draw on Judith Butler, who in turn cited Foucault's *History of Sexuality* to refute Julia Kristeva's Lacanian derived notion of motherhood as a precultural instinct and prediscursive form of ontology. Butler argues that neither personal maternal agency nor its discursive and symbolic signification by patriarchal culture exist prior to one another (*Gender Trouble,* 115–19).

2. Wrightson, "Infanticide in Earlier Seventeenth-Century England," 10–22; Piers, *Infanticide,* 21, 34.

3. Morrissey, *When Women Kill,* 3, 57. For popular depictions of the Medea-figure in early English plays, see Travitsky, "Child Murder in English Renaissance Life and Drama," 71–76.

4. Malcolmson, "Infanticide in Eighteenth-Century England," 246–69; Sharpe, *Crime in seventeenth-century England,* 135–37; Beattie, *Crime and the Courts,*

113–24; Sharpe, *Crime in Early Modern England*, 87–88, 157–58; Walker, *Crime, Gender and Social Order*, 148–58.

5. The term is sometimes parsed to distinguish the killing of newborn children (neonaticide) from children less than twenty-four hours old (filicide), to those up to one year (infanticide). See Hoffer and Hull, *Murdering Mothers*, 145–64. Mark Jackson notes that early modern people did not use "infanticide" and prefers the more precise term "new-born infant murder" (*New-Born Child Murder*, 6–7). But Garthine Walker argues that it is historically useful to be able to extend the term "infanticide" to include recently born infants (*Crime, Gender and Social Order*, 148, n. 152). I shall also use the term this way. "Child murder" refers to subjects beyond infant years.

6. See Gladfelder, *Criminality and Narrative in Eighteenth-Century England*.

7. Clark, *Women and Crime*, 164; Walker, "Demons in female form," 131–32.

8. Dickinson and Sharpe, "Infanticide in Early Modern England," 49.

9. Lake, "Deeds Against Nature," 282.

10. See the discussion of Arthur Golding's *A briefe discourse* and related wonder news in ch. 3, pp. 81–88.

11. For instance, in addition to Medea, Shakespeare's "she-wolf of France," Margaret of Anjou (*Henry VI* and *Richard III*) was alluded to as an exemplum of unnatural motherhood in several early pamphlets (e.g., *Three Bloodie Murders* [1613], C1v–C2r).

12. Possibly with an antiforeigner subtext: the maid, her employers, and their relations were all Dutch immigrants.

13. Daston and Park, *Wonders and the Order of Nature*, 294.

14. Munday's analogies from ancient natural history and traditional assumptions about universal maternal instincts, female frailty, feminine modesty and its whorish opposites, were reinforced in more learned contexts by conduct books (e.g., Gouge, *Of Domesticall Duties* [1622, 1634]).

15. Laura Gowing discusses how ambiguities and misunderstandings about the birthing process could validate such claims in "Secret Births," 108–09.

16. Wrightson, "Infanticide in Earlier Seventeenth-Century England;" Clark, *Women and Crime*, 44–51; Gowing, "Secret Births," 90–108.

17. This aesthetic touch and other features (a third [unoriginal] woodcut of a mother stabbing her right breast as three dead children lie at her feet, the eleven-leaf quarto format) indicated the book was not hastily or cheaply produced and would have sold at a higher price than most news pamphlets. The left-hand title page image showed a man digging a shallow grave in a garden or orchard while a well-dressed woman holds out a naked infant and a tiny skull and bones lie at their feet. Given the pamphlet's other apparently symbolic visual features, the thick cloud cover and seemingly disturbed sky may have been intended to convey "the Foggs & cloudes of [Adamson's] dissembling and priuie contriuing," behind which God's punishment waited "like the Sun [to] burst out" (C1v).

18. Clark, *Women and Crime*, 51.

19. Kristeva, *The Powers of Horror*, 4.

20. This statement contradicted the traditional view mentioned earlier ("And as I was mishapt by kind, / Deformed also was my mind," B1r) and drew attention to the perceptual instability of both assumptions.

21. Laura Gowing notes that this belief served to distinguish legitimate from illicit births: "poor women, and in particular the mothers of bastards, bore their children quickly and more easily than those fully prepared for a lying-in: stories of illegitimate births and the murder of new-borns created a culture in which such labours were meant to be shamefully easy" ("Secret Births," 99).

22. Wrightson, "Infanticide in Early Seventeenth-Century England," 12; Gowing, "Secret Births," 89; Walker, *Crime, Gender and Social Order*, 148–49.
23. The [Toronto] *Globe and Mail*, May 4, A10.
24. Travitsky, "'A Pittilesse Mother'?," 62 ,68, 73.
25. Gouge, *Of Domesticall Duties*, Q2r.
26. PRO SP 14/87/24, reproduced in Travitsky, "'A Pittilesse Mother'?," 59.
27. PRO SP 14/87/25, cited in Travitsky, "'A Pittilesse Mother'?," 58–59. This item was not included in Chamberlain's *Letters*, ed. McClure.
28. Bellany, *The Politics of Court Scandal*, 140, 184–88. Also ch. 4, p. 141.
29. Chamberlain, *Letters*, ed. McClure, 2:15.
30. Jackson, *Law, Fact and Narrative Coherence*, 132, cited in Morrissey, *When Women Kill*, 11.
31. These work to settle the new assumptions and choices into another state of temporary closure until the process begins afresh. Fish, "Force," *Doing What Comes Naturally*, 513, 516.
32. Two older definitions of "discovery" are in play here: (1) information or evidence that brings anything to light, and (2) the action of discovering or divulging (anything secret or unknown); revelation, disclosure (*OED, sb.*, 2, 4).
33. Possibly Thomason, from whose collection the single extant British Library copy of *Bloody Newes* derives.
34. Baker, "Thomas Edwards," 5–6.
35. The pamphlet opened "Murder is a crying sin, and of it self, commonly its own discoverer" (A2r).
36. Edwards, *Gangraena*, Part Two, ch. 8, p. 146; Baker, "Thomas Edwards," 6.
37. Walker, *Crime, Gender and Social Order*, 156.
38. Morrissey, *When Women Kill*, 12.
39. Walker, *Crime, Gender and Social Order*, 152, 155–56.
40. Morrissey, *When Women Kill*, 12, citing Douglas Maynard's phrase in "Narratives and Narrative Structure in Plea-Bargaining," in Papke, ed., *Narrative and the Legal Discourse*, 129.
41. "But common it is that such common pieces, can beare it out better then true and lawfull bearers of children can" (Brewer, *The Bloudy Mother*, B2r). "Beare it out" resonates with sexual double meaning.
42. "Matronly" suggests both the appearance of a married woman, and one who is knowledgeable about pregnancy, childbirth, and midwifery (*OED*, Matron, *sb.*, 1–2).
43. The image was recycled in a ballad, *Inhumane, & Cruel Bloody News from Leeds in York-Shire*, published by Francis Coles and others in 1676. Coles published Goodcole's *Natures Cruell Step-Dames*.
44. Clark, *Women and Crime*, 49; Birch (?), *Fair Warning to the Murderers of Infants* (1692); *The Cruel Midwife* (1697). See below pp. 174–75.
45. Piers, *Infanticide*, 17.
46. Bowers, *The Politics of Motherhood*, 94.
47. Bowers, *The Politics of Motherhood*, 94–95.
48. The author was possibly visitor of Newgate, who may have written one or both of these earlier accounts.
49. "An Act to prevent the Destroying and Murthering of Bastard Children," 21 James I, c. 27, reproduced in Jackson, *New-Born Child Murder*, 32.
50. Following the execution of Jane Hattersley and grisly death of Adam Adamson in July and November 1609, a nonextant ballad of their lives was entered in the Stationers' Register on 8 February 1610 (Arber, ed., *Stationers' Register*, 3:428).
51. Jackson, *New-Born Child Murder*, 29–31; Jackson, ed., *Infanticide*, 5–7.

52. Ingram, *Church Courts*, 152.

53. Jackson, *New-Born Child Murder*, 32–33.

54. Reproduced in Rollins, ed., *A Pepysian Garland*, 425–30.

55. Dickinson and Sharpe, "Infanticide in Early Modern England," 47–48.

56. Walker, *Crime, Gender and Social Order*, 153–56.

57. Rob. Mathew, Fellow of New College, on Anne Greene's revival, in *Newes from the Dead*, C2r.

58. Raymond, ed., *Making the News*, 172.

59. Sinclair and Robb-Smith, *A Short History of Anatomical Teaching at Oxford*, 12.

60. Sharpe, "The People and the Law," 249.

61. *Newes from the Dead*; Gowing, "Greene, Anne," 1, citing BL Add. MS 72892, fol. 2.

62. Plot's *The Natural History of Oxford-shire* contrasted Greene's story with that of a woman named Elizabeth, servant to a Mrs. Cope, who hanged a long time for killing her bastard child but revived after being cut down. "But having no *friends* to appear for *her, she* was barbarously dragg'd the night following by the order of one *Mallory* then one of the *Baliffs* of the *City*, to *Glocester-green*, and there drawn up over one of the arms of the *Trees*, and hang'd a second time till she was dead" (200).

63. Herrup, *The Common Peace*, 2, and *passim*; Sharpe, "People and the Law," 248.

64. Raymond, ed., *Making the News*, 125; Thomas, "Women and the Civil War Sects," 46–49.

65. *Newes from the Dead*; Gowing, "Greene, Anne," 2. The pamphlet ends, again conventionally, by contrasting this joyful "wonder" with a sad example of the "great work of God:" the news of a pregnant Derbyshire woman who seemed to die in labor, was buried, and then hastily exhumed with her now delivered baby, "but both dead," after passers-by had allegedly heard a child's cries (6).

66. Nedham's reports are both reproduced in Raymond, ed., *Making the News*, 182–83.

67. Petty also claimed Greene recovered her speech not by slow degrees "but in a manner altogether, beginning to speak just where she had left off on the Gallows." This claim seemed to confirm the providentialist detail in *A Wonder* and *A Declaration* that Greene burst out "Behold God's providence" (or something similar) when she revived, because all accounts mention her making pious speeches and prayers on the gallows ladder.

68. For the development of seventeenth-century skepticism, see Shapiro, *Probability and Certainty in Seventeenth-Century England*. For Bathurst, see DeMaria, "Bathurst, Richard," and Derham, *Physico-Theology*, 157.

69. Plot, *Natural History*, Book 7, ch. 52.

70. Sharpe, *Crime in seventeenth-century England*, 61; Gowing, "Secret Births," 88–89; Walker, *Crime, Gender and Social Order*, 150–51.

71. Malcolmson, "Infanticide in the Eighteenth-Century," 187–209; Dickinson and Sharpe, "Infanticide in Early Modern England," 38–39. Essex assize records between 1620 and 1680 indicated that the rate for convictions reached 55% in 1630–34 and 10% in 1655–59 (Sharpe, *Crime in seventeenth-century England*, 134). Examinations and informations relating to Northern Circuit Assizes between 1642 and 1680 produce seventy cases of neonatal infanticide. Surviving indictment files raise the number of prosecutions by "at least another 25 per cent of cases" (Gowing, "Secret Births," 88–89).

72. Walker, *Crime, Gender and Social Order*, 150–57.

73. Beattie, *Crime and the Courts*, 116.
74. Hoffer and Hull, *Murdering Mothers*, 23–25, citing Essex assize records.
75. Jackson, *New-Born Child Murder*, 36.
76. Dickinson and Sharpe, "Infanticide in Early Modern England," 39.
77. Walker, *Crime, Gender and Social Order*, 150–51 citing Hindle, *State and Social Change*, 142.
78. The lead item of the paper's inaugural number was a secret murder of a naval purser found hanging by the arms in the woods between Greenwich and Woolwich with his hands and head cut off and his bowels ripped out. Since 30 to 31 shillings were reported to be left in his pockets, the killing was presumed to be a "private revenge" rather than a random robbery. The *Domestick Intelligence* ended its report by assuring readers that the murderers were being sought, implicitly requesting further information from the public about the murder to solve the case (the absence of a follow-up story from the next Old Bailey or Surrey assize suggests the killers were never found).
79. Raymond, ed., *Making the News*, 123–24.
80. Walker, *Crime, Gender and Social Order*, 155.
81. *News From The Sessions-house In The Old-Bayly . . . With the Condemnation of a Woman that murthered her Childe*, A3v.
82. *News from Tyburn . . . the 19th of this Instant April*, 1676.
83. *A true Narrative Of the Proceedings . . . On April 25, and 26*, A2r–A3v; *The Confession and Execution Of the Seven Prisoners . . . On Fryday the 4th of May*, 1677.
84. Walker, *Crime, Gender and Social Order*, 152.
85. This scenario was called into question by a later report, *The Last Dying Speeches and Confession Of the Six Prisoners . . . This 17th of September, 1680*, which suggested that Bucknell did not technically give birth secretly because the other woman heard some noise, woke up, and asked her what was wrong. Bucknell said she had eaten too many damsons and vomited. The other woman allegedly went back to sleep.
86. *The True Narrative Of The Proceedings at The Sessions-House . . . on Fryday the 10th of this instant September; The Account Of several of the most Remarkable Tryals . . . on Friday the Tenth of this instant September*, 2. See also Margaret Adams in the undated *Tryals At the Sessions In the Old-Bailey . . . on Wednesday the 8th of this instant December* (ca.1680); *The Loyal Protestant and True Domestick Intelligence*, No. 17, Saturday May 3, 1681: "On Thursday [sic] last a Maid-servant was committed to Newgate for murdering her Bastard Child; The discourse goes, that it was begot by a certain Brazier in the City, who was then a Batchellour, (but since married,) and that he promised her 10 l. for so doing;" *The Loyal Protestant and True Domestick Intelligence*, No. 54, Saturday September 10, 1681: "London, September 9 . . . Susanna Powell for murthering her Bastard."
87. See also one of two accounts about Mary Clark (discussed below), *The True Narrative of the Confession And Execution Of the eight Prisoners . . . On Wednesday the 14th of this instant July* (1680), which claimed that Clark cried out but nobody heard; "but upon the statute of King James she was found Guilty of wilful Murder." Also *The Tryal and Condemnation of Several Notorious Malefactors . . . Beginning August the 31* about Elizabeth Powel of St. Martins-in-the-Fields, who "desiring the people to be good to her, for that it was Still-born, but she not calling any to her Labor, to testify the same, [was] found guilty according to the statute of King James, which there was read." As far as I am aware, this is the last news account informing readers that the 1624 act was read in court. Several new stories after this date mention women charged with infanticide avoiding the application of the 1624 law by proving

they were married and the child was not a bastard, thus allowing the circumstances to be understood as accidental death; for example, Mary Naples and Barbara French in 1682, Margaret Benson in 1683.

88. See Gowing, "Secret Births," 90–94.

89. *The Proceedings at the Sessions . . . on Wednesday the Sixteenth of July, 1679.*

90. *The Narrative Of the most Material Proceedings . . . Begun July the Seventh, 1680.*

91. *The True Narrative of the Proceedings . . . on Wednesday the 13th of this Instant April and ended on Thursday the 14th following.* Also *The Protestant (Domestick) Intelligence*, No.111, Tuesday April 5, 1681; *The Loyal Protestant and True Domestic Intelligence*, No. 9, Tuesday April 5, 1681.

92. C. E., *Strange and Wonderful News from Durham. Or The Virgins Caveat Against Infant-Murther.* An alternative version of Mary Clark's crime claimed she had strangled her newborn infant "with both her hands" before throwing it in a privy (*The True Narrative of the Confession And Execution Of the eight Prisoners . . . On Wednesday the 14th of this instant July 1680*). The phrase "with . . . hands" sounds like an indictment formula. The case of maidservant Mary Read in 1683 is uncertain, but her reported prosecution and indictment on the testimony of "William Apps, Gent. and Coroner for the county" suggested she was charged with murdering her newborn bastard by violence rather than concealment (*A True Narrative of the Proceedings at the Assizes, held at Kingston upon Thames . . . on Thursday the 26th. Of the Instant July* [1683]).

93. *An Exact and True Account of the Proceedings of the Sessions . . . On Wednesday January the 17th. 1682*, A1r.

94. Bowers, *The Politics of Motherhood*, 28–30. As always, there were exceptions to the general picture; *viz. Fair Warning for Murderers of Infants*, a Calvinist gallows-conversion pamphlet probably written by a nonconformist prison visitor, Mr Birch, echoed themes and attitudes going back to Golding's *A briefe discourse*. As a format for infanticide news, the single-story pamphlet had been largely overtaken by assize-trial and execution reports. *Fair Warning's* overweening focus on moral condemnation appears obsolescent.

95. *The Proceeding on the King's Commissions of the Peace . . . The 16th, and 17th. of January, 1684/5.*

96. *The Last Dying Speeches, Confession, and Execution of Rice Evans.* The context of a publishers' war between George Croom and Elizabeth Mallet, who had continued in business after the death of her husband David, may explain the two unconventional reports of alleged infanticide which Croom reported from the May Old Bailey sessions. Mary Stanes was charged (in language quoting the indictment) with "feloniously, malicitiously and of her Malice afore-thought, she did make an Assault, and the said Child between a Pair of Blankets did put, and thrust, with Intent to smother and strangle it, and that of the said Choaking, Smothering, and Strangling, the said Child instantly died." But some witnesses spoke in her favor and she was acquitted (*An Account of the Proceedings on the King's Commissions . . . The 15th and 16th Days of May, 1684*). Jane Cross was also indicted for "throwing [her bastard child] into a House of Easement, filled with Urine and other Excrements." But the child was found alive and lived for "12 Dayes in a languishing Condition" (2). At the trial, however, searchers and neighbors testified the child died of a convulsion after "thriv[ing] very well four Dayes" after it was rescued. Cross also claimed it had fallen in accidentally and she was unable to get it out. She too was acquitted. Mallet accused Croom publicly of publishing far-fetched (and old-fashioned) "wonder" stories. The twist in both accounts of Cross's trial

may reflect Croom's strategy of varying his narrative repertoire to strengthen his journalistic reputation for accuracy. The acquittals also reflect the mitigating trends in infanticide trials documented by court records in the final decades of the century.

97. *The True Account of the Behaviour and Confessions Of The Condemned Criminals in Newgate . . . October 23d. 1685.*

98. *The True Account of the Behaviour and Confession Of the Condemned Criminals, at Justice-Hall in the Old-Baily; on the 8th. Day of April 1687.*

99. *The Proceedings on the King and Queens Commissions . . . the 9th, 10th, and 11th. Days of December, 1691.*

100. Jackson, *New-Born Child Murder*, 120–27; Walker, *Crime, Gender and Social Order*, 156–57)

101. Or "her Masters Child," according to a newspaper version of the crime (*The Protestant (Domestick) Intelligence*, No. 88, Friday January 14, 1680/1).

102. *A True and Wonderful Relation of A Murther Committed in . . . Newington*. A marginal title page annotation in the Harvard copy reads: "14 Jan. 1680."

103. *A True and Perfect Account of the Proceedings . . . the 15. and 16. of January Instant.*

104. *A true Narrative Of the Proceedings . . . On Wednesday the 17th of January 1676/7.* This sounds like another newborn sacrificed to improve its siblings' chances of survival in straitened circumstances. See Elizabeth Hazard in *The Unnatural Grand Mother*, above p. 175.

105. Gowing, "Secret Births," 114; Walker, *Crime, Gender and Social Order*, 156–57.

106. *The Behaviour, Confession, & Execution of The several prisoners . . . On Friday the ninth of May, 1679*, 8. Smith's euphemistic language betrays slightly softened attitudes.

107. Linebaugh, "The Ordinary of Newgate and His *Account*."

108. Smith, *The True Account of the Behaviour . . . Of the Criminals Condemned, on Saturday the 16th of October, 1686; The Proceedings on the King's Commissions of the Peace . . . The 13th 15th And 16th days of October, 1686.*

109. Blackwell's name was the first to appear in *A True Relation of the Names and Suspected Crimes Of Prisoners now in Newgate . . . Jane Blackwel, for Murdering her Child [et al.]* (1679), which also mentioned "*Elizabeth Dyke, for Murdering her Child*." The *Domestic Intelligence*, Number 31, for Tuesday, 21 October 1679 referred to "A young Woman was Condemned for Murthering her Bastard Child'. I have found nothing further about Dyke.

110. Gowing, "Secret Births," 98.

111. Making use of very poor women was another widely recognized practice for disposing of illegitimate children (Wrightson, "Infanticide in Earlier Seventeenth-Century England," 16).

112. The identification of the mother only by her initials shields a gentlewoman's reputation and defers to collusive attitudes that had suppressed previous public discussion of baby disposal activities serving better-off women and patriarchal interests.

113. Gowing, "Secret Births," 91, 103–04.

114. The publication was a new model for reporting trials mandated by the Old Bailey recorder. He had been commanded by the court to provide more information about "*Convicts and their Crimes, and who were fit for Mercy*," to make better decisions about royal pardons and mitigation (verso).

115. He did so because of some under-explained dispute between them. Compton later alleged she had been or was about to be arrested by Drake "in an Action of 40 *l.* at the suit of one *Stone*" (verso) and was forced to stay away from the house.

NOTES TO CHAPTER SIX

1. Hindle, *The State and Social Change*, 14–15, 29–30, conveniently summarizes. Also Sharpe, *Crime in Early Modern England*, 9–10.
2. Hay, "Property, Authority, and the Criminal Law;" Lawson, "Lawless Juries?."
3. Hindle, *The State and Social Change*, 116–45.
4. Sarat and Kearns, *History, Memory, and the Law*, 2–8.
5. Sommerville, "Time and Play," *The Secularization of Early Modern England*, ch. 3, 33–42, and 181–87; Gladfelder, *Criminality and Narrative*, 45.
6. Gladfelder, *Criminality and Narrative*, 9–10, 52, 71.
7. *The Dialogic Imagination*, ed. Michael Holquist, trans. Caryl Emerson and M. Holquist (Austin: University of Texas Press, 1981), 272.
8. Amussen, "'Being Stirred to Much Unquietness,'" "Punishment, Discipline, and Power;" Cowen Orlin, "Patriarchalism and Its Discontents," *Private Matters and Public Culture*, ch. 2, 85–130; Dolan, "Home-rebels and House-traitors," *Dangerous Familiars*, ch. 1, 20–58; Lawson, "Patriarchy, Crime, and the Courts;" Sharpe, "Domestic Homicide in Early Modern England;" Staub, "Bloody Relations," 125; Walker, *Crime, Gender and Social Order*, 75–96, 138–58.
9. "'Those Eyes Are Made So Killing,'" 49–80; "Voices of Record," 287–308; Staub, "Bloody Relations," 128.
10. Bellany, "News Culture and the Overbury Affair," *The Politics of Court Scandal*, ch. 2, 74–132.
11. Hindle, *The State and Social Change*, 139.
12. Sharpe, *Judicial Punishment*, 40; Gaskill, *Crime and Mentalities in Early Modern England*, 10–12, 242–64.
13. *The Secularization of Early Modern England*.
14. *Crime in Early Modern England*, 208.
15. *Crime and Mentalities in Early Modern England*, 240.
16. *A true Narrative Of the Proceedings ... in the Old-bayly, The 10th and 11th days of May, 1676* reported, for instance, that an unnamed woman was indicted for bigamy. Found guilty "and her sex not being capable of the benefit of Clergy, [she] was likewise condemned to dye" (A3r). When sentenced, however, she was probably one of the six convicts who were transported, since she is not mentioned as one of those executed in the follow-up *The Confession and Execution Of the Prisoners at Tyburn On Wednesday the 17th of this Instant May, 1676*.
17. *A true Narrative Of the Proceedings At the Sessions-house in the Old-Bayly ... 23–25 August* (1676).

Bibliography

EARLY MODERN MANUSCRIPT SOURCES

United Kingdom, The British Library (BL)

Reports and letters relating to the trial of Mervin Touchet, 2nd Earl of Castlehaven, 1631, BL Add. MS 22,591/81–93.
Dr. William Petty's papers, BL Add. MS 72892.

United Kingdom, Corporation of London Record Office

Repertories of the minutes of the Court of Aldermen (Rep.).
City Cash Account.
Remembrancia, 1614–15: Letter 53.

United Kingdom, London Metropolitan Archives (MJ)

Session Roll, Indictment, 1573, George Browne, MJ/SR/0179/21.
Session Roll, Indictment, 1635, Thomas Shearwood, Elizabeth Evans, theft, MJ/SR/778/48.
Session Roll, Coroner's report, 1635, on the body of Thomas Claxton, MJ/SR/778/49.
Session Roll, Coroner's report, 1635, on the body of Rowland Holt, MJ/SR/778/50.
Session Roll, Indictment, 1635, Thomas Shearwood, burglary, MJ/SR/778/55.
Session Roll, Indictments, 1635, Thomas Shearwood, Elizabeth Evans, theft, battery, MJ/SR/778/76–78.
Session Roll, Indictment, 1635, Thomas Shearwood, Elizabeth Evans, murder of Thomas Claxton, MJ/SR/778/85.
Session Roll, Indictment, 1635, Thomas Shearwood, Elizabeth Evans, murder of Rowland Holt, MJ/SR/778/86.
Session Roll, Recognizance, 1637, Elizabeth Barnes, MJ/SR/819/25.
Session Roll, Indictment, 1637, Elizabeth Barnes, MJ/SR/819/38.
Session Roll, Gaol delivery calendar, 1641, Anne Hamton, MJ/SR/897/136.
Session Roll, Indictment, 1641, Anne Hamton, MJ/SR/900.
Session Roll, Gaol delivery calendar, indictment, 1675, Elizabeth Lillyman, MJ/SR/1489.
Session Roll, Indictment, 1681, Leticia Wigington, John Sadler, MJ/SR/1590.
Session Roll, Gaol delivery calendar, Coroner's report, indictment, 1687/8, Mary Hobry (or Aubrey), MJ/SR/1722.

Henry Goodcole's will and testament, 24 January 1641/2, Consistory Court Records.

United Kingdom, National Archives

Gaol Book for 1676, Anne Evans, Philippa Carey, ASSI 23/I.
Gaol Book for 1686, Ester Ives, ASSI 23/3.
Sessions Roll, Indictment, 1680, Margaret Osgood, ASSI 35/122/5.
Palatinate of Chester Crown Book, 1603–04, Elizabeth Caldwell, Jeffrey Bownd, Isabel Hall, CHES 21/2.

Early Modern Printed Sources

I have included STC or Wing numbers as well as UMI microfilm reels for most early printed sources, since the use of serialized or near identical titles (e.g., *The True Narrative Of The Proceedings at The Sessions-House*) can make identifying individual items difficult. Because many are not yet available on EEBO, I have also retained such details as names, dates, and locations in listing titles to help differentiate similar-sounding reports.
Shelfmarks identify particular copies consulted by this study, preceded by standard library abbreviations derived from STC and Wing (e.g., L = The British Library, O = Bodleian Library, Oxford, etc.).
Names in square brackets at the end of entries refer to women criminals of interest in the news item.
An Account Of the Manner, Behaviour and Execution of Mary Aubry, Who was Burnt to Ashes, in Leicester Fields, On Friday the 2d Day of March, 1687. London, 1687/8. STC A319D. Reel 1802. O Ashmole F 5 (25). [Mary Hobry (or Aubrey)]
An Account of the Proceedings on the King's Commissions of the Peace, And Oyer and Terminer, and Goal-Delivery [sic] of Newgate . . . at Justice-Hall, in the Old-Bayly, The 10, 11, and 12th. Days of October, 1683. London, 1683. Another edition of Wing A362. Not on EEBO. HN 79216 (E–PV 79180–225). O Ashm. 1677 (98). [Elizabeth Hare]
An Account of the Proceedings on the King's Commissions Of the Peace, And Oyer and Terminer, and Goal-Delivery [sic] of Newgate . . . at Justice-Hall, in the Old-Bayly. The 15th and 16th Days of May, 1684. London, 1684. In *ESTC* but not Wing or on *EEBO*. L 1480.c.25 (13). [Mary Stanes, Jane Cross]
An Account of the Proceedings At The Sessions Of Oyer and Terminer . . . the 10. of October 1683. and ended the 13th of the same Instant. London, 1683. Wing A362. Reel 47:12. L 515.l.2.(76). [Elizabeth Hare, Mary Phelps]
An Account of the Tryals of Several Notorious Malefactors . . . Which began on the 16. of this Instant January, and ended the 17. London, 1683. Wing A417E. Reel 2281:07. [Elizabeth Crossman]
The Account Of several of the most Remarkable Tryals That were Tryed at the Sessions-house in the Old-Bailey . . . begun on Friday the Tenth of this instant September, and ending on Munday the Thirteenth of the same. London, 1680. Not in Wing or *ESTC*. MH *fEC65 A100 680a3 (annotated "14 Sept.1680"). O Godw. Pamph. 2209 (24). [Mary Bucknell]
Alleine, Richard, and Robert Franklin. *A Murderer Punished, and Pardoned. Or, A True Relation of the Wicked Life, and shameful-happy Death of Thomas Savage . . . The Thirteenth Edition: With the Addition of the leud Life, and shameful Death of Hannah Blay*. London, 1671. Wing A997. Reel 1298:10. L 4903.cc.13. [Hannah Blay]

The Apprehension, Arraignement, and execution of Elizabeth Abbot. London, 1608.
STC 23. Reel 1783:01. MH HV6535.E5 L3 1608. [Elizabeth Abbot]

The Araignement & burning of Margaret Ferne-seede. London, 1608. STC 10826.
Reel 724:11. L C.21.b.5. [Margaret Ferneseede]

Assize Records Hertfordshire, James I. Hertford, August 1, 1606. Edited by J. S.
Cockburn, 1975. 35/48/2. 30. [George Dell, Agnes Dell]

Assize Records Surrey, James I. Southwark, February 18, 1608. Edited by J. S. Cockburn, 1975. 35/50/7. 32. [Margaret Ferneseede]

Assize Records Surrey, James I. Southwark, July 1, 1613. Edited by J. S. Cockburn,
1975. 35/55/6. 34. [Elizabeth James]

Babington, Zachary. *Advice to Grand Jurors in Cases of Blood.* London, 1677. Wing
B248. Reel 50:12.

Bathurst, Richard. *Newes from the Dead. Or A True and Exact Narration of the
miraculous deliverance of Anne Greene, Who being Executed at Oxford Decemb.
14. 1650. afterwards revived.* Oxford, 1651. Wing W1074. Reel 2023:08. O
Wood 516 (7). [Anne Greene]

Beard, Thomas. *The Theatre of Gods Iudgements.* London, 1597. STC 1659. HN
289276. [Alice Arden]

*The Behaviour, Confession, & Execution Of The several Prisoners that suffered at
Tyburn On Friday the ninth of May, 1679. Viz. . . . Sarah Dent.* London, 1679.
Wing B1706. Reel 835:03. LG A.7.6. no. 69. [Sarah Dent]

*The Behaviour of the Condemned Criminals in Newgate, Viz; . . . Anne Parker, and
Jane Arnock . . . On Friday the 17th. of October 1684.* London, 1684. Wing
B1709B. No reel. L C.175.e.16.(8). [Anne Parker]

*The Behaviour of the Condemned Criminals in Newgate, Who were Executed On
Friday the 19th of this Instant December.* London, 1684. Not in Wing or ESTC.
L C.175.e.16.(10). [Jenny Voss]

*The Behaviour of the five Prisoners in Newgate . . . Together with their Last Dying
Words at Tyburn. On Friday the 19th. of this Instance December, 1684.* London,
1684. Wing B1709C. L C.175.e.16 (11). [Jenny Voss]

*The Behaviours, Confessions, Last Speeches, and Execution of Seven Notoriovs
Malefactors, who were On the 24th. of this Instant October, Executed at Tyburn.*
London, 1683. Wing B1710. Reel 203:03. O Ashm. 1677 (99). [Mary Phelps]

Birch, Mr.(?). *Fair Warning to Murderers of Infants: Being an Account of the Tryal,
Codemnation [sic] and Execution of Mary Goodenough at the Assizes held in
Oxon, in February 1691/2.* London, 1692. Wing F105. Reel 1009:33. O Wood
365 (34). [Mary Goodenough]

*The Bloody downfall of Adultery. [sic] Murder, Ambition, At the end of which are
added Westons and Mistris Turners last Teares, shed for the Murder of Sir Thomas
Ouerbury poysoned in the Tower.* London, 1615. STC 18919.3. Reel 1148:05.
HN 60225. [Anne Turner]

The Bloody minded Midwife. ca. 1693. Wing B3258D. No reel. *Pepys Ballads.* Edited
by W. G. Day, 1987. 5:10. [Mary Compton]

*The Bloody Murtherer, Or, The Unnatural Son His Just Condemnation. At the
Assizes Held at Monmouth, March 8. 1671/2.* London, 1672. Wing B3259. Reel
168:04. [Mary Jones]

*Bloody Newes from Dover. Being A True Relation Of The great and bloudy Murder,
committed by Mary Champion.* London, 1646/7. Wing B3267. Reel Thomason
60: E.375 (20). [Mary Champion]

*Bloody News from Clarken-well. Being A true Relation of . . . a Bloody murther com-
mitted by a Soldiers wife on her husband.* London, 1661. Wing B3264. Reel 14:18.

Brewer, Thomas. *The Bloudy Mother, Or The most inhumane murthers, committed
by Iane Hattersley vpon diuers infants.* London, 1610. STC 3717.3. Reel 1982:
13. MH *52–2413. [Jane Hattersley]

————. *Mistres Turners Repentance, Who, about the poysoning of that Ho: Knight Sir Thomas Overbvry, Was executed the fourteenth day of Nouember, last.* London, 1615. STC 3720. No reel. Society of Antiquaries Lemon 144. [Anne Turner]

A Briefe Discovrse of Two most cruell and bloudie murthers, committed bothe in Worcestershire. London, 1583. STC 25980. Reel 1264:06. L C.27.a.28. [Mrs. Beast]

Britains Triumphs, Or, A Brief History Of The Warres And Other State-Affairs Of Great Britain. London, 1656. Wing B4813. Reel 2244:04.

Burdet, W. *A Wonder of Wonders. Being A faithful Narrative and true Relation, of one Anne Green.* London, 1651.Wing B5620. Reel Thomason 95: E.621 (11). [Anne Greene]

A Cabinet of Grief: Or, The French Midwife's Miserable mean for the Barbarous Murther committed upon the Body of her Husband. London, 1688. Wing C188. Reel 1611:04. O Wood 284 (10). [Mary Hobry (or Aubrey)]

Clarke, Samuel. *The Marrow of Ecclesiastical History.* London, 1654. 3rd ed., 1675. Wing C4545. Reel 656:09.

Coke, Edward. *The Third Part of the Institutes Of the Laws of England: concerning High Treason, and other Pleas of the Crown.* London, 1644. Wing C4960. Reel 659:02.

[*The*] *Complaint and lamentation of Mistresse Arden . . . who for the loue of one Mosbie, hired certaine Ruffians* [*and*] *Villaines most cruelly to murder her Husband.* London, ca.1633. STC 732. Reel 867:12. L Rox. 3:156. [Alice Arden]

A Compleat Narrative of the Tryal of Elizabeth Lillyman. Found Guilty of Petty Treason . . . To be Burned to Death, For the Barbarous and Bloody Murther of William Lillyman her late Husband. London, 1675. Wing C5647. Reel 1630:14. LG A5.4 34(9). [Elizabeth Lillyman]

Concealed murther reveild . . . on the body of Hannah Jones an Infant. London, 1699. Wing C5693. Tract supplement C17:1(515.l.2[5]). [Mary Anderson]

The Confession and Execution of Elizabeth Lillyman. London, 1675. L D-6496.a.39 (destroyed). [Elizabeth Lillyman]

The Confession and Execution of Leticia Wigington Of Ratclif . . . written by her own hand in the Goal [*sic*] *of Newgate, two days before her death, being Condemned for whiping her Apprentice Girl to death.* London, 1681. Wing W2110. Reel 950:32. L Cup21.g.32/63. O Ashm. 1677 (65). HN 133524. [Leticia Wigington]

The Confession and Execution Of the Five Prisoners that suffered at Tyburn On Wednesday the 19th of Decemb. 1677. London, 1677. Wing C5747A. Reel 2287:13. HN 303477. [Margaret Riggs]

The Confession and Execution Of the Five Prisoners that suffered at Tyburn On Wednesday the 23d of January 1677/8. London, 1678. Wing C5747B. Reel 2287:14. HN 303478.

The Confession and Execution of the Prisoners at Tyburn On Fryday the 9th of this Instant May. London, 1679. L D-6495.aa.5 (destroyed). [Sarah Dent]

The Confession and Execution Of the Seven Prisoners suffering at Tyburn On Fryday the 4th of May, 1677. Viz. . . . Margaret Spicer, For murthering her Bastardchilde. London, 1677. Wing C5754. Reel 1186:11. [Margaret Spicer]

A Continuation of the Inquest after Blood, and Goal-Delivery [*sic*] *of Newgate, April 13. 1670.* London, 1670. Wing C5966. Reel 1148:55. [Mary Line, Hannah Whitford]

Cooper, Thomas. *The Cry and Reuenge of Blood. Expressing the Nature and haynousnesse of wilful Murther.* London, 1620. STC 5698. Reel 1133:03.

Cruel and Barbarous News From Cheapside in London: Being a True and Faithful Relation Of an horid Fact, acted by an unhuman Mistriss upon the body of her Apprentice. London, 1676. Wing C7415. Reel 1737:10. O Wood 365 (24).

The Cruel French Lady: Or, A true and perfect Relation of the most execrable Murthers committed by a French Lady upon the persons of her own Father, two brothers and Sister. London, 1673. Wing C7418. Reel 1631:08. LG A 1.2 no. 68(9). O Wood 365 (23).

The Cruel Midwife. Being a True Account of a most Sad and Lamentable Discovery ... in the Village of Poplar in the Parish of Stepney. London, 1693. Wing C7419A. Reel 2652:11. L 1132.f66. [Mary Compton]

The Cruel Mother; being A true Relation of the Bloody Murther Committed by M. Cook, upon her Dearly beloved Child. London, 1670. Wing C7420. Reel 2865:20. CLC *HV6541 G7L8c. L RB.23.a.7784 (destroyed). [Mary Cook]

The Cry of Blood: Or, The Horrid Sin of Murther Display'd. London, 1692. Wing C7449aA. Reel 2387:03. LG Bside 16.87.

Dalton, Michael. *The Covntrey Ivstice.* London, 1618. STC 6205. Reel 1095:01.

A Declaration from Oxford, of Anne Green, A young woman that was lately, and unjustly hanged in the Castle-yard; but since recovered. London, 1651. Wing D585A. Reel 2352:06. HN 123781. [Anne Greene]

Deeds Against Natvre, and Monsters by kinde ... The other of a lasciuious yong Damsell named Martha Scambler. London, 1614. STC 809. Reel 809. O 4⁰ L 68(7) Art. [Martha Scambler]

Deloney, Thomas. *The Complaint of Mrs. Page, for causing her Husband to be murthered, for the love of Strangwidge.* London, ca. 1591, pr. 1663–74. Wing C5613A. Reel 1548: 20. Printed on the same page as *The Lamentation of George Strangwidge* (see next entry). L Rox. I. 553 is a variant version. [Eulalia Page]

———. *The Lamentation of George Strangwidge.* London, ca. 1591, pr. 1663–74. Wing D955E. Reel 1548:20. [Eulalia Page]

———. *The Lamentation of Mr. Pages Wife of Plimouth: Who being enforced to wed against her will, did consent to his Murder for the love George Strangwidge.* London, 1609. STC 6557.4. Reel 1637:08. MH *EBB65h v.3. Also Wing D955E and D957B. MH Child 25242 68.5PF* and Pierce 25242.9* are variant versions. (See Lane, *Bibliographical Contributions,* 1905.) [Eulalia Page]

Derham, William. *Physico-Theology: or, A Demonstration of the Being and Attributes of God, from his Works of Creation.* London, 1713.

Domestic Intelligence, no. 31, Tuesday, October 21, 1679 [Jane Blackwell]

Domestic Intelligence, no. 33, Tuesday, October 28, 1679 [Jane Blackwell]

Domestic Intelligence, no. 40, Friday, November 21, 1679 [Susanna Parslow]

Domestic Intelligence, no. 51, Tuesday, December 30, 1679.

Domestic Intelligence, no. 61, Tuesday, February 3, 1679/80. 1680 [Margaret Clark]

Domestic Intelligence, no. 74, March 19, 1679/80. 1680 [Margaret Clark]

Domestic Intelligence, no. 75, March 23, 1679/80. 1680 [Margaret Clark]

Domestic Intelligence, no. 76, March 26, 1680. [Margaret Clark]

Domestic Intelligence, no. 79, April 6, 1680. [Margaret Clark]

Domestick Intelligence, no. 5, Tuesday, July 22, 1679 [Katherine Tumince]

Domestick Intelligence, no. 6, Thursday, July 24, 1679 [Katherine Tumince]

Domestick Intelligence, no. 9, Tuesday, August 5, 1679 [Katherine Tumince]

The Domestick Intelligence, no. 32, Thursday, September 8–Monday, September 12, 1681 [Leticia Wigington]

The Domestick Intelligence, no. 69, Tuesday, January 16–Friday, January 19, 1681/2. 1682 [Elizabeth Crossman]

Dreadful News from Southwark: Or, A true Account of the Most Horrid Murder committed By Margaret Osgood, On her Husband Walter Osgood. London, 1680. Not in Wing. Misidentified as D2153 and Reel 1401:19. L Cup21.g.32/27. O Godw. Pamph. 2209 (25). [Margaret Osgood]

Dugdale, Gilbert. *The Time Triumphant.* London, 1604. STC 7292. Reel 955:17.

————. *A True Discourse Of the practises of Elizabeth Caldwell*. London, 1604. STC 7293. Reel 955:18. HN 60571. O Art 4° C. 16 BS(43). [Elizabeth Caldwell]

E., C. *Strange and Wonderful News from Durham. Or The Virgins Caveat Against Infant-Murther*. London, 1679. Wing E6A. Reel 2705:28. O Wood 365 (30). [Elizabeth B.]

E., T. *The Lawes Resolutions of Womens Rights*. London, 1632. STC 7437.

Edwards, Thomas. *Gangraena: Or A catalogue and Discovery of many of the Errours, Heresies, Blasphemies and pernicious Practices of the Sectaries of this time*. London, 1646. Wing E228. Reel 142:01.

Of the endes and deathes of two Prisoners / lately pressed to death in Newgate. London, 1569. STC 18492. Reel 387:06.

An Exact Narrative of the Bloody Murder, and Robbery Committed, By Stephen Eaton, Sarah Swift . . . upon the Person of Mr. John Talbot, Minister. London, 1669. Wing E3665. Reel 914:21. LG A 9.3 no. 71. HN 54786. [Sarah Swift]

An Exact Relation of the Barbarous Murder Committed on Lawrence Corddel . . . Also the Examination and Confession of His Land-Lord and Land-Lady. London, 1661. Wing E3682. Reel 1331:03. MH *EC65.A100.661e3. [Sarah Cook]

An Exact Relation Of The Bloody and Barbarous Murder, committed by Miles Lewis, and his Wife . . . upon their Prentice. London, 1646. Wing E3684. Reel Thomason 58: E.364 (2). L W.P.1594/31. [Mrs. Lewis]

An Exact and True Account of the Proceedings of the Sessions, Begun at the Old-Bayly, On Wednesday January the 17th. 1682. London, 1682. Wing E3608B. Reel 2048:34. [Elizabeth Neal]

Fair Warning from Tybvrn: Or, the Several Confessions and Execution of The Fifteen notorious Malefactors That suffered there on Munday the 8 of March, 1679/80. London, 1680. Wing F103. Reel 1716:09. O Godw. Pamph. 2209 (21). L Cup21.g.32/54. [Frances Lewis, Dorothy Clark, Dorothy Hall]

Foxe, John. *Actes and monuments of these latter and perillous dayes touching matters of the Church*. London, 1563. STC 11222. Reel 230:08.

A Full Relation Of The Birth, Parentage, Education, Life and Conversation of Mrs. Margaret Martel, The Barbarous French-Woman, Who was Executed . . . for a most Bloody Murther committed by her on the Body of Madam Pvllen. London, 1697. Wing F2360A. Reel 1829:31. L 518.f.47. [Margaret Martel]

A Full and True Account Of A Most Barbarous and Bloody Murther, Committed By Esther Ives, . . . on the Body of William Ives, her Husband. London, 1686. Wing F2293D. Reel 2572:27. O Ashmole 739 (31). [Esther Ives]

A Full and True Account of the Proceedings . . . At the Sessions-House in the Old-Bayly, On Thursday, Iune 1st. and Ended on Fryday Iune 2d. London, 1682. Wing F2310. Reel 2029:23. [Jane Kent]

The Full and True Relation Of All The Proceedings at the Assizes Holden at Chelmsford . . . Monday the 29th of this instant March, and ended on Thursday the 1st of April. London, n.d., but MH copy annotated "Printed 3 Aprill 1680." Wing F2316. Reel 1461:25. MH KD 370 F88. O Godw. Pamph. 2209 (48). [Sara Bell]

Fuller, Thomas. *Abel Redevivus or The dead yet speaking*. London, 1651. Wing F2400. Reel 316:27.

Gods Mercy and Justice Displayed, In The Wicked Life and Penitential Death of Dorothy Livingstone, Executed the 7. Of April, 1679 . . . for Murthering her Bastard-Childe. London, 1679. Wing G960B. Reel 1831:14.

Golding, Arthur. *A briefe discourse of the late murther of master George Saunders*. London, 1573. STC 11985. Reel 568:09. L C.40.a.36. Second edition 1577. STC 11986. Reel 568:10. L C.33.a.30. [Anne Saunders]

————. *A discourse vpon the earthquake that hapned throughe this Realme of Englande . . . the sixt of Aprill. 1580*. London, 1580. STC 11987. Reel 545:02.

———. *A briefe treatise concerning the burnynge of Bucer and Phagius . . . Translated into Englyshe by Arthur Goldyng.* London, 1562. STC 3966. Reel 181:04.

Goodcole, Henry. *The Adultresses Funerall Day: In flaming, scorching, and consuming fire: Or The burning downe to ashes of Alice Clarke.* London, 1635. STC 12009. Reel 1852:19. MH *54–1207. HV6535.E5 G6. [Alice Clarke]

———. *The Case of Sodomy, in the Tryal of Mervin Lord Audley, Earl of Castlehaven.* London, 1708. Possibly based on BL Add. MS 22,591/81–93.

———. *The good treasvrer. Or heaven and earths day of iubile in finding the most pretious hidden treasures: Preached at Pauls Crosse on Whitson-Monday the 2. of Iune.* London, 1623. STC 12009.5. No reel.

———. *Heavens Speedie Hue and Cry sent after Lust and Murther.* London, 1635. STC 12010. Reel 2184:08. Second edition STC 12010.5. Reel 1946:09. O Ashmole 739(1) is a transitional edition (STC 12010.3). [Elizabeth Evans (Canberry Bess)]

———. *London's Cry: Ascended to God, and entred into the hearts, and eares of men for Reuenge of Bloodshedders, Burglaiers, and Vagabounds. Manifested the Last Sessions, holden at Iustice Hall in the old Baily the 9.10.11.12. of December, Anno Dom. 1619.* London, 1620. STC 12011. Reel 1101:05.

———. *Natures Cruell Step-Dames: Or, Matchlesse Monsters of the Female Sex: Elizabeth Barnes and Anne Willis.* London, 1637. STC 12012. Reel 578:08. [Elizabeth Barnes, Anne Willis, Anne Holden]

———. *The Prodigals Teares. With a Heavenly New yeeres Gift sent to the soule.* London, 1620. STC 3580. Reel. 1477:07.

———. *A True Declaration of the happy Conuersion, contrition, and Christian preparation of Francis Robinson, Gentleman.* London, 1618. STC 12013. Reel 888:08. L C.122.e.10.

———. *The wonderfull discouerie of Elizabeth Sawyer a Witch, late of Edmonton, her conuiction and condemnation and Death. Together with the relation of the Diuels accesse to her, and their conference together.* London, 1621. STC 12014. Reel 838:05. L C.27.b.38. [Elizabeth Sawyer]

Goodman, Peter. *Crueltie Unvailed; Or, The State of the Case of Several Persons, committed Close-Prisoners to the Gate-house, Westminster.* London, 1661. Wing G1141C. Tract Supp. A3:5.(C.161.f.2 [48]). [Mrs. Cook]

Goodwin, John. *Cretensis: Or A Briefe Answer To an ulcerous Treatise.* London, 1646. Wing G1161. Reel 1149:29.

Gouge, William. *Of Domesticall Duties.* London, 1622. STC 12119. Second edition 1634. STC 12121.

Great and Bloody News, From Farthing-Ally . . . Or the True and Faithful Relatjon [sic] Of a Horid and Barbarous Murther, Committed on the Body of Walter Osily [sic], by his own Wife. London, 1680. Wing G1645A. Reel 1403:17. MH *fEC65.A100.680g2 (annotated "August: 2: 1680"). L Cup21.g.32/53. [Margaret Osgood]

Great News from Middle-Row in Holbourn: Or A True Relation of a Dreadful Ghost. London, 1679. Wing G1727. Reel 1403:18. O G.Pamph. 2203 (19). MH BF1473.G47.

Hatton, Sir Christopher. *A Treatise Concerning Statues.* London, 1677. Wing H1142. Reel 420:08.

Heath, James. *A Brief Chronicle Of the Late Intestine Warr In The Three Kingdoms of England, Scotland, and Ireland.* London, 1663. Wing H1319. Reel 1094:03. O Wood 145. [Anne Greene]

His Majesties Most Gracious Pardon, Pleaded at Justice-Hall, in the Old-Bayly, On Monday the 7th. of March, 1687. London, 1687. Wing J221. Reel 1852:15. O Ashmole F 5 (66). [Arabella Reeves]

His Majesties Most Gracious Pardon Which was Pleaded by the Prisoners . . . on Monday the 26th. of July, 1686. London, 1686. Wing J224. Tract supplement C17: 1(515.l.2[118]). O Ashmole F 5 (58).

Holinshed, Raphael. *The Chronicles of England, Scotland, and Ireland*, London, 1577.

The Horrible Murther of a young Boy of three yeres of age, whose Sister had her tongue cut out. London, 1606. STC 6552. Reel 986:07. L 1104.b.51. [Annis Dell]

Horrid News from St. Martins: Or, Vnheard-of Murder and Poyson. London, 1677. Wing H2864. Reel 1528:11.

I., T. *A World of wonders. A Masse of Murthers. A Covie of Cosonages*. London, 1595. STC 14068.5. Reel 1604:02.

Inhumane, & Cruel Bloody News from Leeds in York-Shire. London, 1674–9. Wing I188B. Reel 1851:21.

The Injured Children, Or, The Bloudy Midwife. London, ca. 1693. Wing I190A. No reel. *Pepys Ballads*. Edited by W.G. Day. 1987. 2:193. [Mary Compton]

Inquest after Blood. Being a Relation Of the several Inquisitions Of All That have Died by any violent Death . . . Commencing from Jan. 1. 1669 to the Conclusion of the last Sessions holden at the Old Baily, Feb. 21. And the Assizes for Surrey, March 1. London, 1670. Wing I209b. Reel 498:32. HN 68847. [Mary Cook, Susan Emery]

The iust Downefall of Ambition,. [sic] Adultery, Murder, At the end of which are added Westons, and Mistris Turners last Teares, shed for the Murder of Sir Thomas Ouerbury poysoned in the Tower. London, 1615. STC 18919.7. Reel 1552:21. O Wood 365 (5). [Anne Turner]

Jonson, Ben. *Every Man Out of His Humor*. London, 1600.

——. *The Staple of News*. London, 1626.

A Just Account Of the Horrid Contrivance of John Cupper, and Judith Brown his Servant, In poysoning his Wife. London, 1684. Wing S4261A. Reel 2295:03. L 0915.d.04 (07). [Judith Brown]

The Last Dying Speeches, Confession, and Execution of . . . Mary Williamson . . . Executed at Tyburn, the 5th. of March, 1684. London, 1684. Wing L482B. Reel 1742:21. L C.175.e.16 (15). [Mary Williamson]

The Last Dying Speeches, Confession, and Execution of Rice Evans, Margaret Corbet [et al.] . . . Executed . . . The 19th of March 1683/4. London, 1684. Wing L482C. Reel 1742:22. O Ashmole F 5 (133). L C.175.e.16 (5). [Margaret Corbet]

The Last Dying Speeches and Confession Of the Six Prisoners Who were Executed at Tybvrn This 17th of September, 1680. London, 1680. Wing L481A. Reel 2430:17. F L481.5. O Godw. Pamph. 2209 (23). [Mary Bucknell]

The Last Dying Speeches And Confessions of the Three Notorious Malefactors who were Executed at Tybvrn, on the 4th. of this Instant March, 1681. London, 1681. Wing L482A. Reel 1339:29. [Leticia Wigington]

The Last Speech and Confession of Sarah Elestone At the place of Execution: Who was Burned For Killing her Husband, April 24. 1678. London, 1678. Wing L504F. Reel 1953:04. [Sarah Elstone]

The last Speech, Confession and Execution of the two Prisoners at Tyburn, On Friday the 23d. of this Instant May, 1684. London, 1684. Wing L505cA. Reel 1742:26. L C.175.e.16.(6).

The last Words and Confession of Margaret Inglis, who was executed at Edinburgh the 6th. of April 1709. London, 1709. L J/12350.m.18 (5). [Margaret Inglis]

L'Estrange, Roger. *A Hellish Murder Committed by a French Midwife, On the Body of her Husband, Jan. 27 1687/8*. London, 1688. Wing H1384. Reel 1060:8. HN 303482. O Wood 365 (33). [Mary Hobry (or Aubrey)]

The Liues, Apprehension, Araignment & Execution, Of Robert Throgmorton. William Porter. Iohn Bishop. London, 1608. STC 24053.5. Reel 941:11. L C.123.e.21. [Margaret Ferneseede]

The Loyal Protestant and True Domestick Intelligence, no. 1, Wednesday, March 19, 1681. [Leticia Wigington]

The Loyal Protestant and True Domestick Intelligence, no. 6, Saturday, March 26, 1681.

The Loyal Protestant and True Domestick Intelligence, no. 9, Tuesday, April 5, 1681. [Anne Price]

The Loyal Protestant and True Domestick Intelligence, no. 17, Saturday, May 3, 1681.

The Loyal Protestant and True Domestick Intelligence, no. 41, Tuesday, July 26, 1681.

The Loyal Protestant and True Domestick Intelligence, no. 52, Saturday, September 3, 1681. [Leticia Wigington]

The Loyal Protestant and True Domestick Intelligence, no. 53, Tuesday, September 6, 1681. [Leticia Wigington]

The Loyal Protestant and True Domestick Intelligence, no. 54, Saturday, September 10, 1681. [Leticia Wigington]

The Loyal Protestant and True Domestick Intelligence, no. 147, Thursday, April 27, 1682. [Elizabeth Fitzpatrick]

The Loyal Protestant and True Domestick Intelligence, no. 198, Thursday, August 24, 1682.

Lykosthenes, Konrad. *The Doome warning all men to the Iudgemente.* Translated by Stephen Bateman. London, 1581. STC 1582. Reel 376:08.

Mary Aubrey A French Midwife who murdered her Husband in Long Acre. Anno 1687–8. London, 1798. LG p7500059. [Mary Hobry (or Aubrey)]

Mercurius Publicus, Comprising The Sum of all Affairs now in agitation in England, Scotland, and Ireland, no. 21, Thursday, May 22–Thursday, May 29, 1662. Reel Thomason 34: E.195 (127). L 1609/420. [Elizabeth Powle]

The Midwife of Poplar's Sorrowful Confession and Lamentation in Newgate. London, ca. 1693. Wing M2001B. No reel. *Pepys Ballads.* Edited by W.G. Day. 1987. 2:192. [Mary Compton]

Mistris Turners Farewell to all women. London, 1615. STC 24341.5. Reel 1861:90. Society of Antiquaries Lemon 143. [Anne Turner]

Morgan, Joseph. *Phoenix Britannicus: Being a Miscellaneous Collection of Scarce and Curious Tracts.* London, 1731.

The Most Cruell and Bloody Mvrther committed by . . . Annis Dell, and her Sonne George Dell, Foure yeeres since. On the bodie of a Childe. London, 1606. STC 6553. Reel 986:08. MH 006204604. [Annis Dell]

Mrs. Elizabeth Gaunt's Last Speech, who was Burnt at London, Oct. 23. 1685. London, 1685. Wing G381A. Reel 1830:24. L J/8052 i 1. [Elizabeth Gaunt]

Munday, Anthony. *A View of sundry Examples. Reporting many straunge murthers . . . since the murther of Maister Saunders by George Browne.* London, 1580. STC 18281. Reel 2049:09. [Amy Harrison, Margaret Dorington]

Murder and Petty-Treason: Or, Bloody News from Southwark. Being A lamentable Relation of a barbarous Murder committed by a Wife upon the person of her Husband. London, 1677. Not in Wing or on *EEBO*. L RB.23.1.8837.

Murder upon Murder, committed by Thomas Sherwood, alias, Countrey Tom: and Elizabeth Evans, alias Canbrye Besse. London, 1635. STC 22431. Reel 1117:01. O Wood 401 (129). [Elizabeth Evans]

The Murderous Midwife, With Her Roasted Punishment . . . for having found in Her House-of-office no less than Sixty two Children, at Paris. London, 1673. Wing M3097. Reel 2192:04. LG Bay H.1.1 no. 18.

Murther, Murther. Or, A bloody Relation how Anne Hamton ... by poyson mur-thered her deare husband Sept. 1641 being assisted and counselled thereunto by Margeret Harwood. London, 1641. Wing M3084. Reel Thomason 255: E.172 (7). LG A.1.2 no. 12. Sig. A2r headed "A bloody Relation of *Katherine Web*, who poysoned her husband at Westminster". L Thomason E.172 (7) and HN 432834 copies read "*Anne Hamton*"] [Anne Hamton]

Murther will out, Or, A True and Faithful Relation of an Horrible Murther com-mitted Thirty Three Years ago, by an unnatural Mother, upon the body of her own Child about a Year Old. London, 1675. Wing M3093. Reel 2709:02. L 1132.a.42.

The Narrative Of the most Material Proceedings At The Sessions ... Begun July the Seventh, 1680. London, 1680. Wing N199C. Reel 2432:10. L Cup21.g.32/49. O Godw. Pamph. 2209 (28). [Mary Clark]

A Narrative Of the Proceedings at the Sessions-House in the Old-Bayly, From Wednesday the 7th of July instant, to Saturday the 10th ... And also an Account of the Tryal and Condemnation of Eliz. Lillyman, who killed her Husband. Lon-don, 1675. Wing N210A. Reel 1817:10. LG A5.4 34(8). [Elizabeth Lillyman]

The Narrative Of the Proceedings at the Sessions ... at the Old-Bailey on Wednes-day the 10th of December, 1679. London, 1679. Wing N209. Reel 1407:05. L Cup21.g.32/48.

A Narrative of the Process Against Madam Brinvilliers; and of Her Condemnation and Execution, For having Poisoned Her Father and Two Brothers. London, 1676. Wing N220. Reel 872:20. HN 54792. [Madam Brinvilliers]

Newes come latle[y] frō Pera. London, 1561. STC 4102.3. Reel 1982:20.

Newes From Perin in Cornwall: Of A most Bloody and vn-exampled Murther very lately committed by a Father on his owne Sonne ... at the Instigation of a merci-lesse Step-mother. London, 1618. STC 19614. Reel 1031:05. L C.40.d.13, O 4⁰ G 29(2) Art.

News from Fleetstreet. London, 1675. Wing B3261A. Reel 2419:11. LG A.5.4 34 (13).

News from Newgate: A Gaol-delivery for the City of London and the County of Middlesex ... At the Sessions begun at Hicks-Hall on Wednesday the third of September ... till Wednesday the 10th of the same Moneth. London, 1673. Wing N985. Reel 1955:12. LG A.7.7. no. 55.

News from Newgate: Or, a true Relation Of the manner of taking Seven persons ... Upon Munday the 13 of this instant November, 1677. London, 1677. Wing N986. Reel 1995:02. L C.27.c.14.

News from Scotland, Declaring the Damnable life and death of Doctor Fian, a nota-ble Sorcerer. London, 1592. STC 10841a. Reel 226:04.

News from the Sessions-House in the Old Baily ... begun on Wednesday the 13th. of this instant April: and ending on the 17th. day. London, 1675. N1017A. Reel 1955:13. LG A5.4 34(7).

News From The Sessions-house In The Old-Bayly ... With the Condemnation of a Woman that murthered her Childe. London, 1676. Wing N1017B. Reel 1955:14. LG A5.4 34(17). [Elizabeth Simmons]

News from Tybourn ... Three Bayliffs And the rest of the Malefactors that Died with them. London, 1675. Wing N1026. Reel 2035:04. LG A.5.4. 34 (5).

News from Tyburn: Or a true Relation of the Confession and Execution of ... Eliz. Simmons For Murthering her Bastard Childe. Who were executed the 19th of this Instant April, 1676. London, 1676. Wing N1025. No reel. LG A5.4 34(18). [Elizabeth Simmons]

News from Tybvrn ... on Wednesday the 16. of this Instant September 1674. London, 1674. Wing N1024. Reel 1955:15. LG A5.4 34(3). [Frances Bennet, Ellen Bayly]

Newton, John. *The Penitent Recognition of Joseph's Brethren: A Sermon Occasion'd by Elizabeth Ridgeway*. London, 1684. Wing N1073. Reel 393:21. L 694.k.2.(6.). [Elizabeth Ridgeway]

Niccols, Richard. *Sir Thomas Overbvries Vision*. London, 1616. STC 18524. Reel 1250:05. [Anne Turner]

The ordre of the Hospital of .S. Bartholomewes in Westsmythfielde in London. London, 1552. STC 21557. Reel 975:03.

Parker, Martin. *No naturall mother, but a monster. Or the exact relation of one, who for making away her owne new borne childe . . . was hang'd at Teyborne, on Wednesday the 11. Of December 1633*. London, 1634. STC 19261. No reel and not on *EEBO*, but reproduced in *A Pepysian Garland*, no. 75. Edited by H.R. Rollins. 1971. 428.

A Particular and Exact Account of the Trial of Mary Compton . . . also of her Maid . . . who were both Arraigned in one Indictment for Felony and Murder . . . also Ann Davis as Accessary. London, 1693. Wing P558A. Reel 2268:09. [Mary Compton, Anne Davis]

Partridge, N., and J. Sharp. *Blood for Blood, Or, Justice Executed For Innocent Blood-Shed. Being a true Narrative of that late horrid Murder, committed by Mary Cook, upon her own and beloved Child*. London, 1670. Wing P630. Reel 1154:02. [Mary Cook]

Patrick, Simon. *The Devout Christian Instructed How to Pray and give Thanks to God*. London, 1673. Wing P780. Reel 1337:09.

Pen, George. *Newes out of Germanie. A most wonderfull and true discourse of a cruell murderer*. London, 1584. STC 11720. Reel 568:05. L C.27.a.27.

A Perfect Account of the daily Intelligence, no. 67, April 7–14, 1652. Wing W3137. Reel Thomason 101: E.659 (26). [Joan Peterson]

A Perfect Narrative of the Robbery and Murder Committed near Dame Annis so Cleer, on Friday night, the second of July, 1669. Vpon the Person of Mr. John Talbot . . . Together With their Examinations, Tryal, and Confession. London, 1669. Wing P1503. Reel 1154:07. HN 54787. [Sarah Swift]

Perkins, William. *A Golden Chaine, or The Description of Theologie*. London, 1592. STC 19660. HN 62912. Reel 387:17.

———. *A Reformed Catholike*. London, 1598. STC 19736. Reel 388:02.

———. *ΕΠΙΕΙΈΙΑ [Hepieíkeia]: or, A Treatise of Christian Equitie and moderation*. London, 1604. STC 19699. Reel 581:05.

———. *The Whole Treatise of the Cases of Conscience*. London, 1608. STC 19670. Reel 1181:06. IIN 62906.

Petau, Denis. *The History of the World: Or, An Account of Time . . . To the Year of Our Lord, 1659*. London, 1659. Wing P1677. Reel 545:03; 1975:11. O Fol. BS. 127. [Anne Greene]

A pittilesse Mother. That most vnnaturally at one time, murthered two of her owne Children . . . Beeing a Gentlewoman named Margret Vincent. London, 1616. STC 24757. Reel 1013:02. MH 25276.43.342*. O 4⁰ G 29(4) Art. [Margaret Vincent]

Plat, Hugh. *Delightes for Ladies*. London, 1602. STC 19978. Reel 1733:06.

———. *The Jewel House of Art and Nature . . . with Sundry New Experiments in the Art of Husbandry, Distillation, and Moulding*. London, 1653. Wing P2390. Reel 701:25.

Platte, T. *Anne Wallens Lamentation*. London, 1616. STC 19997. Reproduced in *A Pepysian Garland*, no. 14. Edited by H.R. Rollins. 1971. 84. [Anne Wallen]

Plot, Robert. *The Natural History of Oxford-shire, Being an Essay toward the Natural History of England*. London, 1677. Wing P2585. Reel 2625:21. [Anne Greene]

The Popish Forgery Detected. Remarks on the Paper delivered by Margaret Martel to the Under-Sheriff at the Time and Place of her Execution . . . For the Barbarous Murther of Elizabeth Pullen. London, 1697. Wing P2950A. Reel 2234:18. LPL OB55 8.12. [Margaret Martel]

The Proceedings At The Assizes in Sovthwark . . . Begun on Thursday the 21th [sic], of March, and not ended till Tuesday the 26 of the same month, 1678. London, 1678. Wing P3557A. Reel 1510:12. MH Soc 2985.69*. O Gough Surrey 30 (11). [Sarah Elstone]

The Proceedings at the Sessions for London & Middlesex, Holden at the Old-Bailey: Beginning on Wednesday the Sixteenth of July, 1679. London, 1679. Wing P3562A. Reel 1408:36. HN 489432. [Katherine Tumince]

The Proceedings on the King and Queens Commissions . . . at Justice-Hall in the Old-Bayly. On Wednesday, Thursday, and Friday, being the 9th, 10th, and 11th. Days of December, 1691. London, 1691. Wing P3606A. Reel 138:28. HN 79995. [G.B., Anne Richardson, Jane Bromley, Mary Mott]

The Proceedings on the King's Commissions of the Peace . . . The 16th, and 17th. of January, 1684/5. London, 1685. Not in Wing (see general entry under title in *ESTC*). O Ashmole F 5 (86). [Jane Langworth, Elizabeth Stoaks]

The Proceedings on the King's Commissions of the Peace . . . The 20th. 21st. and 22d. days of May, 1686. London, 1686. Not in Wing (see general entry under title in *ESTC*). O Ashmole F 5 (56). [Alice Millikin, David Millikin, Mary Millikin, Martha Morgan]

The Proceedings on the King's Commissions of the Peace . . . The 13th 15th And 16th days of October, 1686. London, 1686. Not in Wing (see general entry under title in *ESTC*). O Ashmole F 5 (62). [Anne Philmore]

The Proceedings on the King's Commissions of the Peace . . . the 6th. 7th. and 8th of April. 1687. London, 1687. Not in Wing (see general entry under title in *ESTC*). L 1480.c.25 (17). [Elizabeth Clarke, Elizabeth Creed, Catherine Jones, Anne Trahern]

The Proceedings on the King's Commissions of the Peace . . . The 23th. and 25th. of February. 1686/7. London, 1687. Not in Wing (see general entry under title in *ESTC*). O Ashmole F 5 (64). [Margaret Torrel, Martha White, Elizabeth Barly, Jane English]

A Proclamation for Reformation of abuses, in the Gaole of New-gate. London, 1617. STC 16727.1. Reel 1997:08.

Protestant Domestic Intelligence, no. 84, Friday, December 31, 1680.

Protestant Domestic Intelligence, no. 88, Friday, January 14, 1680/81. 1681.

Protestant Domestic Intelligence, no. 87, Tuesday, January 11, 1680/81. 1681.

The Protestant (Domestick) Intelligence. Or, News both from City and Country, no. 88, Friday, January 14, 1680/1. 1681. [Charity Philpot]

The Protestant (Domestick) Intelligence, no. 90, Friday, January 21, 1680/1. 1681. [Leticia Wigington]

The Protestant (Domestick) Intelligence, no. 91, Tuesday, January 25, 1680/1. 1681. [Leticia Wigington]

The Protestant (Domestick) Intelligence, no. 111, Tuesday, April 5, 1680/1. 1681. [Anne Price]

Quick, John. *Hell Open'd, Or, The Infernal Sin of Murther Punished, Being A True Relation of the Poysoning of a whole Family in Plymouth.* London, 1676. Wing Q207. Reel 397:12. [Anne Evans, Philippa Cary]

A Rehearsall both straung and true, of hainous and horrible actes committed by Elizabeth Stile. London, 1579. STC 23267. Reel 1035:16. L C.27.a.11. [Elizabeth Stile]

[A] *Relation of The most Remarkable Proceedings at the late Assizes at Northampton.* London, 1674. Wing R855B. Reel 2176:26. MH 24246.63*.

A Representation of the bloody murder committed by Mary Aubry, a french midwife, which was burnt to death the 2d day of March 1687/8. London, 1798. LG Pr L. 42.021. Another version of *Mary Aubrey A French Midwife* [1798]).

A Sad and Sorrowfull Relation of Laurence Cauthorn, Butcher; who was Buried whilest he was Alive. London, 1661. Wing S244E. No reel. O Wood 365 (18). [Sarah Cook]

Saint German, Christopher. *The Dialogues in Englysshe / bytwene a Doctour of dyuinyte & a Studēt in the lawes of Englēde.* London, 1543. STC 21570. Reel 145:02.

Scot, Reginald. *The Discouerie of witchcraft.* London, 1584. STC 21864. Reel 1116:07.

Settle, Elkanah. *An Epilogue to the French Midwife's Tragedy. Who was Burnt in Leicester-Fields, March 2. 1687/8. For the Barbarous Murder of her Husband Denis Hobry.* London, 1688. Wing S2680A. Reel 2294:21. O Ashmole G 15 vol. 5 (135). MH *pEB65 A100 B675b v. 3. [Mary Hobry (or Aubrey)]

Smith, Samuel. *The Behaviour of the Condemned Criminals in Newgate, Who were Executed On Wednesday, the Sixth of May, 1685.* London, 1685. In *ESTC* but not in Wing. No reel. L C.175.e.16.(16.). [Katherine Brown]

———. *The True Account Of The Behaviour And Confession Of Alice Millikin, Who was Burnt in Smithfield On Wednesday the 2d. of June, 1686.* London, 1686. Wing T2343. Reel 2002:19. O Ashmole F 5 (54).

———. *The True Account of the Behaviour and Confession Of the Condemned Criminals, at Justice-Hall in the Old-Baily; on the 8th. Day of April 1687.* London, 1687. Not in Wing or *ESTC*. O Ashmole F 5 (76). [Ann Trahern, Elizabeth Clarke]

———. *The True Account of the Behaviour and Confessions Of The Condemned Criminals in Newgate, Viz. . . . Katherine Browne . . . October 23d. 1685.* London, 1685. Wing S4202. Reel 1130:23. HN 72908. O Ashmole F 5 (43). [Katherine Brown]

———. *The True Account of the Behaviour and Confession Of the Criminals Condemned, on Monday the 14th. 15th. and 17th. of January 1687. These Nine Persons Received the Sentence of Death, viz. . . . Arabella Reeves.* London, 1687. Not in Wing or *ESTC*. O Ashmole F 5 (63). [Arabella Reeves]

———. *The True Account of the Behaviour and Confession Of the Criminals, Condemned on Saturday the 22th. of May, 1686 . . . viz. . . . Alice Millikin.* London, 1686. Not in Wing or *ESTC*. O Ashmole F 5 (55). [Alice Millikin]

———. *The True Account of the Behaviour and Confessions Of the Criminals Condemned, on Saturday the 16th of October, 1686. At Justice-Hall in the Old-Bayly.* London, 1686. Not in Wing or *ESTC*. O Ashmole F 5 (59). [Anne Philmore]

Smith, William. *The Vale-Royall of England. Or, The County Palatine of Chester Illustrated.* London, 1656. Wing K488. Reel 1858:10.

The sorrowful complaint of Susan Higges, who for twenty yeeres, maintained her selfe by robberies on the high-way side. London, ca. 1630. STC 13440b.5. No reel. *Pepys Ballads.* Edited by W.G. Day. 1987. 1:113. [Susan Higges]

A Strange and wonderfull Discovery Of a horrid and cruel Murther Committed fourteen years since, upon the Person of Robert Eliot. London, 1662. Wing S5845. Reel 852:20. HN 307437. O Wood 365 (20). [Mary Burton, Alice Colson]

Strange Newes out of Kent. London, 1609. STC 14934. Reel 802:18.

Stubbes, Phillip. *A Christal Glas for christian Women.* London, 1592. STC 23382. Reel 861:02.

Sundrye strange and inhumaine Murthers, lately committed. London, 1591. STC 18286.5. Reel 1800:13. LPL (ZZ)1594.16.10. [Eulalia Page]

T., I. *A World of wonders. A Masse of Murthers. A Covie of Cosonages.* London, 1595. STC 14068.5. Reel 1604:02. HN 88838. [Alice Arden, Anne Saunders, Margaret Davie, Rebecca Chambers]

Three Bloodie Murders . . . The Second, committed by Elizabeth Iames, on the body of her Mayde. London, 1613. STC 18287. Reel 1211:12. O Wood 365 (4). [Elizabeth James]

A True account of the Behaviour, and Manner of the Execution of six persons. London, 1685. Wing T2345. Reel 1537:39. MH f EC65 A100 685t3. [Catherine Brown]

A True Account of the Behaviour, Confessions, and Last Dying Words, Of . . . Jane Langworth, and Elizabeth Stoaks. At Tyburn, On Wednesday the 21th. [*sic*] *of December, 1684.* London, 1684. Wing T2354. Reel 2083:15. O Ashmole F 5 (87). [Jane Langworth, Elizabeth Stoaks]

A True Account of the Proceedings at the Assizes . . . for the County of Surrey . . . on Wednesday the 28th, of February, 1683. London, 1683. Wing T2392aA. Reel 2557:24. [Alice Fergison]

A True Account of the Proceedings on the Crown-Side at this Lent Assize Held for the County of Surrey . . . Thursday the 13th of March, 1683, and ending on Saturday the 15th. London, 1684. Wing T2395. Reel 2220:05. L 1480.c.25 (12). [Margaret Corbet, Elizabeth Tymon]

A True and Perfect Account of the Examination, Confession, Tryal, Condemnation, and Execution of Joan Perry. London, 1676. Wing O614. Reel 1621:05. O Wood 365 (25). [Joan Perry]

A True and Perfect Account of the Proceedings . . . for London and Middlesex, Upon the 15. and 16. of January Instant. Or the Tryals, Examination and Confession of the Woman that Burned her Child. London, 1674. Wing T2521. Reel 617:11 (Union Theological Seminary copy missing sig. A2v–3v about this crime). LG A5.4 34(1).

A True and Sad Relation Of Two Wicked and Bloody Murthers, The one done by the Earl of Pembrook . . . The other was done by one Jane Lawson . . . upon her self, and Two small Children. London, 1680. Wing T2581A. Reel 2083:19. L 1132.g.55. [Jane Lawson]

A true and sad Reration [*sic*] *Of the great and bloudy Murder Committed At Ratcliff . . . upon the body of John Hunter . . . by one Mr. Smith and his wife, and a young Maid.* London, 1647. Wing T2581. Reel Thomason 59: E.372 (5). [Mrs. Smith]

A True and Wonderful Relation of A Murther Committed in . . . Newington, The 12th. Day of this present January. By A Maid who Poysoned her self, and Cut the Throat of a Child. London, 1681. Wing T2586. Reel 519:36. MH *fEC65 A100 681t6. [Charity Philpot]

A True Copy of the Paper Delivered by Margaert [*sic*] *Martels own Hand Before she went to the Place of Execution. July the 16th. 1697.* London, 1697. Wing M817A. Reel 2251:23. [Margaret Martel]

A True Discourse. Declaring the damnable life and death of one Stubbe Peeter. London, 1590. STC 23375. Reel 1010:05. L C.27.a.9.

The True Narrative And The Confession of Elizabeth Hare which is burnt for High-Treason. London, 1683. Wing T2777bA. Reel 2318:32. L C.175.e.16 (4). O Ashm. 1677 (100). [Elizabeth Hare]

The True Narrative Of The Confession And Execution Of the eight Prisoners at Tyburn, On Wednesday the 14th of this instant July, 1680. Viz. . . . Mary Clark for Murthering her Bastard-Child. London, 1680. Wing T2782. Reel 1344:07. L Cup21.g.32/28. O Godw. Pamph. 2209 (27). [Mary Clark]

The True Narrative Of The Confession And Execution Of the fifteen Prisoners at Tyburn, On Monday the 8th of this Instant March 1670 [*sic*]. London, 1680. Wing T2779. Reel 1558:36. MH *fEC65 A100 680t7 (annotated "1679/80"). L Cup21.g.32/72 (annotated "the 8th of March, 1679"). [Frances Lewis, Dorothy Clark, Dorothy Hall]

A True Narrative of the Confession and Execution Of the four Prisoners . . . On Wednesday the 5th of this Instant February 1684. London, 1684. Wing T2779bA. Reel 2557:27. O Ashmole F 5 (121). L C.175.e.16. (14). [Joan Nicholas, Mary Defoe]

The True Narrative of the Confession and Execution Of the Prisoners at Kingstone-upon-Thames, on Wednesday the 16th of this Instant March, 1681 . . . But more particular of the Confession and Burning of Margaret Osgood. London, 1681. Wing T2780A. Reel 2258:17. O Ashm. 1677 (58). HN 478344. MH *fEC65 A100 68lt7. [Margaret Osgood]

The True Narrative of the Confession and Execution Of the Prisoners at Tyburn, on Friday the 17th of this instant September, 1680. Viz. . . . Mary Bucknel, for murdering her Bastard Child. London, 1680. Wing T2780. No reel. L Cup21.g.32/29. [Mary Bucknell]

The True Narrative Of The Confession And Execution of the seven Prisoners At Tyburn On Wednesday the 24th. of this Instant October, 1683. London, 1683. Wing T2780D. Reel 2374:27. L C.175.e.16.(9). [Mary Phelps]

The True Narrative of the Confession and Execution Of the three Prisoners at Kingstone upon Thames . . . On Monday the 22th [sic] of March, 1679. London, 1680. Wing T2781aA. Reel 2100:23. O Godw. Pamph. 2209 (6). [Margaret Clark]

A true Narrative Of the Proceedings . . . at Kingston upon Thames, On the 4, 5, and 6th of July, 1676 . . . Likewise the Tryal of two Women . . . for killing of a Man that was fighting with her Husband. London, 1676. Wing T2833B. No reel. O Gough Surrey 30 (9).

A True Narrative of the Proceedings at the Assizes, held at Kingston upon Thames . . . on Thursday the 26th. Of the Instant July, and ended on Saturday the 28th. London, 1683. Wing T2812B. No reel. L Cup. 21.g.32/30. [Mary Read]

The True Narrative of the Proceedings at the Assizes Holden at Kingstone-upon-Thames, for the County of Surry. Which began on Monday the 7th of this Instant March, and ended on Tuesday the 10th following. London,1681. Wing T2813A. Reel 2083:26 (also 2116:11 reproducing O Ashm.1677 (56)]. MH copy annotated "12 March 1680/1" and identified as Wing 2812A on Reel 2083, according to *ESTC*). [Margaret Osgood]

The True Narrative Of The Procedings [sic] At The Assizes Holden for the County of Surry: Which began on Fryday the 12th of this instant March 1679. and ended on the Wednesday following. London, 1680. Wing T2813. Reel 1344:09. L Cup21.g.32/66. O Godw. Pamph. 2209 (5). [Margaret Clark]

The True Narrative Of The Procedings [sic] At The Session-House In The Old-Bayly. Which began on Thursday the 26th of this February last past. London, 1680. Wing T2827AC. Reel 2374:30. L Cup21.g.32/75. [Dorothy Clark]

A true Narrative Of the Proceedings at the Sessions-house in the Old-Bayly . . . On April 25, and 26. London, 1677. Wing T2820B. Reel 2827:29. O Gough Surrey 30 (10). [Margaret Spicer]

A true Narrative Of the Proceedings at the Sessions-house in the Old-Bayly . . . On Wednesday the 17th of January 1676/7 . . . As also the Tryals and Condemnation of a Woman for Killing her Bastard-Child. London, 1677. Wing T2820. Reel 2220:13. LG A5.4 34(16).

A true Narrative Of the Proceedings at the Sessions-house in the Old-Bayly . . . on Wednesday the 13th of this Instant Decemb. and ended on Saturday the 16th, 1676 . . . With the Tryal of the Maid that set her Master's Barns on fire. London, 1676. Wing T2819A. Reel 2220:12.

A true Narrative Of the Proceedings At the Sessions-house in the Old-Bayly . . . Wednesday the 23d. of this Instant August, and ended on Fryday the 25th. London, 1676. Wing T2818. Reel 2220:11. LG A5.4 34(22).

The True Narrative Of The Proceedings at The Sessions House in the Old-Bayly which began on Fryday the 23th of this Instant February and ended on Saturday the 24th following. London, *ca.* 1682–1683. Wing T2830A (misidentified on *EEBO*). Reel 2594:11. Cup21.g.32/33. [Margaret Benson]

The True Narrative Of The Proceedings at The Sessions-House in the Old-Baly, Which began on Fryday the 10th of this instant September, and ended on Mnnday [sic] the 13 following. London, 1680. Wing T2827E. No reel. L Cup21.g.32/32. [Mary Bucknell]

The True Narrative Of The Procedings [sic] At The Sessions-house In The Old-Baylx [sic]. Which began on Wednesday the 26th of this Instant April, 1680. and ended on Fryday the 28th following. London, 1680. Wing T2827BA. Reel 2220:15. L 1480.c.25 (8). [Ellenor David, Ann Rye, Elizabeth Brown, Elizabeth Oliver, Mary Bird]

The True Narrative Of The Proceedings Of The Sessions-House in the Old-Bayly Which began on Wednesday the 13th of this Instant April and ended on Thursday the 14th following. London, 1681. Wing T2829. Reel 2220:17. HN 489444b. [Anne Price]

The True Narrative Of The Sessions Begun at the Old Bayley On Wednesday the Fifteenth of October, 1679. London, 1679. Wing T2840. Reel 1344:16. L Cup21.g.32/35. [Joan Blackwell]

A True Narrative Of Three Wicked and Bloody Murthers . . . The Second in London, done by a Young Lady upon her Lover. London, 1680. Wing T2840BA. Reel 2100:24.

The True Protestant Mercury, no. 7, Saturday, January 15–Tuesday, January 18, 1680/1. 1681. [Leticia Wigington]

The True Protestant Mercury, no. 18, Wednesday, February 23–Saturday, February 26, 1680/1. 1681. [Leticia Wigington]

The True Protestant Mercury, no. 24, Wednesday, March 16–Saturday, March 19, 1680/1. 1681. [Margaret Osgood]

The True Protestant Mercury, no. 137, Wednesday, April 26–Saturday, April 29, 1682. [Elizabeth Fitzpatrick]

A True Relation Of Four most Barbarous and Cruel Murders Committed in Leicester-shire by Elizabeth Ridgway. London, 1684. Wing T2905. Reel 853:62. MH *EC65.A100.684t. HN 437416. [Elizabeth Ridgeway]

A true Relation of one Susan Higges . . . and how shee lived 20. yeeres, by robbing on the High-wayes. London, 1640. STC 13441. Reel 1631:10. L Rox.1:424–5. [Susan Higges]

A True Relation Of the Life and Conversation of Margaret Martel, that Murder'd Mistress Pvllyn. London, 1697. Wing T2994A. Reel 2396:17. [Margaret Martel]

A true Relation Of the most Horrid and Barbarous murders committed by Abigall [sic] Hill . . . on the persons of foure Infants. London, 1658. Wing T3008. Reel Thomason 234: E.1881 (2). [Abigail Hill]

A True Relation of the most Inhumane and bloody Murther, of Master Iames . . . Committed by one Lowe his Curate, and consented vnto by his Wife. London, 1609. STC 14436. Reel 720:02. L C.143.b.18. [Mrs. James]

A True Relation of the Names and Suspected Crimes Of Prisoners now in Newgate . . . Jane Blackwel, for Murdering her Child [et al.]. London, 1679. Wing T3012. Reel 2374:43. O Godw. Pamph. 2209 (3). [Jane Blackwell, Elizabeth Dyke, Rebecca Rudd]

The True Relation Of The Tryals At the Sessions of Oyer and Terminer . . . which began in the Old-Bailey the 17th of this instant January, and ended the 18th of the same. As particularly of Elizabeth Wigenton For Whipping a Girl to Death.

London, 1681. Wing T3063. Reel 2067:25. MH *EB65. O Godw. Pamph. 2209 (46). [Leticia Wigington]

A True report of the horrible Murther, which was committed in the house of Sir Ierome Bowes. London, 1605. STC 3434. Reel 656:03.

A true report of the late horrible murther committed by William Sherwood. London, 1581. STC 22432. Reel 1156:07. LPL (ZZ)1584.24.03.

A true Translation of a Paper written in French, delivered by Margaret Martell to the Vnder-Sheriff at the Time and Place of her Execution . . . for the barbarous murther of Elizabeth Pullen. London, 1697. Wing M817B. Reel 2251:24. [Margaret Martel]

The Truest News From the Sessions; Or, An Exact Account of the Tryal & Condemnation Of . . . Mrs. Ann Petty . . . the 12th of Decemb, 1674. London, 1674. Wing T3135A. Reel 1876:15. HN 303473. [Ann Petty]

The Truest News From Tyburn, Or, An Exact Account of the Tryal . . . At Justice-Hall in the Old Baily, the [9-]12th of Decemb. 1674. London, 1674. Not in Wing. LG A5.4 34(4). [Ann Petty]

The trueth of the most wicked and secret murthering of Iohn Brewen . . . committed by his owne wife. London, 1592. STC 15095. Reel 2025:10. LPL (ZZ)1594.16.11. [Anne Welles]

A Trve Discovrse Of A cruell fact committed by a Gentlewoman towardes her Husband, her Father, her Sister and two of her Nephewes. London, 1599. STC 3469. Reel 411:11. L 1104.b.49. [Anna de Boyse]

A Trve Relation of two most strange and fearefull Accidents, lately happening. London, 1618. STC 4932. Reel 1229:17.

The Tryal and Condemnation Of Several notorious Malefactors, at a Sessions of Oyer and Terminer . . . And most remarkably of John Sadler, who Whipt the Child to Death at Ratcliffe. London, 1681. Wing T2147A (misidentified under this title on *ESTC* and *EEBO* as T2149). Reel 1344:02. MH *fEC65.A100.681t2 (annotated "28 Feb. 1680/1"). [Leticia Wigington]

The Tryal and Condemnation Of Several Notorious Malefactors . . . Beginning August the 31. Ending September the 1. 1681. London, 1681. Wing T2150. Reel 648:04. L Cup21.g.32/45. O Ashm. 1677 (64). [Elizabeth Powel]

The Tryal and Condemnation Of Several Notorious Malefactors . . . Beginning July 6. 1681. London, 1681. Wing T2151. Reel 677:10. Godw. Pamph. 2209 (43). [Mary Naples]

The Tryal and Condemnation Of Several Notorious Malefactors . . . Beginning May 20. 1681. Ending the 21 of the same Month. London, 1681. Wing T2149. No reel. L Cup21.g.32/44. [Alice Enterys, Elizabeth Messenger]

The Tryals and Condemnation of Several Persons . . . Which began on the 16th of this instant July 1679. and ended on Fryday the 18th. London, 1679. Wing T2248A. No reel. [Katherine Tumince]

The Tryal And Conviction Of Mary Butler, alias Strickland . . . on the 12th Day of October, 1699. London, 1700. Wing T2162. Reel 2158:05. L 518.f.26. [Mary Butler]

The Tryall and Examination of Mrs. Joan Peterson . . . for her supposed Witchcraft, and poysoning of the Lady Powel at Chelsey. London, 1652. Wing T2167. Reel Thomason 101: E.659 (15). [Joan Peterson]

The Tryals At the Sessions In the Old-Bailey . . . on Wednesday the 8th of this instant December, and ended on Thursday the 10th of the same. London, *ca.* 1680. Wing T2248B. Reel 2374:19. L Cup21.g.32/43. O Godw. Pamph. 2209 (44). [Elizabeth Owen, Margaret Adams]

Tuke, Thomas. *A Discovrse Against Painting and Tincturing of Women*. London, 1616. STC 24316a. Reel 1191:02. HN 60715.

Two most vnnaturall and bloodie Murthers: The one by Maister Cauerley . . . The other, by Mistris Browne . . . vpon her husband. London, 1605. STC 18288. Reel 997:02. O 4⁰ C 16(27) Art. BS. [Mrs. Browne]

Twyne, Thomas. *A Shorte and Pithie Discourse.* London, 1580. STC 24413. Reel 1158:12.

The Unnatural Grand Mother, Or a true Relation Of a most barbarous Murther Committed by Elizabeth Hazard . . . on her Grand childe . . . on Friday the 15. of Iuly 1659. London, 1659. Wing U86. Reel 441:04. HN 148125. [Elizabeth Hazard]

The Unnatural Mother: Being a Full and True Account of One Elizabeth Kennet . . . who . . . privately Deliver'd her self, and afterwards flung her Infant in the Fire. London, 1697. Wing U86B. Reel 2258:34. [Elizabeth Kennet]

The vnnaturall Wife: Or, The lamentable Murther, of one goodman Dauis . . . who was stabbed to death by his Wife. London, 1628. STC 6366. Reel 1410:01. Reproduced in *A Pepysian Garland*, no. 49. Edited by H.R. Rollins. 1971. 283. [Alice Davies]

W., W. *The Black Book Of Newgate: Or, An Exact Collection Of The Most material Proceedings At All The Sessions in the Old baily, For Eighteen months last past.* London, 1677. Wing W140A. Reel 2259:02. LG A5.4 34(25). [Elizabeth Simmons, Margaret Spicer]

A warning for all desperate Women. By the example of Alice Dauis. London, 1628. STC 6367. Reel 1410:02. Reproduced in *A Pepysian Garland*, no. 50. Edited by H. R. Rollins. 1971. 288. [Alice Davies]

A Warning for Bad Wives: or, The Manner of the Burning of Sarah Elston. London, 1678. Wing W918A. Reel 2161:06. L 1132.a.21. O Ashmole 739 (22). [Sarah Elstone]

A Warning for Faire Women. Containing, The Most Tragicall and lamentable murther of Master George Sanders. London, 1599. STC 25089. Reel 400:09. MH 14434.76.210. [Anne Saunders]

A Warning for Maidens. London, ca. London, 1650. Wing W921. Reel 2123:501.

Warning for Servants: And a Caution to Protestants. Or, the Case of Margret Clark. London, 1680. Wing C4483. Reel 87:08. HN 440993. [Margaret Clark]

A Warning-Piece to All Married Men and Women. Being the Full Confession of Mary Hobry, The French Midwife, Who Murdered her Husband on the 27th. of January 1687/8. London, 1688. Wing W935. Reel 1559:10. O Ashmole G 15 vol. 5 (134). [Mary Hobry (or Aubrey)]

The Whole Confession And Speech Of Mr. Nathaniel Tompkins. London, 1643. Wing T1865. Reel Thomason 10: E.59 (9). [Nathaniel Tompkins]

The Witch of Wapping. Or An Exact and Perfect Relation, of the Life and Devilish Practises of Joan Peterson . . . With the Confession of Prudence Lee . . . for the murthering her Husband. London, 1652. Wing W3137. Reel Thomason 101: E.659 (18). [Joan Peterson, Prudence Lee]

The wofull lamentacon of mrs. Anne Saunders, which she wrote with her own hand, being prisoner in newgate, Justly condemned to death. Manuscript version of what originally was probably a printed ballad, now lost. L Sloane MS 1896 fol. 8–11. Reproduced in *Old English Ballads 1553–1625.* Edited by H. R. Rollins, 1920. 340–48.

Wright, Thomas. *The Glory of God's Revenge Against the Bloody and Detestable Sins of Murther and Adultery, Express'd in Thirty Modern Tragical Histories.* London, 1685. Wing W3708. Reel 2122:13. MH *EC65 W9366.685g.

Yarington, Robert. *Two Lamentable Tragedies.* London, 1601. STC 26076. Reel 1018:06. HN K-D 464.

Yearwood, Randolph. *The Penitent Murderer. Being an Exact Narrative Of the Life and Death of Nathaniel Bvtler.* London, 1657. Wing Y23. Reel Thomason 208: E.1660 (2).

Modern Sources

Aelian, Claudius. *On the Characteristics of Animals*. Translated by A. F. Scolfield. 3 vols. London: Heinemann, 1958–59.

Amos, Andrew. *The Great Oyer of Poisoning: The Trial of the Earl of Somerset for the Poisoning of Sir Thomas Overbury*. London: Richard Bentley, 1846.

Amussen, Susan Dwyer. "'Being Stirred to Much Unquietness': Violence and Domestic Violence in Early Modern England." *Journal of Women's History* 6 (1994): 70–89.

———. *An Ordered Society: Gender and Class in Early Modern England*. Oxford: Basil Blackwell, 1988.

———. "Punishment, Discipline, and Power: The Social Meanings of Violence in Early Modern England." *Journal of British Studies* 34 (1995): 1–34.

Anderson, Jennifer, and Elizabeth Sauer. "Current Trends in the History of Reading." In *Books and Readers in Early Modern England: Material Studies*, edited by J. Anderson and E. Sauer, 1–22. Philadelphia, PA: University of Pennsylvania Press, 2002.

Andrews, Alexander. *The History of British Journalism*. 2 vols. London: Bentley, 1859.

Arber, Edward, ed. *A Transcript of the Registers of the Company of Stationers of London 1554–1640*. 5 vols. London: privately printed, 1875–94.

Aristotle. *Nichomachean Ethics*. Translated by H. Rackam. 1926. Rev. ed. Cambridge, MA: Harvard University Press, 1934.

Bacon, Francis. *The Works*. Edited by James Spedding, Robert Leslie Ellis, and Douglas Denon Heath. 15 vols. London: Longmans and Co., 1857–74.

Baker, P. R. S. "Thomas Edwards." *ODNB*.

Beattie, J. M. *Crime and the Courts in England 1660–1800*. Princeton: Princeton University Press, 1986.

———. "The Criminality of Women in Eighteenth-Century England." *Journal of Social History* 8 (1975): 80–116.

———. "The Courts in Surrey 1736–1753." In *Crime in England, 1550–1800*, edited by J. S. Cockburn, 155–86. London: Methuen, 1977.

———. "Judicial Records and the Measurement of Crime in Eighteenth-Century England." In *Crime and Criminal Justice in Europe and Canada*, edited by Louis A. Knafla, 127–45. Waterloo, ON: Wilfrid Laurier University Press, 1981.

———. "London Juries in the 1690s." In *Twelve Good Men and True: The Criminal Trial Jury in England, 1200–1800*, edited by J. S. Cockburn and Thomas A. Green, 214–53. Princeton, NJ: Princeton University Press, 1988.

———. "Towards the Study of Crime in 18th Century England: A Note on Indictments." In *The Triumph of Culture: 18th Century Perspectives*, edited by Paul Fritz and David Williams, 299–314. Toronto: A. M. Hakkert, 1977.

———. "Women and Crime in Augustan London." In *Women & History: Voices of Early Modern England*, edited by Valerie Frith, 103–15. Toronto: Coach House Press, 1995.

Beck, Ulrich. *Risk Society: Towards a New Modernity*. Translated by Mark Ritter. London: Sage Publications, 1992.

Bellamy, John G. *Criminal Law and Society in Late Medieval and Tudor England*. Gloucester: Alan Sutton, 1984.

Bellany, Alastair. "Mistress Turner's Deadly Sins: Sartorial Transgression, Court Scandal, and Politics in Early Modern England." *Huntington Library Quarterly* 58.2 (1996): 179–210.

———. *The Politics of Court Scandal in Early Modern England*. Cambridge: Cambridge University Press, 2002.

Belsey, Catherine. *The Subject of Tragedy: Identity and Difference in Renaissance Drama*. London: Methuen, 1985.

Bennett, W. Lance, and Martha S. Feldman. *Reconstructing Reality in the Courtroom*. New Brunswick, NJ: Rutgers University Press, 1981.

Birch, Thomas, ed. *The Court and Times of James the First*. 2 vols. London: Henry Colburn, 1849.

Blackstone, William. *Commentaries on the Laws of England: A Facsimile of the First Edition of 1765–1769*. With an Introduction by Thomas A. Green. 4 vols. Chicago: University of Chicago Press, 1979.

Bowers, Toni. *The Politics of Motherhood: British Writing and Culture, 1680–1760*. Cambridge: Cambridge University Press, 1996.

Boyer, Allen D. "Coke, Sir Edward (1552–1634), lawyer, legal writer, and politician." *ODNB*.

Breward, Ian, ed. *The Work of William Perkins*. Abingdon, UK: The Sutton Courtenay Press, 1970.

Briggs, John, Christopher Harrison, Angus McInnes, and David Vincent. *Crime and Punishment in England: An Introductory History*. London: UCL Press, 1996.

Brittain, Robert P. "Cruentation in Legal Medicine and in Literature." *Medical History* 9.1 (January 1965): 82–88.

Brooks, E. St. John. "A Pamphlet by Arthur Golding: The Murder of George Saunders." *Notes and Queries* 174 (1938): 182–84.

Brown, Pamela Allen. *Better a Shrew than a Sheep: Women, Drama, and the Culture of Jest in Early Modern England*. Ithaca, NY: Cornell University Press, 2003.

Burford, E. J., and Sandra Shulman. *Of Bridles and Burnings: The Punishment of Women*. New York: St. Martin's, 1992.

Burke, Peter. "Popular Culture in Seventeenth-Century London." In *Popular Culture in Seventeeth-Century England*, edited by Barry Reay, 31–58. London: Croom Helm, 1985.

———. "Reflections on the Origins of Cultural History." In *Interpretation and Cultural History*, edited by Joan H. Pittock and Andrew Wear, 5–24. Basingstoke: Macmillan, 1990.

Burnett, Mark Thornton. *Constructing 'Monsters' in Shakespearean Drama and Early Modern Culture*. Basingstoke: Palgrave, 2002.

Butler, Judith. *Gender Trouble: Feminism and the Subversion of Identity*. 1990. New York: Routledge, 1999.

Calhoun, Craig, ed. *Habermas and the Public Sphere*. Cambridge, MA: MIT Press, 1992.

Calkins, Susanna. "Cholmondeley, Mary, Lady Cholmondeley." *ODNB*.

Calvert, F. Crace. "On Poisons." *Transactions of the Historic Society of Lancashire and Cheshire* 12 (1859–60): 193–208.

Campbell, Ruth. "Sentence of Death by Burning for Women." *The Journal of Legal History* 5 (1984): 44–59.

Cannon, Charles Dale, ed. *A Warning for Fair Women. A Critical Edition*. The Hague: Mouton, 1975.

Capp, Bernard. "Popular Literature." In *Popular Culture in Seventeenth-Century England*, edited by Barry Reay, 198–243. London: Croom Helm, 1985.

de Certeau, Michel. *The Practice of Everyday Life*. Translated by Steven Rendell. Berkeley, CA: University of California Press, 1984.

Chamberlain, Sir John, *Letters*. Edited by N. E. McClure. 2 vols. Philadelphia, PA: The American Philosophical Society, 1939.

Chapman, Christopher. "Smith, Samuel (1620–1698), Church of England clergyman." *ODNB*.

Chartier, Roger. *Cultural History: Between Practices and Representations*. Translated by Lydia G. Cochrane. Cambridge: Polity/Blackwell, 1998.

———. *The Cultural Uses of Print*. Translated by Lydia G. Cochrane. Princeton, NJ: Princeton University Press, 1987.

———. "Texts, Printing, Readings." In *The New Cultural History*, edited by Lynn Hunt, 154–75. Berkeley, CA: University of California Press, 1989.

Cioni, Maria L. *Women and Law in Elizabethan England, With Particular Reference to the Court of Chancery*. New York: Garland, 1985.

Clark, Sandra. *The Elizabethan Pamphleteers: Popular Moralistic Pamphlets 1580–1640*. Rutherford, NJ: Fairleigh Dickinson University Press, 1983.

———. *Women and Crime in the Street Literature of Early Modern England*. Basingstoke: Palgrave Macmillan, 2003.

Cockburn, J. S., ed. *Calendar of Assize Records: Home Circuit Indictments Elizabeth I and James I*. London: H.M.S.O., 1985.

———. "Early Modern Assize Records as Historical Evidence." *Journal of the Society of Archivists* 5 (1975): 215–31.

———. *A History of English Assizes 1558–1714*. Cambridge: Cambridge University Press, 1972.

———. "Patterns of Violence in English Society: Homicide in Kent, 1560–1985." *Past and Present* 130 (February 1991): 70–106.

———. "Twelve Silly Men? The Jury Trial at Assizes, 1560–1670." In *Twelve Good Men and True: The Criminal Trial Jury in England, 1200–1800*, edited by J. S. Cockburn and Thomas A. Green, 158–181. Princeton, NJ: Princeton University Press, 1988.

Cohen, Charles Lloyd. *God's Caress: The Psychology of Puritan Religious Experience*. New York: Oxford University Press, 1986.

Collington, Philip D. "Leticia Wigington, *The Confession and Execution of Leticia Wigington*." In *Reading Early Modern Women: an Anthology of Texts in Manuscript and Print, 1550–1700*, edited by Helen Ostovich and Elizabeth Sauer, 50–53. London: Routledge, 2004.

Collins, D.C. *A Handlist of News Pamphlets, 1590–1610*. London: Southwest Essex Technical College, 1943.

Cook, Judith. *Dr Simon Forman: A Most Notorious Physician*. London: Chatto & Windus, 2001.

Cressy, David. *Literacy and the Social Order: Reading and Writing in Tudor and Stuart England*. Cambridge: Cambridge University Press, 1980.

———. "Literacy in Context: Meaning and Measurement in Early Modern England." In *Consumption and the World of Goods*, edited by John Brewer and Roy Porter, 305–19. London: Routledge, 1993.

Curtis, T. C., and F. M. Hale. "English Thinking About Crime, 1530–1620." In *Crime and Criminal Justice in Europe and Canada*, edited by Louis A. Knafla, 111–26. Waterloo, ON: Wilfrid Laurier University Press, 1981.

Cust, Richard. "News and Politics in Early Seventeenth-Century England." *Past & Present* 112 (August 1986): 60–90.

Daly, Kathleen, and Lisa Maher. "Crossroads and Intersections: Building from Feminist Critique." In *Criminology at the Crossroads: Feminist Readings in Crime and Justice*, edited by Kathleen Daly and Lisa Maher, 1–17. New York: Oxford University Press, 1998.

Daston, Lorraine, and Katharine Park. *Wonders and the Order of Nature, 1150–1750*. New York: Zone Books, 2001.

Davies, Marie-Hélène. *Reflections of Renaissance England: Life, Thought and Religion Mirrored in Illustrated Pamphlets 1535–1640*. Allison Park, PA: Pickwick Publications, 1986.

Davis, Natalie Zemon. *Fiction in the Archives: Pardon Tales and their Tellers in Sixteenth-Century France*. Stanford, CA: Stanford University Press, 1987.

Day, W. G., ed. *The Pepys Ballads*. 5 vols. Cambridge: D.S. Brewer, 1987.

DeMaria, Robert. "Bathurst, Richard (1722/3–1762), physician and writer." *ODNB*.

Derrida, Jacques. "Force of Law: The 'Mystical Foundation of Authority.'" In *Deconstruction and the Possibility of Justice*, edited by Drucilla Cornell, Michel Rosenfeld, and David Gray Carlson, 3–67. New York: Routledge, 1992.

Dickinson, J. R., and J. A. Sharpe. "Infanticide in Early Modern England: The Court of Great Sessions at Chester, 1650–1800." In *Infanticide: Historical Perspectives on Child Murder and Concealment, 1550–2000*, edited by Mark Jackson, 35–51. Aldershot, UK: Ashgate, 2002.

Dobb, C. "Henry Goodcole, Visitor of Newgate." *The Guildhall Miscellany* 4 (1955): 15–21.

Dolan, Frances E. *Dangerous Familiars: Representation of Domestic Crime in England, 1550–1700*. Ithaca, NY: Cornell University Press, 1994.

———. "Gender, Moral Agency, and Dramatic Form in *A Warning For Fair Women*." *Studies in English Literature* 29 (1989): 201–18.

———. "'Gentlemen, I have one thing more to say': Women on Scaffolds in England, 1563–1680." *Modern Philology* 92 (1994): 157–78.

———. "Taking the Pencil Out of God's Hand: Art, Nature, and the Face-Painting Debate in Early Modern England." *PMLA* 108 (1993): 224–39.

Doody, Margaret. "'Those Eyes Are Made So Killing': Eighteenth-Century Murderesses and the Law." *Princeton University Library Chronicle* 46.1 (Fall 1984): 49–80.

———. "Voices of Record: Women as Witnesses and Defendants in the *Old Bailey Sessions Papers*." In *Representing Women: Law, Literature and Feminism*, edited by Susan Sage Heinzelman and Zipporah Batshaw Wiseman, 287–308. Durham, NC: Duke University Press, 1994.

Drew-Bear, Annette. *Painted Faces on the Renaissance Stage: The Moral Significance of Face-Painting Conventions*. Lewisburg, PA: Bucknell University Press, 1994.

Eden, Kathy. *Poetic and Legal Fiction in the Aristotelian Tradition*. Princeton, NJ: Princeton University Press, 1986.

Eisenstien, Elizabeth L. *The Printing Press as an Agent of Change: Communications and Cultural Transformations in Early-Modern Europe*. Cambridge: Cambridge University Press, 1979.

Elliot, Vivien Brodsky. "Single Women in the London Marriage Market: Age, Status and Mobility, 1598–1619." In *Marriage and Society: Studies in the Social History of Marriage*, edited by R. B. Outhwaite, 90–94. London: Europa, 1981.

Emsley, John. *The Elements of Murder*. Oxford: Oxford University Press, 2005.

Erickson, Amy Louise. *Women and Property in Early Modern England*. London: Routledge, 1993.

Evelyn, John. *The Diary of John Evelyn*. Edited by E. S. de Beer. 6 vols. Oxford: Clarendon Press, 1955.

Farrell, Michael. *Poisons and Poisoners: An Encyclopedia of Homicidal Poisoners*. London: Bantam, 1994.

Fish, Stanley. "Force." In *Doing What Comes Naturally: Change, Rhetoric, and the Practice of Theory in Literary and Legal Studies*, 503–24. Durham, NC: Duke University Press, 1989.

Foucault, Michel. *Discipline and Punish: The Birth of the Prison*. Translated by Alan Sheridan-Smith. New York: Pantheon Books, 1977.

———. *The Order of Things: An Archaeology of the Human Sciences*. Translated by Alan Sheridan-Smith. New York: Pantheon Books, 1970.

Fox, Adam. "Popular Verses and Their Readership in the Early Seventeenth Century." In *The Practice and Representation of Reading in England*, edited by James Raven, Helen Small, and Naomi Tadmor, 125–37. Cambridge: Cambridge University Press, 1996.

Frank, Joseph. *The Beginnings of the English Newspaper 1620–1660*. Cambridge, MA: Harvard University Press, 1961.

Fraser, Nancy. "Rethinking the Public Sphere: A Contribution to the Critique of Actually Existing Democracy." In *Habermas and the Public Sphere*, edited by Craig Calhoun, 109–42. Cambridge, MA: MIT Press, 1992.

Frearson, Michael. "The Distribution and Readership of London Corantos in the 1620s." In *Serials and their Readers, 1620–1914*, edited by Robin Myers and Michael Harris, 1–26. Winchester, UK: St. Paul's Bibliographies, 1993.

Gaskill, Malcolm. *Crime and Mentalities in Early Modern England*. Cambridge: Cambridge University Press, 2000.

Geertz, Clifford. *The Interpretation of Cultures*. New York: Basic Books, 1973.

Gladfelder, Hal. *Criminality and Narrative in Eighteenth-Century England: Beyond the Law*. Baltimore, MD: Johns Hopkins University Press, 2001.

Golding, Louis Thorn. *An Elizabethan Puritan: Arthur Golding, the Translator of Ovid's Metamorphoses and also of John Calvin's Sermons*. New York: R. R. Smith, 1971.

Gordon, Alexander, and Stephen Wright. "Quick, John (*bap.* 1636, *d.* 1706)." *ODNB*.

Gowing, Laura. "'The Freedom of the Streets': Women and Social Space, 1560–1640." In *Londinopolis: Essays in the Cultural and Social History of Early Modern London*, edited by Paul Griffiths and Mark S.R. Jenner, 130–51. Manchester: Manchester University Press, 2000.

———. "Greene, Anne (*c.* 1628–1659), survivor of execution." *ODNB*.

———. "Secret Births and Infanticide in Seventeenth-Century England." *Past & Present* 156 (August 1997): 87–115.

Green, Ian. "Career Prospects and Clerical Conformity in the Early Stuart Church." *Past & Present* 90 (February 1981): 71–115.

———. *Protestantism and Print in Early Modern England*. Oxford: Oxford University Press, 2000.

Green, Thomas A. "The Jury and the English Law of Homicide, 1200–1600." *Michigan Law Review* 74 (1976): 413–99.

———. "Societal Concepts of Criminal Liability for Homicide in Medieval England." *Speculum* 47 (1972): 669–94.

———. *Verdict According to Conscience: Perspectives on the English Criminal Trial Jury, 1200–1800*. Chicago: University of Chicago Press, 1985.

Grieve, Mrs. M. *A Modern Herbal*. 1931. Edited by C.F. Leyal. Harmondsworth: Penguin, 1980.

Griffiths, Paul. *Youth and Authority: Formative Experiences in England 1560–1640*. Oxford: Oxford University Press, 1996.

Habermas, Jürgen. *The Structural Transformation of the Public Sphere: An Inquiry into a Category of Bourgeois Society*. Translated by Thomas Burger and Frederick Lawrence. Cambridge, MA: MIT Press, 1989.

Harris, B. E., ed. *A History of the County of Chester*. 2 vols. Oxford: Oxford University Press, 1979.

Harris, Michael. "The Structure, Ownership and Control of the Press, 1620–1780." In *Newspaper History from the Seventeenth Century to the Present Day*, edited by George Boyce, James Curran, and Pauline Wingate, 82–97. London: Constable, 1978.

———. "Trials and Criminal Biographies: a Case Study in Distribution." In *Sale and Distribution of Books from 1700*, edited by Robin Myers and Michael Harris, 1–36. Oxford: Oxford Polytechnic Press, 1982.

Harrison, Thomas R. "The Literary Background of Renaissance Poisons." *Texas University Studies in English* 27 (1948): 35–67.

Hartshorne, Albert. *Hanging in Chains*. New York: Cassell, 1893.

Hay, Douglas. "Property, Authority, and the Criminal Law." In *Albion's Fatal Tree: Crime and Society in Eighteenth-Century England*, edited by Douglas Hay *et al.*, 17–63. New York: Pantheon Books, 1975.

Helgerson, Richard. *Adulterous Alliances: Home, State, and History in Early Modern European Drama and Painting*. Chicago: University of Chicago Press, 2000.
———. "Murder in Faversham: Holinshed's Impertinent History." In *The Historical Imagination in Early Modern Britain: History, Rhetoric, and Fiction 1500–1800*, edited by Donald R. Kelly and David Harris Sacks, 133–58. Cambridge, MA: Woodrow Wilson Center Press, 1997.
———. Review of Annabel Patterson's *Reading Holinshed's "Chronicles"* (Chicago: University of Chicago Press, 1994), *Journal of English and Germanic Philology* 95 (1996): 237–40.
Henslowe, Philip. *Henslowe's Diary*. Edited by R.A. Foakes and R.T. Rickert. Cambridge: Cambridge University Press, 1961.
Herrup, Cynthia B. *The Common Peace: Participation and the Criminal Law in Seventeenth-Century England*. Cambridge: Cambridge University Press, 1987.
———. *A House in Gross Disorder: Sex, Law, and the 2nd Earl of Castlehaven*. New York: Oxford University Press, 1999.
———. "Law and Morality in Seventeenth-Century England." *Past & Present* 106 (February 1985): 102–23.
Hill, Christopher. "William Perkins and the Poor." In *Puritanism and Revolution: Studies in Interpretation of the English Revolution of the 17th Century*, 215–38. London: Secker & Warburg, 1958.
Hindle, Steve. *The State and Social Change in Early Modern England, c. 1550–1640*. Basingstoke: Palgrave Macmillan, 2000.
Hoffer, Peter C., and N. E. H. Hull. *Murdering Mothers: Infanticide in England and New England, 1558–1803*. New York: New York University Press, 1981.
Hoffman, David. *The Holistic Herbal*. Shaftesbury, UK: Element Books, 1983.
Holmes, O.W. "Early English Equity." *The Law Quarterly Review* 2 (1885): 162–74.
Hovenden, Robert, ed. *A True Register of All the Christenings, Mariages, and Burialles in the Parishe of St. James, Clarkenwell*. Vol. 9, Harleian Society Registers. London: Harleian Society, 1884.
Hunter, Lynette. "Women and Domestic Medicine: Lady Experimenters, 1570–1620." In *Women, Science and Medicine 1500–1700*, edited by Lynette Hunter and Sarah Hutton, 89–107. Stroud, Gloucestershire, UK: Sutton, 1997.
———. "'Sweet Secrets' from Occasional Receipt to Specialised Books: The Growth of a Genre." In *"Banquetting Stuffe" The Fare and Social Background of the Tudor and Stuart Banquet*, edited by C. Anne Wilson, 36–59. Edinburgh: Edinburgh University Press, 1991.
Ingram, Martin. *Church Courts, Sex and Marriage in England, 1570–1640*. Cambridge: Cambridge University Press, 1987.
Jackson, Bernard S. *Law, Fact and Narrative Coherence*. Roby, UK: Deborah Charles, 1988.
Jackson, Mark, ed. *Infanticide: Historical Perspectives on Child Murder and Concealment, 1550–2000*. Aldershot, UK: Ashgate, 2002.
———. *New-Born Child Murder: Women, Illegitimacy and the Courts in Eighteenth-Century England*. Manchester: Manchester University Press, 1996.
James, Mervyn. *English Politics and the Concept of Honour, 1485–1642. Past & Present Supplement No. 3*. Oxford: Oxford University Press, 1978.
Johnson, Francis R. "Notes on English Retail Book-prices, 1550–1640." *The Library*, 5th series, 5 (1950): 83–112.
Jones, Ann Rosalind, and Peter Stallybrass. *Renaissance Clothing and the Materials of Memory*. Cambridge: Cambridge University Press, 2000.
Kaye, J. M. "The Early History of Murder and Manslaughter." *Law Quarterly Review* 83 (1967): 365–77, 587–601.
Kelleher, Michael D., and C. L. Kelleher. *Murder Most Rare: The Female Serial Killer*. Westport, CN: L. Praeger, 1998.

Kerrigan, John. "The Editor as Reader: Constructing Renaissance texts." In *The Practice and Representation of Reading in England*, edited by James Raven, Helen Small, and Naomi Tadmor, 102–24. Cambridge: Cambridge University Press, 1996.

Kesselring, Krista. "A Draft for the 1531 'Acte for Poysoning.'" *English Historical Review* 468 (2001): 894–99.

King, Helen. "Cellier, Elizabeth (fl. 1668–1688)." *ODNB*.

Kitchin, George. *Sir Roger L'Estrange: a contribution to the history of the press in the seventeenth century*. London: Kegan Paul & Co., 1913.

Kristeva, Julia. *Powers of Horror: An Essay on Abjection*. Translated by Leon S. Rondiez. New York: Columbia University Press, 1982.

Lake, Peter. "Deeds Against Nature: Cheap Print, Protestantism and Murder in Early Seventeenth-Century England." In *Culture and Politics in Early Stuart England*, edited by Kevin Sharpe and Peter Lake, 257–67. Basingstoke: Macmillan, 1994.

———. "Ministers, Magistrates and the Production of 'Order' in *Measure for Measure*." *Shakespeare Survey* 54 (2001): 165–81.

———. "Popular Form, Puritan Content? Two Puritan Appropriations of the Murder Pamphlet from Mid-seventeenth-century London." In *Religion, Culture and Society in Early Modern Britain*, edited by Anthony Fletcher and Peter Roberts, 313–34. Cambridge: Cambridge University Press, 1994.

———, with Michael Questier. *The Antichrist's Lewd Hat: Protestants, Papists and Players in Post-Reformation England*. New Haven, CT: Yale University Press, 2002.

Lane, William Coolidge, ed. *Bibliographical Contributions*. No. 56, Catalogue of English and American Chap-books and Broadside Ballads in Harvard College Library. Cambridge, MA: Harvard University Press, 1905.

Laqueur, Thomas W. "Crowds, Carnival and the State in English Executions, 1604–1868." In *The First Modern Society: Essays in English History in Honour of Lawrence Stone*, edited by A. L. Beier, David Cannadine, and James M. Rosenheim, 305–55. Cambridge: Cambridge University Press, 1989.

Lawson, P. G. "Lawless Juries? The Composition and Behavior of Hertfordshire Juries, 1573–1624." In *Twelve Good Men and True: The Criminal Trial Jury in England, 1200–1800*, edited by J. S. Cockburn and Thomas A. Green, 117–57. Princeton, NJ: Princeton University Press, 1988.

Lawson, Peter. "Patriarchy, Crime, and the Courts: The Criminality of Women in Late Tudor and Early Stuart England." In *Criminal Justice in the Old World and the New*, edited by Greg T. Smith, Allyson N. May, and Simon Devereaux, 16–57. Toronto: Centre of Criminology, University of Toronto, 1998.

Lehmburg, Stanford. "Nowell, Alexander (c.1516/17–1602), dean of St. Paul's." *ODNB*.

Levy, Fritz. "The Decorum of News." In *News, Newspapers, and Society in Early Modern England*, edited by Joad Raymond, 12–38. London: F. Cass, 1999.

———. "How Information Spread among the Gentry 1550–1640." *Journal of British Studies* 21 (1992): 11–34.

Lieblein, Leanore. "The Context of Murder in English Domestic Plays, 1590–1610." *Studies in English Literature* 23 (1983): 181–96.

Lindley, David. *The Trials of Frances Howard: Fact and Fiction at the Court of King James*. London: Routledge, 1993.

Linebaugh, Peter. "The Ordinary of Newgate and His *Account*." In *Crime in England, 1550–1800*, edited by J. S. Cockburn, 246–69. London: Methuen, 1977.

———. "The Tyburn Riot Against the Surgeons." In *Albion's Fatal Tree: Crime and Society in Eighteenth-Century England*, edited by Douglas Hay *et al.*, 65–117. New York: Pantheon Books, 1975.

Loomis, Catherine. "Elizabeth Abbot, *The Apprehension, Arraignment, and Execution of Elizabeth Abbot.*" In *Reading Early Modern Women: An Anthology of Texts in Manuscript and Print, 1550–1700*, edited by Helen Ostovich and Elizabeth Sauer, 29–31. London: Routledge, 2004.

Love, Harold. "L'Estrange, Sir Roger (1616–1704), author and press censor." *ODNB*.

Luborsky, Ruth Samson. "Connections and Disconnections Between Images and Texts: The Case of Secular Tudor Book Illustration." *Word & Image* 3 (1987): 74–85.

Lupton, Deborah. *Risk*. London: Routledge, 1999.

Maclean, Ian. *The Renaissance Notion of Woman*. Cambridge: Cambridge University Press, 1980.

Maitland, F. W. *Equity: A Course of Lectures*. Edited by John Brunyate. 1936. Reprint, Cambridge: Cambridge University Press, 1969.

Malcolmson, R. W. "Infanticide in Eighteenth-Century England." In *Crime in England, 1550–1800*, edited by J. S. Cockburn, 246–69. London: Methuen, 1977.

Markham, Gervase. *The English Housewife*. Edited by Michael R. Best. Kingston, ON: McGill-Queen's University Press, 1986.

Marshall, Cynthia. *The Shattering of the Self: Violence, Subjectivity, and Early Modern Texts*. Baltimore, MD: Johns Hopkins University Press, 2002.

Marshburn, Joseph H. "'A Cruell Murder Donne in Kent' and its Literary Manifestations." *Studies in Philology* 46 (1949): 131–40.

———. *Murder & Witchcraft in England, 1550–1640*. Norman, OK: University of Oklahoma Press, 1971.

Martin, Randall. "The Autobiography of Grace, Lady Mildmay," *Renaissance and Reformation* 18 (1994): 33–81.

———. "Henry Goodcole, Visitor of Newgate: Crime, Conversion, and Patronage." *The Seventeenth Century* 20.2 (Autumn 2005): 153–84.

———. ed. *Women and Murder in Early Modern News Pamphlets and Broadside Ballads, 1573–1697*. Aldershot, UK: Ashgate, 2005.

———. "'The Cat' Gets Its Nine Tails." *Notes and Queries* 53.1 (March 2006): 31–34.

May, Allyson. "'She at first denied it': Infanticide Trials at the Old Bailey." In *Women & History (Voices of Early Modern England)*, edited by Valerie Frith, 19–50. Toronto: Coach House Press, 1995.

McElwee, Thomas. *The Murder of Sir Thomas Overbury*. London: Faber and Faber, 1952.

McGowen, Randall. "The Changing Face of God's Justice: The Debates over Divine and Human Punishment in Eighteenth-Century England." *Criminal Justice History* 9 (1988): 63–98.

McKenzie, Andrea. "Making Crime Pay: Motives, Marketing Strategies, and the Printed Literature of Crime in England." In *Criminal Justice in the Old World and the New: Essays in Honour of J.M. Beattie*, edited by Greg T. Smith, Allyson N. May, and Simon Devereaux, 235–69. Toronto: Centre of Criminology, University of Toronto, 1998.

McLaughlin, Terence. *The Coward's Weapon*. London: Robert Hale, 1980.

McMullan, John L. "Crime, Law and Order in Early Modern England." *British Journal of Criminology* 27.3 (Summer 1987): 252–74.

Meldrum, Tim. *Domestic Service and Gender 1660–1750: Life and Work in the London Household*. London: Longman, 2000.

Morgan, Paul. "The Provincial Book Trade Before the End of the Licensing Act." In *Six Centuries of the Provincial Book Trade in Britain*, edited by Peter Isaac, 31–37. Winchester, UK: St. Paul's Bibliographies, 1990.

Morrissey, Belinda. *When Women Kill: Questions of Agency and Subjectivity*. London: Routledge, 2003.

O'Connell, Sheila. *The Popular Print in England 1550–1850*. London: British Museum Press, 1999.

Oldham, James C. "On Pleading the Belly: A History of the Jury of Matrons." *Criminal Justice History* 6 (1985): 1–64.

Omerod, George. *The History of the County Palatine and City of Chester*. Edited by Thomas Helsby. 2nd rev. ed. 2 vols. London: Lackington, 1882.

Orlin, Lena Cowen. "A Case for Anecdotalism in Women's History: The Witness Who Spoke When the Cock Crowed." *English Literary Renaissance* 31 (2001): 52–77.

———. *Private Matters and Public Culture in Post-Reformation England*. Ithaca, NY: Cornell University Press, 1994.

Ostovich, Helen, and Elizabeth Sauer, eds. *Reading Early Modern Women: An Anthology of Texts in Manuscript and Print, 1550–1700*. London: Routledge, 2004.

Oxford Dictionary of National Biography. Oxford: Oxford University Press, 2004–05.

Papke, David R., ed. *Narrative and the Legal Discourse*. Liverpool, UK: Deborah Charles, 1991.

Paster, Gail Kern. *The Body Embarrassed: Drama and the Disciplines of Shame in Early Modern England*. Ithaca, NY: Cornell University Press, 1993.

Peck, Linda Levy. *Court Patronage and Corruption in Early Stuart England*. Boston, MA: Unwin Hyman, 1990.

Pennell, Sara. "Perfecting Practice? Women, Manuscript Recipes and Knowledge in Early Modern England." In *Early Modern Women's Manuscript Writing*, edited by Victoria E. Burke and Jonathan Gibson, 237–55. Aldershot, UK: Ashgate, 2004.

Piers, Maria W. *Infanticide*. New York: W.W. Norton, 1978.

Pittock, Joan H., and Andrew Wear, eds. *Interpretation and Cultural History*. Basingstoke: Macmillan, 1990.

Posner, Richard A. *Law and Literature*. Rev. ed. Cambridge, MA: Harvard University Press, 1998.

Powys, Llewelyn. *The Life & Times of Anthony à Wood*. London: Wishart & Company, 1932.

Pugh, R. B. "Newgate Between Two Fires." *Guildhall Miscellany* 3–4 (1978): 137–63, 199–222.

Purkiss, Diane. *The Witch in History: Early Modern and Twentieth-Century Representations*. London: Routledge, 1996.

Questier, Michael C. *Conversion, Politics and Religion in England, 1580–1625*. Cambridge: Cambridge University Press, 1996.

———, and Peter Lake. "Agency, Appropriation and Rhetoric Under the Gallows: Puritans, Romanists and the State in Early Modern England." *Past & Present* 153 (November 1996): 64–107.

Radzinowicz, Leon. *A History of the English Criminal Law and its Administration from 1750*. London: Stevens & Sons, 1948.

Raven, James, Helen Small, and Naomi Tadmor, eds. Introduction to *The Practice and Representation of Reading in England*, 1–21. Cambridge: Cambridge University Press, 1996.

Ravenhill, W. W. "Murder in the Seventeenth Century." *The Wiltshire Archaeological and Natural History Magazine* 22 (1885): 39–69.

Raymond, Joad, ed. *Making the News: An Anthology of the Newsbooks of Revolutionary England 1641–1660*. Moreton-in-Marsh, UK: Windrush Press, 1993.

———, ed. *News, Newspapers, and Society in Early Modern England*. London: F. Cass, 1999.

———. "The Newspaper, Public Opinion, and the Public Sphere in the Seventeenth Century." In *News, Newspapers, and Society in Early Modern England*, edited by J. Raymond, 109–40. London: F. Cass, 1999.

Reinhard, J. R. "Burning at the Stake in Mediaeval Law and Literature." *Speculum* 16 (1941): 186–209.

Reynolds, Bryan. *Becoming Criminal: Transversal Performance and Cultural Dissidence in Early Modern England*. Baltimore, MD: Johns Hopkins University Press, 2002.

Roberts, Clayton. *The Logic of Historical Explanation*. University Park, PA: Pennsylvania State University Press, 1996.

Roberts, M. "Women and Work in Sixteenth-Century English Towns." In *Work in Towns 850–1850*, edited by P. Corfield and D. Keene, 92–3. London: Leicester University Press, 1999.

Rollins, Hyder E. "The Black-Letter Broadside Ballad." *PMLA* 34.2 (1919): 258–339.

———. *Old English Ballads 1553–1625: Chiefly from Manuscripts*. Cambridge: Cambridge University Press, 1920.

———. *A Pepysian Garland: Black-Letter Broadside Ballads of the Years 1595–1639*. Cambridge, MA: Harvard University Press, 1971.

Rowley, William, Thomas Dekker, and John Ford. *The Witch of Edmonton, A Critical Edition*. Edited by E. S. Onat. New York: Garland, 1980.

Rublack, Ulinka. *The Crimes of Women in Early Modern Germany*. Oxford: Clarendon Press, 1994.

Sarat, Austin, and Thomas R. Kearns, eds. Introduction to *History, Memory, and the Law*. 1–24. Ann Arbor, MI: University of Michigan Press, 2002.

Sawday, Jonathan. *The Body Emblazoned: Dissection and the Human Body in Renaissance Culture*. London: Routledge, 1996.

Scarry, Elaine. *The Body in Pain: The Making and Unmaking of the World*. New York: Oxford University Press, 1985.

Schwoerer, Lois G. "Liberty of the Press and Public Opinion: 1660–1695." In *Liberty Secured? Britain Before and After 1688*, edited by J. R. Jones. 199–230. Stanford, CA: Stanford University Press, 1992.

Shaaber, Matthias A. *Some Forerunners of the Newspaper in England, 1476–1622*. Philadelphia, PA: University of Pennsylvania Press, 1929.

Shapiro, Barbara J. *Probability and Certainty in Seventeenth-Century England: A Study of the Relationships Between Natural Science, Religion, History, Law, and Literature*. Princeton, NJ: Princeton University Press, 1983.

Sharpe, J. A. "Civility, Civilizing Processes, and the End of Public Punishment in England." In *Civil Histories: Essays Presented to Sir Keith Thomas*, edited by Peter Burke, Brian Harrison, and Paul Slack, 215–30. Oxford: Oxford University Press, 2000.

———. *Crime in seventeenth-century England: A county study*. Cambridge: Cambridge University Press, 1983.

———. *Crime in Early Modern England 1550–1750*. 2nd ed. London: Longman, 1999.

———. "Domestic Homicide in Early Modern England." *Historical Journal* 24 (1981): 29–48.

———. "The History of Violence in England: Some Observations." *Past & Present* 108 (August 1985): 206–15.

———. *Instruments of Darkness: Witchcraft in England 1550–1750*. London: Hamish Hamilton, 1996.

———. *Judicial Punishment in England*. London: Faber and Faber, 1990.

———. "'Last Dying Speeches': Religion, Ideology and Public Execution in Seventeenth-Century England." *Past & Present* 107 (May 1985): 144–67.

———. "The People and the Law." In *Popular Culture in Seventeenth-Century England*, edited by Barry Reay, 244–70. London: Croom Helm, 1985.

Sidney, Sir Philip. *An Apology for Poetry*. Edited by Geoffrey Shepherd. London: Thomas Nelson and Sons, 1965.

Siebert, Fredrick Seaton. *Freedom of the Press in England, 1476–1776: The Rise and Decline of Government Controls*. Urbana, IL: University of Illinois Press, 1952.

Simmons, R. C. "ABCs, Almanacs, Ballads, Chapbooks, Popular Piety and Textbooks." In *The Cambridge History of the Book in Britain*, vol. 4, edited by John Barnard and D.F. McKenzie, 504–13. Cambridge: Cambridge University Press, 2002.

Sinclair, H. M., and A. H. T. Robb-Smith. *A Short History of Anatomical Teaching at Oxford*. Oxford: Oxford University Press, 1950.

Singleton, Robert R. "English Criminal Biography, 1651–1722." *Harvard Library Bulletin* 18 (1970): 63–83.

Smith, Abbot E. *Colonists in Bondage: White Servitude and Convict Labor in America, 1607–1776*. Chapel Hill, NC: University of North Carolina Press, 1947.

Smith, Lacey Baldwin. "English Treason Trials and Confessions in the Sixteenth Century." *Journal of the History of Ideas* 15 (1954): 471–98.

———. "Theory and the History of Criminal Justice." In *Crime and Criminal Justice in Europe and Canada*, edited by Louis A. Knafla, 319–28. Waterloo, ON: Wilfrid Laurier University Press, 1981.

Somerset, Anne. *Unnatural Murder: Poison at the Court of James I*. London: Weidenfeld & Nicolson, 1997.

Sommerville, John. *The Secularization of Early Modern England: From Religious Culture to Religious Faith*. New York: Oxford University Press, 1992.

Spierenburg, Pieter. *The Spectacle of Suffering: Executions and the Evolution of Repression*. Cambridge: Cambridge University Press, 1984.

Spufford, Margaret. "First Steps in Literacy: the Reading and Writing Experiences of the Humblest Seventeenth-Century Autobiographers." *Social History* 4 (1979): 407–35.

———. *Small Books and Pleasant Histories: Popular Fiction and its Readership in Seventeenth-Century England*. London: Methuen, 1981.

Staub, Susan C. "Bloody Relations: Murderous Wives in the Street Literature of Seventeenth-Century England." In *Domestic Arrangements in Early Modern England*, edited by Kari Boyd McBride, 124–46. Pittsburgh, PA: Dusquesne University Press, 2002.

———. *Nature's Cruel Stepdames: Murderous Women in the Street Literature of Seventeenth Century England*. Pittsburgh, PA: Duquesne University Press, 2005.

Stone, Lawrence. "The History of Violence in England: A Rejoinder." *Past & Present* 108 (August 1985): 216–24.

———. "Interpersonal Violence in English Society, 1300–1980." *Past & Present* 101 (November 1983): 22–33.

Strachniewski, John. *The Persecutory Imagination: English Puritanism and the Literature of Religious Despair*. Oxford: Oxford University Press, 1991.

Stretton, Timothy. *Women Waging Law in Elizabethan England*. Cambridge: Cambridge University Press, 1998.

Sutherland, James. *The Restoration Newspaper and its Development*. Cambridge: Cambridge University Press, 1986.

Thomas, Keith. "Women and the Civil War Sects." *Past and Present* 13 (April 1958): 42–62.

———. "The Meaning of Literacy in Early Modern England." In *The Written Word: Literacy in Transition*, edited by Gerd Baumann, 97–131. Oxford: Clarendon Press, 1986.

Thompson, C. J. S. *Poisons and Poisoners: With Historical Accounts of Some Famous Mysteries in Ancient and Modern Times*. London: Harold Shaylor, 1931.

Thorne, Samuel E., ed. *A Discourse upon the Exposicion & Understandinge of Statutes (ca. 1567–71)*. San Marino, CA: Huntington Library, 1942.

The Tragedy of Master Arden of Faversham, edited by M. L. Wine. London: Methuen, 1973.

Travitsky, Betty S. "Child Murder in English Renaissance Life and Drama." *Medieval and Renaissance Drama in England* 6 (1993): 63–84.

———. "'A Pittilesse Mother'?: Reports of A Seventeenth-Century English Filicide." *Mosaic* 27.4 (1994): 55–79.

Underdown, David. "The Taming of the Scold: The Enforcement of Patriarchal Authority in Early Modern England." In *Order and Disorder in Early Modern England*, edited by A.J. Fletcher and John Stevenson, 116–36. Cambridge: Cambridge University Press, 1985.

Vinogradoff, Paul. "Reason and Conscience in Sixteenth-Century Jurisprudence." *Law Quarterly Review* 24 (1908): 373–84.

Walker, Garthine. *Crime, Gender and Social Order in Early Modern England*. Cambridge: Cambridge University Press, 2003.

———. "'Demons in female form': Representations of Women and Gender in Murder Pamphlets of the Late Sixteenth and Early Seventeenth Centuries." In *Writing and the English Renaissance*, edited by William Zander and Suzanne Trill, 123–39. London: Longman, 1996.

Wall, Wendy. *Staging Domesticity: Household Work and English Identity in Early Modern Drama*. Cambridge: Cambridge University Press, 2002.

Walsham, Alexandra. *Providence in Early Modern England*. Oxford: Oxford University Press, 1999.

Watson, Katherine D. *Poisoned Lives: English Poisoners and their Victims*. London: Hambledon and London, 2004.

Watt, Tessa. *Cheap Print and Popular Piety 1550–1640*. Cambridge: Cambridge University Press, 1991.

———. "Publisher, Pedlar, Pot-poet: The Changing Character of the Broadside Ballad, 1550–1640." In *Spreading the Word: The Distribution Networks of Print 1550–1850*, edited by Robin Myers and Michael Harris, 61–81. Winchester, UK: St. Paul's Bibliographies, 1990.

Whigham, Frank. *Ambition and Privilege: The Tropes of Elizabethan Courtesy Theory*. Berkeley, CA: University of California Press, 1984.

White, R. S. *Natural Law in English Renaissance Literature*. Cambridge: Cambridge University Press, 1996.

Wiener, Carol Z. "Is a Spinster an Unmarried Woman?" *American Journal of Legal History*, 20.1 (1976): 27–31.

Wiggins, Martin. *Journeymen in Murder: the Assassin in English Renaissance Drama*. Oxford: Oxford University Press, 1991.

Wiles, David. *Shakespeare's Clown: Actor and Text in the Elizabethan Playhouse*. Cambridge: Cambridge University Press, 1987.

Williams, Abigail. "Settle, Elkanah (1648–1724), playwright." *ODNB*.

Wiltenburg, Joy. *Disorderly Women and Female Power in the Street Literature of Early Modern England and Germany*. Charlottesville, VA: University Press of Virginia, 1992.

Woodbridge, Linda. *Women and the English Renaissance*. Urbana, IL: University of Illinois Press, 1984.

Woolf, D. R. "The Rhetoric of Martyrdom: Generic Contradiction and Narrative Strategy in John Foxe's *Acts and Monuments*." In *The Rhetorics of Life-Writing in Early Modern Europe*, edited by Thomas F. Mayer and D. R. Woolf, 243–82. Ann Arbor, MI: University of Michigan Press, 1995.

Wrightson, Keith. "Infanticide in Earlier Seventeenth-Century England." *Local Population Studies* 15 (1975): 10–22.

Young, Sidney. *The Annals of the Barber-Surgeons of London.* 2 vols. London: Blades, East & Blades, 1890.

Zaret, David. "Religion, Science, and Printing in the Public Spheres in Seventeenth-Century England." In *Habermas and the Public Sphere*, edited by Craig Calhoun, 212–35. Cambridge, MA: MIT Press, 1992.

Unpublished Dissertations

Dobb, Clifford. "Life and Conditions in the London Prisons 1543–1643, with Special Reference to Contemporary Literature." B.Litt. thesis, University of Oxford, 1953.

Foskett, Marjorie Lamont. "A Survey of the First English Newspapers 1620–1650." MA thesis, University of Southern California, 1934.

Linebaugh, Peter. "Tyburn. A Study of Crime and the Labouring Poor in London During the First Half of the Eighteenth Century." Ph.D. diss., Centre for the Study of Social History, University of Warwick, 1975.

Sheehan, W. J. "The London Prison System 1666–1795." Ph.D. diss., University of Maryland, 1975.

Index

For Product Safety Concerns and Information please contact our EU
representative GPSR@taylorandfrancis.com
Taylor & Francis Verlag GmbH, Kaufingerstraße 24, 80331 München, Germany